About the Authors

Maureen Child is the author of more than 130 romance novels and novellas that routinely appear on bestseller lists and have won numerous awards, including the National Reader's Choice Award. A seven-time nominee for the prestigous RITA® award from Romance Writers of America, one of her books was made into a CBS-TV movie called *The Soul Collecter*. Maureen recently moved from California to the mountains of Utah and is trying to get used to snow.

USA Today bestselling author **Kat Cantrell** read her first Mills & Boon novel in third grade and has been scribbling in notebooks since she learned to spell. She's a former Mills & Boon So You Think You Can Write winner and former RWA Golden Heart finalist. Kat, her husband and their two boys live in north Texas.

As an Air Force officer, **Merline Lovelace** served at bases all over the world. When she hung up her uniform for the last time, she combined her love of adventure with a flare for storytelling. She's now produced more than ninety-five action-packed novels. Over twelve million copies of her works are in print in thirty countries. Named Oklahoma's Writer of the Year and Female Veteran of the Year, Merline is also a recipient of Romance Writers of America's prestigious RITA® Award.

Billionaire Boss

Billionaire Boss: The Billion Dollar Deal

MAUREEN CHILD

KAT CANTRELL

MERLINE LOVELACE

MILLS & BOON

First Published in Great Britain 2020
By Mills & Boon, an imprint of HarperCollins*Publishers*
1 London Bridge Street, London, SE1 9GF

BILLIONAIRE BOSS: THE BILLION DOLLAR DEAL
© 2020 Harlequin Books S.A.

An Outrageous Proposal © 2012 Maureen Child
Matched to a Billionaire © 2014 Kat Cantrell
A Business Engagement © 2013 Merline Lovelace

ISBN: 978-0-263-28173-6

Printed and bound in Spain
by CPI, Barcelona

AN OUTRAGEOUS
PROPOSAL

MAUREEN CHILD

For two wonderful writers
who are fabulous friends,
Kate Carlisle and Jennifer Lyon.
Thank you both for always being there.

One

"For the love of all that's holy, *don't push!*" Sean Connolly kept one wary eye on the rearview mirror and the other on the curving road stretching out in front of him. Why the hell was *he* the designated driver to the hospital?

"Just mind the road and drive, Sean," his cousin Ronan complained from the backseat. He had one arm around his hugely pregnant wife, drawing her toward him despite the seat belts.

"He's right," Georgia Page said from the passenger seat. "Just drive, Sean." She half turned to look into the back. "Hang on, Laura," she told her sister. "We'll be there soon."

"You can all relax, you know," Laura countered. "I'm not giving birth in the car."

"Please, God," Sean muttered and gave the car more gas.

Never before in his life had he had reason to curse the

narrow, winding roads of his native Ireland. But tonight, all he wanted was about thirty kilometers of smooth highway to get them all to the hospital in Westport.

"You're not helping," Georgia muttered with a quick look at him.

"I'm driving," he told her and chanced another look into the rearview mirror just in time to see Laura's features twist in pain.

She moaned, and Sean gritted his teeth. The normal sense of panic a man felt around a woman in labor was heightened by the fact that his cousin was half excited and half mad with worry for the wife he doted on. A part of Sean envied Ronan even while the larger part of him was standing back and muttering, *Aye, Ronan, better you than me.*

Funny how complicated a man's life could get when he wasn't even paying attention to it. A year or so ago, he and his cousin Ronan were happily single, each of them with an eye toward remaining that way. Now, Ronan was married, about to be a father, and Sean was as involved in the coming birth of the next generation of Connollys as he could be. He and Ronan lived only minutes apart, and the two of them had grown up more brothers than cousins.

"Can't you go any faster?" Georgia whispered, leaning in toward him.

Then there was Laura's sister. Georgia was a smart, slightly cynical, beautiful woman who engaged Sean's brain even while she attracted him on a much more basic level. So far, he'd kept his distance, though. Getting involved with Georgia Page would only complicate things. What with her sister married to his cousin, and Ronan suddenly becoming insanely protective about the women he claimed were in "his charge."

Damned old-fashioned for a man who had spent most

of his adult years mowing through legions of adoring females.

Still, Sean was glad to have Georgia along. For the sanity she provided, if nothing else. Georgia and Sean would at least have each other to turn to during all of this, and he was grateful for it.

Sean gave her a quick glance and kept his voice low. "I go much faster on these roads at night, we'll *all* need a room in hospital."

"Right." Georgia's gaze fixed on the road ahead, and she leaned forward as if trying to make the car speed up through sheer force of will.

Well, Sean told himself, if anyone could pull that off, it would be Georgia Page. In the light from the dashboard, her dark blue eyes looked fathomless and her honey-colored hair looked more red than blond.

He'd first met her at Ronan and Laura's wedding a year or so ago, but with her many trips to Ireland to visit her sister, he'd come to know Georgia and he liked her. He liked her quick wit, her sarcasm and her sense of family loyalty—which he shared.

All around them, the darkness was complete, the headlights of his car illuminating the narrow track winding out in front of them. This far from the city, it was mainly farmland stretching out behind the high, thick hedges that lined the road. The occasional lighted window in a farmhouse stood out like beacons, urging them on.

At last, a distant glow appeared and Sean knew it was the lights of Westport, staining the night sky. They were close, and he took his first easy breath in what felt like hours.

"Nearly there," he announced, and glanced at Georgia. She gave him a quick grin, and he felt the solid punch of it.

From the backseat, Laura cried out and just like that, Sean's relief was cut short. They weren't safe yet. Focusing on the task at hand, he pushed his car as fast as he dared.

What felt like days—and was in reality only hours and hours later—Sean and Georgia walked out of the hospital like survivors of a grueling battle.

"God," Sean said, as they stepped into the soft rain of an Irish afternoon in winter. The wind blew like ice, and the rain fell from clouds that looked close enough to touch. He tipped his face back and stared up into the gray. It was good to be outside, away from the sounds and smells of the hospital. Even better to know that the latest Connolly had arrived safely.

"That was the longest night and day of my life, I think," he said with feeling.

"Mine, too," Georgia agreed, shrugging deeper into the navy blue coat she wore. "But it was worth it."

He looked over at her. "Oh, aye, it was indeed. She's a beauty."

"She is, isn't she?" Georgia grinned. "Fiona Connolly. It's a good name. Beautiful, but strong, too."

"It is, and by the look of her, she's already got her da wrapped around her tiny fingers." He shook his head as he remembered the expression on his cousin's face as Ronan held his new daughter for the first time. Almost enough to make a jaded man believe in—never mind.

"I'm exhausted and energized all at the same time."

"Me, as well," Sean agreed, happy to steer his mind away from dangerous territory. "Feel as though I've been running a marathon."

"And all we did was wait."

"I think the waiting is the hardest thing of all."

Georgia laughed. "And I think Laura would disagree."

Ruefully, he nodded. "You've a point there."

Georgia sighed, stepped up to Sean and threaded her arm through his. "Ronan will be a great father. And Laura…she wanted this so much." She sniffed and swiped her fingers under her eyes.

"No more crying," Sean said, giving her arm a squeeze. "Already I feel as though I've been riding a tide of tears all day. Between the new mother and father and you, it's been weepy eyes and sniffles for hours."

"I saw your eyes get a little misty, too, tough guy."

"Aye, well, we Irish are a sentimental lot," he admitted, then started for the car park, Georgia's arm still tucked through his.

"It's one of the things I like best about you—"

He gave her a look.

"—the Irish in general, I mean," she qualified.

"Ah, well then." He smiled to himself at her backtracking. It was a lovely afternoon. Soft rain, cold wind and new life wailing in the hospital behind them. "You've been to Ireland so often in the last year, you're very nearly an honorary Irishman yourself, aren't you?"

"I've been thinking about that," she admitted. They walked up to his car, and Sean hit the unlock button on his keypad.

"What's that then?" he asked, as he opened the passenger door for her and held it, waiting. Fatigue clawed at him, but just beneath that was a buoyant feeling that had him smile at the woman looking up at him.

"About being an honorary Irishman. Or at least," she said, looking around her at the car park, the hospital and the city beyond, "moving here. Permanently."

"Really?" Intrigued, he leaned his forearms on the top

of the door. "And what's brought this on then? Is it your brand-new niece?"

She shrugged. "Partly, sure. But mostly, it's this country. It's gorgeous and friendly, and I've really come to love being here."

"Does Laura know about this?"

"Not yet," she admitted, and shifted her gaze back to him. "So don't say anything. She's got enough on her mind at the moment."

"True enough," he said. "But I'm thinking she'd be pleased to have her sister so close."

She flashed him a brilliant smile then slid into her seat. As Sean closed the door after her and walked around the car, he was forced to admit that *he* wouldn't mind having Georgia close, either.

A half hour later, Georgia opened the door to Laura and Ronan's expansive stone manor house and looked back over her shoulder at Sean. "Want to come in for a drink?"

"I think we've earned one," he said, stepping inside and closing the door behind him. "Or even a dozen."

She laughed and it felt good. Heck, *she* felt good. Her sister was a mother, and Georgia was so glad she had made the decision to come to Ireland to be present for the baby's birth. She hated to think about what it would have been like, being a half a world away right now.

"Ronan's housekeeper, Patsy, is off in Dublin visiting her daughter Sinead," Georgia reminded him. "So we're on our own for food."

"It's not food I want at the moment anyway," Sean told her.

Was he flirting with her? Georgia wondered, then

dismissed the notion. She shook her head and reminded herself that they were here for a drink. Or several.

As he spoke, a long, ululating howl erupted from deep within the house. Georgia actually jumped at the sound and then laughed. "With the rain, the dogs have probably let themselves into the kitchen."

"Probably hungry now, too," Sean said, and walked beside her toward the back of the house.

Georgia knew her sister's house as if it were her own. Whenever she was in Ireland, she stayed here at the manor, since it was so huge they could comfortably hold a family reunion for a hundred. She opened the door into a sprawling kitchen with top-of-the-line appliances and what looked like miles of granite countertops. Everything was tidy—but for the two dogs scrambling toward her for some attention.

Deidre was a big, clumsy English sheepdog with so much hair over her eyes, it was a wonder she didn't walk into walls. And Beast—huge, homely—the best that could be said about him was what he lacked in beauty he made up for in heart. Since Beast reached her first, Georgia scratched behind his ears and sent the big dog into quivers of delight. Deidre was right behind him, nudging her mate out of her way.

"Okay then, food for the dogs, then drinks for us," Georgia announced.

"Already on it," Sean assured her, making his way to the wide pantry, stepping over and around Beast as the dog wound his way in and out of Sean's feet.

Within a few minutes, they had the dogs fed and watered and then left them there, sleeping on their beds in front of the now cold kitchen hearth. Cuddled up together, the dogs looked snug and happy.

Then Georgia led the way back down the hall, the

short heels of her shoes clicking against the wood floor. At the door to the parlor, Sean asked, "So, Patsy's in Dublin with her daughter. Sinead's doing well then, with her new family?"

"According to Patsy, everything's great," Georgia said.

Laura had told her the whole story of the pregnant Sinead marrying in a hurry. Sinead was now the mother of an infant son and her new husband was, at the moment, making a demo CD. He and his friends played traditional Irish music and, thanks to Ronan's influence with a recording company, had a real chance to do something with it. "She misses Sinead living close by, but once they get the demo done, they'll all be coming back to Dunley."

"Home does draw a body back no matter how far you intend to roam," Sean mused, as he followed her into the front parlor. "And yet, you're thinking of leaving your home to make a new one."

"I guess I am."

Hearing him say it aloud made the whole idea seem more real than it had in the past week or so that it had been floating around in her mind. But it also felt…right. Okay, scary, but good. After all, it wasn't as if she was giving up a lot. And the plus side was, she could leave behind all of the tension and bad memories of a marriage that had dissolved so abruptly.

Moving to Ireland was a big change, she knew. But wasn't change a good thing? Shake up your life from time to time just to keep it interesting?

At that thought, she smiled to herself. Interesting. Moving to a different country. Leaving the familiar to go to the…okay, also familiar. Since Laura had married Ronan and moved to Ireland, Georgia had made the long trek to visit four times. And each time she came, it was harder to leave. To go back to her empty condo in Huntington Beach, California. To sit at her desk, alone in the real estate office she and Laura had opened together.

Not that she was feeling sorry for herself—she wasn't. But she had started thinking that maybe there was more to life than sitting behind a desk hoping to sell a house.

In the parlor, Georgia paused, as she always did, just to enjoy the beauty of the room. A white-tiled hearth, cold now, but stacked with kindling that Sean was already working to light against the chill gloom of the day. Pale green walls dotted with seascapes and oversize couches facing each other across a low table that held a Waterford crystal bowl filled with late chrysanthemums in tones of russet and gold. The wide front windows looked out over a sweep of lawn that was drenched with the rain still falling softly against the glass.

When he had the fire going to his satisfaction, Sean stood up and brushed his palms together, then moved to the spindle table in the corner that held a collection of crystal decanters. Ignoring them, he bent to the small refrigerator tucked into the corner behind the table.

"Now, about that celebratory drink," he muttered.

Georgia smiled and joined him at the table, leaning her palms on the glossy top as she watched him open the fridge. "We earned it all right, but I wouldn't have missed it. The worry, the panic—" She was still smiling as he glanced up at her. "And I was seriously panicked. It was hard knowing Laura was in pain and not being able to do anything about it."

"Would it make me seem less manly to you if I admitted to sheer terror?" he asked, as he reached into the refrigerator.

"Your manhood is safe," Georgia assured him.

In fact, she had never known a man who needed to worry less about his manhood than Sean Connolly. He was gorgeous, charming and oozed sex appeal. Good thing, she thought, that she was immune. Well, nearly.

Even she, a woman who knew better, had been tempted by Sean's charms. Of course, it would be much better—safer—to keep him in the "friend" zone. Starting up anything with him would not only be dangerous but awkward, as well. Since her sister was married to his cousin, any kind of turmoil between them could start a family war.

And there was *always* turmoil when a man was involved, she thought with an inner sigh. But she'd learned her lesson there. She could enjoy Sean's company without letting herself get...involved. Her gaze skimmed over his tall, nicely packed yet lanky body, and something inside her sizzled like a trapped flame struggling to grow into a bonfire. She so didn't need that.

Nope, she told herself, just enjoy looking at him and keep your hormones on a tight leash. When he sent her a quick wink and a wild grin, Georgia amended that last thought to a tight, *short,* leash.

To divert herself from her own thoughts, Georgia sighed and asked, "Isn't she beautiful? The baby?"

"She is indeed," Sean agreed, pulling a bottle of champagne from the fridge and holding it aloft like a hard-won trophy. "And she has a clever father, as well. Our Ronan's stocked the fridge with not one but three bottles of champagne, bless him."

"Very thoughtful," she agreed.

He grabbed two crystal flutes from the shelf behind the bar, then set them down on the table and worked at the champagne wire and cork. "Did you get hold of your parents with the news?"

"I did," Georgia said, remembering how her mother had cried over the phone hearing the news about her first grandchild. "I called from Laura's room when you took Ronan down to buy flowers. Laura got to talk to them and they heard the baby cry." She smiled. "Mom cried along with her. Ronan's already promised to fly them in whenever they're ready."

"That's lovely then." The cork popped with a cheerful sound, and Sean poured out two glasses. Bubbling froth filled the flutes, looking like liquid sunshine. "So, champagne?"

"Absolutely."

She took a glass and paused when Sean said, "To Fiona Connolly. May her life be long and happy. May she be a stranger to sorrow and a friend to joy."

The sting of tears burned Georgia's eyes. Shaking her head, she took a sip of champagne and said, "That was beautiful, Sean."

He gave her a grin, then took her free hand in his and led her over to one of the sofas. There, he sat her down and then went back to the bar for the bottle of champagne. He set it on the table in front of them, then took a seat beside Georgia on the couch.

"A hell of a day all in all, wouldn't you say?"

"It was," she agreed, then amended, *"is."* Another sip of champagne and she added, "I'm tired, but I don't think I could close my eyes, you know? Too much left-over adrenaline pumping away inside."

"I feel the same," he told her, "so it's lucky we can keep each other company."

"Yeah, I guess it is," Georgia agreed. Kicking her shoes off, she drew her feet up onto the sofa and idly rubbed her arches.

The snap and hiss of the fire along with the patter of rain on the window made for a cozy scene. Taking a sip of her champagne, she let her head fall back against the couch.

"So," Sean said a moment or two later, "tell me about this plan of yours to move to Ireland."

She lifted her head to look at him. His brown hair was tousled, his brown eyes tired but interested and the half smile on his face could have tempted a saint. Georgia took another sip of champagne, hoping the icy liquor would dampen the heat beginning to build inside.

"I've been thinking about it for a while," she admitted, her voice soft. "Actually since my last visit. When I left for home, I remember sitting on the airplane as it was taxiing and wondering why I was leaving."

He nodded as if he understood completely, and that settled her enough to continue.

"I mean, you should be happy to go home after a trip, right?" She asked the question more of herself than of Sean and answered it the same way. "Looking forward to going back to your routine. Your everyday life. But I wasn't. There was just this niggling sense of disappointment that seemed to get bigger the closer I got to home."

"Maybe some of that was just because you were leaving your sister," he said quietly.

"Probably," she admitted with a nod and another sip of champagne. "I mean, Laura's more than my sister, she's my best friend." Looking at him, she gave him a small smile. "I really miss having her around, you know?"

"I do," he said, reaching for the champagne, then topping off their glasses. "When Ronan was in California, I found I missed going to the pub with him. I missed the laughter. And the arguments." He grinned. "Though if you repeat any of this, I'll deny it to my last breath."

"Oh, understood," she replied with a laugh. "Anyway, I got home, went to our—*my*—real estate office and stared out the front window. Waiting for clients to call or come in is a long, boring process." She stared down into her champagne. "And while I was staring out that window, watching the world go by, I realized that everyone outside the glass was doing what they wanted to do. Everyone but me."

"I thought you enjoyed selling real estate," Sean said. "The way Laura tells it, the two of you were just beginning to build the business."

"We were," she agreed. "But it wasn't what either of us wanted. Isn't that ridiculous?" Georgia shifted on the couch, half turning to face Sean more fully.

Wow, she thought, *he really is gorgeous.*

She blinked, then looked at the champagne suspiciously. Maybe the bubbles were infiltrating her mind, making her more susceptible to the Connolly charm and good looks. But no, she decided a moment later, she'd always been susceptible. Just able to resist. But now...

Georgia cleared her throat and banished her wayward thoughts. What had she been saying? Oh, yeah.

"I mean, think about it. Laura's an artist, and I was an interior designer once upon a time. And yet there we were, building a business neither of us was really interested in."

"Why is that?" He watched her out of those beautiful brown eyes and seemed genuinely curious. "Why would you put so much of yourselves into a thing you'd no interest in?"

"Well, that's the question, isn't it?" she asked, gesturing with her glass and cringing a little when the champagne slopped over the brim. To help fix that situation, she sipped the contents down a bit lower. "It started simply enough," she continued. "Laura couldn't make a living painting, so she took classes and became a real estate agent because she'd rather be her own boss, you know?"

"I do," he said with a knowing nod.

Of course he understood that part, Georgia thought. As the owner of Irish Air, a huge and growing airline, Sean made his own rules. Sure, their situations were wildly different, but he would still get the feeling of being answerable only to oneself.

"Then my marriage dissolved," she said, the words still tasting a little bitter. Georgia was mostly over it all, since it had been a few years now, but if she allowed herself to remember… "I moved out to live with Laura, and rather than try to build up a brand-new business of my own—and let's face it, in California, you practically stumble across an interior designer every few steps, so they didn't really need another one—I took classes and the two of us opened our own company."

Shaking her head, she drank more of the champagne and sighed. "So basically, we both backed into a business we didn't really want, but couldn't think of a way to get out of. Does that make sense?"

"Completely," Sean told her. "What it comes down to is, you weren't happy."

"*Exactly.*" She took a deep breath and let it go again. What was it about him? she wondered. So easy to talk to. So nice to look at, a tiny voice added from the back of her mind. Those eyes of his seemed to look deep inside her, while the lilt of Ireland sang in his voice. A heady combination, she warned herself. "I wasn't happy. And, since I'm free and on my own, why shouldn't I move to Ireland? Be closer to my sister? Live in a place I've come to love?"

"No reason a'tall," he assured her companionably. Picking up the champagne bottle he refilled both of their glasses again, and Georgia nodded her thanks. "So, I'm guessing you won't be after selling real estate here then?"

"No, thank you," she said on a sigh. God, it felt wonderful to know that soon she wouldn't have to deal with recalcitrant sellers and pushy buyers. When people came to her for design work, they would be buying her talent, not whatever house happened to be on the market.

"I'm going to open my own design shop. Of course, I'll have to check everything out first, see what I have to do to get a business license in Ireland and to have my interior design credentials checked. And I'll have to have a house..."

"You could always stay here," he said with a shrug. "I'm sure Ronan and Laura would love to have you here with them, and God knows the place is big enough..."

"It is that," she mused, shifting her gaze around the parlor of the luxurious manor house. In fact, the lovely old house was probably big enough for two or three families. "But I'd rather have a home of my own. My own place, not too far. I'm thinking of opening my shop in Dunley..."

Sean choked on a sip of champagne, then laughed a second later. "*Dunley?* You want to open a design shop in the *village?*"

Irritated, she scowled at him. And he'd been doing so nicely on the understanding thing, too. "What's wrong with that?"

"Well, let's just say I can't see Danny Muldoon hiring you to give the Pennywhistle pub a makeover anytime soon."

"Funny," she muttered.

"Ah now," Sean said, smile still firmly in place, "don't get yourself in a twist. I'm only saying that perhaps the city might be a better spot for a design shop."

Still frowning, she gave him a regal half nod. "Maybe. But Dunley is about halfway between Galway and Westport—two big cities, you'll agree—"

"I do."

"So, the village is centrally located, and I'd rather be in a small town than a big one anyway. And I can buy a cottage close by and walk to work. Living in the village, I'll be a part of things as I wouldn't if I lived in Galway and only visited on weekends. *And,*" she added, on a roll, "I'd be close to Laura to visit or help with the baby. Not to mention—"

"You're right, absolutely." He held up both hands, then noticed his champagne glass was nearly empty. He refilled his, and hers, and then lifted his glass in a toast. "I'm sorry I doubted you for a moment. You've thought this through."

"I really have," she said, a little mellower now, thanks not only to the wine, but to the gleam of admiration in Sean's gaze. "I want to do this. I'm *going* to do this," she added, a promise to herself and the universe at large.

"And so you will, I've no doubt," Sean told her, leaning forward. "To the start of more than *one* new life this day. I wish you happiness, Georgia, with your decision and your shop."

"Thanks," she said, clinking her glass against his, making the heavy crystal sing. "I appreciate it."

When they'd both had a sip to seal the toast, Sean mused, "So we'll be neighbors."

"We will."

"And friends."

"That, too," she agreed, feeling just a little unsettled by his steady stare and the twisting sensation in the pit of her stomach.

"And as your friend," Sean said softly, "I think I should tell you that when you're excited about something, your eyes go as dark as a twilight sky."

Two

"What?"

Sean watched the expression on her face shift from confusion to a quick flash of desire that was born and then gone again in a blink. But he'd seen it, and his response to it was immediate.

"Am I making you nervous, Georgia?"

"No," she said and he read the lie in the way she let her gaze slide from his. After taking another sip of champagne, she licked a stray drop from her lip, and Sean's insides fisted into knots.

Odd, he'd known Georgia for about a year now and though he'd been attracted, he'd never before been tempted. Now he was. Most definitely. Being here with her in the fire-lit shadows while rain pattered at the windows was, he thought, more than tempting. There was an intimacy here, two people who had shared a hellishly long day together. Now, in the quiet shadows, there was something new and...compelling rising up between them.

He knew she felt it, too, despite the wary gleam in her eyes as she watched him. Still, he wanted her breathless, not guarded, so he eased back and gave her a half smile. "I'm only saying you're a beautiful woman, Georgia."

"Hmm..." She tipped her head to one side, studying him.

"Surely it's not the first time you've heard that from a man."

"Oh, no," she answered. "Men actually chase me down the street to tell me I have twilight eyes."

He grinned. He did appreciate a quick wit. "Maybe I'm just more observant than most men."

"And maybe you're up to something," she said thoughtfully. "What is it, Sean?"

"Not a thing," he said, all innocence.

"Well, that's good." She nodded and reached down absently to rub at the arch of her foot. "I mean, we both know anything else would just be...complicated."

"Aye, it would at that," he agreed, and admitted silently that complicated might be worth it. "Your feet hurt?"

"What?" She glanced down to where her hand rubbed the arch of her right foot and smiled ruefully. "Yeah, they do."

"A long day of standing, wasn't it?"

"It was."

She sipped at her champagne and a log shifted in the fire. As the flames hissed and spat, she closed her eyes— a little dreamily, he thought, and he felt that fist inside him tighten even further. The woman was unknowingly seducing him.

Logic and a stern warning sounded out in his mind, and he firmly shut them down. There was a time for a cool head, and there was a time for finding out just where the road you found yourself on would end up. So far, he liked this particular road very much.

He set his glass on the table in front of them, then sat back and dragged her feet onto his lap. Georgia looked at him and he gave her a quick grin. "I'm offering a one-night-only special. A foot rub."

"Sean…"

He knew what she was thinking because his own mind was running along the same paths. Back up—or, stay the course and see what happened. As she tried to draw her feet away, he held them still in his lap and pushed his thumbs into her arch.

She groaned and let her head fall back and he knew he had her.

"Oh, that feels too good," she whispered, as he continued to rub and stroke her skin.

"Just enjoy it for a bit then," he murmured.

That had her lifting her head to look at him with the wariness back, glinting in those twilight depths. "What're you up to?"

"Your ankles," he said, sliding his hands higher to match his words. "Give me a minute, though, and ask again."

She laughed as he'd meant her to, and the wariness edged off a bit.

"So," she asked a moment later, "why do I rate a foot rub tonight?"

"I'm feeling generous, just becoming an uncle and all." He paused, and let that settle. Of course, he and Ronan weren't actually brothers, but they might as well have been. "Not really an uncle, but that's how it feels."

"You're an uncle," she told him. "You and Ronan are every bit as tight as Laura and I are."

"True," he murmured, and rubbed his thumb into the arches of her small, narrow feet. Her toes were painted a dark pink, and he smiled at the silver toe ring she wore on her left foot.

She sighed heavily and whispered, "Oh, my...you've got great hands."

"So I've been told," he said on a laugh. He slid his great hands a bit higher, stroking her ankles and then up along the line of her calves. Her skin was soft, smooth and warm, now that the fire had chased away the chill of the afternoon.

"Maybe it's the champagne talking," she said softly, "but what you're doing feels way too good."

"'Tisn't the champagne," he told her, meeting her eyes when she looked at him. "We've not had enough yet to blur the lines between us."

"Then it's the fire," she whispered, "and the rain outside sealing us into this pretty room together."

"Could be," he allowed, sliding his hands even higher now, stroking the backs of her knees and watching her eyes close as she sighed. "And it could just be that you're a lovely thing, here in the firelight, and I'm overcome."

She snorted and he grinned in response.

"Oh, yes, overcome," she said, staring into his eyes again, as if trying to see the plans he had, the plans he might come up with. "Sean Connolly, you're a man who always knows what he's doing. So answer me this. Are you trying to seduce me?"

"Ah, the shoe is on the other foot entirely, Georgia," he murmured, his fingertips moving higher still, up her thighs, inch by inch. He hadn't thought of it earlier, but now he was grateful she'd been wearing a skirt for their mad ride to the hospital. Made things so much simpler.

"Right," she said. "I'm seducing you? You're the one

giving out foot rubs that have now escalated—" her breath caught briefly before she released it on a sigh "—to *thigh* rubs."

"And do you like it?"

"I'd be a fool not to," she admitted, and he liked her even more for her straightforwardness.

"Well then…"

"But the question remains," she said, reaching down to capture one of his hands in hers, stilling his caresses. "If you're seducing me, I have to ask, why now? We've known each other for so long, Sean, and we've never—"

"True enough," he murmured, "but this is the first time we've been alone, isn't it?" He set her hand aside and continued to stroke the outsides of her thighs before slowly edging around to the inside.

She squirmed, and he went hard as stone.

"Think of it, Georgia," he continued, though his voice was strained and it felt as though there were a rock lodged in his throat. "'Tis just us here for the night. No Ronan, no Laura, no Patsy, running in and out with her tea trays. Even the dogs are in the kitchen sleeping."

Georgia laughed a little. "You're right. I don't think I've ever been in this house alone before. But…"

"No buts," he interrupted, then leaned out and picked up the champagne bottle. Refilling her glass and then his own, he set the bottle down again and lifted his glass with one hand while keeping her feet trapped in his lap with the other. "I think we need more of this, then we'll…*talk* about this some more."

"After enough champagne, we won't want to talk at all," she said, though she sipped at the wine anyway.

"And isn't that a lovely thought?" he asked, giving her a wink as he drained his glass.

She was watching him, and her eyes were filled with

the same heat that burned inside him. For the life of him, Sean couldn't figure out how he'd managed to keep his hands off of her for the past year or more. Right now, the desire leaping inside him had him hard and eager for the taste of her. The feel of her beneath his hands. He wanted to hear her sigh, hear her call his name as she erupted beneath him. Wanted to bury himself inside her heat and feel her surrounding him.

"That look in your eyes tells me exactly what you're thinking," Georgia said, and this time she took a long drink of champagne.

"And are you thinking the same?" he asked.

"I shouldn't be."

"That wasn't the question."

Never breaking her gaze from his, Georgia blew out a breath and admitted, "Okay, yes, I'm thinking the same."

"Thank the gods for that," he said, a smile curving his mouth.

She chuckled, and the sound was rich and full. "I think you've got more in common with the devils than you do with the gods."

"Isn't that a lovely thing to say then?" he quipped. Reaching out, he plucked the champagne flute from her hand and set it onto the table.

"I wasn't finished," she told him.

"We'll have more later. *After,*" he promised.

She took a deep breath and said, "This is probably a mistake, you know."

"Aye, probably is. Would you have us stop then, before we get started?" He hoped to hell she said no, because if she said yes, he'd have to leave. And right now, leaving was the very last thing he wanted to do.

"I really should say yes, because we absolutely should stop. Probably," she said quietly.

He liked the hesitation in that statement. "But?"

"But," she added, "I'm tired of being sensible. I want you to touch me, Sean. I think I've wanted that right from the beginning, but we were being too sensible for me to admit to it."

He pulled her up and over to him, settling her on his lap where she'd be sure to feel the hard length of him pressing into her bottom. "You can readily see that I feel the same."

"Yeah," she said, turning her face up to his. "I'm getting that."

"Not yet," he teased, "but you're about to."

"Promises, promises…"

"Well then, enough talking, yes?"

"Oh, yes."

He kissed her, softly at first, a brush of the lips, a connection that was as swift and sweet as innocence. It was a tease. Something short to ease them both into this new wrinkle in their relationship.

But with that first kiss, something incredible happened. Sean felt a jolt of white-hot electricity zip through him in an instant. His eyes widened as he looked at her, and he knew the surprise he read on her face was also etched on his own.

"That was… Let's just see if we can make that happen again, shall we?"

She nodded and arched into him, parting her lips for him when he kissed her, and this time Sean fed that electrical jolt that sizzled between them. He deepened the kiss, tangling his tongue with hers, pulling her closer, tighter, to him. Her arms came up around his neck and held on. She kissed him back, feverishly, as if every ounce of passion within her had been unleashed at once.

She stabbed her fingers through his hair, nails dragging along his scalp. She twisted on his lap, rubbing her behind against his erection until a groan slid from his throat. The glorious friction of her body against his would only get better, he thought, if he could just get her out of these bloody clothes.

He broke the kiss and dragged in a breath of air, hoping to steady the racing beat of his heart. It didn't help. Nothing would. Not until he'd had her, all of her. Only then would he be able to douse the fire inside. To cool the need and regain his control.

But for now, all he needed was her. Georgia Page, temptress with eyes of twilight and a mouth designed to drive a man wild.

"You've too many clothes on," he muttered, dropping his hands to the buttons on her dark blue shirt.

"You, too," she said, tugging the tail of his white, long-sleeved shirt free of the black jeans he wore. She fumbled at the buttons and then laughed at herself. "Can't get them undone, damn it."

"No need," he snapped and, gripping both sides of his shirt, ripped it open, sending small white buttons flying around the room like tiny missiles.

She laughed again and slapped both palms to his chest. At the first touch of her skin to his, Sean hissed in a breath and held it. He savored every stroke, every caress, while she explored his skin as if determined to map every inch of him.

He was willing to lie still for that exploration, too, as long as he could do the same for her. He got the last of her buttons undone and slid her shirt off her shoulders and down her arms. She helped him with it, and then her skin was bared to him, all but her lovely breasts, hidden behind the pale, sky-blue lace of her bra. His mouth went dry.

Tossing her honey-blond hair back from her face, Georgia met his gaze as she unhooked the front clasp of that bra and then slipped out of it completely. Sean's hands cupped her, his thumbs and forefingers brushing across the rigid peaks of her dark pink nipples until she sighed and cupped his hands with her own.

"You're lovely, Georgia. More lovely than I'd imagined," he whispered, then winked. "And my imagination was pretty damned good."

She grinned, then whispered, "My turn." She pushed his shirt off and skimmed her small, elegant hands slowly over his shoulders and arms, and every touch was a kiss of fire. Every caress a temptation.

He leaned over, laying her back on the sofa until she was staring up at him. Firelight played over her skin, light and shadow dancing in tandem, making her seem almost ethereal. But she was a real woman with a real need, and Sean was the man to meet it.

Deftly, he undid the waist button and the zipper of the skirt she wore, then slowly tugged the fabric down and off before tossing it to the floor. She wore a scrap of blue lace panties that were somehow even more erotic than seeing her naked would have been. Made him want to take that elastic band between his teeth and—

"Sean!" She half sat up and for a dark second or two, Sean was worried she'd changed her mind at the last. The thought of that nearly brought him to his knees.

"What is it?"

"Protection," she said. "I'm not on the pill, and I don't really travel with condoms." Worrying her bottom lip with her teeth, she blurted, "Maybe Ronan's got some old ones upstairs…"

"No need," he said and stood. "I've some in the glove box of the car."

She just looked at him. "You keep condoms in the glove compartment?"

Truthfully, he hadn't used any of the stash he kept there for emergencies in longer than he cared to admit. There hadn't been a woman for him in months. Maybe, he thought now, it was because he'd been too tangled up in thoughts of twilight eyes and kissable lips. Well, he didn't much care for the sound of that, so he told himself that maybe he'd just been too bloody busy getting his airline off the ground, so to speak.

"Pays to be prepared," was all he said.

Georgia's lips twitched. "I didn't realize Ireland *had* Boy Scouts."

"What?"

"Never mind," she whispered, lifting her hips and pulling her panties off. "Just…hurry."

"I bloody well will." He scraped one hand across his face, then turned and bolted for the front door. It cost him to leave her, even for the few moments this necessary trip would take.

He was through the front door and out to his car in a blink. He hardly felt the misting rain as it covered him in an icy, wet blanket. The night was quiet; the only light came from that of the fire within the parlor, a mere echo of light out here, battling and losing against the darkness and the rain.

He tore through the glove box, grabbed the box of condoms and slammed the door closed again. Back inside the house, he staggered to a stop on the threshold of the parlor. She'd moved from the couch, and now she lay stretched out, naked, on the rug before the fire, her head on one of the countless pillows she'd brought down there with her.

Sean's gaze moved over her in a flash and then again,

more slowly, so he could savor everything she was. Mouth dry, heartbeat hammering in his chest, he thought he'd never seen a more beautiful picture than the one she made in the firelight.

"You're wet," she whispered.

Sean shoved one hand through his rain-soaked hair, then shrugged off his shirt. "Hadn't noticed."

"Cold?" she asked, and levered herself up on one elbow to watch him.

The curve of her hip, the swell of her breasts and the heat in her eyes all came together to flash into an inferno inside him. "Cold? Not likely."

Never taking his gaze from hers, he pulled off the rest of his clothes and simply dropped them onto the colorful rug beneath his feet. He went to her, laser-focused on the woman stretched out beside him on the carpet in the firelight.

She reached up and cupped his cheek before smiling. "I thought we'd have more room down here than on the couch."

"Very sensible," he muttered, kissing her palm then dipping to claim her lips in a brief, hard kiss. "Nothing more sexy than a smart woman."

"Always nice to hear." She grinned and moved into him, pressing her mouth to his. Opening for him, welcoming the taste of him as he devoured her. Bells clanged in his mind, warning or jubilation he didn't care which.

All that mattered now was the next touch. The next taste. She filled him as he'd never been filled before and all Sean could think was *Why had it taken them so bloody long to do this?*

Then his thoughts dissolved under an onslaught of sensations that flooded his system. He tore his mouth from hers to nibble at the underside of her jaw. To drag lips and tongue along the line of her throat while she sighed with pleasure and slid her hands up and down his back.

She was soft, smooth and smelled of flowers, and every breath he took drew her deeper inside him. He lost himself in the discovery of her, sliding his palms over her curves. He took first one nipple, then the other, into his mouth, tasting, suckling, driving her sighs into desperate gasps for air. She touched him, too, sliding her hands across his back and around to his chest and then down, to his abdomen. Then further still, until she curled her fingers around his length and Sean lifted his head, looked down into her eyes and let her see what she was doing to him.

Firelight flickered, rain spattered against the windows and the wind rattled the glass.

Her breath came fast and heavy. His heart galloped in his chest. Reaching for the condoms he'd tossed to the hearth, he tore one packet open, sheathed himself, then moved to kneel between her legs.

She planted her feet and lifted her hips in invitation and Sean couldn't wait another damn minute. He needed this. Needed *her* as he'd never needed anything before.

Scooping his hands beneath her butt, he lifted her and, in one swift push, buried himself inside her.

Her head fell back, and a soft moan slid from her lips. His jaw tight, he swallowed the groan trying to escape his throat. Then she wrapped her legs around his middle, lifted her arms and drew him in deeper, closer. He bent over her and kissed her as the rhythm of this ancient, powerful dance swept them both away.

They moved together as if they'd been partners for years. Each seemed to know instinctively what would most touch, most inflame, the other. Their shadows moved on the walls and the night crowded closer as Sean pushed Georgia higher and higher.

His gaze locked with hers, he watched her eyes flash, felt her body tremble as her release exploded inside her. Lost himself in the pleasure glittering in her twilight eyes and then, finally, his control snapped completely. Taking her mouth with his, he kissed her deeply as his body shattered.

Georgia felt...fabulous.

Heat from the fire warmed her on one side, while Sean's amazing body warmed her from the other. And of the two, she preferred the heat pumping from the tall, gorgeous man laying beside her.

Turning to face him, she smiled. "That was—"

"Aye, it was," he agreed.

"Worth waiting for," she confessed.

He skimmed a palm along the curve of her hip and she shivered. "And I was just wondering why in the hell we waited as long as we did."

"Worried about complications, remember?" she asked, and only now felt the first niggling doubt about whether or not they'd done the right thing. Probably not, she mused, but it was hard to regret any of it.

"There's always complications to good sex," he said softly, "and that wasn't just good, it was—"

"Yeah," she said, "it was."

"So the question arises," he continued, smoothing his hand now across her bottom, "what do we do about this?"

She really hadn't had time to consider all the options, and Georgia was a woman who spent most of her life looking at any given situation from every angle possible. Well, until tonight anyway. Now, her brain was scrambling to come up with coherent thoughts in spite of the fact that her body was still buzzing and even now hoping for more.

Still, one thing did come to mind, though she didn't much care for it. "We could just stop whatever this is. Pretend tonight never happened and go back to the way things were."

"And is that what you really want to do?" he asked, leaning forward to plant a kiss on her mouth.

She licked her lips as if to savor the taste of him, then sighed and shook her head. "No, I really don't. But those complications will only get worse if we keep doing this."

"Life is complicated, Georgia," he said, smoothing his hand around her body to tug playfully at one nipple.

She sucked in a gulp of air and blew it out again. "True."

"And, pretending it didn't happen won't work, as every time I see you, I'll want to do this again…"

"There is that," she said, reaching out to smooth his hair back from his forehead. Heck, she *already* wanted to do it all again. Feel that moment when his body slid into hers. Experience the sensation of his body filling hers completely. That indescribable friction that only happened when sex was done really well. And this *so* had been.

His eyes in the firelight glittered as if there were sparks dancing in their depths, and Georgia knew she was a goner. At least for now, anyway. She might regret it all later, but if she did, she would still walk away with some amazing memories.

"So," he said softly, "we'll take the complications as they come and do as we choose?"

"Yes," she said after giving the thought of never being with him again no more than a moment's consideration.

"We'll take the complications. We're adults. We know what we're doing."

"We certainly seemed to a few minutes ago," he said with a teasing grin.

"Okay, then. No strings. No expectations. Just...*us*. For however long it lasts."

"Sounds good." He pushed himself to his feet and walked naked to the table where they'd abandoned their wineglasses and the now nearly empty bottle of champagne.

"What're you doing?"

He passed her the glasses as she sat up, then held the empty bottle aloft. "I'm going to open another of Ronan's fine bottles of champagne. The first we drank to our new and lovely Fiona. The second we'll drink to *us*. And the bargain we've just made."

She looked up at him, her gaze moving over every square inch of that deliciously toned and rangy body. He looked like some pagan god, doused in firelight, and her breath stuttered in her chest. She could only nod to his suggestion because her throat was so suddenly tight with need, with passion, with...other things she didn't even want to contemplate.

Sean Connolly wasn't a forever kind of man—but, Georgia reminded herself as she watched him move to the tiny refrigerator and open it, she wasn't looking for forever. She'd already tried that and had survived the crash-and-burn. Sure, he wasn't the man her ex had been. But why even go there? Why try to make more out of this than it was? Great sex didn't have to be forever.

And as a right-now kind of man, Sean was perfect.

Three

The next couple of weeks were busy.

Laura was just settling into life as a mother, and both she and Ronan looked asleep on their feet half the time. But there was happiness in the house, and Georgia was determined to find some of that happy for herself.

Sean had been a big help in navigating village society. Most of the people who lived and worked in Dunley had been there for generations. And though they might like the idea of a new shop in town, the reality of it slammed up against the whole aversion-to-change thing. Still, since Georgia was no longer a complete stranger, most of the people in town were more interested than resentful.

"A design shop, you say?"

"That's right," Georgia answered, turning to look at Maeve Carrol. At five feet two inches tall, the seventy-year-old woman had been Ronan's nanny once upon a long-ago time. Since then, she was the self-appointed

chieftain of the village and kept up with everything that
was happening.

Her white hair was piled at the top of her head in a lopsided bun. Her cheeks were red from the wind, and her
blue eyes were sharp enough that Georgia was willing
to bet Maeve didn't miss much. Buttoned up in a Kelly
green cardigan and black slacks, she looked snug, right
down to the soles of her bright pink sneakers.

"And you'll draw up pictures of things to be done to
peoples' homes."

"Yes, and businesses, as well," Georgia said, "just
about anything. It's all about the flow of a space. Not
exactly feng shui but along the same lines."

Maeve's nose twitched and a smile hovered at the corners of her mouth. "Fing Shooey—not a lot of that in the
village."

Georgia smiled at Maeve's pronunciation of the design philosophy, then said, "Doesn't matter. Some will
want help redecorating, and there will be customers for
me in Westport and Galway…"

"True enough," Maeve allowed.

Georgia paused to take a look up and down the main
street she'd come to love over the past year. There really
wasn't much to the village, all in all. The main street held
a few shops, the Pennywhistle pub, a grocer's, the post
office and a row of two-story cottages brightly painted.

The sidewalks were swept every morning by the shop
owners, and flowers spilled from pots beside every doorway. The doors were painted in brilliant colors, scarlet,
blue, yellow and green, as if the bright shades could offset the ever-present gray clouds.

There were more homes, of course, some above the
shops and some just outside the village proper on the narrow track that wound through the local farmers' fields.

Dunley had probably looked much the same for centuries, she thought, and liked the idea very much.

It would be good to have roots. To belong. After her divorce, Georgia had felt so...untethered. She'd lived in Laura's house, joined Laura's business. Hadn't really had something to call *hers*. This was a new beginning. A chapter in her life that she would write in her own way in her own time. It was a heady feeling.

Outside of town was a cemetery with graves dating back five hundred years or more, each of them still lovingly tended by the descendants of those who lay there. The ruins of once-grand castles stubbled the countryside and often stood side by side with the modern buildings that would never be able to match the staying power of those ancient structures.

And soon, she would be a part of it.

"It's a pretty village," Georgia said with a little sigh.

"It is at that," Maeve agreed. "We won the Tidy Town award back in '74, you know. The Mayor's ever after us to win it again."

"Tidy Town." She smiled as she repeated the words and loved the fact that soon she would be a part of the village life. She might always be called "the Yank," but it would be said with affection, she thought, and one day, everyone might even forget that Georgia Page hadn't always been there.

She hoped so, anyway. This was important to her. This life makeover. And she wanted—needed—it to work.

"You've your heart set on this place, have you?" Maeve asked.

Georgia grinned at the older woman then shifted her gaze to the empty building in front of them. It was at the end of the village itself and had been standing empty for a couple of years. The last renter had given up on making a go of it and had left for America.

"I have," Georgia said with a sharp nod for emphasis. "It's a great space, Maeve—"

"Surely a lot of it," the older woman agreed, peering through dirty windows to the interior. "Colin Ferris now, he never did have a head for business. Imagine trying to make a living selling interwebbing things in a village the size of Dunley."

Apparently Colin hadn't been able to convince the villagers that an internet café was a good idea. And there hadn't been enough of the tourist trade to tide him over.

"'Twas no surprise to me he headed off to America." She looked over at Georgia. "Seems only right that one goes and one comes, doesn't it?"

"It does." She hadn't looked at it that way before, but there was a sort of synchronicity to the whole thing. Colin left for America, and Georgia left America for Dunley.

"So you've your path laid out then?"

"What? Oh. Yes, I guess I have," Georgia said, smiling around the words. She had found the building she would rent for her business, and maybe in a couple of years, she'd be doing so well she would buy it. It was all happening, she thought with an inner grin. Her whole life was changing right before her eyes. Georgia would never again be the same woman she had been when Mike had walked out of her life, taking her self-confidence with him.

"Our Sean's been busy as well, hasn't he?" Maeve mused aloud. "Been a help to you right along?"

Cautious, Georgia slid a glance at the canny woman beside her. So far she and Sean had kept their…relationship under the radar. And in a village the size of Dunley, that had been a minor miracle. But if Maeve Carrol was paying attention, their little secret could be out.

And Maeve wasn't the only one paying attention. Laura was starting to give Georgia contemplative looks that had to mean she was wondering about all the time Georgia and Sean were spending together.

Keeping her voice cool and her manner even cooler, Georgia said only, "Sean's been great. He's helped me get the paperwork going on getting my business license—" Which was turning out to be more complicated than she'd anticipated.

"He's a sharp one, is Sean," Maeve said. "No one better at wangling his way around to what he wants in the end."

"Uh-huh."

"Maggie Culhane told me yesterday that she and Colleen Leary were having tea at the pub and heard Sean talking to Brian Connor about his mum's cottage, it standing empty this last year or more."

Georgia sighed inwardly. The grapevine in Dunley was really incredible.

"Yes, Sean was asking about the cottage for me. I'd really like to live in the village if I can."

"I see," Maeve murmured, her gaze on Georgia as sharp as any cop's, waiting for a confession.

"Oh, look," Georgia blurted, "here comes Mary Donohue with the keys to the store."

Thank God, she thought, grateful for the reprieve in the conversation. Maeve was a sweetie, but she had a laserlike focus that Georgia would just as soon avoid. And she and Sean were keeping whatever it was between them quiet. There was no need for anyone else to know, anyway. Neither one of them was interested in feeding the local gossips—and Georgia really didn't want to hear advice from her sister.

"Sorry I'm late," Mary called out when she got closer. "I was showing a farm to a client, and wouldn't you know he'd be late and then insist on walking over every bloody blade of grass in the fields?"

She shook her mass of thick red hair back from her face, produced a key from her suitcase-sized purse and opened the door to the shop. "Now then," she announced, standing back to allow Georgia to pass in front of her. "If this isn't perfect for what you're wanting, I'll be shocked."

It *was* perfect, Georgia thought, wandering into the empty space. The floor was wood, scarred from generations of feet tracking across its surface. But with some polish, it would look great. The walls were in need of a coat of paint, but all in all, the place really worked for Georgia. In her mind, she set up a desk and chairs and shelves with samples stacked neatly. She walked through, the heels of her boots clacking against the floor. She gave a quick look to the small kitchen in the back, the closet-sized bath and the storeroom. She'd already been through the place once and knew it was the one for her. But today was to settle the last of her nerves before she signed the rental papers.

The main room was long and narrow, and the window let in a wide swath of daylight even in the gray afternoon. She had a great view of the main street, looking out directly across the road at a small bakery where she could go for her lunch every day and get tea and a sandwich. She'd be a part of Dunley, and she could grow the kind of business she'd always wanted to have.

Georgia breathed deep and realized that Mary was giving her spiel, and she grinned when she realized she would never have to do that herself, again. Maeve wandered the room, inspecting the space as if she'd never seen it before. Outside, two or three curious villagers began to gather, peering into the windows, hands cupped around their eyes.

Another quick smile from Georgia as she turned to Mary and said, "Yes. It's perfect."

Sean came rushing through the front door just in time to hear her announcement. He gave her a wide smile and walked across the room to her. Dropping both hands onto her shoulders, he gave her a fast, hard kiss, and said, "That's for congratulations."

Georgia's lips buzzed in reaction to that spontaneous kiss even while she worried about Maeve and Mary being witnesses to it. Sean didn't seem to mind, though. But then, he was such an outgoing guy, maybe no one would think anything of it.

"We used handshakes for that in my day," Maeve murmured.

"Ah, Maeve my darlin', did you want a kiss, too?" Sean swept the older woman up, planted a quick kiss on her mouth and had her back on her feet, swatting the air at him a second later.

"Go on, Sean Connolly, you always were free with your kisses."

"He was indeed," Mary said with a wink for Georgia. "Talk of the village he was. Why when my Kitty was young, I used to warn her about our Sean here."

Sean slapped one hand to his chest in mock offense. "You're a hard woman, Mary Donohue, when you know Kitty was the first to break my heart."

Mary snorted. "Hard to break a thing that's never been used."

No one else seemed to notice, but Georgia saw a flash of something in Sean's eyes that made her wonder if

Mary's words hadn't cut a little deeper than she'd meant. But a moment later, Sean was speaking again in that teasing tone she knew so well.

"Pretty women were meant to be kissed. You can't blame me for doing what's expected, can you?"

"You always did have as much brass as a marching band," Maeve told him, but she was smiling.

"So then, it's settled." Sean looked from Georgia to Mary. "You'll be taking the shop."

"I am," she said, "if Mary's brought the papers with her."

"I have indeed," that woman said and again dipped into her massive handbag.

Georgia followed her off a few steps to take care of business while Sean stood beside Maeve and watched her go.

"And just what kind of deviltry are you up to this time, Sean Connolly?" Maeve whispered.

Sean didn't look at the older woman. Couldn't seem to tear his gaze off of Georgia. Nothing new there. She had been uppermost in his mind for the past two weeks. Since the first time he'd touched her, Sean had thought about little else but touching her again. He hadn't meant to kiss her like that in front of witnesses—especially Maeve—but damned if he'd been able to help himself.

"I don't know what you mean, Maeve."

"Oh, yes," the older woman said with a knowing look, "it's clear I've confused you…"

"Leave off, Maeve," he murmured. "I'm here only to help if I can."

"Being the generous sort," she muttered right back.

He shot her a quick look and sighed. There was no putting anything over on Maeve Carrol. When they were boys, he and Ronan had tried too many times to count to get away with some trouble or other only to be stopped short by the tiny woman now beside him.

Frowning a bit, he turned to watch Georgia as she read over the real estate agent's papers. She was small but, as he knew too well, curvy in all the right places. In her faded blue jeans and dark scarlet, thickly knit sweater, she looked too good. Standing here in this worn, empty store, she looked vivid. Alive. In a way that made everything else around her look as gray as the skies covering Dunley.

"Ronan says you haven't been by the house much," Maeve mentioned.

"Ah, well, I'm giving them time to settle in with Fiona. Don't need people dropping in right and left."

"You've been *dropping* in since you were a boy, Sean." She clucked her tongue and mused, "Makes a body wonder what you've found that's kept you so busy."

"I've got a business to run, don't I?" he argued in a lame defense, for Maeve knew as well as he did that his presence wasn't required daily at the offices of Irish Air. There was plenty of time for him to stop in at Ronan's house as he always had. But before, he hadn't been trying to cover up an affair with his...what was Georgia to him? A cousin-in-law? He shook his head. Didn't matter. "I'll go to the house, Maeve."

"See that you do. Ronan's wanting to show off his baby girl to you, so mind you go to there soon."

"I will and all," he assured her, then snatched at his ringing cell phone as he would a lifeline tossed into a churning sea. Lifting one finger to Maeve as if to tell her one moment, he turned and answered, "Sean Connolly."

A cool, dispassionate voice started speaking and he actually *felt* a ball of ice drop into the pit of his stomach.

"Repeat that if you please," he ordered, though he didn't want to hear the news again. He had to have the information.

His gaze moved to Georgia, who had turned to look at him, a question in her eyes. His tone of voice must have alerted her to a problem.

"I understand," he said into the phone. "I'm on my way."

He snapped the phone closed.

Georgia walked up to him. "What is it?"

Sean could hardly say the words, but he forced them out. "It's my mother. She's in hospital." It didn't sound real. Didn't feel real. But according to the nurse who'd just hung up on him, it was. "She's had a heart attack."

"Ah, Sean," Maeve said, sympathy rich in her voice.

He didn't want pity. More than that though, he didn't want to be in a position to need it. "She's in Westport. I have to go."

He headed for the door, mind already racing two or three steps ahead. He'd get to the hospital, talk to the doctors, then figure out what to do next. His mother was hale and hearty—usually—so he wouldn't worry until he knew more. An instant later, he told himself *Bollocks to that,* as he realized the worry and fear had already started.

Georgia was right behind him. "Let me come with you."

"No." He stopped, looked down into her eyes and saw her concern for him and knew that if she were with him, her fears would only multiply his own. Sounded foolish even to him, but he had to do this alone. "I have to go—"

Then he hit the door at a dead run and kept running until he'd reached his car.

* * *

Ailish Connolly was not the kind of woman to be still.

So seeing his mother lying in a hospital bed, hooked up to machinery that beeped and whistled an ungodly tune was nearly enough to bring Sean to his knees. Disjointed but heartfelt prayers raced through his mind as he reached for the faith of his childhood in this time of panic.

It had been too long since he'd been to Mass. Hadn't graced a church with his presence in too many years to count. But now, at this moment, he wanted to fling himself at the foot of an altar and beg God for help.

Sean shoved one hand through his hair and bit back the impatience clawing inside him. He felt so bloody helpless, and that, he thought, was the worst of it. Nothing he could do but sit and wait, and as he wasn't a patient man by nature...the waiting came hard.

The private room he had arranged for his mother smelled like her garden, since he'd bought every single flower in the gift shop. That was what he'd been reduced to. Shopping for flowers while his mother lay still and quiet. He wasn't accustomed to being unable to affect change around him.

Sean Connolly was a man who got things done. Always. Yet here, in the Westport hospital, he could do not a bloody thing to get action. To even get a damned doctor to answer his questions. So far, all he'd managed to do was irritate the nurses and that, he knew, was no way to gain cooperation. Irish nurses were a tough bunch and took no trouble from anyone.

Sitting beside his mother's bed in a torture chair designed to make visiting an ordeal, Sean braced his elbows on his knees and cupped his face in his palms. It had been only his mother and he for so long, he couldn't remember his life any other way. His father had died when Sean was just a boy, and Ailish had done the heroic task of two parents.

Then when Ronan's parents had died in that accident, Ailish had stepped in for him, as well. She was strong, remarkably self-possessed and until today, Sean would have thought, invulnerable. He lifted his gaze to the small woman with short, dark red hair. There was gray mixed with the red, he noticed for the first time. Not a lot, but enough to shake him.

When had his mother gotten old? Why was she here? She'd been to lunch with her friends and had felt a pain that had worried her enough she had come to the hospital to have it checked. And once the bloody doctors got their hands on you, you were good and fixed, Sean thought grimly, firing a glare at the closed door and the busy corridor beyond.

They'd slapped Ailish in to be examined and now, several hours later, he was still waiting to hear what the dozens of tests they'd done would tell them. The waiting, as he had told Georgia not so very long ago, was the hardest.

Georgia.

He wished he had brought her with him. She was a calm, cool head, and at the moment he needed that. Because what he was tempted to do was have his mother transferred to a bigger hospital in Dublin. To fly in specialists. "To *buy* the damned hospital so *someone* would come in and talk to me."

"Sean," his mother whispered, opening her eyes and turning her face toward him, "don't swear."

"Mother." He stood up, curled one hand around the bar of her bed and reached down with the other to take hers in his. "How are you?"

"I'm fine," she insisted. "Or I was, having a lovely nap until my son's cursing woke me."

"Sorry." She still had the ability to make him feel like a guilty boy. He supposed all mothers had that power, though at the moment, only *his* mother concerned him. "But no one will talk to me. No one will tell me a bloody—" He cut himself off. "I can't get answers from anyone in this place."

"Perhaps they don't have any to give yet," she pointed out.

That didn't ease his mind any.

Her face was pale, her sharp green eyes were a little watery, and the pale wash of freckles on her cheeks stood out like gold paint flicked atop a saucer of milk.

His heart actually ached to see her here. Like this. Fear wasn't something he normally even considered, but the thought of his mother perhaps being at death's bleeding door with not a doctor in sight cut him right down to the bone.

"Do you know what I was thinking," she said softly, giving her son's hand a gentle squeeze, "when they were sticking their wires and such to me?"

He could imagine. She must have been terrified. "No," he said. "Tell me."

"All I could think was, I was going to die and leave you alone," she murmured, and a single tear fell from the corner of her eye to roll down her temple and into her hair.

"There'll be no talk of dying," he told her, instinctively fighting against the fear that crouched inside him. "And I'm not alone. I've friends, and Ronan and Laura, and now the baby…"

"And no family of your own," she pointed out.

"And what're you then?" Sean teased.

She shook her head and fixed her gaze with his. "You

should have a wife. A family, Sean. A man shouldn't live his life alone."

It was an old argument. Ailish was forever trying to marry off her only child. But now, for the first time, Sean felt guilty. She should have been concerned for herself; instead she was worried for him. Worried *about* him. He hated that she was lying there so still and pale, and that there was nothing he could do for her. Bloody hell, he couldn't even get the damn doctor to step into the room.

"Ronan's settled and happy now," Ailish said softly. "And so should you be."

Her fingers felt small and fragile in his grip, and the fear and worry bottled up inside Sean seemed to spill over. "I am," he blurted before he was even aware of speaking.

Her gaze sharpened. "You are what?"

"Settled," he lied valiantly. He hadn't planned to. But seeing her worry needlessly had torn something inside Sean and had him telling himself that this at least, he could do for her. A small lie couldn't be that bad, could it, if it brought peace? And what if she *was* dying, God forbid, but how was he to know since no one would tell him anything. Wouldn't it be better for her to go believing that Sean was happy?

"I'm engaged," he continued, and gave his mother a smile. "I was going to tell you next week," he added, as the lie built up steam and began to travel on its own.

Her eyes shone and a smile curved her mouth even as twin spots of color flushed her pale cheeks. "That's wonderful," she said. "Who is she?"

Who indeed?

Brain racing, Sean could think of only one woman who would fit this particular bill, but even he couldn't drag Georgia into this lie without some warning. "I'll tell you as soon as you're fit and out of here."

Now those sharp green eyes narrowed on him. "If this is a trick…"

He slapped one hand to his chest and hoped not to be struck down as he said, "Would I lie about something this important?"

"No," she said after a long moment, "no, you wouldn't."

Guilt took another nibble of his soul.

"There you are then," he pronounced. "Now try to get some sleep."

She nodded, closed her eyes and still with a smile on her face, was asleep in minutes. Which left Sean alone with his thoughts—

A few hours later the doctor finally deigned to make an appearance, and though Sean was furious, he bit his tongue and was glad he had. A minor heart attack. No damage to her heart, really, just a warning of sorts for Ailish to slow down a bit and take better care of herself.

The doctor also wanted a few more tests to be sure of his results, which left Sean both relieved and worried. A minor heart attack was still serious enough. Was she well enough to find out he'd…*exaggerated* his engagement?

She would be in hospital for a week, resting under doctor's orders, so Sean wouldn't have to decide about telling her the truth right away. But he *did* have to have a chat with Georgia. Just in case.

Four

He left his mother sleeping and made his way out of the hospital, grateful to leave behind its smell of antiseptic and fear. Stepping into a soft, evening mist, Sean stopped dead when a familiar voice spoke up.

"Sean?"

He turned and felt a well of pleasure open up inside as Georgia walked toward him. "What're you doing here?" he asked, wrapping both arms around her and holding on.

She hugged him, then pulled her head back to look up at him. "When we didn't hear anything, I got worried. So I came here to wait for you. How's your mom?"

Pleasure tangled with gratitude as he realized just how much he'd needed to see her. He'd been a man alone for most of his adult life, never asking for anything, never expecting anyone to go an extra meter for him. Yet here she was, stepping out of the mist and cold, and Sean had never been happier to see anyone.

"She's well, though the doctor's holding on to her for a week or so. More tests, he says, and he wants her to rest. Never could get my mother to slow down long enough to *rest,* so God help the nurses trying to hold her down in that bed," he said, dropping a quick kiss on her forehead. "Scared me, Georgia. I don't even remember the last time anything has."

"Family does that to you," she told him. "But she's okay?"

"Will be," he said firmly. "It was a 'minor' heart attack, they say. No permanent damage, though, so that's good. She's to take it easy for a few weeks, no upsets. But yes, she'll be fine."

"Good news." Georgia's gaze narrowed on him. "So why do you look more worried than relieved?"

"I'll tell you all. But first, I've a need to get away from this place. Feels like I've been here for years instead of hours." Frowning, he looked out at the car park. "How did you get here?"

"Called a cab." She shrugged. "Laura was going to drive me, but I told her and Ronan that I'd be fine and you'd bring me home."

"As I will," he said, taking her arm and steering her toward his car. "But first, we'll go to my house. We need to talk."

"You'll tell me on the way?"

"I think not," he hedged. "I'm a man in desperate need of a beer, and I'm thinking you'll be needing wine to hear this."

There wasn't enough wine in the world.

"Are you insane?" Georgia jumped off the comfortable sofa in Sean's front room and stared down at him in stunned shock. "I mean, seriously. Maybe we should have had *you* examined at the hospital while we were there."

Sean huffed out a breath and took a long drink of the beer he'd poured for himself as soon as they reached his home. Watching him, Georgia took a sip of her Chardonnay, to ease the tightness in her own throat.

Then he leaned forward and set the glass of beer onto the table in front of him. "I'm not insane, no. Crazy perhaps, but not insane."

"Fine line, if you ask me."

He pushed one hand through his hair and muttered, "I'm not explaining this well a'tall."

"Oh, I don't know." Georgia sipped at her wine, then set her own glass down beside his. Still standing, she crossed both arms over her chest and said, "You were pretty clear. You want me to *pretend* to be engaged to you so you can lie to your mother. That about cover it?"

He scowled and stood up, Georgia thought, just so he could loom over her from his much greater height.

"Well, when you put it like that," he muttered, "it sounds—"

"Terrible? Is that the word you're looking for?"

He winced as he scrubbed one hand across his face. Georgia felt a pang of sympathy for him even though a part of her wanted to kick him.

"I thought she was dying."

"So you lied to her to give her a good send-off?"

He glared at her, and for the first time since she'd known him, she wasn't seeing the teasing, laughing, charming Sean...but instead the hard-lined owner of Irish Air. This was the man who'd bought out a struggling airline and built it into the premier luxury line in the world. The man who had become a billionaire through sheer strength of will. His eyes flashed with heat, with temper, and his mouth, the one she knew so well, was now flattened into a grim line.

Georgia, who had a temper of her own and just as hard a head, was unimpressed.

"If you think I enjoy lying to her, you're wrong."

"Well, good, because I *like* your mother."

"As do I," he argued.

"Then tell her the truth."

"I will," he countered, "as soon as the doctor says she's well again. Until then, would it really be so bad to let her believe a small lie?"

"Small." She shook her head and walked toward the wide stone hearth, where a fire burned against the cold night. On the mantel above the fire were framed family photos. Sean and Ronan. Sean and his mother. Laura and Georgia captured forever the day Ronan and Sean had taken them to the Burren—a lonely, desolate spot just a few miles outside Galway. Family was important to him, she knew that. Seeing these photos only brought that truth back to her.

She turned her back to the flames and looked at him, across the room from her. Sean's and Ronan's houses were both huge, sprawling manors, but Sean's was more…casual, she supposed was the right word. He'd lived alone here, but for his housekeeper and any number of people who worked on the estate, so he'd done as he pleased with the furniture.

Oversize sofas covered in soft fabric in muted shades of gray and blue crowded the room. Heavy, carved wooden tables dotted the interior, brass-based reading lamps tossed golden circles of light across gleaming wood floors and midnight-blue rugs. The walls were stone as well, interspersed with heavy wooden beams, and the wide front windows provided a view of a lawn that looked as if the gardener had gone over it on his knees with a pair of scissors, it was so elegantly tended.

"Is it really such a chore to pretend to be mad about me?" he asked, a half smile curving his mouth.

She looked at him and thought, no, pretending to be crazy about him wasn't a problem. Which should probably *be* a problem, she told herself, but that was a worry for another day.

"You want me to lie to Ailish."

"For only a while," he said smoothly. "To give me time to see her settled." He frowned a bit and added quietly, "She's…important to me, Georgia. I don't want her hurt."

God, was there anything sexier than a man unafraid to show his love for someone? Knowing how much Ailish meant to Sean touched Georgia deeply, but she was still unconvinced that his plan was a good one. Still, she remembered clearly how devastated she had been when she'd discovered all of her ex-husband's lies to her. Wouldn't Ailish feel the same sort of betrayal?

She shook her head slowly. "And you don't think she'll be hurt when she discovers she's been tricked?"

"Ah, but she won't find that out, will she?" Sean said, and he was smiling again, his temper having blown away as fast as it had come. "When the time is right, you'll throw me over, as well you should, and I'll bravely go on with my heart shattered to jagged pieces."

She snorted a laugh before she could stop it.

"So I get to be the bad guy, too?" She walked back, picked up her wine and took another sip. "Wow, I'm a lucky woman, all right. You remember I'm moving to Dunley, don't you? I'll see Ailish all the time, Sean, and she's going to think I'm a hideous person for dumping her son."

"She won't blame you," he assured her, "I'll see to it."

"Uh-huh."

"Georgia love," he said with a sigh, "you're my only chance at pulling this off."

"I don't like it."

"Of course you don't, being an honest woman." He plucked the wineglass from her fingers and set it aside. Then, stroking his hands up and down her arms, he added, "But being a warm-hearted, generous one as well, you can see this is the best way, can't you?"

"You think you can smooth me into this with a caress and a kiss?"

He bent down until his eyes were fixed on hers. "Aye, I do." Before she could respond to that arrogant admission, he added, "But I don't think I'll have to, will I? You've a kind heart, Georgia, and I know you can see why I've to do this."

Okay, yes, she could. Irritating to admit that even to herself. She understood the fear that must have choked him when he thought his mother was going to die. But damn it. Memories fluttered in her mind like a swarm of butterflies. "Lies never go well, Sean."

"But we're not lying to each other now, are we? So between the two of us, everything is on the up and up, and my mother will get over the disappointment—when she's well."

"It's not *just* your mother, though," she said. "The whole village will know. They'll all think I'm a jerk for dumping you."

"Hah!" Sean grinned widely. "Most of those in Dunley will think you a fool for agreeing to marry me in the first place and will swear you've come to your senses when we end it. And if that doesn't do the job, I'll take the blame entirely."

She laughed, because he looked so pleased with that statement. "You're completely shameless, aren't you?"

"Absolutely," he agreed, with that grin that always managed to make her stomach take a slow bump and roll. "So will you do it then, Georgia? Will you pretend to be engaged to me?"

She was tempted, she could admit that much to herself. It was a small thing, after all. Just to help her lover out of a tight spot. And oh, he was a wonderful lover, she thought, her heart beginning to trip wildly in her chest. The time spent with him in the past couple of weeks had been…fabulous. But this was something else again.

"I can help you get your business license," he offered. "You're bogged down in the mire of bureaucratic speak, and I don't know as you'd noticed or not, but things in Ireland move at their own pace. You could be a woman with a walker by the time you got that license pushed through on your own."

She gave him a hard look. "But you're a magician?"

"I've a way about me, that's true. But also, I know some of those that are in charge of these things and frankly, as the owner of Irish Air, I carry a bit more weight to my words than you would."

He could. Darn it. She'd already seen for herself that working her way through the reams of paperwork was going to be mind-boggling.

"I could see you settled and ready for business much faster than you could do it on your own."

"Are you trying to bribe me?"

He grinned, unashamed. "I am and doing a damn fine job of it if you ask me."

Staring up into his brown eyes, shining now with the excitement for his plan, Georgia knew she was pretty much done. And let's face it, she told herself, he'd had her from the jump. Not only was it a great excuse to keep their affair going—but she knew how worried he was about Ailish and she felt for him. He had probably never doubted for a moment that he'd be able to talk her into joining him in his insanity. Even *before* the really superior bribe.

He was unlike anyone she'd ever known, Georgia thought. Everything about him was outrageous. Why wouldn't a proposal from Sean Connolly be the same?

"And, did you know there's a cottage for sale at the edge of the village?"

"Is that the one I hear you were talking to someone named Brian about?"

"Ah, the Dunley express," he said with a grin. "Talk about it in the pub and it's as good as published in the paper. No, this isn't Brian's mum's place. He's rented it just last week to Sinead and Michael when they come home."

"Oh." Well, there went a perfectly good cottage. "I spoke to Mary this afternoon, and she didn't say a thing about a cottage for sale."

"She doesn't know all," Sean said, bending to plant one quick, hard kiss on her lips. "For example, I own two of the cottages near the close at the end of main. Not far from your new shop…"

That last bit he let hang there long enough for Georgia to consider it. Then he continued.

"They're small, but well kept. Close to the village center and with a faery wood in the back."

She shook her head and laughed. "A what?"

He smiled, that delicious, slow curve of his mouth that promised wickedness done to perfection. "A faery wood, where if you stand and make a wish on the full of the moon, you might get just what your heart yearns for." He paused. "Or, the faeries might snatch you away to live forever in their raft beneath the trees."

With the song of Ireland in his voice, even the crazy sounded perfectly reasonable. "Faeries."

"You'd live in Ireland and dismiss them?" he challenged, his eyes practically twinkling now with good humor and banked laughter.

"Sean…"

"I could be convinced to make you a very good deal on either of the cottages, if…"

"You're evil," she said softly. "My mother used to warn me about men like you."

"An intelligent woman to be sure. I liked her very much when we met at Ronan's wedding."

Her mother had liked him, too. But then, her mom liked everybody. Georgia could remember being like that once upon a time. Before her ex-husband had left her for her cheerleader cousin and cleaned out their joint accounts on his way out of town. Just remembering the betrayal, the hurt, stiffened her spine even while her mind raced. Too many thoughts piling together were jumbled up in possibilities and possible disasters.

She was torn, seriously. She really did like Sean's mother and she hated the thought of lying to her. But Sean would be the *real* liar, right? Oh, man, even she couldn't buy that one. She would be in this right up to her neck if she said yes. But how could she not? Sean was offering to help her get her new life started, and all she had to do was pretend to be in love with him.

And that wasn't going to be too difficult, she warned herself. Just standing here beside him was dangerous. She knew all too well what it was like to have his hands and his mouth on her. Having a lover like Sean—much less a fiancé, pretend or not—was really a slippery slope toward something she had to guard against.

She wasn't interested in trusting another man. Giving her heart over to him. Giving him the chance to crush her again. Sure, Sean was nothing like her ex, but he was still *male*.

"What do you say, Georgia?" he asked, reaching down to take her hands in his and give them a squeeze. "Will you pretend-marry me?"

She couldn't think. Not with him holding on to her. Not with his eyes staring into hers. Not with the heat of him reaching for her, promising even *more* heat if she let him get any closer. And if she did that, she would agree to anything, because she well knew the man could have her half out of her mind in seconds.

Georgia pulled her hands free of his and took one long step back. "This isn't the kind of thing I can decide on in a minute, Sean. There's a lot to consider. So I'll think about it and let you know tomorrow, okay?"

He opened his mouth as if to argue, then, a moment later, changed his mind. Nodding, he closed the distance between them again and pulled her into the circle of his arms. Georgia leaned into him, giving herself this moment to feel the rush of something spectacular that happened every time he touched her.

Kissing the top of her head, he whispered, "Fine then. That'll do. For now."

With him holding on to her, the beat of his heart beneath her ear, Georgia was tempted to do all sorts of things, so she looked away from him, out the window to the rain-drenched evening. Lamps lining the drive shone like diamonds in the gray. But the darkness and the incessant rain couldn't disguise the beauty that was Ireland.

Just like, she thought, looking up at Sean, a lie couldn't

hide what was already between the two of them. She didn't know where it was going, but she had a feeling the ride was going to be much bumpier than she had planned.

"I feel like I haven't slept in years," Laura groaned over her coffee the following morning.

"At least you can have caffeine again," Georgia said.

"Yes." Her sister paused. "Is it wrong to be nearly grateful that Fiona had no interest in nursing just so I can have coffee again?"

"If it is, I won't tell."

"You're the best." Laura slouched in a chair near the end of the couch where Georgia sat, checking email on her computer tablet.

Though she'd never been much of a morning person, it was hard to remain crabby when you got to sit in this beautiful parlor sipping coffee every morning. Of course, the baby had jumbled life in the manor, but she had to admit she loved being around her niece. Georgia glanced out the window at a sun-washed vista of sloping yard and trees beginning to lose their leaves for winter. For the first time in days, the sky was clear, but the cold Irish wind was tossing leaves into the air and making the trees dance and sway.

"I'm so excited that you're moving to Ireland," Laura said. "I really miss you when you're not around."

Georgia smiled at her sister. "I know, me, too. And it is exciting to move," she said, as she reached out for the silver pot on the rolling tea table in front of them. Hefting it, she refilled both her own and Laura's cups. Tea might be the big thing over here, but thankfully Patsy Brennan was willing to brew a pot of coffee for the Page sisters every morning. "Also, moving is terrifying. Not only going to a new place and starting over, but it's all the logistics of the thing. Canceling mail and utilities, starting them up somewhere else, and the packing."

Georgia shuddered and took a sip of coffee to bolster her.

"I get that. I was worried when I first moved here with Ronan, but everything went great."

"You had Ronan."

"And you have *me*."

"Ever the optimist," Georgia noted.

"No point in being a pessimist," Laura countered. "If you go around all grim, expecting the worst, when it happens, you've been suffering longer than you had to."

Georgia just blinked at her. "I'll work on that one and let you know when I figure it out."

Laura grinned, then sobered up again. "I wish you'd reconsider living here with us. There's plenty of room."

She knew her sister meant it, and having her offer was really wonderful. Even though having a secret affair was hard to manage when you were living with your sister. "I know, and I appreciate the offer. Just like I appreciate you letting me stay here when I visit. But I want my own place, Laura."

"Yeah, I know."

Morning light filtered into the room, and the winter sunshine was pale and soft. The baby monitor receiver that Laura carried with her at all times sat on the coffee table in front of them, and from it came the soft sounds of Fiona's breathing and the tiny sniffling sounds she made as she slept.

"Yesterday, Sean told me he owns a couple of cottages at the edge of the village," Georgia said. "He's going to sell me one of them."

"And that," Laura said thoughtfully, "brings us to the

main question for the day. What's going on with you and Sean?"

She went still and dropped her gaze to the black coffee in her cup. "Nothing."

"Right. What am I, blind? I gave birth in the hospital, Georgia," her sister pointed out, "I didn't have a lobotomy."

"Laura…" Georgia had known this was coming. Actually, it was probably only because Laura was so wrapped up in Fiona that she hadn't noticed earlier. Laura wasn't stupid and as she just mentioned, not blind, either.

"I can see how you guys are around each other," Laura was saying, tapping her fingernails lightly against the arm of the chair. "He watches you."

"Oooh, that's suspicious."

"I said he *watches* you. Like a man dying of thirst and you're a fountain of ice-cold water."

Something inside her stirred and heat began to crawl through Georgia's veins, in spite of her effort to put a stop to it. After that proposal Sean had made last night, he'd kissed her senseless, then dropped her off here at the manor, leaving Georgia so stirred up she'd hardly slept. Now, just the thought of Sean was enough to light up the ever-present kindling inside her.

Shaking her head, she said only, "Leave it alone, Laura."

"Sure. I'll do that. I'm sorry. Have we met?" Laura leaned toward her. "Honey, don't get me wrong. I'm glad you're having fun finally. God knows it took you long enough to put what's-his-name in the past—"

At the mention of Georgia's ex, she frowned. Okay, fine. It had taken her some time to get past the fury of being used, betrayed and then finally, publicly *dumped*.

But she figured most women would have come out of that situation filled with righteous fury.

"Gee, thanks."

"—I just don't want you to get crushed again."

"What happened to that optimism?"

Laura frowned at her. "This is different. What if you guys crash and burn? Then you'll be living here, with Sean right around the corner practically and seeing him all the time and you'll be miserable. I don't want that for you."

Georgia sighed and gave her sister's hand a pat. "I know. But you don't get to decide that, Laura. And we're not going to crash and burn. We're just…"

"…yeah?"

"I was going to say we're just lovers."

"There's no 'just' about it for you, Georgia," Laura sputtered. "Not for either one of us. We're not built that way. We don't do 'easy.'"

"I know that, too," Georgia argued, "but I did the cautious thing for years, and what did it get me? I thought Mike was the one, remember? Did everything right. Dated for two years, was engaged for one of those two. Big wedding, nice house, working together to build something, and what happened?"

Laura winced.

Georgia saw it and nodded. "Exactly. Mike runs off with Misty, who, if she had two thoughts running around in that tiny brain of hers, would rattle like BBs in a jar."

Laura smiled, but sadly. "That's no reason to jump into something with a man like Sean."

Suddenly forced to defend the man she was currently sleeping with, Georgia said, "What does that mean, 'a man like Sean'? He's charming and treats me great. We have fun together, and that's all either one of us is looking for."

"For now."

Georgia shook her head and smiled. "All I'm interested in at the moment is 'for now,' Laura. I did the whole cautious thing for way too long. Maybe it's time to cut loose a little. Stop thinking nonstop about the future and just enjoy today."

A long moment passed before Laura sighed and said, "Maybe you're right. Sean is a sweetie, but Georgia—"

"Don't worry," she said, holding up one hand to stave off any more advice. "I'm not looking for marriage and family. I don't know that I ever will."

"Of course you will," Laura told her, sympathy and understanding shining in her eyes. "That's who you are. But if this is what you need right now, I'm on your side."

"Thanks. And," Georgia added, "as long as we're talking about this, you should know that last night Sean asked me to help him out."

In a few short sentences, she explained Sean's plan and watched Laura's mouth drop open. "You can't be serious."

"I think I am."

"Let me count the ways this could go bad."

"Do me a favor and don't, okay?" Georgia glanced down at her email and idly deleted a couple of the latest letters from people offering to send her the winnings to contests she'd never entered. "I've thought about it, and I understand why he's doing it."

"So do I. That doesn't make it a good idea."

"What's not a good idea?" Ronan asked, as he walked into the room and paused long enough to kiss his wife good morning before reaching out to grab a cup and pour himself some coffee.

"Your idiot cousin," Laura started, firing a glare at her

husband as if this were all his fault, "wants my sister to pretend they're engaged."

While Laura filled Ronan in, Georgia sat back and concentrated on her coffee. She had a feeling she was going to need all the caffeine she could get.

Five

When Laura finally wound down and sat in her chair, alternately glowering at Ronan and then her sister, Georgia finally spoke up.

"Sean can sell me a cottage," she said calmly. "He can help push through my business license and speed things up along the bureaucratic conga line."

"Ronan can do that, too, you know."

"I know he can," Georgia said with a smile for her brother-in-law. "Sean's already volunteered."

"And…" Laura said.

"And what?"

"And you're already lovers, so this is going to complicate things."

"Oh," Ronan muttered, "when did that happen? No. Never mind. I don't need to know this."

"It's not going to get complicated," Georgia insisted.

"Everything gets complicated," Laura argued. "Heck,

look at me! I broke up with Ronan last year, remember? Now here I sit, in Ireland, married, with a baby daughter."

Ronan asked wryly, "Are you complaining?"

Laura shot a look at the man studying her through warm brown eyes. "No way. Wouldn't change a thing. I'm just saying," she continued, shifting her gaze back to Georgia, "that even when you think you know what's going to happen, things suddenly turn upside down on you."

A warbling cry erupted from the baby monitor on the table in front of Laura. Picking it up, she turned off the volume and stood.

"I have to go get the baby, but we're not done here," she warned, as she left the dining room.

"Laura's just worried for you." Ronan poured himself more coffee, then sat back and crossed his legs, propping one foot on the opposite knee.

"I know." She looked at him and asked, "But you've known Sean forever. What do you think?"

"I think I warned Sean to keep his distance from you already, for all the good that's done." Then he thought about it for a moment or two, and said, "It's a good idea."

Georgia smiled and eased back in her chair. "Glad to hear you say that."

"But," he added.

"There's always a *but,* isn't there?"

"Right enough," he said. "I can see why Sean wants to do this. Keep his mother happy until she's well. And you helping him is a grand thing as long as you remember that Sean's not the man to *actually* fall for."

"I'm not an idiot," Georgia reminded him.

"And who knows that better than I?" Ronan countered with a smile. "You helped me out last year when Laura was making my life a misery—"

"You're welcome."

"—and I'll do the same now. Sean is a brother to me, and so if he hurts you and I'm forced to kill him, it would pain me."

Georgia grinned. "Thanks. I never had a big brother threaten to beat up a boy who was mean to me."

He toasted her with his coffee cup. "Well, you do now."

She laughed a little. "Good to know."

"You'd already made up your mind to go along with Sean's plan, even before you told Laura, hadn't you?"

"Just about," she admitted. But until Ronan had thrown in on her side, she had still had a few doubts. Being close with Sean was no hardship, but getting much closer could be dangerous to her own peace of mind. Laura was right. Georgia wasn't the "take a lover, use him and lose him" kind of woman. So her heart would be at risk unless she guarded it vigilantly.

"So you've signed your rental agreement on the shop?"

"I did, and I'm going into Galway this morning to look at furnishings." She glanced down at her computer tablet as a sound signaled an incoming email. "I'm really excited about the store, too. Of course it needs some fresh paint and—" She broke off as her gaze skimmed the e-vite she had just received. "You have *got* to be kidding me."

"What is it?" All serious now, Ronan demanded, "What's wrong?"

Georgia hardly heard him over the roaring in her ears. She read the email again and then once more, just to be sure she was seeing it right. She was.

"That miserable, rotten, cheating, lying…"

"Who's that then?"

"My *ex*-husband and my *ex*-cousin," Georgia grumbled. "Of all the— I can't believe this. I mean seriously, could this be any more tacky? Even for *them?*"

"Ah," Ronan muttered. "This may be more in Laura's line…"

Georgia tossed her computer tablet to the couch cushion beside her, set her coffee cup down with a clatter and stood up, riding the wings of pure rage. "I'll see you later, Ronan."

"What?" He stood too and watched as she headed for the back door that led to the stone patio, the garden and the fields beyond. "Where are you going? What am I to tell Laura?"

"Tell her I just got engaged."

Then she was through the door and across the patio.

She could have taken a car and driven along the narrow, curving road to Sean's place. But as angry as she was, Georgia couldn't have sat still for that long. Instead, she took the shortcut. Straight across a sunlit pasture so green it hurt her eyes to look at it. Stone fences rambled across the fields, and she was forced to scramble over them to go on her way.

Normally, she loved this walk. On the right was the round tower that stood near an ancient cemetery on Ronan's land. To her left was Lough Mask, a wide lake fringed by more trees swaying in the wind. In the distance, she heard the whisper of the ocean and the low grumbling of a farmer's tractor. The sky above was a brilliant blue, and the wind that flew at her carried the chill of the sea.

Georgia was too furious to feel the cold.

Her steps were quick, and she kept her gaze focused on her target. The roof of Sean's manor house was just visible above the tips of the trees, and she headed there with a steely determination.

She crossed the field, walked into the wood and only then remembered Sean saying something about the faeries and how they might snatch her away.

"Well, I'd like to see them try it today," she murmured.

Georgia came out of the thick stand of trees at the edge of Sean's driveway. A wide gravel drive swung in a graceful arch in front of the stone-and-timber manor. Leaded windows glinted in the sunlight. As she neared the house, Sean stepped out and walked to meet her. He was wearing black slacks, a cream-colored sweater and a black jacket. His dark hair ruffled in the wind, and his hands were tucked into his pockets.

"Georgia!" He grinned at her. "I was going to stop to see you on my way to hospital to check in on my mother."

She pushed her tangled hair back from her face and stomped the dew and grass from her knee-high black boots. She wore her favorite, dark green sweater dress, and the wind flipped the hem around her knees. She had one short flash that for something this big, she should have worn something better than a dress she'd had for five years. But then, she wasn't really getting engaged, was she? It was a joke. A pretense.

Just like her first marriage had been.

"Are you all right?" he asked, his smile fading as he really looked at her. Walking closer, he pulled his hands from his pockets and reached out to take hold of her shoulders.

"Really not." Georgia took a deep breath of the cold Irish air and *willed* it to settle some of the roaring heat she still felt inside. It didn't work.

"What's wrong then?"

There was real concern on his face and for that, she

was grateful. Sean was exactly who he claimed to be. There was no hidden agenda with him. There were no secrets. He wouldn't cheat on a woman and sneak out of town with every cent she owned. It wouldn't even occur to him. She could admire that about him since she had already survived the man who was the exact opposite of Sean Connolly.

That thought brought her right back to the reason for her mad rush across the open field.

"You offered me a deal yesterday," she said.

"I did."

"Now I've got one for you."

Sean released her, but didn't step back. His gaze was still fixed on her and concern was still etched on his face. "All right then, let's hear it."

"I don't even know where to start," she said suddenly, then blurted out, "I just got an email from my cousin Misty. The woman my ex-husband ran off with."

"Ah." He nodded as if he could understand now why she was so upset.

"Actually, the email was an e-vite to their *wedding*."

His jaw dropped, and she could have kissed him for that alone. That he would *get* it, right away, no explanation necessary, meant more to Georgia than she could have said.

"She sent you an e-vite?" He snorted a laugh, then noted her scowl and sobered up fast. "Bloody rude."

"You think?" Shaking her head, Georgia started pacing back and forth on the gravel drive, hearing the grinding noise of the pebbles beneath her boots. "First, that she's tacky enough to use e-vites as wedding invitations!" She shot him a look and threw both hands in the air. "Who does that?"

"I wouldn't know."

"Of course you wouldn't, because *no one* does that!" Back to pacing, the *crunch, crunch* of the gravel sounding out in a rapid rhythm. "And really? You send one of your stupid, tacky e-vites to the woman your fiancé cheated on? The one he left for *you?*"

"The pronouns are starting to get confusing, in case you were wondering," Sean told her.

She ignored that. "And Mike. What the hell was *he* thinking?" Georgia demanded. "He thinks it's okay to invite me to his wedding? What're we now? Old *friends?* I'm supposed to be civilized?"

"What fun is civilized?" Sean asked.

"Exactly!" She stabbed a finger at him. "Not that I care who the creep marries and if you ask me, the two of them deserve each other, but why does either one of them think I want to be there to watch the beginning of a marriage that is absolutely doomed from the start?"

"Couldn't say," Sean said.

"No one could, because it doesn't make sense," Georgia continued, letting the words rush from her on a torrent of indignation. Then something occurred to her. "They probably don't expect me to actually *go* to the wedding."

"No?"

"No." She stopped dead, faced Sean and said, "Misty just wants me to *know* that she finally got Mike to marry her. Thinks it'll hurt me somehow."

"And of course she's wrong about that," Sean mused.

She narrowed her eyes on him. "Do I look hurt to you?"

"Not a bit," he said quickly. "You look furious and well you should be."

"Damn right." She set both hands on her hips and tapped the toe of one boot against the gravel, only absently noting the rapid *tappity, tappity, tap* sound. "But you know what? I'm *going* to that wedding. I'm going to be the chill kiss of death for those two at the happy festivities."

Sean laughed. "I do admire a woman with fire in her eyes."

"Then stick around," she snapped. "I'm going to show them just how little they mean to me."

"Good on you," Sean said.

"And the kicker is, I'm going to be arriving at their wedding in Brookhollow, Ohio, with my gorgeous, fabulously wealthy Irish fiancé."

One corner of his mouth tipped up. "Are you now?"

"That's the deal," Georgia said calmly, now that the last of her outrage had been allowed to spill free. "I'll help you keep your mom happy until she's well if you go to this wedding with me and convince everyone there that you're nuts about me."

"That's a deal," he said quickly and walked toward her.

She skipped back a step and held up one hand to keep him at bay. "And you'll help me get my license and sell me that cottage, too, right?"

"Absolutely."

"Okay, then." She huffed out a breath as if she'd been running a marathon.

"We've a deal, Georgia Page, and I think we'll both come out of this for the better."

"I hope you're right," she said and held out her right hand to take his in a handshake.

He smirked and shook his head. "That's no way to seal a deal between lovers."

Then he swooped in, grabbed her tightly and swung her into a dip that had her head spinning even *before* he kissed her blind.

* * *

The next few days flew past.

Georgia could even forget, occasionally, that what was between she and Sean wasn't actually *real*. He played his part so well. The doting fiancé. The man in love. Seriously, if she hadn't known it was an act, she would have tumbled headfirst into love with him.

And wouldn't that be awkward?

True to his word, Sean had pushed through the paperwork for her business license, and in just a week or two she would have it in hand. He sold her one of the cottages he owned and made her such a good deal on it she almost felt guilty, then she reminded herself that it was all part of the agreement they had struck. And with that reminder came the annoying tug of memory about her ex and the wedding Sean would be attending with her.

Georgia squared her shoulders and steeled her spine. She'd made her decision and wouldn't back away now. Besides, her new life was coming together. She had her lover. A shop. A new home.

And all of it built on a tower of lies, her mind whispered.

"The question is," she asked herself aloud, "what part of it will survive when the tower collapses?" Frowning at the pessimistic thoughts that she was determined to avoid, she added, "Not helping."

She had chosen her road and wouldn't change directions now. Whatever happened, she and Sean would deal with it. They were two adults after all. They could have sex. Have…whatever it was they had, without destroying each other. And then, there was the fact that even if she had been willing to consider ending their deal, she was in too deep to find a way out anyway. So instead, she would suck it up, follow the plan Sean had laid out and hope for the best.

Meanwhile, she had a shop to get ready and a new cottage to decorate and furnish.

She stepped back to take a look at her handiwork and smiled at the wash of palest yellow paint on one of the walls of her new office. It was cheerful and just bright enough to ease back the gray days that seemed to be a perpetual part of the Irish life. The smell of paint was strong, so she had propped open the front door. That cold wind she was so accustomed to now whipped through the opening and tugged at her hair as she worked.

All morning, people in the village had been stopping in, to offer help—which Georgia didn't need, since she wanted to do this part herself—or to offer congratulations on her upcoming marriage. So she hardly jumped when a voice spoke up from the doorway.

"It's lovely."

Georgia turned to smile at Ailish as Sean's mother walked into the shop just a step or two ahead of her son.

"Thanks." Georgia smiled at both of them. "I didn't know you were stopping by. Ailish, it's so good to see you out of the hospital."

"It's even better from my perspective," she answered quickly, a soft smile curving her mouth. "I can't tell you how badly I wanted to be home again. Of course, I was planning on going back to my own home in Dublin, but my son insists I stay at the family manor until I'm recovered—which I am even now, thanks very much."

"You're not recovered yet and you'll take it easy as the doctor advised," Sean told her.

"Take it easy," Ailish sniffed. "How'm I to do that with you and everyone else hovering?"

Georgia grinned at the expression of helpless frustration on Sean's face. She understood how he was feeling, but she really identified with Ailish. Georgia didn't appreciate hovering, either. "How're you feeling?"

The smaller woman hurried across the tarp-draped floor and took Georgia in a hard, brief hug. "I'm wonderful is what I am," she said. "Sean's told me your news and I couldn't be happier."

Guilt flew like an arrow and stabbed straight into Georgia's heart. She looked into Ailish's sharp green eyes and felt *terrible* for her part in this lie. But at the same time, she could see that Sean's mother's face was pale and there were shadows beneath those lovely eyes of hers. So she wasn't as well as she claimed and maybe, Georgia thought wildly, that was enough of a reason to carry on with the lie.

"Isn't it lovely that you and your sister both will be here, married and building families?" Ailish sighed at the romance of it. "I couldn't ask for a more perfect daughter-in-law."

"Thank you, Ailish," Georgia said and simply embraced the guilt, accepting that it would now be a part of her life. At least for a while.

"Now," Ailish said, grabbing Georgia's left hand. "Let me see the ring…"

There was no ring.

Georgia curled her fingers into her palm and threw a fast look at Sean who mimed slapping his hand to his forehead.

"We've not picked one out yet," he said quickly. "It has to be just right, doesn't it?"

"Hmm…" Ailish patted Georgia's hand even as she slid a curious look at her son. "Well, I'll look forward to seeing it."

"So," Georgia said into the quiet, "you're not heading home to Dublin?"

"Not for a bit yet," she said, "though I do long for my own things about me."

"The manor was your home until four years ago, mother," Sean reminded her. "There's plenty of your things there, as well. And someone to look after you."

"I don't need a keeper," Ailish told him. "Though there were plenty of times I was convinced you did. Until you had the sense to become engaged to Georgia."

"Thanks very much," Sean muttered, stuffing his hands into the pockets of his slacks.

"Now, if you don't mind, I think I'll go sit in the car again until you're ready to leave, Sean. Georgia," she added, leaning in to kiss her cheek, "I couldn't be happier for the both of you. It'll be a lovely wedding, and you know I think this one should be held in Dunley, as Ronan and Laura were married in California."

"Um, sure," Georgia said, as the pile of lies she was standing on grew higher and higher. "Only fair."

"Exactly." Ailish took a breath and let it slide from her lungs as she smiled. "Have you thought about when the wedding will be?"

"We really haven't gotten that far yet," Sean told her. "What with Georgia opening a new business and moving here and all, we've been too busy to set a date."

"Sometime soon then," Ailish went on in a rush. "Perhaps a Christmas wedding? Wouldn't that be lovely? Sean will send a plane for your parents of course, and perhaps they'd like to come out early, so we could all work on the wedding preparations together."

"I'll, um, ask them."

"Wonderful." Ailish smiled even wider, then turned

for a look at her son. "I'll speak to Father Leary tomorrow and see about having the banns read at Mass."

"All right then," Sean said stiffly, "I'll leave it in your hands."

"Good. That's settled. Now," Ailish added, "you two don't mind me. I'll be in the car, Sean, whenever you're ready."

They watched her through the window to make sure she was all right, and once she was safely in the car again, Georgia grabbed his arm. "The priest? She's going to have the banns read in church?"

This was suddenly way more complicated. For three weeks running, the priest would read the names of the couples wanting to be married, giving anyone with a legal or civil objection a chance to speak up. But that just meant the news would fly around Dunley even faster than they'd expected.

He pushed one hand through his hair. "Aye, well, that's the way it's done, isn't it?"

"Can't you ask her to wait?"

"And use what for a reason?" He shook his head. "No, the banns will be read but it changes nothing. We'll still call it off when you break up with me. It'll all be fine, Georgia. You'll see." He grabbed her left hand and ran his thumb over her ring finger. "I'm sorry though, that I forgot about a ring."

"It isn't important."

His gaze locked with hers. "It is, and it'll be taken care of today. I'll see to it."

"Sean," she whispered, moving in close, then sliding a quick look at Ailish to make absolutely certain the woman couldn't overhear them, "are you really *sure* we're doing the right thing?"

"I am," he insisted, dipping his head to hers. "She's

tired, Georgia. I've never seen my mother so pale, and I've no wish to give her a setback right now. Let's see her up and moving around and back to herself before we end this. We have a deal, right?"

She sighed miserably. "We do."

"Good then." He kissed her hard and fast. "I'll just take mother to the manor house, then I'll come back and help you paint."

Surrendering, she smiled and asked, "Are you a good painter?"

"I'm a man of many talents," he reminded her.

And as he walked out of the shop, Georgia thought, he really hadn't needed to remind her of that at all.

Six

"I've an itch between my shoulder blades," Sean confessed the following day, as he followed Ronan into the front parlor of his cousin's house.

He felt as if he were surrounded by women lately. Ordinarily, not a bad thing at all. But just now, between Georgia and his mother and his housekeeper and even Laura, who was giving him a glare every time they met up, he was ready for some strictly male company. And his cousin was the one to understand how he was feeling. Or so he thought.

"Not surprising." Ronan walked to the corner, where an elegant table stood in for a bar, and headed for the small refrigerator that held the beer he and Sean both needed. "It's probably much what a rabbit feels when the hunter's got his gun trained on it."

Sean winced and glared at his cousin's back. "Thanks for that. I've come to you looking for solidarity and you turn on me like a snake. Are you going to be no comfort to me in this?"

"I won't." Ronan bent to the fridge, opened it and pulled out two beers. As he closed the door again, he spotted something small and white beside it on the floor and picked it up. "A shirt button?"

"What?"

"A shirt button," Ronan repeated, standing up and glancing down at his own shirt front as if expecting to see that one of the buttons had leaped free of the fabric. "Where did that come from?"

Sean knew exactly where. It was one of his, after all, torn from his shirt the first night he and Georgia had made love, right here in this room, before a roaring fire. At the thought of that, he went hard as stone and covered his discomfort by snapping, "How'm I to know why your shirt button is on the bloody floor? Did you not hear me, Ronan? I said I'm in trouble."

Frowning still at the button, Ronan tossed it onto the table, then crossed the room and handed one of the beers to Sean. "'Tis no more than you deserve," he said, tearing off the bottle cap and taking a long drink. "I warned you, didn't I, at my own bleeding wedding, to keep your hands off our Georgia?"

Sean uncapped his beer as well and took a long, thirsty drink. Ronan had indeed warned him off, but even now, when things had gotten so completely confused, he couldn't bring himself to regret ignoring that warning.

"When a man's tempted by a woman like her," Sean mused, "he's hard put to remember unwanted advice."

"And yet, when the shite hits the fan, you come to me for more of that advice."

Sean scowled at his cousin. He'd thought to find a little male solidarity here in this house that had been as much his home as Ronan's since he was a child. Seems he'd been wrong. "When you've done gloating, let me know."

"I'll be a while yet," Ronan mused and dropped onto the sofa. Propping his booted feet up on the table in front of him, he glanced up at Sean and said, "What's got you so itchy, then?"

"What hasn't?" Shaking his head, Sean wandered the room, unable to settle. Unable to clear his mind enough to examine exactly why he felt as though he were doing a fast step-toe dance on a hot skillet—barefoot.

"Then pick one out of the bunch to start with."

"Fine." Sean whirled around, back to the fire, to face his cousin. Heat seared him from head to toe, and still there was a tiny chill inside it couldn't reach. "Father Leary dropped in on me this morning, wanting to have a 'pre-marriage' chat."

Ronan snorted. "Aye, I had one with the old man, as well. Always amazed me, bachelor priests thinking they know enough about marriage to be handing out counsel on how to treat a wife."

"Worse than that, he wanted to tell me all about how sex with a wife is different from sex with a mistress."

Ronan choked on a sip of beer, then burst out laughing. "That's what you get for having a reputation as quite the ladies' man. Father didn't feel it necessary to warn me of such things." As Ronan considered that, he frowned, clearly wondering whether or not he should be insulted.

"Fine for you," Sean grumbled. "I don't know which of us was more uncomfortable with that conversation— me, or the good father himself."

"I'd bet on you."

"You'd win that one, all right," Sean said, then took another drink of his beer. Shaking his head, he pushed that confrontation with the village priest out of his head. "Then there's Katie—"

"Your housekeeper?"

"No, the other Katie in my life, of *course* my bloody housekeeper," Sean snapped. "She's buying up bridal magazines and bringing them to Mother, who's chortling over them as if she's planning a grand invasion. She's already talked to me about flowers, as if I know a rose from a daisy, and do we want to rent a canvas to stretch over the gardens for the reception in case of rain—"

"Shouldn't be news to you," Ronan said mildly. "Not the first time you've been engaged, after all."

"'Tisn't the same," Sean muttered.

"Aye, no, because that time it wasn't a game, was it? And when Noreen dumped your ass and moved on, you couldn't have cared less."

All true, Sean thought. He'd asked Noreen Callahan to marry him more than three years ago now. It had seemed, he considered now, the thing to do at the time. After all, Noreen was witty and beautiful, and she liked nothing better than going to all the fancy dos he was forced to attend as Irish Air made a name for itself.

But he hadn't put in the time. He'd spent every minute on his business, and finally Noreen had had enough. She'd come to understand that not even getting her mitts on Sean's millions was enough motivation to live with a man who barely noticed her existence.

Sean had hardly noticed when she left. So what did that say about him? He'd decided then that he wasn't the marrying sort and nothing yet had happened to change his mind.

"This was all your idea," Ronan reminded him.

"Do you think I don't know that?" He scrubbed one hand across his face, then pushed that hand through his hair, fingers stabbing viciously. The longer this lie went on, the more it evolved. "There's a pool at the Pennywhistle, you know. Picking out dates for the wedding *and* the birth of our first child."

"I've five euros on December twenty-third myself." Ronan studied the label on his bottle of Harp.

"Why the bloody hell would you do that? You *know* there's not to be a wedding!"

"And if I don't enter a pool about your wedding, don't you think those in the village would wonder why?"

"Aye, I suppose." Sean shook his head and looked out the window at the sunny afternoon. Shadows slid across the lawn like specters as the trees that made them swayed in the wind. "No one in the village was this interested in my life when it was Noreen who was the expected bride."

"Because no one in the village could stand the woman," Ronan told him flatly. "A more nose-in-the-air, pretentious female I've never come across."

Hard to argue with that assessment, Sean thought, so he kept his mouth shut.

"But everyone around here *likes* Georgia. She's a fine woman."

"As if I didn't know that already."

"Just as you knew this would happen, Sean. It can't be a surprise to you."

"No, it's not," he admitted, still staring out the glass, as if searching for an answer to his troubles. "But it all feels as though it's slipping out of my control, and I've no idea how to pull it all back in again."

"You can't," Ronan said easily, and Sean wanted to kick him.

"Thanks for that, too." He sipped at his beer again and got no pleasure from the cold, familiar taste. "I'm seeing this whole marriage thing get bigger and bigger, and I've no idea what's going to happen when we finally call it off."

"Should've thought of that before this half-brained scheme of yours landed you in such a fix."

"Again, you're a comfort to me," he said, sarcasm dripping in his tone. "I've told Georgia I'll see to it that everyone blames me. But now I'm seeing that it's more complicated than that. Did you know, my assistant's already fielding requests for wedding invitations from some of my business associates?"

"Lies take on a life of their own," Ronan said quietly.

"True enough." Sean's back teeth clenched, as he remembered exactly how he'd gotten into this whole thing, and for the life of him, he couldn't say for sure now that he would have done it differently if given a chance. "You didn't see my mother lying in that hospital bed, Ronan. Wondering if she'd recover—or if, God forbid, I was going to lose her. Seeing her face so pale and then the tears on her cheeks as she worried for me." He paused and shook his head. "Scared me."

"Scared me, too," Ronan admitted. "Your mother's important to me, you know."

"I do know that." Sean took a deep breath, shook off the tattered remnants of that fear and demanded, "So out of your fondness for my mother, why not help save her son?"

"Ah no, lad. You're on your own in this."

"Thanks for that, as well."

"I will say that if Georgia ends up shedding one tear over what you've dragged her into," Ronan told him, "I will beat you bloody."

"I know that, too." Sean walked back and sat down beside Ronan. He kicked his feet up onto the table and rested his bottle of beer on his abdomen. "I'd expect nothing less."

"Well then, we're agreed." Ronan reached over and clinked the neck of his beer against Sean's. "You're in a hole that's getting deeper with every step you take, Sean. Mind you don't go in over your head."

As he drank to that discomforting toast, Sean could only think that Ronan was too late with this particular warning. He knew damn well he was already so deep, he couldn't see sky.

From Georgia's cottage kitchen downstairs came the incredible scent of potato-leek soup and fresh bread.

Georgia inhaled sharply, then sighed as she looked at her sister. "I think I'm going to keep Patsy here with me. You go on home to Ronan and have him cook for you."

"Never gonna happen," Laura told her on a laugh. "Besides, Patsy wouldn't leave now even if I wanted her to—which I don't—she's too crazy about Fiona."

Georgia looked down at the tiny baby cuddled in her arms and smiled wistfully. Milk-white skin, jet-black eyelashes lying in a curve on tiny, round cheeks. Wisps of reddish-brown hair and a tiny mouth pursed in sleep. A well of love opened in Georgia's heart, and she wondered how anything so young, so helpless, could completely change the look of the entire world in less than a month.

"Can't blame Patsy for that. I know I'm Fiona's aunt, but really, isn't she just beautiful?"

"I think so," Laura answered, and plopped down onto Georgia's new bed. "It's so huge, Georgia. The love I have for her is so immense. I just never knew anything could feel like this."

A trickle of envy wound its way around Georgia's heart before she recognized it, then banished it. She didn't begrudge her sister one moment of her happiness. But Georgia could admit, at least to herself, that she wished for some of the same for herself.

But maybe that just wasn't going to happen for her. The whole "husband and family" thing. A pang of regret sliced through her at that thought, but she had to accept that not everyone found love. Not everyone got to have their dreams come true. And sometimes, she told herself, reality just sucked.

"It's terrific," Georgia said, and jiggled the baby gently when she stirred and made a soft mewing sound. "You've got Ronan, Fiona, you're painting again..." As Georgia had given up on her design dreams to sell real estate, Laura had set aside her paints and easel in favor of practicality. Knowing that she'd rediscovered her art, had found the inspiration to begin painting again, made Georgia's heart swell. "I'm really happy for you, Laura."

"I know you are," her sister said. "I want *you* to be happy, too, you know."

"Sure I know. But I am happy," Georgia said, adding a smile to the words to really sell it. "Honest. I'm starting a new business. I'm moving to a new country. I've got a brand-new niece and a new home   what's not to be happy about?"

"I notice you didn't mention your new faux fiancé."

Georgia frowned a bit. "I don't *have* Sean."

"As far as the whole village of Dunley is concerned you do."

"Laura..." Georgia sighed a little, then crossed the bedroom and handed the baby back to her mother. She understood why her sister was concerned, but hearing about it all the time didn't help and it didn't change anything.

"All I'm saying is," Laura said, as she snuggled her

daughter close, "well, I don't really know what I'm saying. But the point is, I'm worried about you."

"Don't be."

"Oh, okay. All better." Laura blew out an exasperated breath. "I love Sean and all, but *you're* my sister, and I'm worried that this is going to blow up in your face. The whole village is counting on this wedding now. What happens when you call it off?"

Niggling doubts had Georgia chewing at her bottom lip. Hadn't she been concerned about the same thing from the very beginning? Everyone in Dunley was excited about the "wedding." Ailish had ordered a cake from the baker and then gleefully told Georgia that it was all taken care of.

"I don't know, but it's too late to worry about that now," she said firmly, and crossed the room to tug at the hem of the new curtains over one of the three narrow windows overlooking Sean's faery wood. A smile curved her mouth as she thought of him.

"I see that."

"What?"

"That smile. You're thinking about him."

"Stop being insightful. It's disturbing."

Laura laughed and shook her head. "Fine. I'll back off. For now."

"It's appreciated." Georgia didn't need her sister's worries crowding into her head. She barely had room for her own.

"So, do you need help packing?"

Now it was Georgia's turn to laugh. "For a trip I'm not taking until next week?"

"Fine, fine." Laura sighed a little. "I'm just trying to help out. I want you settled in and happy here, Georgia."

"I *am*." She looked around the bedroom of her new cottage.

It really helped knowing the owner, since Sean had given her the keys so she could move in *before* escrow closed on the place. It was good to have her own home, even though it wouldn't really feel like hers until she had some of her own furniture and things around her. Thank God, though, as a rental it had come furnished, so she at least had a place to sit and sleep, and pots and pans for the kitchen.

She'd taken the smaller of the two cottages Sean had shown her. The other one had been a row cottage, differentiated from the homes on either side of it only by the shade of emerald green painted on the front door. It was bigger and more modern, but the moment Georgia had seen *this* one, she'd been lost.

Mainly because this cottage appealed to her sense of whimsy.

It was a freestanding home, with a thatched roof and white-washed walls. Empty flower boxes were attached to the front windows like hope for spring. The door was fire-engine red, and the back door opened onto a tiny yard with a flower bed and a path that led into the faery wood.

The living room was small, with colorful rugs strewn across a cement floor that was painted a deep blue. A child-sized fireplace was tucked into one wall with two chairs pulled up in front of it. The kitchen was like something out of the forties, but everything worked beautifully. The staircase to the second floor was as steep as a ladder, and her bedroom was small with her bed snuggled under a sloping ceiling. But the windows looked out over the woods, and the bathroom had been updated recently to include a tub big enough to stretch out in.

It was a fairy-tale cottage, and Georgia already loved it.

This would be her first night in her new place, and she was anxious to nudge Laura on her way so that she could relax in that beautiful tub and pour herself a glass of wine to celebrate the brand-new chapter in her life.

"It is a great cottage." Laura looked at her for a long minute then frowned and asked, "You sure you don't want Fiona and me along for the trip back to California?"

"Absolutely not." On this, Georgia was firm. "I'm not going to be there for long, and all I have to do is sign the papers to put the condo up for sale. After that, when they find a buyer for the place, they can fax me the paperwork and I'll handle it from here. Then I'll arrange for my stuff to be shipped to Ireland and I'll be done. Besides," she added with a grim nod, "when I leave California, I'll be stopping in Ohio for the wedding."

Laura shook her head. "Why you're insisting on going to that is beyond me. I mean come on. You're over Mike, so what do you care?"

"I don't." And she realized as she said it that she really didn't care about her ex-husband and his soon-to-be wife, the husband-stealing former cheerleader. After all, if Mike hadn't been willing to cheat on his wife, Misty never would have gotten him in the first place.

So Georgia figured she was much better off without him anyway. "It's the principle of the thing, really. You know damn well Misty only sent me that tacky invitation to rub in my face that she and Mike are getting married. They never for a minute expect me to show up. So why shouldn't I? At the very least I should be allowed the pleasure of ruining their big day for them."

Laura chuckled. "I guess you're right. And seriously? Misty deserves to be miserable."

"She will be," Georgia promised with a laugh. "She's

marrying Mike, after all. May they be blessed with a dozen sons, every one of them just like their father."

"Wow," Laura said, obviously impressed, "you're really getting the hang of being Irish. A blessing and a curse all at the same time."

"It's a gift."

Georgia glanced down at her ring finger. She still wasn't entirely accustomed to the weight of the emerald and diamond ring Sean had given her for the length of their "engagement."

The dark green of the stone swam with color, and the diamonds winked in the light. It occurred to her then that while her new life was beginning with a lie—Mike was apparently *happy* with his. It didn't matter so much to her anymore, though Georgia could admit, if only to herself, that she'd spent far too much time wrapped up in anger and bitterness and wishing a meteor to crash down on her ex-husband's head.

It was irritating to have to acknowledge just how much time she had wasted and how much useless energy had been spent thinking about how her marriage had ended while the man who had made her so miserable wasn't suffering at all.

She had locked her heart away to avoid being hurt again, which was just stupid. She could see that now. Being hurt only meant that you were alive enough to feel it. And if her soul wasn't alive, then why bother going through the motions trying to pretend different? At least, she told herself, using her thumb against the gleaming gold band of the ring on her finger, she'd gotten past it, had moved on.

Then a voice inside her laughed. Sure, she'd moved on. To a ring that meant nothing and planning a fake future with a fake fiancé.

Wow. How had all of this happened anyway?

Still befuddled by her train of thought, she didn't notice Laura scooting off the bed until her sister was standing beside her.

"I should gather up Patsy and go," she said. "It's nearly time to feed Fiona, and Ronan's probably starving, as well."

Pleased at the idea of having some time to herself, Georgia lovingly nudged her sister to the door. "Go home. Feed the baby. Kiss your husband. I've got a lot to do around here before I leave for my trip next week. Don't worry, you'll have plenty of time to nag me before I leave. And then I'll be back before you even miss me."

"Okay." Laura gave her a one-armed hug and kissed her cheek. "Be careful. And for heaven's sake, take a picture of Misty's wedding gown. That's bound to be entertaining."

Laughing, Georgia vowed, "I will."

"And about Sean—"

"You said you were backing off."

"Right." Laura snapped her mouth shut firmly, took a breath and said, "Okay, then. Enjoy your new house and the supper Patsy left for you. Then have a great trip with your pretend fiancé and hurry home."

When her sister had gone down the stairs and she and Patsy had both shouted a goodbye, Georgia dropped onto the edge of her bed, relishing the sudden silence.

Home, she thought with a sigh. This cottage, in Dunley, Ireland, was now *home*.

It felt good.

She took a long bath, savored a glass of wine in the stillness, then dressed in what she thought of as her Ireland winter wear—jeans, sneakers and a shirt with one of her thick, cable-knit sweaters, this one a dark red, over it—and went downstairs.

Restless, she wandered through her new home, passing through the kitchen to break off a piece of the fresh bread Patsy had left for her. Walking back to the small living room, she paused in the center and did a slow turn.

There were still changes to be made, of course. She wouldn't bring all of her things from America, but the few items she loved would fit in here and make it all seem more *hers* somehow. Though already she felt more at home here than she ever had in the plush condo in Huntington Beach.

The fire in the hearth glowed with banked heat, its red embers shining into the room. Outside her windows, the world was dark as it could be only in the country. The streetlights of the village were a faint smudge in the blackness.

Georgia turned on the television. Then, the instant the sound erupted, turned it off again. She hugged herself and wished for company. Not the tinny, artificially cheerful voice of some unknown news anchor.

"Maybe I should get a dog," she mused aloud, listening to the sound of her own voice whisper into the stillness around her. She smiled at the thought of a clumsy puppy running through the cottage, and she promised herself that when she left America to come home to Dunley for good, she would find a puppy. She missed Beast. And Deidre. And the sound of Ronan's and Laura's voices. And the baby's cries. And Patsy's quiet singing when she was working in the kitchen.

She wanted another heartbeat in the house.

Georgia frowned as she realized the hard truth. What she wanted was Sean.

She could call him, of course, and actually started

for her phone before stopping again. Not a good idea to turn to him when she was lonely. He wouldn't always be there, right? Better she stand on her own, right from the beginning.

Plus, if she was making Dunley her home now, then she might as well get used to going about the village on her own. With that thought in mind, she snagged her jacket off the coat tree by the door and headed for the Pennywhistle.

It was a short walk from her door to the main street of the village, and from there only a bit more to the pub, but she fought for every step. The wind roared along the narrow track, pushing at Georgia and the few other hardy souls wandering the sidewalks with icy hands, as if trying to steer them all back to their homes.

Finally, though, she reached the pub, yanked open the heavy door and stepped into what felt like a *wall* of sound. The silence of the night was shattered by the rise and fall of conversations and laughter, the quick, energetic pulse of the traditional music flowing from the corner and the heavy stomp of booted feet dancing madly to the tune.

Just what I need, Georgia thought, and threw herself into the crush.

Seven

Georgia edged her way to the bar, slipping out of her jacket as she went. The heat inside was nearly stifling, what with the crowd of people and the fire burning merrily in the corner. Waitresses moved through the mob of people with the sort of deft grace ballet dancers would envy, carrying trays loaded with beer, whiskey, soft drinks and cups of tea.

A few people called hello to her as she made her way to the bar and Georgia grinned. This was just what she needed, she thought, to remind herself that she *did* have a real life; it merely also included a fake fiancé. She had friends here. She belonged, and that felt wonderful.

Jack Murphy, the postmaster, a man of about fifty with graying hair and a spreading girth, leaped nimbly off his stool at the bar and offered it to her. She knew better than to wave off his chivalry, though she felt a bit guilty for chasing him out of his seat.

"Thanks, Jack," she said, loud enough to be heard. "Looks like a busy night."

"Ah, well, on a cold night, what's better than a room full of friends and a pint?"

"Good point," she said, and, still smiling, turned to Danny Muldoon, the proprietor of the Pennywhistle.

A big man with a barrel chest, thinning hair and a mischievous smile, he had a bar towel slung over one shoulder and a clean white apron strung around his waist. He was manning the beer taps like a concert pianist as he built a Guinness with one hand and poured a Harp with another. He glanced up at her and asked, "Will it be your usual then, love?"

Her usual.

She loved that. "Yes, Danny, thanks. The Chardonnay when you get a minute."

He laughed, loud and long. "That'll be tomorrow morning by the looks of this crowd, but I'll see you put right as soon as I've finished with this."

Georgia nodded and turned on her stool to look over the crowd. With her jacket draped across her knees, she studied the scene spread out in front of her. Every table was jammed with glassware, every chair filled, and the tiny cleared area closest to the musicians was busy with people dancing to the wild and energetic tunes being pumped out furiously by a fiddle, a flute and a bodhran drum. Georgia spotted Sinead's husband, Michael, and watched as he closed his eyes and tapped his foot to the reel spinning from his fiddle. Sinead sat close by, her head bent to the baby in her arms as she smiled to the music her husband and his friends made.

Here was Dunley, Georgia thought. Everyone was welcome in Irish pubs. From the elderly couple sitting together and holding hands to the tiny girl trying to step-dance like her mother, they were all here. The village. The sense of community was staggering. They were part of each other's lives. They had a connection, one to the other, and the glorious part of it all, in Georgia's mind, was that they had included *her* in their family.

When the incredibly fast-paced song ended, the music slid into a ballad, the notes of which tugged at Georgia's heart. Then one voice in the crowd began to sing and was soon joined by another until half the pub was singing along.

She turned and saw her wine waiting for her and Georgia lifted it for a sip as she listened to the song and lost herself in the beauty of the moment.

She was so caught up, she didn't even notice when Sean appeared at her side until he bent his head and kissed her cheek.

"You've a look of haunted beauty about you," he whispered, and Georgia's head spun briefly.

She turned and looked up at him. "It's the song."

"Aye, 'The Rising of the Moon' is lovely."

"What's it about?"

He winked and grinned. "Rebellion. What we Irish do best."

That song ended on a flourish, and the musicians basked in applause before taking a beer break.

"What'll it be for you then, Sean?" Danny asked.

"A Jameson's if you please, Danny. *Tá sé an diabhal an oíche fuar féin.*"

"It is indeed," the barman answered with a laugh.

"What was that?" Georgia asked. "What did you say?"

Sean shrugged, picked up his glass and laid money down for both his and Georgia's drinks. "Just a bit of the Gaelic. I said it's the devil's own cold night."

"You speak *Gaelic?*"

"Some," he said.

Amazing. Every time she thought she knew him, she found something new. And this was touching, she thought. "It sounds…musical."

"We've music in us, that's for sure," Sean acknowledged. "A large part of County Mayo is Gaeltacht, you know. That means 'Irish-speaking.' Most of those who live here have at least a small understanding of the language. And some speak it at home as their first language."

She'd heard snippets of Gaelic since she first came to Ireland, but it had never occurred to her that it was still a living language. And, to be honest, some of the older people here spoke so quickly and had such thick accents, at first she'd thought they were speaking Gaelic—though it was English.

"Of course," she said after a sip of wine. "The aisle signs in the grocery store are in both English and Gaelic. And the street signs. I just thought maybe it was for the tourists, you know…"

He tapped one finger to her nose. "It's for us. The Irish language was near lost not so very long ago. After the division and the Republic was born, the government decided to reclaim all we'd nearly lost. Now our schools teach it and our children will never have to worry about losing a part of who they are."

Georgia just looked at him. There was a shine of pride in his eyes as he spoke, and she felt a rush of something warm and delicious spread through her in response.

"We're a small country but a proud one," he went on, staring down into his glass of whiskey. "We hang on to what we have and fight when another tries to take it." He shot a quick look at the man on the stool beside Georgia. "Isn't that so, Kevin Dooley?"

The man laughed. "I've fought you often enough for a beer or a woman or just for the hell of it."

"And never won," Sean countered, still grinning.

"There's time yet," Kevin warned companionably, then smiled and turned back to his conversation.

Georgia laughed, too, then leaned into Sean as the musicians picked up their instruments again and the ancient pub came alive with music that filled the heart and soul. With Sean's arm around her, Georgia allowed herself to be swept into the magic of the moment.

And she refused to remember, at least for tonight, that Sean was only hers temporarily.

Two hours later, Sean walked her to the cottage and waited on the step while she opened the door. Georgia went inside, then paused and looked at him.

For the first time in days, they were alone together. With his mother recuperating at his house and her at Ronan and Laura's, they'd been able to do little more than smile at each other in passing.

Until tonight.

Earlier that night, she'd been wishing for him and now, here he was.

He stood in the doorway, darkness behind him, lamplight shining across his face, defining the desire quickening in his eyes. The cold night air slipped inside, twisted with the heat from the banked fire and caused Georgia to shiver in response.

"Will you invite me in, Georgia?"

Her heartbeat sped up, and her mouth went dry. There was something about this man that reached her on levels she hadn't even been aware of before knowing him. He'd made a huge difference in her life, and she was only now realizing how all-encompassing that difference was.

Just now, just this very minute, she stared up at Sean and felt everything within her slide into place, like jagged puzzle pieces finally creating the picture they were meant to be.

There was more here, she thought, than a casual affair. There was affection and danger and excitement and a bone-deep knowledge that when her time with Sean was done, she'd never be the same again.

It was far too late to pull back, she thought wildly. And though she knew she'd be hurt when it was all over, she wouldn't have even if she could.

Because what she'd found with Sean was what she'd been looking for her whole life.

She'd found out who she was.

And more importantly, she *liked* the woman she'd discovered.

"Is it so hard then, to welcome me into your home?" Sean asked softly, when her silence became too much for him.

"No," she said, reaching out to grab hold of his shirt-front. She dragged him inside, closed the door then went up on her toes. "It's not hard at all," she said, and then she kissed him.

At the first long taste of him, that wildness inside her softened. Her bones seemed to melt until she was leaning into him, the only thing holding her up was the strength of Sean's arms wrapped around her.

Her body went up like a torch. Heat suffused her, swamping Georgia with a need so deep, so all-consuming, she could hardly draw breath. When he tore his mouth from hers, she groaned.

"You've a way about you, Georgia," he whispered, dipping his head to nibble at her ear.

She shivered and tipped her head to one side, giving

him easier access. "I was just thinking the same thing about you…" She sighed a little. "Oh, that feels so good."

"You taste of lemons and smell like heaven."

Georgia smiled as her eyes closed and she gave herself up to the sensations rattling through her. "I had a long soak in that wonderful tub upstairs."

"Sorry to have missed that," he murmured, dragging his lips and tongue and teeth along the line of her neck until she quivered in his arms and trembled, incredibly on the brink of a climax. Just his touch. Just the promise of what was to come was enough to send her body hurtling toward completion.

The man had some serious sexual power.

"I thought about you today," he whispered, turning her to back her up against the front door. He lifted his head, looked her dead in the eye and fingered her hair as he spoke. "Thought I'd lose my mind at the office today, trying to work out the figures on the new planes we've ordered… Galway city never seemed so far from Dunley before." He dropped his hands to her waist, pulled up the hem of her sweater and tugged at the snap of her jeans. "And all I could think about was you. Here. And finally having you all to myself again."

The brush of his knuckles against the bare skin of her abdomen sent a zip of electricity shooting through her veins. Releasing him long enough to shrug out of her jacket, she let it fall to the floor, unheeded.

"You're here now," she told him, reaching up to push his jacket off, as well. He helped her with that, then went back to the waistband of her jeans and worked the zipper down so slowly she wanted to scream.

"I am," he said, dipping his head for a kiss. "And so're you."

He had the fly of her jeans open, and he slid one hand

down across her abdomen, past the slip of elastic on her panties and down low enough to touch the aching core of her.

The moment his hand cupped her, she shattered. She couldn't stop it. Didn't want to. She had been primed and ready for his touch for days. Georgia cried out and rocked her hips into his hand. While her body trembled and shook, he kissed her, whispering bits and pieces of Gaelic that seemed to slide into her heart. He stroked her, his fingers dipping into her heat while she rode his hand feverishly, letting the ecstasy she'd found only with him take her up and then under.

When it was done and she could breathe again, she looked up into his eyes and found him watching her with a hunger she'd never seen before. His passion went deeper and gleamed more darkly in his eyes. He held her tenderly, as if she were fragile and about to splinter apart.

"Shatter tú liom," he said softly, gaze moving over her face like a touch.

Still trying to steady her breathing, she reached up to cup his cheek in her palm. The flash of her ring caught her eye but she ignored it. This wasn't fake, she thought. This, what she and Sean shared when they were together, was *very* real. She had no idea what it meant—and maybe it didn't have to *mean* anything. Maybe it was enough to just shut off her mind and enjoy what she had while she had it.

"What does that mean?"

He turned his face into her palm and kissed her. "'You shatter me,' that's what I said."

Her heartbeat jolted, and a sheen of unexpected tears welled up in her eyes, forcing her to blink them back before she could make a fool of herself and cry.

"I watch you tremble in my arms and you take my

knees out from under me, Georgia. That's God's truth."
He kissed her, hard, fast, and made her brain spin. "What
you do to me is nothing I've ever known before."

She knew exactly what he meant because she felt
the same. What she had with Sean was unlike any previous relationship. Sometimes, she felt as though she
were stumbling blindly down an unfamiliar road and
the slightest misstep could have her falling off a cliff.
How could anything feel so huge? How could it not be
real? And still, this journey was one she wouldn't have
missed for anything.

"Say something else," she urged. "In Gaelic, say something else."

He gave her a smile and whispered, *"Leat mo anáil
uaidh."*

She returned his smile. "Now translate."

"'You take my breath away.'"

To disguise the quick flash of feelings too deep to explore at the moment, Georgia quipped, "Back atcha. That
means 'same to you.'"

He chuckled, rested his forehead against hers, pulled
his hand from her jeans and wrapped both arms around
her. "I've got to have you, Georgia. It feels like years
since I've felt your skin against mine. You're a hunger
in me, and I'm a starving man."

Her stomach did a fast roll and her heartbeat leaped
into a gallop. And still she teased him because she'd discovered she liked the teasing, flirtatious way they had
together. "Starving? Patsy Brennan left some bread and
soup in the kitchen."

"You're a hard woman," he said, but the curve of his
mouth belied the words.

"Or," she invited, taking his hand in hers and heading

for the stairs, "you can come up with me and we'll find something else to ease your appetite."

"Lá nó oíche, Tá mé do fear."

She stopped and looked at him. "Now you're just doing that because you know what it does to me."

"I am indeed."

"What did you say that time?"

"I am indeed."

Her lips quirked at the humor in his eyes. "Funny. Before that, what did you say?"

"I said," he told her, swooping in to grab her close and hold on tight like a drowning man clinging to the only rope in a stormy sea, "'Day or night, I'm your man.'"

Then his mouth came down on hers and every thought but one dissolved.

Her man. Those two words repeated over and over again in her mind while Sean was busy kissing her into oblivion. He was hers. For now. For tonight. For however long they had together.

And that was going to have to be enough.

When he let her up for air, she held his hand and shakily led the way up the steep flight of stairs. The ancient treads groaned and squeaked beneath them, but it was a cozy sound. Intimate. At the head of the stairs, Georgia pulled Sean into her room and then turned to look up at him.

He glanced around the bedroom and smiled as he noted everything she'd done to it. "You've made it nice in here. In just a day."

She followed his gaze, noting the fresh curtains at the windows, the quilt on the bed and the colorful pillows tossed against the scrolled iron headboard.

"Laura and Patsy brought a few things over from the manor."

"You've made it a home already."

"I love it already, too," she confessed. "And when I get some of my own things in here, it'll be perfect."

"'Tis perfect right now," he said, moving in on her with a stealthy grace that made her insides tremble. "There's a bed after all."

"So there is."

"I've a need to have you stretched across that bed," he told her, undoing the buttons of his shirt so he could tear it off and throw it onto a nearby chair. "I've a need to touch every square inch of that luscious body of yours and then, when I've finished, to begin again."

Georgia drew a long, unsteady breath and yanked her sweater up and off, before throwing it aside with Sean's shirt. Her fingers were shaky as she tugged at the buttons on her blouse, but Sean's hands were suddenly there, making fast work of them. Then he pushed the fabric off her shoulders and let it slide down her arms to puddle on the floor.

Outside, the night was clear for a change. No rain pinged against the windows, but moonlight did a slow dance through the glass. Inside, the house was still, only the sounds of their ragged breathing to disturb the quiet.

Georgia couldn't hear anything over the pounding of her own heart, anyway. Sean undid the front clasp of her bra, and she slipped out of it eagerly. His hands at her waist, her hands at his, and he pushed her jeans down her hips as she undid the hook and zipper of his slacks, then pushed them down, as well.

In seconds they were naked, the rest of their clothes discarded as quickly as possible. Georgia threw herself into his arms, and when he lifted her off her feet she felt a thrill in her bones. He tucked her legs around his waist, and she hooked her ankles together at the small of his back.

He took two long steps to the nearest wall and braced her back against it. With her arms around his neck, she looked down into his eyes and said breathlessly, "I thought we needed the bed."

"And so we will," he promised. "When we're too tired to stand."

Then he entered her. His hard, thick length pushing into her welcoming body. Georgia could have sworn he went deep enough to touch the bottom of her heart. She felt him all through her, as if he'd laid claim to her body and soul and was only now letting her in on it.

The wall was cold against her back, but she didn't feel it. All she was aware of was the tingling spread of something miraculous inside her. Her body was spiraling into that coil of need that would tighten until it burst from the pressure and sent jagged shards of sensation rippling through her.

Bracing one hand on the dresser beside her, Georgia clapped the other to his shoulder and moved with him as he set a frenetic pace. She watched his eyes glaze over, saw the mix of pleasure and tension etch themselves onto his features. Again and again he took her, pushing her higher and higher, faster and faster.

Her heels dug into his back, urging him on, and when the first hard jolt of release slammed into her, she shouted his name and clung desperately to him. She was still riding the ripples of her climax when he buried his face in the curve of her neck and joined her there.

A few miles away at Laura's house, the phone rang and Laura picked it up on the run. She had just gotten the baby down for the night and she had a gorgeous husband waiting for her in the front parlor with a bottle of wine.

"Hello?"

"Laura, love," Ailish said. "And how's our darling Fiona this night?"

Sean's mother. Why was she calling? Did she suspect something? *This* was why Laura didn't like lies. They tangled everything up. Made her unsure what she could say and what she couldn't. Sean and Georgia were trying to protect Ailish, and what if Laura said something that blew the whole secret out of the water? What if she caused Ailish a heart attack? What if—

Laura stepped into the parlor, gave her husband a silent *Oh Dear God* look and answered, "The baby's wonderful, Ailish. I've just put her down."

"Lovely, then you have a moment?"

"Um, sure," she said desperately, "but wouldn't you like to say hello to Ronan?"

At that, her devoted husband shot out of his chair, shaking his head and waving both hands.

Laura scowled at him and mouthed the word *coward*.

He bowed at the waist, accepting the insult as if it were a trophy.

"No, dear, this is better between us, I think," Ailish told her through the phone.

Uh-oh. She didn't want to talk to Ronan? *Better between us?* That couldn't be good.

Deserted by the man she loved, Laura took a breath and waited for the metaphorical ax to fall.

"I just want to ask you one question."

No, no, no. That wasn't a good idea at all.

"Oh!" Laura interrupted her frantically, with one last try for escape. "Wait! I think I hear Fiona—"

"No, you don't. And there's no point trying to lie to me, Laura Connolly. You've no talent for it, dear."

It was the Irish way. A compliment and a slap all in the same sentence.

"Yes, ma'am," she said, throwing a trapped look at her husband. Ronan only shrugged and poured each of them a drink. When he was finished, he handed her the wine and Laura took a long gulp.

"Now then," Ailish said and Laura could picture the tiny, elegant woman perfectly. "I know my son, and I've a feeling there's more going on between him and Georgia than anyone is telling me."

"I don't—"

"No point in lying, Laura dear, remember?"

She sighed.

"That's better." Then to Sean's housekeeper, Ailish said, "Thank you, Katie. A cup of tea would be wonderful. And perhaps one or two of your scones? Laura and I are just settling down for a long chat."

Oh, God, Laura thought. A long chat? That wasn't good. Wasn't good at all. Quickly, she drained her glass and handed it to her husband for a refill.

Eight

For the entire next week, Sean felt that itch between his shoulder blades. And every day, it got a little sharper. A little harder to ignore. Everywhere he went, people in the village were talking about the upcoming wedding. It shouldn't have bothered him, as he'd known full well what would happen the moment he began this scheme. But knowing it and living it were two different things.

The pool in the pub was more popular than ever— with odds changing almost daily as people from outlying farms came in to make their bets on the date of the wedding. Even the Galway paper had carried an engagement announcement, he thought grimly, courtesy of Ailish.

From her sickbed, his mother had leaped into the planning of this not-to-be wedding with such enthusiasm, he shuddered to think what she might do once she was cleared by her doctor.

When the article in the paper had come out, it had

taken Sean more than an hour of fast talking with Georgia to smooth that particular bump in the road. She was less and less inclined to keep up the pretense as time went by, and even Sean was beginning to doubt the wisdom of the whole thing.

But then, he would see his mother moving slowly through the house and tell himself that he'd done the right thing. The only thing. Until Ailish was well and fit again, he was going to do whatever he had to.

Though to accomplish it, the annoying itch would become his constant companion.

Even Ronan and Laura had been acting strangely the past few days, Laura especially. She had practically sequestered herself in the manor, telling Georgia she was simply too exhausted with caring for the baby to be good company.

Frowning, Sean told himself there was definitely something going on there, but he hadn't a clue what it was. Which made this trip with Georgia to the States seem all the more attractive.

At the moment, getting away from everyone in Ireland for a week or so sounded like a bloody vacation. Going to California to close out Georgia's house and then on to Ohio, of all places, for the wedding, would give both of them a chance to relax away from the stress of the lies swarming around them like angry bees.

Or maybe it was the muted roar of the plane's engines making him think of swarming bees. He and Georgia had the jet to themselves for this trip, but for the pilots and Kelly, the flight attendant who had already brought them coffee right after takeoff and then disappeared into the front of the jet, giving them privacy.

He looked at Georgia, sitting across from him, and Sean felt that quick sizzle of heat and need that he'd become accustomed to feeling whenever he was close to her. Oh, since the moment he first met her at Ronan's wedding, he had felt the zing of attraction and interest any man would feel for a woman like Georgia.

But in the past few weeks, that zing had become something else entirely. He spent far too much time thinking about her. And when he was with her, he kept expecting to feel the edge of his need slackening off as it always had before with the women he was involved with. It hadn't happened, of course. Instead, that need only became sharper every time he was with her. As if feeding his hunger for her only defined his appetite, not quenched it.

It wasn't just the sex, either, he mused, studying her profile in the clear morning light. He liked the way her short, honey-blond hair swung at her chin. He liked the deep twilight of her eyes and how they darkened when he was inside her. He liked her sense of style—the black skirt, scooped-neck red blouse and the high heels that made her legs look bloody amazing. And he liked her mind. She had a quick wit, a sharp temper and a low tolerance for bullshit—all of which appealed to him.

She was on his mind all the bloody time and he couldn't say he minded it overmuch. The only thing that *did* bother him was the nagging sensation that he was coming to care for her more than he'd intended. Sean knew all too well that a man in love lost all control over a situation with his woman, and he wasn't a man who enjoyed that. He'd seen enough of his friends become fools over women. Even Ronan had lost a part of himself when he first tumbled for Laura.

No, Sean preferred knowing exactly what was happening and when, rather than being tossed about on a tide of emotion you couldn't really count on anyway.

And still…

There was a voice inside him whispering that perhaps *real* love was worth the risk. He argued that point silently as he'd no wish to find out.

A knot of something worrisome settled into the pit of his stomach and he determinedly chose to ignore it. No point in examining feelings at the moment anyway, was there? Right now, he was just going to enjoy watching her settle into the plush interior of one of his jets.

Her gaze didn't settle, but moved over the inside of the plane, checking out everything, missing nothing. Another thing to admire about her. She wasn't a woman to simply accept her surroundings. Georgia had enough curiosity to explore them. And Sean could admit that he wanted her opinion of his jets.

He was proud of what he'd built with Irish Air and had a million ideas for how to grow and expand the company. By the time he was finished, when someone thought luxury travel, he wanted Irish Air to be the name that came to mind.

"What do you think?" Sean had noticed how she had tensed up during takeoff, but now that they were at a cruising altitude, she was relaxed enough to ease her white-knuckled grip on the arms of the seat.

"Of the jet? It's great," she said. "Really beats flying coach."

"Should be our new slogan," Sean said, with a chuckle. "I'm glad you like it. Irish Air is a luxury airline. There are no coach seats. Everyone is a first-class passenger."

"A great idea, but I'm sure most of us couldn't afford to travel like this."

"It's not so dear as you'd think," Sean said. In fact, he'd made a point of doing as much as he could to keep the price down.

He was proud of what he'd built, but curious what

Georgia thought of his flagship. This plane was the one he used most often himself. But all of the others in his fleet were much like it.

Sean's idea had been to outfit a smaller plane with luxury accommodations. To give people who wouldn't ordinarily fly first class a chance to treat themselves. And yes, the price was a bit higher than coach, but still substantially less than that of a first-class ticket on an ordinary airline.

"It's cheaper than chartering a jet."

"Yeah," she said, flicking a curtain aside to take a look out the window at the clouds beneath them. "But coach is still way cheaper."

"You get what you pay for, don't you?" he asked, leaning back in his own seat to sip at his coffee. "When you fly Irish Air, your vacation begins the moment you board. You're treated like royalty. You arrive at your destination rested instead of wild-eyed and desperate for sleep."

"Oh, I get it," she said. "Believe me. And it's a great idea…"

He frowned as she left that thought hanging. *"But?"*

Georgia shot him a half grin. "But, okay." She set her coffee on the table. "You say your airline's different. Set apart."

"I do."

"But, inside, it's set up just like every other plane. A center aisle, seats on either side."

There was a shine in her eyes and Sean was paying more attention to that, than he was to her words. When what she'd said at last computed, he asked, "And how else should we have it arranged?"

"Well, that's the beauty of it, isn't it?" she countered. "It's your plane, Sean. You want to make Irish Air different from the crowd, so why even have them furnished like everyone else?"

She ran the flat of her hand across the leather arm rest and for a second, he allowed himself to picture that hand stroking him, instead. As his body tightened, he reminded himself they had a six-hour flight to New York and then another five to L.A. Plenty of time to show Georgia the owner's bedroom suite at the back of the jet. That brought a smile to his face, until he realized that Georgia was frowning thoughtfully.

"What is it you're thinking? Besides the fact that the seats are arranged wrong?"

"Hmm? Oh, nothing."

"It's something," he said, following her gaze as she studied the furnishings of the plane with a clearly critical eye. "Let's have it."

"I was just thinking…you say you started Irish Air as a way of giving people a real choice in flying."

"That's right," he said, leaning forward, bracing his elbows on his knees. "As I said, most can't afford first-class tickets on commercial airlines, and chartering a jet is well beyond them, as well. Irish Air," he said with a proud smile, "is in the buffer zone. I offer luxury travel for just a bit more than coach."

"How much is a bit?"

"More than a little," he hedged, "less than a lot. The theory being, if people save for an important vacation, then they might be willing to save a bit more to start their vacation the moment they board the plane." Warming to his theme, he continued. "You see, you fly coach, say from L.A. to Ireland. By the time you've arrived, you feel as though you've been dragged across a choppy sea. You're tired, you're angry, you're hungry. Then you've to rent a car and drive on a different side of the road when you're already on the ragged edge…"

"All true. I've done it," she said.

He nodded. "But, on Irish Air, you step aboard and you relax. There are fewer seats. The seats are wider, fold out into beds and there's a TV at every one of them. We offer WiFi on board and we serve *real* meals with actual knives and forks. When you arrive at your destination, you're rested, refreshed and feel as though your worries are behind you."

"You should do commercials," Georgia said with a smile. "With the way you look, that accent of yours and the way your eyes shine when you talk about Irish Air, you'd have women by the thousands lined up for tickets."

"That's the idea." He sat back, rested one foot on his opposite knee and glanced around. "By this time next year, Irish Air will be the most talked-about airline in the world. We'll be ordering a dozen new planes soon and—" He broke off when he saw her shift her gaze to one side and chew at her bottom lip. A sure sign that she had something to say and wasn't sure how to do it. "What is it?"

"You want the truth?"

"Absolutely," he told her.

"Okay, you want Irish Air to stand out from the crowd, right?"

"I do."

"So why are you creating such boring interiors?"

"What? Boring, did you say?" He glanced around the main cabin, saw nothing out of line and looked back at her for an explanation.

She half turned in her seat to face him, then slapped one hand against the armrest. "First, I already told you, the arrangement of the seats. There are only ten of them on this plane, but you've got them lined up in standard formation, with the aisle up the middle."

One eyebrow winged up. "There's a better way?"

"There's a *different* way, and that is what you said you wanted."

"True. All right then, tell me what you mean."

A light burned in her eyes as she gave him a quick grin. Unbuckling her seat belt, she stood up, looked down the length of the plane, then back to him.

"Okay. It's not just the seats," she said, "the colors are all wrong."

A bit insulted, as he'd paid a designer a huge sum to come up with a color palette that was both soothing and neutral, he asked, "What the bloody hell is wrong with beige?"

She shook her head sadly. "It's *beige,* Sean. Could any color be more ordinary?"

"I've had it on good authority that beige is calming and instills a sense of trust in the passenger."

"Who told you that?" she asked, tipping her head to one side as she studied him. "A man?"

He scowled. "I'm a man, if you've forgotten."

She gave him a wicked smile. "That's one thing I'm certain of."

He stood up, too, but she skipped back a pace to keep some distance between them. "*But* you're not a designer."

"I'm not, no." Considering, thinking, he watched her and said, "All right, then. Tell me what it is you're thinking, Georgia."

"Okay…" She took a breath and said, "First, the carpeting. It looks like the kind you see in a dentist's office. Trust me when I say *that* is not soothing."

He frowned thoughtfully at the serviceable, easy-to-clean carpet.

"It should be plush. Let a passenger's feet sink into it when they step on board." She wagged a finger at him. "Instant luxurious feel and people *will* notice."

"Thick carpet."

"Not beige," she added quickly. "I think blue. Like the color of a summer sky."

"Uh-huh."

She ran one hand across the back of the leather seat again. "These are comfortable, but again. Beige. Really?"

"You recommend blue again?" he asked, enjoying the animation on her face.

"No, for the seats, gray leather." She looked up at him. "The color of the fog that creeps in from the ocean at night. It'll go great with the blue carpet and it'll be different. Make Irish Air stand out from the crowd. And—" She paused as if she were wondering if she'd already gone too far.

He crossed his arms over his chest. "Go on, no reason to stop now."

"Okay, don't line the seats up like bored little soldiers. Clump them."

"Clump?"

"Yeah," she said. "In conversational groups. Like seats on a train. You said this is the midsize jet, right? So your others are even wider. Make use of that space. Make the interior welcoming. Two seats facing back, two forward. And stagger them slightly too, so the people sitting on the right side of the plane aren't directly opposite those on the left. Not everyone wants strangers listening in to conversations."

She walked down the aisle and pointed. "Have the last two back here, separate from the others. A romantic spot that seems cozy and set apart."

He looked at the configuration of his jet and in his

mind's eye, pictured what she was describing. He liked it. More, he could see that she was right. He'd seen the same sort of design on private corporate jets, of course, but not on a passenger line. Offering that kind of difference would help set Irish Air apart. The congenial airline. The jets that made travel a treat. And gray seats on pale blue carpet would look more attractive than the beige. Why hadn't he thought of that?

Better yet, why hadn't the "expert" he'd hired to design the interiors thought of it?

"Oh, and I hate those nasty little overhead light beams on airplanes. It's always so hard to arrow them down on what you want to read." Georgia looked at the slope of the walls, then back to him. "You could have small lamps attached to the hull. Like sconces. Brass—no, pewter. To go with the gray seats and offset the blue."

She reached down and lifted a table that was folded down into itself. Opening it, she pointed to the space on the wall just above. "And here, a bud vase, also affixed to the hull, with fresh flowers."

Sean liked it. Liked all of it. And the excitement in her eyes fired his own.

"Oh, and instead of the standard, plastic, pull-down shades on the windows, have individual drapes." She leaned over and put her hands to either side of one of the portholes. "Tiny, decorative curtain rods—also pewter—and a square of heavy, midnight-blue fabric…"

Before he could comment on that, she'd straightened up and walked past him to the small galley area. The flight attendant was sitting in the cockpit with the pilot and copilot, so there was no one in her way as she explored the functional kitchen setup.

She stepped out again and studied the wall with a

flat-screen television attached to it. "The bathroom is right here, yes?"

"One of them," he said. "There's another in the back."

"So, if you get rid of the big TV—and you should have individual screens at the seating clumps—and expand the bathroom wall another foot or so into the cabin," she took another quick look around the corner at the galley. "That gives you a matching extra space in the kitchen. And that means you could expand your menu. Offer a variety of foods that people won't get anywhere else."

He could bloody well see it, Sean thought. Frowning, he studied the interior of the jet and saw it not as it was now, but as it could be. As it *would* be, he told himself, the moment they got back to Ireland and he could fire the designer who'd suggested ordinary for his *extraordinary* airline.

Following Georgia's train of thought was dizzying, but the woman knew what she was talking about. She painted a picture a blind man could see and appreciate. Why she'd wasted her talent on selling houses, he couldn't imagine.

"You could even offer cribs for families traveling with babies." She was still talking. "If you bolt it down in the back there and have, I don't know, a harness or something for the baby to wear while it sleeps, that gives the mom a little time to relax, too."

He was nodding, making mental notes, astonished at the flow of brilliant ideas Georgia had. "You've a clever mind," he said softly. "And an artist's eye."

She grinned at him and the pleasure in her eyes was something else a blind man could see.

"What's in the back of the plane, through that door?" she asked, already headed toward it.

"Something I'd planned to show you later," he told her with a wink. Then he took her hand and led her down the narrow, ordinary aisle between boring beige seats. Opening the door, he ushered her inside, then followed her and closed the door behind them.

"You have a bedroom on your jets?" she asked, clearly shocked at the sight of the double bed, bedecked with a dark blue duvet and a half-dozen pillows. The shades were drawn over the windows, filling the room with shadow. Georgia looked up at him, shaking her head.

"This plane is mine," Sean told her. "I use it to fly all over the damn place for meetings and such, and so I want a place to sleep while I travel."

"And the seats that fold into beds aren't enough for you?"

"Call it owner's privilege," he said, walking closer, steadily urging her backward until the backs of her knees hit the edge of the mattress and she plopped down. Swinging her hair back from her face, she looked up at him.

"And do you need help designing this room, too?" she asked, tongue firmly in cheek.

"If I did, I now know who to call," he assured her.

"Does that door have a lock on it?" she asked, sliding her gaze to the closed door and then back to him.

"It does."

"Why don't you give it a turn, then?"

"Another excellent idea," Sean said, and moved to do just that.

Then he looked down at her and was caught by her eyes. The twilight shine of them. The clever mind behind them. Staring into her eyes was enough to mesmerize a man, Sean thought. He took a breath and dragged the scent of her into his lungs, knowing that air seemed empty without her scent flavoring it.

Slowly, she slipped her shoes off, then lay back on the mattress, spreading her arms wide, so that she looked like a sacrifice to one of the old gods. But the welcoming smile on her face told him that she wanted him as much as he did her.

In seconds, then, he was out of his clothes and helping her off with hers. The light was dim in the room, but he saw all he needed to see in her eyes. When he touched her, she arched into him and a sigh teased a smile onto her lips.

"Scáthanna bheith agat," he whispered. Amazing how often he felt the old language well up inside him when he was with her. It seemed only Irish could help him say what he was feeling.

She swept her fingers through his hair and said, "I love when you speak Gaelic. What did you say that time?"

"I said, 'Shadows become you,'" he told her, then dipped his head for a kiss.

"You make my heart melt sometimes, Sean," she admitted, her voice little more than a hush of sound.

That knot in his guts tightened further as words he might have said, but wouldn't, caught in his throat. Right now, more words were unnecessary anyway, he told himself.

Instead, he kissed her again, taking his time, tasting her, tangling his tongue with hers until neither of them were thinking. Until all either of them felt was the need for each other. He would take his time and savor every luscious inch of her. Indulge them both with a slow loving that would ease away the ragged edges they had been living with and remind them both how good they were together.

Well, Georgia told herself later that night, Sean was right about one thing. Flying Irish Air did deliver you to your destination feeling bright-eyed and alert. Of course, great sex followed by a nap on a real bed probably hadn't hurt, either.

Now Sean was out picking up some dinner, and she was left staring into her closet trying to decide what to pack, what to give away and what to toss.

"Who'm I trying to kid?" she asked aloud. "I'm taking my clothes with me. All of 'em."

She glanced at the stack of packing boxes on the floor beside her and sighed. Then her gaze moved around her bedroom in the condo she and Laura used to share.

She'd had good times in this house. Sort of surprising, too, since when she'd arrived here to move in with her sister, she hadn't really been in a good place mentally. Marriage dissolved, bank account stripped and ego crushed, she'd slowly, day by day, rebuilt a life for herself.

"And now," she whispered, "I'm building another."

"Talking to yourself? Not a good sign."

She whirled around to find Sean standing in the open doorway, holding a pizza box that smelled like heaven while he watched her with amusement glittering in his eyes.

In self-defense, she said, "I have to talk to myself, since I'm the only one who really understands me."

"*I* understand you, Georgia."

"Is that right?" She turned her back on the closet, the boxes and everything she had to do. Snatching the pizza box from him, she headed out of the bedroom and walked toward the stairs. He was right behind her. "Well then, why don't you tell me what I'm thinking?"

"Easily enough done," he said, his steps heavy on the stairs behind her. "You're excited, but worried. A bit embarrassed for having me catch you doing a monologue in your bedroom and you're hoping you've some wine in the kitchen to go with that pizza."

She looked over her shoulder at him and hoped the surprise she felt was carefully hidden. "You're right about two of them, but I happen to know I don't have a bottle of wine in the kitchen."

"You do now," he told her, and dropped an arm around her shoulders when they hit the bottom of the stairs. "I picked some up while I was out."

"I do like a man who plans ahead."

"Then you'll love me for the plans I have for later." He took the box from her, walked into the kitchen and set it down on the counter.

She stood in the doorway, her gaze following him as he searched through cupboards for plates and napkins and wineglasses. His hair was shaggy and needed a trim. The jeans he wore now were faded and clung to his butt and legs, displaying what she knew was a well-toned body. He whistled as he opened the bottle of wine and poured each of them a glass of what was probably an outrageously expensive red.

You'll love me for the plans I have for later.

His words echoed in her head, and Georgia tried to shrug them off. Not easy to do, though, when a new and startling discovery was still rattling through her system. Warning bells rang in her mind and a flutter of nerves woke up in the pit of her stomach.

Mouth dry, heart pounding, she looked at Sean and realized what her heart had been telling her for days. Maybe weeks.

She'd done the unthinkable.

She'd fallen in love with Sean Connolly.

Nine

Oh, absolutely not.

She refused to think about it. Simply slammed a wall up against that ridiculous thought and told herself it was jet lag. Or hunger. Probably hunger. Once she got some of that pizza into her, her mind would clear up and she'd be fine again.

"You know, you don't have to do the packing yourself," Sean was saying, and she told herself to pay attention.

"What?"

He snorted a laugh. "Off daydreaming while I'm slaving over a hot pizza box were you?"

"No." God, now she was nervous around him. How stupid was that? He'd seen her naked. She'd made love to the man in every way possible. How could she be nervous over what was, in essence, a blip on the radar?

This wasn't love. This was lust. Attraction. Hell, even *affection*.

But not love.

There, she told herself. Problem solved. *Love* was not a word she was going to be thinking ever again. "What did you say? About the packing?"

"While you take care of putting your house up for sale tomorrow, why don't I make some calls and see about getting movers in here?" He looked around the well-stocked condo kitchen. "You can go through, tell them what you want moved to Ireland and what you're getting rid of, and then stand back and watch burly men do the heavy lifting for you."

Tempting. And expensive. She argued with herself over it for a minute or two, but the truth was, if she did it Sean's way, the whole business could be finished much faster. And wasn't that worth a little extra expense?

Especially if it got her back to Ireland faster? And then hopefully in another week or two, they could end this pretend engagement? She glanced down at the emerald-and-diamond ring on her hand and idly rubbed at the band with her thumb. Soon, it wouldn't be hers anymore. Soon, *Sean* wouldn't be hers anymore.

She lifted her gaze to his and his soft brown eyes were locked on her. Another flutter of something nerve-racking moved in the pit of her stomach, but she pushed it aside. Not love, she reminded herself.

And still, she felt a little off balance. Georgia had to have some time to come to grips with this. To figure out a way to handle it while at the same time protecting herself.

She wasn't an idiot, after all. This hadn't been a part of their deal. It was supposed to be a red-hot affair with no strings attached. A pretend engagement that they would both walk away from when it was over.

And that was just what she would do.

Oh, it was going to hurt, she thought now, as Sean handed her a glass of wine, letting his fingers trail across her skin. When he was out of her life, out of her bed and still in her heart—not that she was admitting he was— it was going to be a pain like she'd never known before.

But she comforted herself with the knowledge that she would be in Ireland, near her sister. She'd have Laura and baby Fiona to help her get over Sean. Shouldn't take more than five or ten years, she told herself with an inner groan.

"So, what do you think?" Sean carried the wine to the table beside the window that overlooked the backyard. "We can have you packed up in a day or two. A lot of your things we can carry back on the jet, what we can't, we'll arrange to ship."

"That's a good idea, Sean." She took a seat, because her knees were still a little weak and it was better to sit down than to fall down. Taking a quick sip of the really great wine, she let it ease the knot in her throat.

Then she picked up the conversation and ran with it. Better to talk about the move. About packers and all of the things she had to do rather than entertain even for a minute that the affection she felt for him could be something else. Losing Sean now was going to hurt. But God help her, if she was really in *love,* the pain would be tremendous.

"There are really only a few things I want to take with me to Ireland," she said. "The rest I'll donate."

That thought appealed to her anyway. She was starting over in Ireland, and the cottage was already furnished, so there was no hurry to buy new things. She could take her time and decide later what she wanted. As for kitchen stuff, it didn't really make sense to ship pots and pans when she could replace them easily enough in Ireland.

All she really wanted from the condo aside from her clothes were family photos, Laura's paintings and a few other odds and ends. What did that say about her, that she'd been living in this condo, surrounded by *stuff* and none of it meant enough to take with her?

She had more of a connection with the cottage than she did with anything here.

"You know," she said, "it's kind of a sad statement that there's so little here I want to take with me. I mean, I was willing to stay here when it clearly didn't mean much to me."

"Why would that be sad?" He sat down opposite her, opened the pizza box and served each of them a slice. "You knew when it was time to move on, is all. Seems to me it's more brave than that. You're moving to a different country, Georgia. Why wouldn't you want to leave the past behind?"

She huffed out a breath and let go of the 'poor me' thoughts that had just begun to form. "How do you do that?"

"What?"

"Manage to say exactly the right thing," she said.

He laughed a little and took a bite of pizza. "Luck, I'd say. And knowing you as I've come to, I thought you might be getting twisted up over all there is to be done and then giving yourself a hard time over it."

Scowling, she told him, "It's a little creepy, knowing you can see into my head so easily."

He picked up his wineglass and toasted her with it. "Didn't say it was easy."

She hoped not, because she *really* didn't want him looking too closely into her mind right now. Twists of emotion tangled inside her and this time she didn't fight them.

Okay, yes. She had feelings for him. Why wouldn't she? He was charming and fun and smart and gorgeous. He was easy to talk to and great in bed, of course she cared about him.

That didn't mean she loved him. Didn't mean anything more than what they had together was important to her.

Even she wasn't buying that one.

Oh, God. No sense in lying to herself, Georgia thought. She'd sew her lips shut and lock herself in a deep dark hole for the rest of her life before she ever admitted the truth to Sean.

This wasn't affection. It wasn't lust. Or hunger.

It was love.

Nothing like the love she had thought she'd found once before.

Now, she couldn't imagine how she had ever convinced herself that she was in love with Mike. Because what she felt for Sean was so much bigger, so much… *brighter,* that it was like comparing an explosion to a sparkler. There simply wasn't a comparison.

This was the kind of love she used to dream of.

And wouldn't you know she'd find it with a man who wouldn't want it? Feelings hadn't been part of their agreement. Love had no place in a secret. A pretense.

So she'd keep her mouth shut and tuck what she felt for him aside until it withered in the dark. It would. Eventually. She hoped.

Oh, God.

She was such an idiot.

"Well," Sean said after a sip of his wine, "I'll admit to you now I've no notion of what you're thinking at this minute. But judging by your expression, it's not making you happy."

Understatement of the century.

"Nothing in particular," she lied smoothly. "Just how much I have to do and how little time I have to do it."

He looked at her for a long minute as if trying to decide to let it lay or not, and finally, thank God, he did.

"So no second thoughts? Being here," he said, glancing around the bright, modern kitchen, "doesn't make you want to rethink your decision?"

She followed his gaze, looking around the room where she'd spent so much alone time in the past year. It was a nice place, she thought, but it had never felt like *hers*. Not like the cottage in Ireland did.

"No," she said, shaking her head slowly. "I came here to live with Laura when my marriage ended and it was what I needed then. But it's not for me now, you know?"

"I do," he said, resting one elbow on the tabletop. "When you find your place, you know it."

"Exactly. What about you? Did you ever want to live somewhere else?"

He grinned. "Leave Dunley?" He shook his head. "I went to college in Dublin and thought it a fine place. I've been all over Europe and to New York several times as well, but none of those bright and busy places tug at me as Dunley does.

"The village is my place, as you said," he told her. "I've no need to leave it to prove anything to myself or anyone else."

"Have you always been so sure of yourself?" She was really curious. He seemed so together. Never doubting himself for a minute. She envied it. At the same time she simply couldn't understand it.

He laughed. "A man who doesn't question himself from time to time's a fool who will soon be slapped down by the fates or whatever gods are paying attention to the jackass of the moment. So of course I question," he said. "I just trust myself to come up with the right answers."

"I used to," she told him and pulled a slice of pepperoni free of the melted cheese and popped it into her mouth. "Then I married Mike and he left me for someone else and I didn't have a clue about it until he was walking out the door." Georgia took a breath and then let it go. "After that, I had plenty of questions, but no faith in my own answers."

"That's changed now, though," he said, his gaze fixed on hers. "You've rebuilt your life, haven't you? And you've done it the way *you* want to. So, I'm thinking your answers were always right, you just weren't ready to hear them."

"Maybe," she admitted. Then, since marriages, both real and pretend, were on her mind, asked, "So, why is it you've never been married?"

He choked on a sip of wine, then caught his breath and said, "There's a question out of the blue."

"Not really. We were talking about my ex—now it's my turn to hear your sad tales. I am your 'fiancée,' after all. Shouldn't I know these things?"

"I suppose you should," he said with a shrug. "Truth is, I was engaged once."

"Really?" A ping of something an awful lot like jealousy sounded inside her. Just went to show her mom was right. She used to tell Georgia, *Never ask a question you don't really want the answer to.*

"Didn't last long." He shrugged again and took a sip of his wine. "Noreen was more interested in my bank account than in me, and she finally decided that she deserved better than a husband who spent most of his time at work."

"Noreen." Harder somehow, knowing the woman's name.

"I let her maneuver me into the thought of marriage," Sean was saying, apparently not clueing in to Georgia's thoughts. "I remember thinking that maybe it was time to be married, and Noreen was there—"

"She was *there?*" Just as *she* had been there, Georgia thought now, when he'd needed a temporary fiancée. Hmm.

He gave her a wry smile. "Aye. I know how it sounds now, but at the time, it seemed easier to let her do what she would than to fight her over it. I was consumed at the time with taking Irish Air to the next level, and I suppose the truth is I didn't care enough to put a stop to Noreen's plans."

Dumbfounded, she just stared at him. "So you would have married her? Not really loving her, you would have married her anyway because it was easier than saying 'no thanks'?"

He shifted uneasily on his chair and frowned a bit at the way she'd put things. "No," he said finally. "I wouldn't have taken that trip down the aisle with her in the end. It wouldn't have worked and I knew it at the time. I was just…"

"Busy?" she asked.

"If you like. Point is," Sean said, "it worked out for the best all around. Noreen left me and married a bank president or some such. And I found you."

Yes, he'd found her. Another temporary fiancée. One he had no intention of escorting down an aisle of any kind. Best to remember that, she told herself.

He lifted his glass and held it out to her, a smile on

his face and warmth in his eyes. Love swam in the pit of her stomach, but Georgia put a lid on it fast. She hadn't planned to love him, and now that she did, she planned to get over it as fast as humanly possible.

So, she'd keep things as they had been between them. Light. Fun. Sexy and affectionate. And when it was over, she'd walk away with her head high, and Sean would never know how she really felt. Georgia tapped her wineglass to his, and when she drank, she thought that the long-gone Noreen had gotten off easy.

Noreen hadn't really loved Sean when she left him, or she'd never have moved on so quickly to someone else.

Georgia on the other hand...it wasn't going to be simple walking away from Sean Connolly.

Georgia was glad they'd come to the wedding. Just seeing the look on Misty's face when she spotted Georgia and Sean had made the trip worthwhile. But it was more than that, too, she told herself. Maybe she'd *had* to attend this wedding. Maybe it was the last step in leaving behind her past so that she could walk straight ahead and never look back.

And dancing with her ex-husband, the groom, was all a part of that. What was interesting was, she felt nothing in Mike's arms. No tingle. No soft sigh of regret for old time's sake. Nothing.

She looked up at him and noticed for the first time that his blue eyes were a little beady. His hair was thinning on top, and she had the feeling that Mike would one day be a comb-over guy. His broad chest had slipped a little, making him a bit thick about the waist, and the whiskey on his breath didn't make the picture any prettier.

Once she had loved him. Or at least thought she had. She'd married him assuming they would be together forever, and yet here she was now, a few years after a divorce she hadn't seen coming and she felt…nothing.

Was that how it would be with Sean one day? Would her feelings for him simply dry up and blow away like autumn leaves in a cold wind?

"You look amazing," Mike said, tightening his arm around her waist.

She did and she knew it. Georgia had gone shopping for the occasion. Her dark red dress had long sleeves, a deep V neckline, and it flared out from the waist into a knee-length skirt that swirled when she moved.

"Thanks," she said, and glanced toward Sean, sitting alone at a table on the far side of the room. Then, willing to be generous, she added, "Misty makes a pretty bride."

"Yeah." But Mike wasn't looking at his new wife. Instead, he was staring at Georgia as if he'd never seen her before.

He executed a fast turn and Georgia had to grab hold of his shoulder to keep from stumbling. He pulled her in even closer in response. When she tried to put a little space between them, she couldn't quite manage it.

"You're engaged, huh?"

"Yes," she said, thumbing the band on her engagement ring. Sean had made quite the impression. Just as she'd hoped, he'd been charming, attentive and, in short, the perfect fiancé. "When we leave here, we're flying home to Ireland."

"Can't believe you're gonna be living in a foreign country," Mike said with a shake of his head. "I don't remember you being the adventurous type at all."

"Adventurous?"

"You know what I mean," he continued, apparently not noticing that Georgia's eyes were narrowed on him thoughtfully. "You were all about fixing up the house.

Making dinner. Working in the yard. Just so—" he shrugged "—boring."

"Excuse me?"

"Come on, Georgia, admit it. You never wanted to try anything new or exciting. All you ever wanted to do was talk about having kids and—" He broke off and sighed. "You're way more interesting now."

Was steam actually erupting from the top of her head? she wondered. Because it really felt like it. Georgia's blood pressure was mounting with every passing second. She had been *boring?* Talking about having kids with your husband was *boring?*

"So, because I was so uninteresting, that's why you slipped out with Misty?" she asked, her voice spiking a little higher than she'd planned. "Are you actually trying to tell me it's *my* fault you cheated on me?"

"Jeez, you always were too defensive," Mike said, and slid his hand down to her behind where he gave her a good squeeze.

Georgia's eyes went wild.

They made a good team.

Sean had been thinking about little else for the past several days. All through the mess of closing up her home and arranging for its sale. Through the packing and the donations to charity and ending the life she'd once lived, they'd worked together.

He was struck by how easy it was, being with her.

Her clever mind kept him on his toes and her luscious body kept him on his knees. A perfect situation, Sean told himself as he sat at the wedding, drinking a beer, considering ways to keep Georgia in his life.

Ever since she'd laid out her ideas to improve the look of his company jets, Sean had been intrigued by possibilities. They got along well. They were a good match. A team, as he'd thought only moments before.

"And damned if I want to lose what we've found," he muttered.

The simplest way, he knew, was to make their engagement reality. To convince her to marry him—not for love, of course, because that was a nebulous thing after all. But because they fit so well. And the more he thought about it, the better it sounded.

Hadn't his cousin Ronan offered very nearly the same deal to his Laura? A marriage based on mutual need and respect. That had worked out, hadn't it? Nodding to himself, he thought it a good plan. The challenge would be in convincing Georgia to agree with him.

But he had time for that, didn't he?

Watching her here, at the wedding of her ex-husband, he was struck again by her courage. Her boldness in facing down those who had hurt her with style and enough attitude to let everyone in the room know that she'd moved on. Happily.

The bride hadn't expected Georgia to show up for the wedding. That had been clear enough when he and Georgia arrived. The stunned shock on the bride's face mingled with the interest from the groom had been proof of that.

Sean frowned to himself and had a sip of the beer sitting in front of him. He didn't much care for the way Georgia's ex-husband took every chance he had to leer at her. But he couldn't blame the man for regretting letting Georgia go in favor of the empty-headed woman he'd now saddled himself with.

Georgia was as a bottle of fine wine while the bride seemed more of a can of flat soda in comparison.

The reception was being held at the clubhouse of a

golf course. Late fall in Ohio was cold, and so the hall was closed up against the night, making the room damn near stifling.

Crepe paper streamers sagged from the corners of the wall where the tape holding them in place was beginning to give. Balloons, as their helium drained away, began to dip and bob aimlessly, as if looking for a way out, and even the flowers in glass vases on every table were beginning to droop.

People who weren't dancing huddled together at tables or crowded what was left of the buffet. Sean was seated near the dance floor, watching Georgia slow dance in the arms of her ex, fighting the urge to go out there and snatch her away from the buffoon. He didn't like the man's hands on her. Didn't like the way Mike bent his head to Georgia and whispered in her ear.

Sean frowned as the music spilled from the speakers overhead and the groom pulled Georgia a bit too tightly against him. Something spiked inside Sean's head and he tightened his grip on the beer bottle so that it wouldn't have surprised him in the least to feel it shatter. Deliberately, he released his hold on the bottle, setting it down carefully on the table.

Then Sean breathed slow and deep, and rubbed the heel of his hand against the center of his chest, unconsciously trying to rub away the hard, cold knot that seemed to have settled there. He gritted his teeth and narrowed his eyes when the groom's hand slipped down to cup Georgia's behind.

Fury swamped his vision and dropped a red haze of anger over his mind. When Georgia struggled to pull free without success, something inside Sean simply snapped. The instinct to protect her roared into life and he went with it. *His* woman, mauled on a dance floor? He bloody well didn't think so.

Sean was halfway out of his chair when Georgia brought the sharp point of one of her high heels down onto the toe of the groom's shoe. While Mike hopped about, whinging about being in pain, Misty ran to her beloved's rescue, and Sean met Georgia halfway between the dance floor and the table.

Her eyes were glinting with outrage, color was high in her cheeks and she'd never been more vividly beautiful to him. She'd saved herself, leaving him nothing to do with the barely repressed anger churning inside him.

His woman, he thought again, and felt the truth of it right down to his bones. And even knowing that, he pulled away mentally from what that might mean. He wouldn't look at it. Not now. Instead, he focused a hard look at the groom and his new bride, then shifted his gaze back to Georgia.

"So then," Sean asked, "ready to leave?"

"Way past ready," Georgia admitted and stalked by him to their table to pick up her wrap and her purse.

He let her go, but was damned if he'd leave this place without making a few things clear to the man he'd like nothing better than to punch into the next week. Misty was clinging to Mike when Sean approached them, but he didn't even glance at the new bride. Instead, his gaze was for the groom, still hobbling unsteadily on one injured foot.

Voice low, eyes hard, Sean said, "I'll not beat a man on his wedding day, so you're safe from me."

Insulted, Mike sputtered, "What the—"

"But," Sean continued, letting the protective instincts rising inside him take over, "you even so much as *think* of Georgia again, I'll know of it. And you and I will have a word."

Misty's mouth flapped open and shut like a baby bird's. Mike flushed dark red, but his eyes showed him for the true coward he was, even before he nodded. Sean left them both standing there, thinking the two of them deserved each other.

When he draped Georgia's wrap about her shoulders, then slid one arm around her waist to escort her from the building, she looked up at him.

"What did you say to him?"

He glanced at her and gave her a quick smile to disguise the fury still pulsing within. "I thanked him for a lovely party and wished him a broken foot."

"I do like your style, Sean," she said, leaning her head against his shoulder.

He kissed the top of her head and took the opportunity to take a long breath of her scent. Then he quipped, "I believe the American thing to say would be, 'back atcha.'"

With the sound of her laughter in his ears, Sean steered her outside to the waiting limousine, and ushered her inside.

With a word to the driver, they were off for the airport so Sean could take his woman home to Ireland.

Ten

A few days later, Sean was standing in Ronan's office in Galway, looking for a little encouragement. Apparently, though, he'd come to the wrong place.

"You're out of your mind," Ronan said.

"Well, don't hold back, cousin," Sean countered, pacing the confines of the office. It was big and plush but at the moment, it felt as if it were the size of a box. There was too much frustrated energy pumping through Sean's brain to let him stand still, and walking in circles was getting him nowhere.

He stopped at the wide window that offered a view of Galway city and the bay beyond. Out over the ocean, layers of dark clouds huddled at the horizon, no doubt bunched up over England but planning their immediate assault on Ireland. Winter was coming in like a mean bitch.

Sean had come into Galway to see Ronan because

his cousin's office was the one place Sean could think of where they could have a conversation without interruptions from the seeming *multitude* of women in their lives. Ronan was, naturally, wrapped up in Laura and baby Fiona. For Sean, there was his mother, nearly recovered now, and there was Georgia. Beautiful Georgia who haunted his sleep and infiltrated his every waking thought.

His woman, he'd thought that night in Ohio, and that notion had stayed with him. There was something there between them. He knew it. Felt it. And he'd finally found a plan to solve his troubles, so he'd needed this time with Ronan to talk it all out. But for all the help he was finding, he might have stayed home.

"How is it crazy to go after what I want?" he argued now. "You did it."

Ronan sat back in the chair behind his uncluttered desk. Tapping the fingers of one hand against that glossy surface, he stared at Sean with a disbelieving gleam in his eyes.

"Aye, I did it, just as you're thinking to, so I'm the man to tell you that you're wrong. You can't ask Georgia to marry you as a sort of business arrangement."

"Why not?" Sean countered, glancing over his shoulder at his cousin before turning his gaze back to the window and the outside world beyond. "For all your calm reason now, you did the same with Laura and look how well that turned out for you."

Ronan scraped one hand across his face. "You idiot. I almost lost Laura through my own foolishness. She wouldn't have me, do you not remember that? How I was forced to chase her down to the airport as she was leaving me?"

Sean waved that off. The point was, it *had* worked out.

A bump or two in the road, he was expecting. Nothing worthwhile came easy, after all, but in the end, Georgia would agree with him. He'd done a lot of thinking about this, and he knew he was right. Georgia was much more sensible, more reasonable than her sister and he was sure she'd see the common sense in their getting married.

He'd worked it out in his mind so neatly, she had to see it. A businesslike offer of marriage was eminently sensible. With his mother on the mend, the time for ending their faux engagement was fast approaching. And Sean had discovered he didn't want his time with Georgia to be over. He wanted her even more now than he had when this had all begun.

He turned around, leaned one hip against the window jamb and looked at his cousin.

"Georgia's buying a house here," Sean pointed out. "She's opening her business. She won't be running off to California to escape me."

"Doesn't mean she'll greet you with open arms, either," Ronan snapped, then huffed out a breath filled with frustration. "She's already been married to a man who didn't treasure her. Why would she choose another who offers her the same?"

Sean came away from the window in a fast lunge and stood glaring down at Ronan. Damned if he'd be put in the same boat as the miserable bastard who'd caused Georgia nothing but pain. "Don't be comparing me to that appalling excuse of a man who hurt her. I'd not cheat on my wife."

"No, but you won't love her, either," Ronan said, jumping up from his chair to match his cousin glare for glare. "And as she's my sister now, I'll stand for her and tell you myself she *deserves* to be loved, and if you're not the man to do it then bloody well step aside and let her find the one who will."

Those words slapped at Sean's mind and heart, and he didn't much care for it. *Love* wasn't a word Sean was entirely comfortable with. He'd tried to be in love with Noreen and he'd failed. What if he tried with Georgia and failed there, as well? No, he wouldn't risk it. What they had now was good. Strong. Warmth beneath the heat. Caring to go with the passion. Affection that wasn't muddled by trying to label it. Wasn't that enough? Wasn't that more than a lot of people built a life around?

And he'd be damned before he stepped aside for some other man to snatch Georgia in front of his eyes. Which was one of the reasons he'd come up with this plan in the first place. If they ended their engagement—and since Ailish was recovering nicely, that time was coming fast— then he'd be forced to let Georgia go. Watch her find a new man. He'd have to imagine that lucky bastard touching her, kissing her, claiming her in the dark of night— and damned if he'd do *that,* either.

He alone would be the man touching Georgia Page, Sean assured himself, because he could accept no other option. If he did, he'd be over the edge and into insanity in no time at all.

"She had a man who promised her love, as you've just said yourself," Sean argued, jamming both hands into his pockets to hide the fists they'd curled into. Thinking about that man, Georgia's ex, made him want to punch something. That a man such as he had had Georgia and let her go was something Sean would never understand.

"What good did the promise of love do her then?" he asked, more quietly now. "I'm not talking of love but of building a life together."

"Without the first, the second's not much good," Ronan told him with a slow shake of his head.

"Without the first, the second is far less complicated,"

Sean argued. He knew Ronan loved his Laura, and good for him. But love wasn't the only answer. Love was too damn ephemeral. Hard to pin down. If he offered her love, why would she believe him? Why would she trust it when that bastard who had offered the same had crushed her spirit with the word?

No. He could offer Georgia what she wanted. A home. Family. A man to stand at her side and never hurt her as she'd been hurt before. Wasn't that worth something?

"You're a jackass if you really believe that bilge you're shoveling."

"Thanks very much," Sean muttered, then said, "You're missing the point of this, Ronan. If there's no love between us, there's no way for her to be hurt. She'll be safe. I'll see to it."

Ronan skewered him with a look. "You're set on this, aren't you?"

"I am. I've thought this through." In fact, he'd thought of little else since going on that trip to the States with Georgia. He wanted this and so, Sean knew, he could make it happen. He'd never before lost when something mattered as this did. Now wouldn't be the first time. "I know I'm right about this, Ronan."

"Ah, well then." Clapping one hand to Sean's shoulder, Ronan said, "I wish you luck with it, because you're going to need it. And when Georgia coshes you over the head with something heavy, don't be coming to me looking for sympathy."

A tiny speck of doubt floated through the river of Sean's surety, but he paid it no attention at all. Instead, he focused only on his plan, and how to present it to Georgia.

It stormed for a week.

Heavy, black clouds rolled in from the sea, riding an

icy wind that battered the village like a bad-tempered child. The weather kept everyone closed up in their own houses, and Georgia was no different. She'd spent her time hanging pictures and paintings, and putting out the other small things she'd brought with her from California until the cottage was cozy and felt more hers every day.

She missed Sean, though. She hadn't seen him in days. Had spoken to him only briefly on the phone. Laura had told her that Sean and Ronan had spent days and nights all over the countryside, helping the villagers and farmers who were having a hard time through the storm. They'd done everything from mending leaking roofs to ferrying a sick child to the hospital just in time for an emergency appendectomy.

Georgia admired their connection to the village and their determination to see everyone safely through the first big storm of the season. But, God, she'd missed him. And though it pained her, she had finally convinced herself that not seeing him, not having him with her, was probably for the best. Soon, she'd have to get accustomed to his absence, so she might as well start getting used to it.

But it was so much harder than she'd thought it would be. She hadn't planned on that, damn it. She'd wanted the affair with the gorgeous Irishman, and who wouldn't have?

But she hadn't wanted the risk of loving him, and the fact that she did was entirely *his* fault. If he hadn't been so blasted charming and sweet and sexy. If he hadn't been such an amazing lover and so much fun to be around, she never would have fallen. So really, Georgia told herself, none of this was her fault at all.

She'd been hit over the head by the Irish fates and the only way out was pain and suffering. He'd become such a part of her life that cutting him out of it was going to be like losing a limb. Which just irritated her immensely. That she could fall in love when she knew she shouldn't, because of the misery that was now headed her way, was both frustrating and infuriating.

The worst of it now was there was nothing she could do about it. The love was there and she was just going to have to hope that, eventually, it would fade away. In hindsight, she probably shouldn't have accepted Sean's bargain in the first place. But if she hadn't…she would have missed so much.

So she couldn't bring herself to wish away what she'd found with him, even though ending it was going to kill her.

When the sun finally came out, people streamed from their homes and businesses as if they were prisoners suddenly set loose from jail. And Georgia was one of them. She was so eager to get out of her own thoughts, and away from her own company, she raced into town to open her shop and start living the life she was ready to build.

The sidewalks were crowded with mothers who had spent a week trapped with bored children. The tea shop did a booming business as friends and neighbors gathered to tell war stories of storm survival. Shop owners were manning brooms, cleaning up the wreckage left behind and talking to friends as they worked.

Georgia was one of them now. Outside her new design shop, she wielded a broom with the rest of them, and once her place was set to rights, she walked back inside to brew some coffee. She might be in Ireland, but she hadn't yet switched her allegiance from coffee to tea.

The bell over the front door rang in a cheery rattle, and she hurried into the main room only to stop dead when she saw Sean. Everything in her kindled into life. Heat, excitement, want and tenderness tangled together making her nearly breathless. It felt like years since she'd seen him though it had only been a few days. Yes. Irritating.

He looked ragged, tired, and a curl of worry opened up in the center of her chest. The shadow of whiskers on his jaws and the way his hair jutted up, no doubt from him stabbing his fingers through it repeatedly, told her just what a hard few days he'd had. He wore faded jeans, a dark, thickly knit sweater and heavy work boots. And, she thought, he'd never looked more gorgeous.

"How are you?" she asked.

He rubbed one hand across his face, blinked a couple of times, then a half smile curved one corner of his mouth. "Tired. But otherwise, I'll do."

"Laura told me what you and Ronan have been up to. Was it bad?"

"The first big storm of the year is always bad," he said. "But we've got most of the problems in the area taken care of."

"I'm glad. It was scary around here for a day or two," she said, remembering how the wind had howled like the shrieks of the dying. At one point the rain had come down so fiercely, it had spattered into the fire in her hearth.

"I'm sorry I wasn't able to be with you during your first real storm in Dunley," he said, as sunlight outlined him in gold against the window.

"I was fine, Sean. Though I am thinking about getting a dog," she added with a smile. "For the company. Besides, it sounds like you and Ronan had your hands full."

"We did at that." He blew out a breath and tucked his hands into the back pockets of his jeans.

How could a man look *that* sexy in old jeans and beat-up work boots?

"Maeve Carrol's roof finally gave up the ghost and caved in on her."

Georgia started. "Oh, my God. Is she okay?"

"She's well," Sean said, walking farther into the shop, letting his gaze move over the room and all the changes she'd made to it. "Madder than the devil with a drop of holy water in his whiskey, but fine."

She smiled at the image and imagined just how furious Maeve was. The older woman was spectacularly self-sufficient. "So, I'm guessing you and Ronan finally talked her into letting you replace her roof."

"The woman finally had no choice as she's a hole in her roof and lots of water damage." He shook his head. "She nearly floated away on a tide of her own stubbornness. She'll be staying with Ronan and Laura until her cottage is livable again."

Georgia folded her arms across her chest to help her fight the urge to go and wrap her arms around him. "I'm guessing she's not happy about leaving her home."

"You'd think we'd threatened to drag her through the village tied to a rampaging horse." He snorted. "The old woman scared us both half to death. Ronan's been after her for years to let us replace that roof."

"I know. It's nice of you to look out for her."

He glanced at her. "Maeve is family."

"I know that, too," she said and felt that flutter of love inside her again. Honestly, who wouldn't be swooning at the feet of a man like this? Even as that thought circled her brain, Georgia steeled herself. If she wasn't careful, she was going to do something stupid that would alert him to just how much she cared about him.

And that couldn't happen. No way would she live in Dunley knowing that Sean was off at the manor feeling sorry for poor Georgia, who'd been foolish enough to fall in love with him.

"Anyway," she said with forced cheer, "my cottage is sound, thanks to the previous owner. So I was fine."

"Aye," he said softly, brown eyes locked on her face. "You are."

A ripple of sensation slid along her spine at the music in his voice, the heat in his eyes. He was temptation itself, she told herself, and she wondered how she was going to manage living in this town over the years, seeing him and not having him. Hearing the gossip in the village about the women he would be squiring around. And again, she wanted to kick herself for ever agreeing to his crazy proposal.

"You've been working here. Your shop looks good," he said, shifting a quick look around the space. "As do you."

Heat flared inside her, but she refused to acknowledge it. Instead, Georgia looked around her shop, letting her gaze slide over the soft gold walls, the paintings of Laura's that Georgia had hung only that morning.

"Thanks," she said. "The furniture I ordered from the shop in Galway should arrive by end of the week."

She could almost see it, a sleek, feminine desk with matching chair. More chairs for clients, and shelves for what would be her collection of design books. She'd have brightly colored rugs strewn across the polished wood floor and a sense of style that customers would feel the moment they stepped inside.

Georgia was excited about the future even as she felt a pang of regret that Sean wouldn't be a part of it. She took a steadying breath before looking into his soft brown eyes again. And still it wasn't enough. Probably never would be, she thought. He would always hold a piece of her heart, whether he wanted it or not.

Still, she forced a smile. "I think it's really coming along. I'm looking forward to opening the shop for business."

"You'll be brilliant," he said, his gaze level on hers.

"Thanks for that, too." She knew his words weren't empty flattery, and his confidence in her was a blossom of warmth inside her. "And as long as I'm thanking you…we'll add on that I appreciate all your help with the business license."

"We had a deal, didn't we?"

"Yeah," she said, biting at her bottom lip. "We did."

"I spoke to Tim Shannon this morning. He told me that your business license should be arriving by end of the week."

A swirl of nerves fluttered in the pit of her stomach, and she slapped both hands to her abdomen as if to still them.

"Never say you're nervous," he said, smiling.

"Okay, I won't tell you. But I am. A little." She turned her gaze on the front window and stared out at the sunlit street beyond. "This is important to me. I just want to do it right."

"And so you will," Sean said, "and to prove it, I want to hire you."

"What?" That she hadn't expected.

"Do you remember how you reeled off dozens of brilliant ideas on how to improve the interior of my planes?"

"Yes…"

He walked closer, tugged his hands from his pockets and laid them on her shoulders. "I want you to redesign the interiors of all the Irish Air jets."

"You…" She blinked at him.

"Not just the fleet we've got at the moment, either," he told her, giving her shoulders a squeeze. "I want you in on my talks with the plane builders. We can get your input from the beginning that way."

"Redesign your…" It was a wild, exciting idea. And Georgia's mind kicked into high gear despite the shock still numbing parts of her brain.

This was huge. Irish Air as her client would give her an instant name and credibility. It would be an enormous job, she warned herself, expecting nerves or fear to trickle in under the excitement, but they didn't come. All she felt was a rush of expectancy and a thrill that he trusted her enough to turn her loose on the business that meant so much to him.

"I can see the wheels in your mind turning," he said, his mouth curving slightly. "So add this to the mix. You'll have a free hand to make whatever changes you think best. We'll work together, Georgia, and together we'll make Irish Air legendary."

Together. Her heart stirred. Oh, she liked the sound of that, even though more time with Sean would only make the eventual parting that much more painful. How could she *not* love him? He was offering her carte blanche to remake Irish Air because he trusted her.

Shaking her head, she admitted, "I don't even know what to say."

He grinned and she felt a jolt.

"Say yes, of course. I'll be your first client, Georgia, but not your last." He pulled her closer and she looked up into deep brown eyes that shone with pleasure and… something else.

"With Irish Air on your résumé, I guarantee other companies will be beating down your door soon."

"It's great, Sean, really. You won't be sorry for this."

"I've no doubts about that, Georgia," he said, then lifted one hand to smooth her hair back from her face.

At his touch, everything in her trembled, but Georgia fought it. She *had* to fight it, for her own sake.

"There's something else I want to talk to you about." His voice was quiet, thoughtful.

And she knew instinctively what he was going to say. She should have known there would be another reason for his incredible offer. He had come here to tell her their engagement was done. Deal finished. Obviously, he'd offered her that job to take the sting out of the whole thing.

"Let me help," she said, pulling back and away from him. How could she think when his hands were on her? When she was looking into those eyes of his? "Laura told me that Ailish is mostly recovered now and I'm really glad."

"Thank you," he said, "and yes, she is. She'll see her doctor this week, then all will be back to normal."

Normal. Back to life without Sean.

"So she'll be headed back to Dublin?"

"No," Sean said. "Mother's decided she wants to come home to Dunley. I offered her the left wing of the manor, but she says she's no interest in living with her son." He shrugged and laughed a little. "So she's opted for moving into the gatehouse on the estate."

"The gatehouse?" Georgia didn't remember ever noticing a gatehouse at Sean's place.

"It's what we call it, anyway," he said with a smile. "It was originally built for my grandmother to live in when she moved out of the manor in favor of my parents. Mother's always loved it, and there's plenty of room there for her friends to visit."

"Oh, okay. Well, it's nice that she'll be closer. I really like your mother."

"I know you do," Sean said. "But the thing is, with mother recovering, it's time we talked about our bargain."

"It's okay." Georgia cut him off. She didn't want him to say the words. "You don't have to say it. Ailish is well, so we're finished with this charade."

She tugged at the ring on her finger, but he reached out and stilled her hand. Georgia looked up at him.

"I don't want to be done with it," he blurted, and hope shot through her like sunlight after the storm they'd just lived through.

She swallowed hard and asked, "What?"

"I want us to marry," he said, curling her fingers into her palm to prevent her from taking off the ring.

"You do?" Love dazzled her. She looked into his eyes and saw them shine. She felt everything in her world setting itself straight again. In one split instant, she saw their lives spiraling out into a wonderful future. The home they'd make. The children. The family. She saw love and happiness and everything she'd ever wished for.

The sad cynic inside her died, and Georgia was glad to see her go.

And then he continued talking.

"It makes sense," he told her, a gorgeous smile on his face. "The village is counting on it. My mother's got the thing half-planned already. We work well together. You must admit we make a hell of a good team. We're great in bed together. I think we should simply carry on with the engagement and go through with the marriage. No one ever has to know we didn't marry for love."

Eleven

There, Sean told himself. He'd done it. Laid out his plan for her, and now she'd see exactly what they could have together. Looking into her eyes, he saw them alight, then watched worriedly as that light dimmed. He spoke up fast, hoping to see her eyes shine again.

"There's no sense in us breaking up when any fool could see we've done well together," he said, words rushing from him as her eyes went cool and a distance seemed to leap up between them.

He moved in closer and told himself she hadn't actually moved *away,* just to one side. "You're a sensible woman, Georgia. Clear-thinking. I admire that about you, along with so many other facets of you."

"Well, how nice for you that I'm such a calm person."

"I thought so." He frowned. "But somehow, I've insulted you."

"Oh, why would I be insulted by *that?*"

"I've no idea," he said, but watched her warily. "I realize I've caught you off guard with this, but you'll see, Georgia. If you'll but take a moment to think it through, you'll agree that this is the best way for both of us."

"You've decided that, have you?" She snapped a look at him that had the hackles at the back of his neck standing straight up.

This wasn't going as he'd thought it would, yet he had no choice but to march on, to lay everything out for her.

"I did. I've done considerable thinking about the two of us since we took that trip to California."

"Have you?"

Her tone was sweet, calm, and he began to relax again. This was the Georgia he knew so well. A temper, aye. What's life without a little seasoning after all, but a reasonable woman at the heart of it.

"I'm saying we work well together and there's no reason for us to separate." When her gaze narrowed, he hurried on. "The entire village is expecting a wedding. If we end things now, there'll be questions and whispers and gossip that will last for years."

"That's not what you said when we started this," she countered. *"Oh, they'll all think you've come to your senses,"* she added in such a true mimic of his own voice and words she had him flinching.

"It's different now," he insisted.

"How? How is it different?"

He rubbed one hand over his face, fatigue clawing at him even as his muddled mind fought for survival. "You're a part of things in Dunley, as am I. They'll wonder. They'll talk."

"Let them," she snapped. "Isn't that what a *sensible* woman would say?"

"Clearly that word upsets you, though I've no idea

why. You're a lovely woman, Georgia, with a sound mind and a clear vision." He pushed on, determined to make her see things his way, though the ground beneath his feet felt suddenly unstable. "You're rational, able to look at a situation and see it for what it is. Which is why I know you'll agree with me on this. Ronan insisted you wouldn't, of course, but he doesn't know you as I do…"

"Ronan?" she asked, turning her head and glancing at him from the corner of her eye. "You discussed this with Ronan?"

"Why wouldn't I?" He stiffened. "He's as close as a brother to me, and I wanted to get it all set in my mind before I came to you with it."

"And now you have?"

"I do," Sean told her, and felt worry begin to slither through him. She wasn't reacting as he'd expected. He'd thought that his sensible Georgia would smile up at him and say, *Good idea, Sean. Let's do it.* Instead, the distance between them seemed to be growing despite the fact she was standing right in front of him.

She looked down at the emerald-and-diamond ring on her finger, and when he caught her hand in his, he felt better. She was considering his proposal, then, though he'd have expected a bit more excitement and a little less biting his damned head off.

"If you'll just take a moment to consider it, I know you'll agree. You're not a woman to muddy your thinking by looking through the wavery glass of emotion."

"Oh, no," she whispered, rubbing her thumb against the gold band of her ring. "I'm cool and calm. That's me. No emotions. Little robot Georgia."

"Robot?" He frowned at her. "What're you talking about?"

"Logical," she repeated. "Rational. If I come when you whistle I could be your dog."

He scrubbed the back of his neck. Maybe he shouldn't have come here first thing this morning. Maybe he should have waited. Gotten some damn sleep before talking to her. For now, he felt as though even his own thoughts were churning. He couldn't lay a finger on how he'd gone wrong here, but he knew he had.

The only way out was to keep talking, hoping he'd stumble on the words he needed so desperately. And why was it, he thought wildly, that when he most needed the words, they'd dried up on him?

"Not a robot now, but a dog?" Sean shook his head. "You've got this all wrong, Georgia. 'Tis my fault you're not understanding me," he said benevolently. "I've not made myself clear enough."

"Oh," she told him with a choked-off laugh, "you're coming through loud and clear."

"I can't be, no, or you wouldn't be standing there spitting fire at me with your eyes."

"Really?" She cocked her head to one side and studied him. "How should I react to this oh-so-generous proposal?"

Temper slapped him. He was offering marriage here, not a year in a dungeon. For all the way she was acting, you wouldn't believe he was trying to make her his wife but instead ordering her to swim her way back to America.

"A kiss wouldn't be out of hand, if you're asking me. It's not every day I ask a woman to marry me, you know."

"And so graciously, too." She fiddled with her ring again, thumb sliding across the big green stone. "I should probably apologize."

"No need for that," he said, worry easing back an inch or so now. "I've caught you by surprise, is all."

"Oh, you could say that." She pulled her hand free of his. "And your proposal to Noreen, was it every bit this romantic?"

"Romantic? What's romance to do with this?"

"Nothing, obviously," she muttered.

"And I never proposed to Noreen," he told her hotly. "That just…happened."

"Poor you," Georgia told him with sarcasm dripping off each word. "How you must have been taken advantage of."

"I didn't say that—" He shook his head and blew out a breath. "I've no idea what I'm saying now, you've got me running in circles so."

"Not sensible enough for you?"

"Not by half, no," he said flatly. "You're behaving oddly, Georgia, if you don't mind my saying." Reaching for her, he blinked when she batted his hands away. "What was that for?"

"Oh, let me count the reasons," she muttered, stalking away from him to pace back and forth across the narrow width of the shop.

The short heels of her boots clacked loudly against the wood floor and sounded to Sean like a thundering heartbeat.

"You want me to marry you because your mother's making plans and the *village* will be disappointed."

"That's only part of it," he argued, feeling control slipping away from him somehow.

"Yes, of course." She snapped him a furious glance. "There's how well we work together, too."

"There is."

"And we're such a good team, right?" Her eyes flashed. "And let's not forget how good we are in bed together."

"It's a consideration, I think you'll agree, when wanting to marry." His tone was as stiff as his spine as he faced the rising fury in her eyes.

"Sure, wouldn't want to waste your time on a sensible, rational, logical woman who sucked in bed."

"A harsh way of putting it—"

She held up one hand to keep him from saying anything else, and he was shocked enough to obey the silent command.

"So basically, you don't want anything as pesky as *love* involved in this at all."

"Who said anything about love?" he demanded, as something cold and hard settled in the center of his chest.

"Exactly my point."

Swallowing his rising anger, he kept his voice calm as he pointed out, "You're not talking sense, Georgia."

"Wow, I'm not?" She flashed him a look out of eyes that had gone as dark as the ocean at night. "How disappointing for you."

Watery winter sunlight slanted into the room through the front windows and seemed to lay across Georgia like a blessing. Her hair shone, her features were golden and the flash in her eyes was unmistakable.

Still, Sean had come here to claim her and he wasn't willing to give up on that. "You're taking this the wrong way entirely, Georgia. You care for me, and I for you—"

"Care for?" she repeated, her voice hitching higher. "Care for? I *love* you, you boob."

Sean was staggered, and for the first time in his life, speechless.

"Hah!" She stabbed one finger in the air, pointing it at him like a blade. "I see you hadn't considered *that* in all of your planning. Why would rational, logical, *sensible* Georgia be in love?"

She loved him? Heat blistered his insides even as words tangled on his tongue.

"Well, I can't explain that. It's really not sensible at all," Georgia muttered, pushing both hands through her hair before dropping her hands to her sides and glaring at him. "At the moment, it feels downright stupid."

"It's not stupid," Sean blurted out, crossing to her and taking hold of her shoulders before she could dodge his touch again. Love? She loved him? This was perfect. "It's more reason than ever for you to marry me. You love me, Georgia. Who the bloody hell else would you marry?"

"Nobody." She yanked free of his grip.

"That makes no sense at all."

"Then you're not paying attention," she snapped. "You think I want to marry a man who doesn't love me? *Again?* No, thanks. I've already had that and am in no way interested in doing it all over."

"I'm nothing like that inexcusable shite you married and you bloody well know it," he argued, feeling the need to defend himself.

"Maybe not, but what you're offering me is a fake marriage."

"It would be real."

"It would be legal," she argued. "Not real."

"What the bloody hell's the difference?"

"If you don't *know* what the difference is," she countered, "then there's no way to explain it to you." She took a long breath and said, "I've come to Ireland to build myself a life. *Myself.* And just because I made the mistake of falling in love with you doesn't mean I'm willing to throw those plans away."

"Who's asking you to?" he demanded, wondering if

she loved him as she claimed, how she could be so stubbornly blind to what they shared. What they *could* share.

"I'm done with you, Sean. It's over. No engagement. No marriage. No nothing." She grabbed his arm and tugged him toward the door.

Sunlight washed the street and, for the first time, Sean noted that a few of the villagers had gathered outside the door. Drawn, no doubt by the rising voices. Nothing an Irishman liked better than a good fight—either participating or witnessing.

"Now get out and go away."

"You're throwing me out of your shop?" He dug in his heels and she couldn't budge him another inch.

"Seems the 'sensible' thing to do," she countered, her gaze simply boiling with temper.

"There's nothing sensible about you at the moment, I'm sorry to say."

"Thank you! I don't feel sensible. In fact, I may never be sensible again." She tapped the tip of her index finger against the center of his chest. "In fact, I feel *great*. It's liberating to say exactly what you're thinking and feeling.

"I've always done the right thing—okay, the sensible thing. But no more. And if you don't want me to redesign Irish Air, that's fine with me." She shook her hair back from her face. "I hear Jefferson King lives somewhere around here—I'll go see *him* about a job if I have to."

"Jefferson King?" The American billionaire who now lived on a sheep farm near Craic? Just the thought of Georgia working in close quarters with another man gave Sean a hard knot in the pit of his belly. Even if that man was married and a father.

Georgia belonged here. With him. Nowhere else.

"There's no need for that," he said sharply. "I don't

break my word. I've hired you to do the job and I'll expect you to do it well."

Surprise flickered briefly in her eyes. At least he had that satisfaction. It didn't last long.

"Good." Georgia gave him a sharp nod. "Then we're agreed. Business. *No* pleasure."

Outside the shop, muttering and conversations rose along with the size of the crowd. All of Dunley would be out there soon, Sean thought, gritting his teeth. Damned if he'd give the village more grist to chew on. If she wouldn't see reason, then he'd leave her now and try again another day to batter his way through that hard head of hers.

He lowered his voice and said, "You've a head like stone, Georgia Page."

"And so is your heart, Sean Connolly," she told him furiously.

Someone outside gasped and someone else laughed.

"This is the way you talk to a man who offers you marriage?" he ground out.

"A man who offered me *nothing*. Nothing of himself. Nothing that matters."

"Nothing? I offer you my name and that's nothing?" His fury spiked as he stared down into those blue eyes flashing fire at him.

She didn't back down an inch and even while furious he could admire that, as well.

"Your name, yes," Georgia said. "But that's all. You don't offer your heart, do you, Sean? I don't think you'd know how."

"Is that right?" Her words slapped at him and a part of him agreed with her. He'd never once in his life risked love. Risked being out of control in that way. "Well, I don't remember hearts being a part of our bargain, do you?"

"No, but with *people,* sometimes hearts get in the way."

"Oooh," someone said from outside, "that was a good one."

"Hush," another voice urged, "we'll miss something."

Sean dragged in a breath and blew it out again, firing a furious glare at their audience then looking back again to Georgia. "I'll be on my way, then, since we've nothing more to talk about."

"Good idea." She folded her arms over her chest and tapped the toe of her shoe against the floor in a rapid staccato that sounded like machine gun fire.

"Fine, then." He turned, stepped outside and pushed his way through the small crowd until he was out on the street. All he wanted now was to walk off this mad and think things through. He stopped when Georgia called his name and turned to her, hoping—foolishly—that she'd changed her mind.

She whipped her right arm back and threw her engagement ring at him. It hit Sean dead in the forehead and pain erupted as she shouted, "No engagement. No marriage!"

She slammed the door to punctuate her less than sensible shout.

Sean heard someone say, "She's a good arm on her for all she's small."

Muttering beneath his breath, Sean bent down to pick up the ring and when he straightened, Tim Casey asked, "So, the wedding'll be delayed, then? If you can keep her angry at you until January, I'll win the pool."

Sean glanced at the closed door of the shop and imagined the furious woman inside. "Shouldn't be a problem, Tim."

* * *

An hour later, Ailish was sitting in Laura's front parlor, a twist of disgust on her lips. "Well, it's happened."

"What?" Laura served the older woman a cup of tea, then took one for herself before sitting down on the couch beside her. "What happened?"

"Just what we've been waiting for," Ailish told her. "I heard from Katie, Sean's housekeeper, that Mary Donohue told her that not an hour ago, your sister threw her engagement ring at Sean. I'd say that ends the 'bargain' you told me about."

Laura groaned. Since the phone call with Ailish, when the sly woman had gotten Laura to confess all about Sean's and Georgia's ridiculous "deal," the two of them had been co-conspirators. Sean's mother was determined to see him married to a "nice" woman and to start giving her grandchildren. Laura was just as determined to see her sister happy and in love. And from what Laura had noted lately, Georgia *was* in love. With Sean. So, if she could...help, she would.

But, this new wrinkle in the situation did not bode well.

Ailish had been convinced that if they simply treated the wedding as a fait accompli, then Sean and Georgia would fall into line. Laura, knowing her sister way better, hadn't bought it for a minute, but she hadn't been able to think of anything else, either. So Ailish had ordered a cake, Laura had reserved canvas tenting for the reception and had already made a few calls to caterers in Galway and Westport.

Not that they would need any of that, now.

"Then it's over," Laura said. "I was really hoping they might actually realize that they belonged together and that it would all work out."

"They *do* belong together," Ailish said firmly, pausing to take a sip of her tea. "We're not wrong about that."

"It doesn't really matter what we think though, does it?" Laura shook her head. "Damn it, I knew Georgia was going to end up hurt."

Ailish gave a delicate, ladylike snort. "From what I heard, I'd say Sean was the one hurt. That was a very big emerald, and apparently she hit him square in the middle of his forehead." Nodding, she added, "Perhaps it knocked some sense into the man."

"Doubt it," Laura grumbled, then added, "no offense."

"None taken." Ailish reached out and patted her hand. "I've never seen my son so taken with a woman as he is with our Georgia, and by heaven, if he's too stubborn to see it, then we'll just have to help the situation along."

"What've you got in mind?" Laura watched the older woman warily.

"A few ideas is all," Ailish said, "but we may need a little help…"

At that moment, Ronan walked into the room, cradling his baby daughter in his arms. He took one look at the two women with their heads together and made a quick about-face, trying for a stealthy escape.

"Not one more step, Ronan Connolly," Ailish called out.

He stopped, turned back and looked at each woman in turn. Narrowing his eyes on them, he said, "You're plotting something, aren't you?"

"*Plotting*'s a harsh word," Laura insisted.

He frowned at her.

"None of your glowering now, Ronan," his aunt told him. "This is serious business here."

"I'll not have a part in a scheme against Sean," he warned.

"'Tis *for* Sean," Ailish corrected him. "Not against him. I am his mother, after all."

"Oh, aye, that makes a difference."

Ailish turned a hard look on her nephew and Laura hid a smile.

"We'll be needing your help, and I want no trouble from you on this," Ailish said.

"Oh, now, I think I'd best be off and out of this—"

"Give it up, Ronan," Laura told him with a slow shake of her head. "You're lost against her and you know it." Turning to the older woman, she said with admiration, "You'd have been a great general."

"Isn't that a lovely thing to say?" Ailish beamed at her and then waved Ronan closer. "Come now, it won't be a bit of trouble to you. You'll see."

Ronan glumly walked forward, but bent his head to his daughter and whispered, "When you're grown, you're not allowed to play with your aunt Ailish."

Twelve

"Damn it Georgia, I knew this was going to happen!" Laura dropped onto the sofa and glared at her sister.

"Well, congrats, you must be psychic!" Georgia curled her legs up under her and muttered, "Better than being sensible, anyway."

"So now what?" Laura reached over and turned up the volume on the baby monitor she'd set on the nearby table. Instantly, the soft sound of Beethoven slipped into the room along with the sighs of a sleeping baby.

Georgia listened to the sounds and felt a jab of something sweet and sharp around her heart. If she hadn't loved Sean, she might have gotten married again someday. But now she was stuck. She couldn't marry the one she loved and wouldn't marry anyone else. Which left her playing the part of favorite auntie to Laura and Ronan's kids.

"Now nothing," Georgia told her and couldn't quite stop a sigh. "It's over and that's the end of it."

"Doesn't make sense," Laura muttered. "I've *seen* the way Sean looks at you."

"If I *pay* you, will you let this go?" Georgia asked.

"I don't know why you're mad at me. You should be fighting with Sean."

"I did already."

"Sounds like you should again."

"To what point?" Georgia shook her head. "We said what we had to say and now we're done."

"Yeah," Laura told her wryly. "I can see that."

"I'll get over it and *him*," Georgia added, remembering Sean's insulting proposal and the look of shock on his face when she told him *thanks, but no, thanks*. Idiot. She dropped her head onto the back of the couch. "Maybe it's like a bad case of the flu. I'll feel like I'm going to die for a few days and then I'll recover." Probably.

"Oh, that's good."

Georgia lifted her head and speared her sister with a dark look. "You could indulge my delusions."

"I'd rather encourage you to go fight for what you want."

"So I can go and beg a man to love me?" Georgia stiffened. "No, thank you. I'll pass on that, thanks."

"I didn't say *beg*. I said *fight*."

"Just leave it alone, okay? Enough already."

She didn't want to keep reliving it all. As it was, her own mind kept turning on her, replaying the scene over and over again. *Why* did she have to tell him she loved him?

Scowling, Laura looked across the room at her husband. "This is your fault."

"And what did I do?"

"Sean's your cousin. You should beat him up or something."

Before Ronan could respond to that, Georgia laughed. "Thanks for the thought, but I don't want him broken and bleeding."

"How about bruised?" Laura asked. "I could settle for bruised."

"No," she said. She was bruised enough for both of them, and she couldn't even blame Sean for it. She was the one who'd fallen in love when she shouldn't have. She was the one who had built up unrealistic dreams and then held them out all nice and shiny for him to splinter. And even now, she loved him. So who was the real idiot? "It's done. It's over. Let's move on."

"Always said you were the sensible one," Ronan piped up from across the room, and then he shivered when Georgia sent him a hard look.

"God, I hate that word."

"I'll make a note of it," Ronan assured her.

"Oh, relax, Ronan," Georgia told him. "I'm not mad at you. I'm mad at *me*."

"For what?" Laura demanded.

"I never should have told him I loved him."

"Why shouldn't you?" her sister argued. "He should know exactly what he's missing out on."

"Yeah," Georgia said, pushing up from the couch, unable to sit still. "I'm sure it's making him crazy, losing me."

"Well, it should!" Laura shot a dark look at her husband and Ronan lifted both hands as if to say, *I had nothing to do with this.*

"Excuse me, Miss Laura."

Patsy Brennan, the housekeeper, walked into the front room. "But Mickey Culhane is here to see Miss Georgia."

Georgia looked to Ronan. "Who's Mickey Culhane?"

"He owns a farm on the other side of Dunley. It was his son Sean drove to hospital during the storm." To Patsy, he added, "Show him in."

"Why would he want to see me?" Georgia wondered.

"How would I know?" Laura asked unconvincingly.

Georgia looked at her sister wish suspicion, then turned to face the man walking into the front parlor.

Mickey was about forty, tall, with thick red hair and weathered cheeks. He nodded to Ronan and Laura, then turned his gaze to Georgia. "I've heard about the troubles you and Sean are having, Miss, and wanted to say that you shouldn't be too hard on him. He's a fine man. Drove thirty kilometers into the teeth of that storm to get my boy to safety."

Georgia felt a flush of heat fill her cheeks. "I know he did, and I'm glad your son's okay."

"He is, yes." Mickey grinned. "Thanks to Sean. Without that Rover of his, we'd never have gotten the boy to help in time. You should probably think more kindly of him, is all I'm saying." He looked to Ronan and nodded. "Well, I've to be off and home for supper."

"G'night, Mickey," Ronan called as the man left.

"What was that all about?" Georgia asked the room in general as she stared after the farmer thoughtfully.

For three days, Sean stayed away from Dunley, from the cottage, giving himself time to settle and giving Georgia time to miss him. And by damn, he thought, she'd better well miss him as he missed her.

During those three days, he threw himself into work. For him, there was no other answer. When his mind was troubled or there was a problem he was trying to solve, work was always the solution.

He had meetings with his engineers, with HR, with contracts and publicity. He worked with pilots and asked for their input on the new planes and tried not to focus on the woman who would be designing their interiors.

He went in to the office early and stayed late. Anything to avoid going home. To Dunley. To the manor. Where the emptiness surrounding him was suffocating. And for three days, despite his best efforts, his mind taunted him with thoughts of Georgia. With the memory of her face as she said *I love you, you boob.*

Had ever a man been both insulted and given such a gift at the same time?

Pushing away from his desk, he walked to the window and stared out over Galway. The city lights shone in the darkness and over the bay, moonlight played on the surface of the water. The world was the same as it had been before Georgia, he thought. And yet...

A cold dark place inside him ached in time with the beat of his heart. He caught his own reflection in the window glass and frowned at the man looking back at him. He knew a fool when he saw one.

Sean Connolly didn't quit. He didn't give up on what he wanted just because he'd hit a hitch in his plans. If he had, Irish Air would be nothing more than a dream rather than being the top private airline in the world.

So a beautiful, strong-willed, infuriating woman wasn't going to stop him either.

But Georgia wasn't his problem and he knew it. The fact was, he'd enjoyed hearing her say she loved him. Had enjoyed knowing that she had said those three words, so fraught with tension and risk, first. It put him more in control, as he'd always preferred being. He hadn't allowed himself to take that step into the unknown. To risk his pride. And yet, he told himself, if there was no risk, there was no reward. He hadn't stepped away from the dare and risk of beginning his airline, had he?

"No, I did not," he told the man in the glass.

Yet, when it had come to laying his heart at the feet of a woman who had looked furious enough to kick it back in his face...he'd balked. Did that make him a coward or a fool?

He knew well that *fool* would be the word Ronan would choose. And his mother. And no doubt Georgia had several apt names for him about now.

But to Sean's way of thinking, what this was, was a matter of control. He would be in charge. He would keep their battle on his turf, so to speak—and since she had up and moved to Ireland she'd helped him in that regard already. What he had to do now was get her to confess her feelings again and then allow that perhaps he might feel the same.

"Perhaps," he sneered. What was the point in lying to himself, he wondered. Of course he loved her. Maybe he always had. Though he hadn't meant to. That certainly hadn't been part of his plan. But there Georgia Page was, with her temper, her wit, her mind. There wasn't a thing about her that didn't tear at him and fire him up all at once. She was the woman for him. Now he'd just to make her see the truth of it.

"And how will you do that when she's no doubt not speaking to you?"

He caught the eye of the man in the glass again and he didn't like what he saw. A man alone. In the dark, with the light beyond, out of reach.

Until and unless he found a way to get Georgia back in his life, he knew the darkness would only grow deeper until it finally swallowed him.

On that thought, he managed a grin as an idea was born. Swiftly, he turned for his desk, grabbed up the phone and made a call.

For the past few days, Georgia had been besieged.

Mickey Culhane had been the first but certainly not the last. Every man, woman and child in Dunley had an opinion on the situation between she and Sean and lined up to share it.

Children brought her flowers and told her how Sean always took the time to play with them. Men stopped in to tell her what a fine man Sean was. He never reneged on a bet and was always willing to help a friend in trouble. Older women regaled her with stories of Sean's childhood. Younger women told of how handsome and charming he was—as if she needed to be convinced of *that*.

In essence, Dunley was circling the wagons, but rather than shutting Georgia out for having turned on one of their own, they were deliberately trying to drag her into the heart of them. To make her see reason and "forgive Sean for whatever little thing he might have done."

The only thing she really had to forgive him for was *not* loving her. Well, okay, that and his terrible proposal. But she wouldn't have accepted a proposal from him even if he'd had violins playing and rose petals at her feet— not if he didn't love her.

But in three days, she hadn't caught even so much as a glimpse of him. Which made her wonder where he was even while telling herself it was none of her business where he was or *who* he was with. That was a lie she couldn't swallow. It ate her up inside wondering if Sean had already moved on. Was he with some gorgeous Irish redhead, already having put the Yank out of his mind?

That was a lowering thought. She was aching for him,

and the bastard had already found someone else? Was she that forgettable, really?

The furniture deliverymen had only just left when the bell over the front door sang out in welcome. Georgia hurried into the main room from the kitchen and stopped dead in her tracks.

"Ailish."

Sean's mother looked beautiful, and even better, *healthy.* She wore black slacks and a rose-colored blouse covered by a black jacket. A small clutch bag was fisted in her right hand.

"Good morning," she said, a wide smile on her face.

Georgia's stomach dropped. First, it was the villagers who'd come to support Sean and now his mother. Georgia seriously didn't know how much more she could take.

"Ailish," she said, "I really like you, but if you've come to tell me all about how wonderful your son is, I'd rather not hear it."

One eyebrow winged up and a smile touched her mouth briefly. "Well, if you already know his good points, we could talk about his flaws."

Georgia laughed shortly. "How much time do you have?"

"Oh, Georgia, I do enjoy you." Ailish chuckled, stepped into the shop and glanced around the room. "Isn't this lovely? Clearly feminine, yet with a strong, clear style that can appeal to a man, as well."

"Thank you." It was the one thing that had gone well this week, Georgia thought. Her furniture was in and she had her shop arranged just as she wanted. Now all she needed were clients. Well, beyond Irish Air. She'd talked to Sean's secretary just the day before and set up an appointment to go into Galway to meet with him.

She was already nervous. She hated that.

"You're in love with him."

"What?" Georgia jolted out of her thoughts to stare at Ailish, making herself comfortable on one of the tufted, blue chairs.

"I said, you're in love with my son."

Awkward. "Well, don't hold that against me. I'm sure I'll get over it."

Ailish only smiled. "Now why would you want to do that?"

Georgia sighed. The woman was Sean's *mother*. How was she supposed to tell the poor woman that her son was a moron? A gorgeous, sexy, funny moron? There was just no polite way to do it, so Georgia only said, "There's no future in it for me, Ailish. Sean's a nice guy—" surely she was scoring Brownie points with the universe here "—but we—I—it just didn't work out."

"Yet." Ailish inspected her impeccable manicure, then folded her hands on her lap. "I've a great fondness for you, Georgia, and I'm sure my son does, as well."

God. Could she just bash her own head against a wall until she passed out? That would be more pleasant than this conversation. "Thank you. I like you, too, really. But Ailish, Sean doesn't love me. There is no happy ending here."

"But if there were, you'd take it?"

Her heart twisted painfully in her chest. A happy ending? Sure, she'd love one. Maybe she should go out into the faery wood and make a wish on the full moon, as Sean had told her.

"Well?" the woman urged. "If my son loved you, then would you have him?"

Oh, she would have him so fast, his head would spin. She would wrap herself around him and let herself drown in the glory of being loved, really loved, by the only man she wanted. Which was about as likely to happen as stumbling across calorie-free chocolate.

"He doesn't, so the question is pointless."

"But I notice you didn't answer it."

"Ailish…" Such a nice woman. Georgia just didn't have the heart to tell her that it had all been a game. A stupid, ridiculous game cooked up by a worried son.

"You've a kind heart, Georgia." Ailish rose, walked to her and gave her a brief, hard hug. Emotion clogged Georgia's throat. She really could have used a hug from her own mother, so Ailish was filling a raw need at the moment. She would have loved this woman as a mother-in-law.

Ailish pulled back then and patted Georgia's cheek. "As I said, you've a kind heart. And a strong spirit. Strong enough, I think, to shake Sean's world up in all the right ways."

Georgia opened her mouth to speak, but Ailish cut her off.

"Don't say anything else, dear. Once spoken, some words are harder to swallow than others." She tucked her purse beneath her arm, touched one hand to her perfect hair and then headed for the door. "I'm glad I came today."

"Me, too," Georgia said. And she was. In spite of everything, these few minutes with Sean's mother had eased a few of the ragged edges inside her heart.

"I'll see you tonight at dinner, dear." Ailish left and the bell over Georgia's door tinkled into the sudden stillness.

It was cold, and the wind blowing in from the ocean was damp. But Laura's house was warm and bright, with a fire burning in the hearth and Beast and Deidre curled up together in front of it. The two dogs were inseparable,

Georgia mused, watching as Beast lay his ugly muzzle down on top of Deidre's head.

Now here was an example of a romance between the Irish and a Yank that had turned out well. So well that, together, the two dogs had made puppies that would be born sometime around Christmas.

Stooping to stroke Beast's head and scratch behind his ears, Georgia told herself that she would adopt one of the pups and she'd have her own Beast junior. She wouldn't be alone then. And she could pour all the love she had stored up to give on a puppy that would love her back.

"Thanks for that," she murmured, and Beast turned his head just far enough to lick her hand.

"Georgia," Laura called, and peeked into the room from the hallway. "Would you do me a favor and go to the wine cellar? Ronan forgot to bring up the red he's picked out for dinner, and I'd like it open and breathing before Ailish gets here."

"Sure," she answered, straightening up. "Where is it?"

"Oh. Um," Laura worried her bottom lip. "He, um, said he set it out, so you should find it easily enough."

"Motherhood's making you a little odd, honey," Georgia said with a smile.

Laura grinned. "Worth every burnt-out brain cell."

"I bet." Georgia was still smiling as she walked down the hall and made the turn to the stairs.

This family dinner idea of Laura's was good, she told herself. Nice to get out of her house. To get away from Dunley and all the well-meaning villagers who continued to sing Sean's praises.

As she opened the heavy oak door and stepped into the dimly lit wine cellar, she thought she heard something behind her. Georgia turned and looked up at Ronan as he stepped out of the shadows. "Ronan?"

He gave her an apologetic look then closed the door.

"Hey!" she called, "Ronan, what're you doing?"

On the other side, the key turned in the lock and she grabbed the doorknob, twisting it uselessly. If this was a joke, it was a bad one. Slapping her hand against the door, she shouted, "Ronan, what's going on here?"

"'Tis for your own good, Georgia," he called back, voice muffled.

"*What* is?"

"I am," Sean said from behind her.

She whirled around so fast, she nearly lost her balance. Sean reached out to steady her but she jumped away from his touch as if he were a leper. He buried the jolt of anger that leaped to the base of his throat and stuffed his hands into his pockets, to keep from reaching for her again only to be rebuffed.

"What're you doing here?" Georgia demanded.

"Waiting for you," he said tightly. Hell, he'd been in the blasted wine cellar for more than an hour, awaiting her arrival for the family dinner he'd had Laura arrange.

The cellar was cool, with what looked like miles of wooden racks filled with every kind of wine you could imagine. Pale lights overhead spilled down on them, creating shadows and the air was scented by the wood, by the wine and, Sean thought…by *her*.

Having Ronan lock her inside with him had been his only choice. Otherwise the stubborn woman would have escaped him and they'd *never* say the things that had to be said.

"I've been waiting awhile for you. Opened a bottle of wine. Would you like some?"

She folded her arms across her middle, pulling at the fabric of her shirt, defining the curve of her breasts in a way that made his mouth water for her. With supreme effort he turned from the view and poured her a glass without waiting for her answer.

He handed it to her and she drank down half of it as if it were medicine instead of a lovely pinot.

"What do you want, Sean?" she said, voice tight, features closed to him.

"Five bloody minutes of your time, if it's all the same to you," he answered, then took a sip of his own wine, telling himself that *he* was supposed to be the cool head here.

But looking at her as she stood in front of him, it took everything in him to stand his ground and not grab her up and kiss her until she forgot how furious she was with him and simply surrendered.

"Fine. Go." She checked the dainty watch on her wrist. "Five minutes."

Unexpectedly, he laughed. A harsh scrape of sound that shot from his throat like a bullet. "By God, you're the woman for me," he said, with a shake of his head. "You'll actually time me, won't you?"

"And am," she assured him. "Four and a half minutes now."

"Right then." He tossed back the rest of his wine and felt a lovely burn of fire in its wake. Setting the glass down, he forgot all about the words he'd practiced and blurted out, "When a man asks a woman to be his wife, he expects better than for her to turn on him like a snake."

She glanced at the watch again. "And when a woman hears a proposal, she sort of expects to hear something about 'love' in there somewhere."

This was the point that had chewed at him for three days. "And did your not-so-lamented Mike, ex-husband and all-around bastard, give you pretty words of love?"

Sean took a step closer and noted with some irritation that she stepped back. "Did he promise to be faithful, to love you always?"

A gleam of tears swamped her eyes and in the pale light, he watched as she ferociously blinked them back. "That was low."

"Aye, it was," he admitted, and cursed himself for the fool Ronan thought him to be. But at the same time, he bristled. "I didn't give you the words, but I gave you the promise. And I *keep* my promises. And if you weren't such a stubborn twit, you'd have realized that I wouldn't propose unless there were feelings there."

"Three and a half minutes," she announced, then added, "Even stubborn twits want to hear about those 'feelings' beyond 'I've a caring for you, Georgia.'"

He winced at the reminder of his own words. She'd given him "love"; he'd given her "caring." Maybe he was a fool. But that wasn't the point. "You should have known what I meant without me having to say it. Let me remind you again that your lying, miserable ex used the word *love* and it meant nothing."

"At least he had the courage to say it, even though his version of love was sadly lacking!"

Her eyes were hot balls of fury and perversely, Sean was as aroused by that as he was by everything else about her.

It tore at him, what she'd said. He *had* lacked the courage to say what he felt. But no more.

Pouring himself more wine, he took a long drink. "I won't be compared to a man who couldn't see you for the treasure you are, Georgia Page. In spite of your miserable temper and your stubbornness that makes a rock look agreeable in comparison."

"And I won't be told what I should do for 'my own

good.' Not by you and not by the villagers you've no doubt *paid* to sing your praises to me for the last three days."

"I didn't pay them!" He took a gulp of wine and set the glass down again. "That was our family's doing. I only found out about it tonight. Ailish and Laura sent Ronan off to do their bidding. He talked to Maeve, who then told every mother's son and daughter for miles to go to you with tales of my wondrousness." He glared at her. "For all the good that seems to have done.

"Besides," he added, "I've no need to bribe anyone because everyone else in my bloody life can plainly see what's in my heart without a bleeding *map!*"

"Yeah?" Georgia snapped with a glance at her watch. "Two minutes. Well, I do need a map. So tell me. Flat out, what *is* in your heart?"

"Love!" He threw both hands high and let them drop again. Irritated, frustrated beyond belief, he shouted it again. "Love! I love you. Have for weeks. Maybe longer," he mused, "but I can't be sure as you're turning me into a crazy man even as we're standing here!"

She smiled at him and his heart turned over.

"Oh, aye," he nodded grimly. "Now she smiles on me with benevolence, now that she's got me just where she wants me. Half mad with love and desire and the crushing worry that she'll walk away from me and leave me to go through the rest of my life without her scent flavoring my every breath. Without the taste of her lingering on my lips. Without the soft brush of her skin against mine. *This* she smiles for."

"Sean…"

"Rather than proposing, I should be committed. What I feel for you has destroyed my control. I feel so much for you, Georgia, it's all I can think of, dream of. I want to *marry* you. Make a family with you. Be your lover, your friend, the father of your children. Because I bloody well *love* you and if you can't see that, then too bloody bad because I won't be walking away from you. Ever."

"Sean…"

"I'm not the bloody clown you once pledged yourself to," he added, stabbing the air with his finger as he jabbed it at her. "You'll not compare me to him ever again."

"No," she said, still smiling.

"How much time have I left?"

"One minute," she said.

"Fine, then." He looked into those twilight eyes, and everything in him rushed toward the only happiness he would ever want or need. "Here it is, all laid out for you. I love you. And you bloody well love me. And you're damn well going to marry me at the first opportunity. And if you don't like that plan, you can spend the next fifty years complaining about it to me. But you *will* be mine. Make no mistake about that."

"You're nuts," Georgia said finally when the silence stretched out, humming with tension, with love, with the fraught emotions tangled up between them.

"I've said as much already, haven't I?"

"You have. And I love it."

He narrowed his gaze on her. "Is that right?"

"I do. I love everything about you, crazy man. I love how you look at me. I love that you think you can tell me what to do."

He scowled but, looking into her eyes, the dregs of his temper drained away, leaving him with only the love that had near choked him since the moment he'd first laid eyes on her.

"And I will marry you," she said, stepping into his arms. "On December twenty-second."

Gathering her up close, he asked, "Why the delay?"

"Because that way, Maeve wins the pool at the pub."

"You're a devious girl, Georgia," he said. "And perfect for me in every way."

"And don't you forget it," she said, grinning up at him.

"How much time have I got left?" he asked.

Never taking her gaze from his, she pulled her wristwatch off and tossed it aside. "We've got all the time in the world."

"That won't be enough," he whispered, and kissed her long and deep, until all the dark places inside him turned to blinding light.

Then he lifted his head and said softly, *"Tá tú an-an croí orm."*

She smiled and smoothed her fingertips across his cheek. "What does that mean?"

He kissed her fingers and told her, "'You're the very heart of me.'"

On a sigh, Georgia whispered, "Back atcha."

* * * * *

MATCHED TO
A BILLIONAIRE

KAT CANTRELL

To Jennifer Hayward, because you're
always there for me. And because you
liked Leo from the beginning.

One

Leo Reynolds wished he could marry his admin. It would make life so much simpler.

Unfortunately, she was already married and nearly twice his age. Plus, women didn't stick around once they figured out he worked a hundred hours a week on a consistent basis. Loneliness was the price of catapulting Reynolds Capital Management into the big leagues of the venture capital game.

"You're a life saver, Mrs. Gordon." Leo shot her a grateful smile and leaned back in his chair.

His laptop was refusing to speak to the printer and a critical document had gotten caught in the middle of the dispute. The signed hard copy now in his hand was due to Garrett Engineering on the other side of Dallas in less than an hour.

"I'd hardly call printing a proposal saving your life." Mrs. Gordon glanced at her watch in a deliberate gesture designed to point out the time. "It's late and it's Friday. Take Jenna to that new restaurant in Victory Park and let me handle the proposal. Relax for once. It'll be good for you."

Leo grimaced as a ping of remorse bloomed and faded. "Jenna and I split up. She's already seeing someone else."

Hopefully, the new relationship would make her happy. She deserved a man who could shower her with attention and affection. He regretted not being able to give her what she wanted, but it would be patently unfair to let Jenna keep hoping he'd ever become a man capable of focusing on a re-lationship. As a result, he'd lost a comfortable companion.

"Of course she is. It's not like she ever saw *you*." Mrs. Gordon crossed her arms and looked down her nose at Leo with a tsk. "Now who are you going to take to the museum dedication?"

Leo groaned. He'd conveniently forgotten about that, but it wasn't as if he could skip the dedication. The new chil-dren's museum in the Dallas Arts District bore his name, after all, since he'd donated the money to build it. "You're free next Saturday, aren't you?"

Mrs. Gordon cackled as though Leo had been joking. "One of these days, I'm going to say yes when you ask me out and really mess with you. If Jenna's not in the picture, find another woman. They seem to be pretty thick on the ground."

Yeah, he tripped over women on a regular basis who would like to go out with him. Or at least they thought they did, right up until they realized they wouldn't be satisfied with what little time and attention he could give. It never took very long to reach that point.

A vague hollow feeling invaded his gut, one he'd ex-perienced more and more lately. He'd written it off as an increased urgency to hit that elusive, unachieved mark of success. But now that it had happened during a discussion about his personal life, he wasn't so convinced.

"I hate dating." *And small talk.* That getting-to-know-you period took time and energy he didn't care to expend. Reynolds Capital Management came first. Always.

"That's because you don't do it often enough."

Here they went, off on her favorite subject. She never got tired of scolding him about the lack of a permanent fe-male in his life.

"Have you been talking to my mother again?"

"We went to lunch Tuesday, as a matter of fact. She says hi." Mrs. Gordon raised her eyebrows and planted guilt simultancously, as Leo was sure she intended. He got it. He should call his mother. And date eligible women.

Problem was, he not only hated dating, he also hated constantly standing up dates and disappointing women who deserved better. But he liked companionship and, well, he *was* a guy—sex was nice, too. Why couldn't the perfect woman fall in his lap so he could focus on work?

"It is late," Leo said in what was no doubt a transparent attempt to change the subject. "Why don't *you* go home and I'll take the proposal to Garrett?"

He had until five o'clock to get it to Garrett Engineering, formally expressing his interest in doing business with them.

What Steve Jobs was to cell phones, Tommy Garrett was to internal combustion engines. Or would be, as soon as funding was in place. Garrett had invented a revolutionary modification to increase the gas mileage of a standard car engine and Leo intended to be Garrett's venture capital firm of choice. The partnership would net a sizable, long-term profit for both men, and Leo could do what he did best—pull strings behind the scenes.

If Leo won the deal.

No, not *if. When.*

Leo would never rest until his company hit that sweet spot of security, where longevity was a given, not a question mark. His first million hadn't done it. Neither had the first eight figures, because his profits went straight back into leveraged investments that wouldn't pay off until some point in the future. So he didn't rest.

"Since you've scared off yet another female with your dogged determination to work yourself into an early grave, be my guest." Mrs. Gordon waved her approval for Leo to deliver the proposal. "I filled up your car with gas this morning. It wouldn't kill you to glance at the gauge once in a while."

"Thanks. You're too good to me. By the way," Leo threw in as Mrs. Gordon pulled her handbag from a desk drawer,

"I was thinking of having a gathering at my house to wine and dine Tommy Garrett. If I ask very nicely, would you plan it?"

"It's not my job to be your stand-in wife." Mrs. Gordon firmed her mouth, which meant she had a lot more to say but didn't know how to do so tactfully. In the eight years she'd been keeping him sane, he'd seen that look a lot.

With a half laugh, Leo said, "Of course not. That's not part of your job description."

Except it had the ring of uncomfortable truth. When his hair grew too long, Mrs. Gordon scheduled a haircut. His mother's birthday—Mrs. Gordon picked out the gift. The wine-and-dine request had been a bit of a blurred line, but based on the set of Mrs. Gordon's mouth, he'd pretty well turned the line into a trapezoid.

Mrs. Gordon shut down her computer for the night. "Well, it should be part of someone's job description."

"What, like a party planner?" Maybe he should hire a professional in some capacity, which wouldn't cover all his social obligations. But it was better than nothing.

"Like a girlfriend. Or someone who might actually still be around in six weeks. Hire a wife," she said with a nod. "You need a good woman to take care of you out-side of the office. Ask *her* to glance at your gas gauge. She can schmooze Garrett and make sure your life is running smoothly. Keep you warm at night."

Her eyebrows waggled but Leo barely noticed.

Hire a wife.

Could you even do such a thing? It seemed too perfect a solution.

He had no time—or the desire—to sift through women until he found one he liked but who also wouldn't expect him to be available. Reynolds Capital Management did not manage itself. His employees and partners depended on him.

A wife couldn't leave him with no notice. It was the ul-timate security.

Leo would have a permanent companion to help fill that occasional hollow feeling, one with no hidden agenda involving his assets and connections. They'd both know from the get-go what to expect—stability. There'd be no hard feelings when she realized he hadn't been kidding about giving 100 percent to his company, leaving nothing left over for her.

All or nothing. Commitment was Leo's kryptonite. Once he latched on to something, he gave it everything and then some. Early on, he'd realized that trait was inherited and tried not to make the same mistakes as his father.

Then he'd met Carmen, who taught him the true depths of his weaknesses, and how easily one obsession could become the center of his existence. He practiced putting everything but the goal aside until it was second nature.

Love or success. His personality didn't allow for both and after clawing his way out of the ghetto, he refused to gamble his future.

If he had an understanding wife, work and his personal life would remain completely separate. And best of all, Leo would never have to engage in small talk with a new woman or experience that sharp pang of guilt over canceling on one ever again.

Leo tugged on his suit jacket and hand delivered the proposal to Garrett's people in their tiny downtown office. It wouldn't be tiny for long. Investors far and wide were clamoring to get in on the ground floor with Garrett's technology. Once the company went public, its worth would shoot to legendary status.

Leo had to land the deal with Tommy Garrett, and the wine-and-dine thing would be a fantastic opportunity to solidify his chances. A wife could handle the logistics, leaving Leo to engage in uninterrupted dialogue with Garrett about what Reynolds Capital could do for him that no one else could. His offer to Garrett didn't expire for several weeks. He had plenty of time to get a wife in place.

When Leo returned to his darkened office, he sat at his

laptop. Within fifteen minutes, Google provided a potential answer to the question of how to hire a wife. He'd had to wade through all the cleaning services and concierge services, then a few distasteful escort services, to find the definitive solution.

A matchmaking service.

Yes. Of course. It was not what he'd had in mind when he started the quest. Actually, he hadn't been sure *what* he'd intended to find. But this was an intriguing answer. Leo had always thought he'd get married one day, when he could afford to transfer his energy to a relationship. Yet here he was on the downside of thirty-five and Reynolds Capital Management still took all of his focus. All of his time.

He stared at the logo for EA International. The website was professional and tasteful, with earth tones and a classic font. Most importantly, this particular matchmaker catered to exclusive clients, promising discretion and a money-back guarantee. Guarantees warmed Leo's heart.

The tagline said it all—*Let us help you find "the one."*

Presumably, "the one" for Leo would fit all his qualifications. EA International would do the screening, the interviewing, the background checks, and ultimately filter out candidates who were looking for some mystical connection. Love didn't pay the bills, and Leo would never allow the power to be turned off on his family, the way his own father had.

It was brilliant. The matchmaker would do everything required to find Leo a wife. One he could never disappoint. All he had to do was make a phone call.

Then, with that settled, he could get back to work.

Daniella White had dreamed of her wedding since the first time she'd created crayon invitations to a ceremony starring Mr. Fourpaws as the tattered velveteen groom and herself as the fairy-tale bride wrapped in dingy sheets. Someday she'd wear a beautiful dress of delicate lace and silver heels. The guests would receive heavy card-stock invitations with a vellum overlay and eat a three-tiered French vanilla cake with fondant flowers.

Best of all, a handsome husband-to-be would wait for her at the end of a church aisle, wearing a tender smile. Later that night, the love of her life would sweep her away to a romantic honeymoon somewhere exotic and breathtaking. Theirs would be a marriage of grand passion and enduring love.

When her real wedding day finally arrived, Dannie could never have envisioned it would involve a groom she'd never met in person. Or that in a few minutes, she'd be marrying Leo Reynolds in the living room of a matchmaker's house in North Dallas, with only a handful of guests in attendance.

"What do you think, Mom?" Dannie beamed at her mother in the cheval mirror and straightened a three-quarter-length sleeve. A dress of any sort usually appealed to Dannie, but this unadorned ecru one would be her wedding dress and she wanted to love it. She didn't. But she'd make the best of it, like always.

EA International's sophisticated computer program had matched her with businessman Leo Reynolds and he expected a wife with a certain refinement—one who dressed the part, acted the part, lived the part. Dannie had spent the past month under the matchmaker's intensive tutelage to become exactly right for that part.

Dannie's mother coughed profusely, hand to her chest as if she'd clear the scar tissue from her lungs through sheer will alone. "You're beautiful, baby," she said when she'd recovered. "Every bit a proper wife. I'm so proud of what you've accomplished."

Yeah, it was really hard to put my name in a database. Dannie bit back the comment. She wasn't a smart aleck anymore. No one ever got her jokes anyway.

Two sharp raps at the door shoved Dannie's heart into her throat. Elise Arundel, Dannie's fairy godmother–slash–

matchmaker, popped into the room, her sleek, dark pageboy swinging. "Oh, Dannie. You look lovely."

Dannie smiled demurely. She needed a lot of practice at being demure.

"Thanks to you."

"I didn't pick out that dress." Elise nodded once. "You did. It's perfect for your willowy frame. I've never had anyone who glommed on to cut and style with such natural talent."

"I made up for it by being hopeless with cosmetics." Dannie frowned. Did that seem too outspoken? Ungrateful? That was the problem with changing your personality to become a society wife—nothing came naturally.

Elise's critical eye swept over Dannie's face and she dismissed the comment with a flick of her manicured hand. "You're flawless. Leo's socks will be knocked off."

And there went her pulse again.

The figure in the mirror stared back at her, almost a stranger, but with her dark brown hair and almond-colored eyes. Would Leo be happy with her sophisticated chignon? The erect posture? The scared-to-death woman in the ecru dress? What if he didn't like brunettes?

She was being silly. He'd seen her picture, of course, as she'd seen his. They'd spoken on the phone twice. Their conversations had been pleasant and they'd worked through several important marital issues: they'd allow the intimate side of their relationship to evolve over time, a clarification that had clinched it since he didn't believe he was buying an "exchange of services," and he was open to eventually having children.

Neither of them had any illusions about the purpose of this marriage—a permanent means to an end.

Why was she so nervous about what was essentially an arranged marriage?

Her mother smoothed a hand over Dannie's hair. "Soon you'll be Mrs. Leo Reynolds and all your dreams will come true. For the rest of your life, you'll have the security and companionship I never had." Racking coughs punctuated the sentiment and the ticking clock in Dannie's mind sped up. Pulmonary fibrosis was killing her mother.

Dannie was marrying Leo to save her.

And she'd never forget what she owed him. What she owed Elise.

Her mom was right. Dannie had always dreamed of being a wife and mother and now she was getting that chance. Marriage based on compatibility would provide security for her and her mom. She had no business being sad that security couldn't be based on love.

Maybe love could grow over time, along with intimacy. She'd hang on to that hope.

With a misty smile, Elise opened the door wider. "Leo's waiting for you in front of the fireplace. Here's your bouquet. Simple and tasteful, with orchids and roses, like you requested."

The clutch of flowers nearly wrenched the tears loose from Dannie's eyes. "It's beautiful. Everything is beautiful. I can't thank you enough."

She still couldn't believe Elise had selected *her* for the EA International matchmaking program. When she'd applied, it had all seemed like such a long shot, but what choice did she have? Her mother needed expensive long-term care, which neither of them could afford, so Dannie gladly did whatever her mother needed—doctor's appointments, cooking, cleaning. Her father had left before she'd been born, so it had been the two of them against the world since the beginning.

Unfortunately, employers rarely forgave the amount of time off Dannie required. After being fired from the third job in a row, her situation felt pretty dire. She'd searched in vain for a work-from-home job or one with a flexible schedule. After hours at the library's computer, she'd been about to give up when the ad for EA International caught her eye.

Have you ever dreamed of a different sort of career? Coupled with a picture of a bride, how could she not click on it?

EA International invited women with superior administrative skills, a desire to better themselves and the drive to become "the woman behind the man" to apply for a bold, innovative training program.

Who had better admin skills than someone managing the care of a perpetually ill mother? Without much to lose, Dannie sent her information into the ether and shock of all shocks, got the call.

It was fate that EA International was based in Dallas, where Dannie lived.

Elise polished Dannie until she shone and then matched her with a man who needed an elegant society wife. In exchange for organizing Leo's household and hosting parties, Dannie could take care of her mother without any more financial worries.

A marriage that was little more than a contract seemed a small price to pay.

"You're one of my most successful graduates." Elise handed Dannie the bouquet and shifted a couple of flowers to face the outside. "I predict you'll be one of my most successful matches, as well. You and Leo couldn't be better suited."

Dannie's stomach lurched. She wanted to like him. To enjoy being married. Would she be attracted to him? What if she wasn't? Would the intimate side of their marriage never happen? Maybe she should have insisted they meet first in spite of their mutual agreement not to.

It hardly mattered. Attraction wasn't a factor here, but surely they'd eventually hold a great deal of affection for each other, regardless of what he looked like.

Nose to the bouquet, Dannie inhaled the sweet scent of her wedding flowers. "We have similar goals and both recognize the practicality of this union. I expect we'll be very happy together."

Leo had gobs of money. She'd have been happy with half a gob. That level of wealth intimidated her, but Elise insisted she could handle it. After all, Dannie would have a valued place in his life and she might eventually be the mother of his children. Her training had made it very clear the woman behind the man worked as hard as women in other careers.

"Happy is exactly what you'll be." Elise pinched the clasp of Dannie's necklace, dragging it to the nape of her neck. The open-heart lavaliere hanging from the chain had been a gift from the matchmaker when Dannie agreed to marry Leo. "My computer program is never wrong."

Dannie's mother chimed in. "This is the best kind of match, one that will last forever, because it's based on compatibility, not feelings. It's everything Dannie wants in a marriage."

Dannie forced a nod, though she wished she could disagree, and spared only a passing thought to Rob. She'd been so gaga over him.

Look where that had gotten her—brokenhearted and determined to make over her temperament so no man could call her opinionated and blunt again. She'd screwed up that relationship but good.

She wasn't going to screw up this one. Her mother couldn't afford it.

"Yes," she agreed. "Security and companionship. What else could I possibly ask for?"

Fairy tales were stories about magical solutions to problems and full of people who fell in love, but whose relationships couldn't possibly stand the test of time. In real life, women had to make sacrifices and Dannie was making hers.

Without any further melancholy and ridiculousness, she marched out the door of the room she'd stayed in during her transformation and went to meet her fate on a prayer that she and Leo would at least grow to care for each other. If there was more, great. She'd consider it a bonus.

Her mother and Elise followed. Dannie paused at the top of the sweeping staircase and took in the scene below.

With cheerful optimism, Elise had placed flower arrangements on the mantel and on each side of the fireplace. Dannie's heart fluttered at the thoughtfulness of the woman who had become her friend. A photographer stood at the back of the room, poised to snap memories at a moment's notice, and the gray-haired minister Elise had recommended waited in front of the fireplace.

To his right was Leo Reynolds. Her husband-to-be.

He looked up and met her gaze.

A shock of…something zapped across her shoulders. He looked exactly like his picture, but in person—*hello*. Dark, straight hair brushed his collar and an expensive, well-designed suit encased a masculine body Leo clearly kept in great shape. Classic, smooth features formed a face handsome enough to sell out an entire print run of *GQ* magazine. More Ashley than Rhett, which was appropriate since she'd banished her inner Scarlett O'Hara to a place where the sun didn't shine.

Leo also looked kind, as though he wouldn't hesitate to carry an elderly lady's groceries to the car. Dannie almost snorted. If Leo Reynolds had ever seen the inside of a grocery store, she'd eat her bouquet. He was a busy man and it was a good thing for her that he was, or he wouldn't need a wife.

Not for the first time, she wondered why he'd resorted to a matchmaker. He was good-looking, rich and well-spoken. By all rights, the eligible-woman line should be wrapped around the block.

Eyes on Leo, she descended the stairs with practiced ease—she'd done it in four-inch heels dozens of times and didn't falter today despite the severity of the occasion. In far too few steps, she reached Leo. In her bone-colored pumps, she and Leo were nearly the same height.

She searched his expression as he did the same to her. What did you say to a man you were about to marry but whom you were seeing for the first time in the flesh? *Hey, fancy meeting you here.*

A hysterical giggle nearly slipped out. Not an auspicious start.

"Hello." Well, that should be reasonably safe.

"Hello," Leo returned and smiled, setting off a nice, warm flutter in her chest.

Up close, he was solid and powerful, capable of carrying a baby in one arm and taking out a carjacker with the other. The flutter that thought set off was a little warmer and little more south than the first one. In theory, she'd known Leo equated to safety. But reality was far more... real. And affecting.

They faced front. Nerves locked Dannie's knees and she tried to loosen them without drawing attention. If she pitched over in the middle of her wedding ceremony, Elise would never forgive her.

"Let's begin." The minister raised a Bible in his wrinkled hands and began reciting the vows Leo had insisted Dannie select.

The words flowed from the minister's mouth, sounding completely different aloud than she would have imagined. For better or worse, richer or poorer. None of that really applied, not in the way it did for most couples. Those vows were a call to remember the reasons you fell in love in the first place when marriage got tough.

From her peripheral vision, she tried to catch a glimpse of Leo to see how all this was registering. Suddenly she wished they'd had a few more conversations so she'd know better what he might be thinking.

It had just seemed so unnecessary. Elise wouldn't have allowed her to marry someone awful. Her screening process was diligent and faultless, matching her with Leo on all forty-seven points of the personality profile. So long as he wasn't a criminal or a wife beater, what did it matter if he had a good sense of humor or liked sweeping historical dramas?

"Do you take Leo as your lawfully wedded husband?" the minister intoned.

Dannie cleared her throat. "I do."

With a trembling hand, she slipped a plain platinum band on Leo's finger. Or tried to. She couldn't get it over the knuckle and when he covered her hand with his to assist, she glanced up to meet his blue eyes.

That same odd shock she'd experienced on the stairs rocked her shoulders. It wasn't awareness, but deeper, as if she'd just seen someone she knew but couldn't place.

She shook it off. Nerves. That's all.

Leo repeated, "I do," his voice even and strong. Because he wasn't nervous. Why would he be, with all that masculine confidence?

The platinum band he slid on her finger matched his and winked in the living room's overhead lighting. She stared at it, transfixed by the sheer weight such a simple band added to her hand.

Divorce wasn't an option.

Both she and Leo had indicated a strong belief in honoring commitments in their profiles and it had been the first thing addressed in their phone conversation. Leo had been far too generous in the original prenuptial agreement and she'd refused to marry him without serious alterations, namely that any future children would be provided for but she'd get nothing. In her mind, that was the best way to demonstrate the seriousness of her word.

Leo represented security, not free money. And in exchange for that security, she'd be the wife he needed.

This marriage was a permanent solution to their problems, not a love match. Which was fine by her. Leo would never leave her the way her father had and she'd never have to worry about whether he'd stop loving her if she screwed up.

The minister signaled the end of the short ceremony with the traditional, "You may kiss the bride."

Oh, why had she asked for that part? It was going to be so weird. But it was her *wedding*. Shouldn't she get a kiss from her husband? A kiss to seal their bargain.

Leo turned to her, his expression unreadable. As his lips descended, she closed her eyes. Their mouths touched.

And held for a shimmering moment, launching a typhoon of flutters in her abdomen. Maybe the possibility of having a whole lot more than just affection between them wasn't as remote as she'd thought.

Then he recoiled as if he'd licked a lemon wedge and stepped away.

Their first kiss. How…disappointingly brief, with a hint of possible sparks she'd had no time to enjoy. Hadn't he felt it? Obviously not.

Her mother and Elise clapped, gathering around her and Leo to gush with congratulations.

Dannie swallowed. What had she expected—Leo would magically transform from a venture capitalist into Prince Charming? Elise's computer program had matched her with the perfect husband, one who would take care of her and her mother and treat Dannie well. She should be happy they'd have a fulfilling partnership.

She should *not* be thinking about how Leo might kiss her if they'd met under different circumstances. If they were getting married because they'd fallen in love, and during the ceremony he'd slid her a sizzling glance that said he couldn't wait for the honeymoon.

She shouldn't be dwelling on it, but the thought wouldn't fade—what would his calm blue eyes look like when they were hot with passion?

TWO

Daniella stood by the door with her hands clasped and chin down. Leo's new wife was refined and unassuming, exactly as he had specified. What he had not expected was to find her picture had lied. And it was a monstrous lie of epic proportions.

She wasn't girl-next-door attractive, as he'd believed. This woman he'd married radiated sensuous energy, as if her spirit was leashed behind a barrier of skin that could barely contain it. If that leash ever broke—look out.

She wasn't merely gorgeous; in person, Daniella defied description.

The stuff of poetry and Michael Bublé songs. If one was inclined toward that sort of thing.

Even her name was exotic and unusual. He couldn't stop looking at her. He couldn't stop thinking about the way-too-short kiss he'd broken off because it felt like the beginning of something that would take a very long time to finish. His entire body buzzed in response to that concentrated energy it badly wanted to explore.

What was he going to do with a woman like *that*?

"I'm ready to leave whenever you are, Leo." Her voice, soft but self-assured, carried across the foyer of Ms. Arundel's house.

He was going to take her home. Regardless of having *distraction* written all over her, they were married.

His recon skills clearly needed help. Why hadn't he met

her first? Because he'd dotted as many *i*'s and crossed as many *t*'s as possible before fully committing to this idea. Or so he'd thought. Leo had spoken with other satisfied clients of EA International and then personally met with Elise Arundel several times. He had confidence in her ability to find the right match, and the thorough background check Ms. Arundel had supplied confirmed her choice.

Daniella White was the perfect woman to be his wife.

Their phone calls had sealed the deal. He'd recognized her suitability immediately and everything fell into place. Why wait to marry when they were like-minded and neither cared if there was any attraction between them? It was better to get on with it.

If he had it to do over, he'd add one more criteria— *doesn't make the roof of my mouth tingle.* It was Carmen all over again, but worse, because he was no longer a lovesick seventeen-year-old and Daniella was his wife. No woman could be allowed to set him on the same catastrophic path as his father, not when Leo knew how hard it was to repurpose himself. What painful test of his inherent all-in personality had he inadvertently set himself up for now?

His marriage was supposed to be about compatibility and convenience, not a headlong sprint into the depths of craziness. It was important to start it off on the right foot.

"Did my driver get all of your belongings?" he asked her and winced.

That wasn't the right foot. *My driver.* As if he regularly employed servants to do his bidding. Was he *really* going to act that pretentious around his new bride? He usually drove himself, for crying out loud. He'd only hired a car because he thought Daniella might enjoy it.

She nodded, taking it in stride. "Yes, thank you."

"Have you said your goodbyes to everyone?"

"Yes. I'm ready."

The conversation was almost painful. This was why he'd rather have a root canal than take a woman to dinner, why he'd opted to skip dating entirely. They were married, well matched and should be able to shoot right past small talk.

Leo waited until they were seated in the town car before speaking again. She crossed her long legs, arranging them gracefully, skin sliding against skin, heels to one side. And he was openly watching her as if it was his own private movie.

Before he started drooling, he peeled his gaze from the smooth expanse of leg below her skirt. "If you don't mind, I'd like to invite my parents over tonight to meet you."

"I would be very happy to meet your parents." She clasped her hands together, resting them in her lap serenely. "You could have invited them to the ceremony. I recall from your profile how important family is to you."

He shrugged, mystified why it pleased him so much that she remembered. "They're less than thrilled about this marriage. My mother would have preferred I marry someone I was in love with."

"I'm sorry." Her hand rested on his sleeve for a brief, reassuring moment, then was gone. "You have to live your life according to what makes sense for you, not your mother."

Everything about her was gracious. Her speech, her mannerisms. Class and style delineated her from the masses and it was hard to believe she'd come from the same type of downtrodden, poverty-stricken neighborhood as he had. She had strength and compassion to spare, and he admired her pledge to care for her mother.

So she possessed a compelling sensuality and he couldn't take his eyes off of her. This was all new. By tomorrow, the edge would surely have worn off.

He relaxed. Slightly.

This marriage was going to work, allowing him to focus on his company guilt-free, while his wife handled wifely things and required none of his attention. He'd paid Ms. Arundel a sizable chunk of change to ensure it.

"Daniella, I realize we barely know each other, but I'd

like to change that. First and foremost, you can always talk to me. Tell me if you need something or have problems. Any problem at all."

"Thank you. That's very kind."

Gratitude beamed from her expression and it made him vaguely uncomfortable, as if he was the lord of the manor, bestowing favors upon the adoring masses. They were equals in this marriage. "As I told you on the phone, I have a lot of social obligations. I'll depend on you to handle them, but you can come to me if you need help or have questions."

"Yes, I understand." She started to say something else and appeared to change her mind, as if afraid to say too much. Probably nervous and unsure.

"Daniella." Leo paused, weighing the best approach to ease the tautness between them. She gazed at him expectantly, her almond-colored eyes bright, with a hint of vulnerability. That nearly undid him. "We're married. I want you to trust me, to feel relaxed around me."

A building was only as good as its foundation.

"I do." She nodded, her expression so serious, he almost told her a joke to see if she'd smile. "You're everything I expected. I'm very happy with Elise's choice."

She was clutching her hands together so tightly, her knuckles had gone white. The art of small talk was not his forte, but surely he could do better than this.

"I'm pleased, as well." Pleased, not happy. This marriage had never been about being happy, but being sensible. "But now we have to live together and it should be comfortable for us both. You can talk to me about anything. Finances. Religion. Politics."

Sex.

His mind had *not* jumped straight to that...but it had, and unashamedly so, with vivid mental images of what her legs looked like under that prim skirt. She glanced at him, held his gaze. A spark flared between them and again, he sensed her energy, coiled and ready to whip out—and his body strained to catch it.

Stop, he commanded his active imagination. He and Daniella had an agreement. A civilized, rational agreement, which did not include sliding a hand over her thigh. His fingers curled and he shoved them under his leg.

She looked down and shifted, angling slightly away. One finger drummed nervously against her skirt. "Thank you. I appreciate that."

His very carnal reaction to a mere glance had obviously upset her.

He cleared his throat. "Are you still okay with letting the intimate side of our relationship unfold naturally?"

Her eyes widened and he almost groaned.

What a fantastic way to set her at ease. He needed to dunk his head in a bucket of cold water or something before he scared her into complete silence. Though that might be better than her constantly starting sentences with *yes,* as if she thought he expected a trained parrot.

"Yes." She met his gaze squarely and earned a couple of points for courage. "Why wouldn't I be?"

Because you feel this draw between us and it's making your palms sweat, too.

Chemistry had been far down the priority list, for both of them.

He just hadn't anticipated having so much of it right out of the gate. Or that it would pose a very real danger of becoming such a distraction, the exact opposite of his intent in hiring a matchmaker.

His focus should be on work. Not on getting his wife naked. Indulgent pleasures weren't on the menu, particularly not for someone with his inability to stop indulging.

"I want to be sure we're on the same page," he said.

"We are. Our marriage will be companionable with a progression toward intimacy when it seems appropriate." Her tone wavered, just a touch, and was coupled with a glint in her eyes he couldn't interpret. "Like we discussed."

His exact words. And suddenly he wished he could take it all back. Wished he could put a glint of happiness in her eyes instead of the look currently drilling a hole through his chest. The unsettling feeling bothered him more than the chemistry, because he had no clue what to do with it.

"We'll have separate bedrooms, for now." That had been his intent from the beginning and seemed even more necessary given her nervousness. It should solve everything. The back of his throat burned with inexplicable disappointment. "Take things slowly."

Separate bedrooms would serve to put some distance between them. Ease the tension, give them both time to acclimate. Give the chemistry time to cool. And definitely allow him to refocus.

Then they'd settle into what he'd envisioned: a marriage where they had fulfilling lives outside of each other and enjoyed a pleasant relationship both in the bedroom and out. No one with his intense personality could have any other kind of marriage.

His phone beeped and he glanced at it. He'd taken a half day to attend his wedding and given his employees the rest of the day off as well, but he was never "out of the office."

The email was a brief courtesy notice from Tommy Garrett's people to let him know Garrett Engineering had narrowed the field to Leo and another firm, Moreno Partners. Excellent. The timing couldn't be better. His new wife could organize the wine and dine for Garrett as soon as she was settled.

"Do you need to make a call?" Daniella asked politely. "I don't mind. Pretend I'm not here."

That wasn't even possible. "Thanks, but it was an email. No response needed."

A different strategy was in order. In light of the wife he'd ended up with, thinking of her as an employee might work best to stave off the urge to spend the weekend in bed, making his wife laugh and then making her gasp with pleasure. And then hitting *repeat* a hundred times.

If he fit Daniella into a predefined box, she'd slide into his life with little disruption and that was exactly what he wanted. What he needed.

Success guaranteed security. It was the only thing that could and no price was too high to ensure he kept his focus on Reynolds Capital Management—even continued solitude.

Dannie kept her mouth shut for the rest of the ride to her new life.

Where she would not share a bedroom with her husband.

She was alternately very glad for the space and very confused. The flash of awareness between them must be one-sided. Or she'd imagined it. Leo could not have been more clear about his lack of interest in her.

Maybe he'd seen right through Elise's makeover.

And now her fantasy about the way he'd kiss if he really meant it had shattered. Such a shame. Her husband was attractive in that unattainable way of movie stars, but in her imagination, he kissed like a pirate on shore leave, and no one could take that away.

She stole a peek at this hard-to-read man she'd married for life.

Her lungs froze. What if Leo decided he didn't like her after all? Just because he claimed to have a strong sense of commitment didn't mean he'd tolerate screwups. And screwups were her specialty.

Her mother was counting on her. She was counting on herself, too. If Leo divorced her, she'd have nothing. One of his first acts upon learning she'd accepted his proposal was to hire a full-time caregiver for her mother who specialized in pulmonary rehabilitation. The nurse was slated to start today.

Without Leo, her mother would surely die a very slow and painful death. And Dannie would be forced to watch helplessly.

Her nails bit into her palm and she nearly yelped. Long nails. Yet another thing she had to get used to, along with all the other things Elise had done to make her over into Leo's perfect wife. Organization and conversation skills came naturally, but the polish—that had taken a while to achieve.

She had to remember her job here was to become the behind-the-scenes support for a successful man. Not to be swept away in a haze of passion for her new husband.

"We're here," Leo said in his smooth voice.

Dannie glanced out the window and tried not to gape. Leo's house practically needed its own zip code.

They'd discussed her comfort level with managing a large house. During the conversation, she'd pictured a two-story, four-bedroom house with a big backyard, located in a quiet suburban neighborhood. That would have been her idea of large after the small two-bedroom apartment she'd shared with her mother.

She'd known the house was in Preston Hollow, one of the most elite neighborhoods of Dallas. But *this* she could never have anticipated.

Wrought-iron gates caught between two large brick-and-stone posts swung open as if by magic and the driver turned the car onto the cobblestone drive leading up to the house. Colossal trees lined the drive, partially blocking the sun and lending a hushed, otherworldly feel to the grounds. And *grounds* was the only fitting term. Neatly manicured grass stretched away on both sides of the car all the way to the high stone wall surrounding Leo's house.

Her house. *Their* house.

The car halted in a semicircular crushed-stone driveway, and the hulking residence immediately cast it in shadow. The manor sprawled across the property, pointy rooflines dominating the brick-and-stone structure. Four—no, five—chimneys stabbed toward the sky.

She should have asked for a picture before agreeing to handle a property this size. What was she *doing* here?

"What do you think?" Leo asked, but it was hardly a question she could answer honestly.

"It's very…" *Gothic.* "Nice."

She bit the inside of her lip. All of Elise's hard work would go up in smoke if Dannie couldn't keep her smart-aleck gene under control. The thought of Elise calmed her. They'd done exhaustive work together to prep Dannie for this, with endless days of learning to set a table, to make proper tea. Practicing how to sit, how to walk, how to introduce people. In between, Elise had transformed Dannie's appearance into something worthy of a magazine cover.

This was it—the test of whether the makeover would stick or Dannie would fail.

With a deep breath, Dannie smiled. "It's beautiful, Leo. I'm very eager to learn my way around."

"Let me show you." He placed a hand at the small of her back as she exited the car and kept it there, guiding and supporting, as they ascended the stone steps to the front door. "Please think of this as your home. Anything you want to change is open for discussion."

Anything. Except the arranged-marriage part.

It was ridiculous to even think that. But her wedding day felt so anticlimactic. And disappointing. She shouldn't be wishing Leo would sweep her up in his arms and carry her over the threshold, Rhett-style. Or wishing they had a timeless romance.

The palm at her back signaled security. Not passion. A partnership based on mutual affection was enough. Dannie was Leo's wife, not the love of his life, and she didn't have the luxury of entertaining daydreams of eventually being both.

Leo led her into the foyer. The interior of the house

opened before her, with soaring ceilings, twenty-foot windows and grand arches leading to long hallways. It reminded her of a cathedral, beautiful and opulent.

The tour of her new home took close to thirty minutes. By the time Leo concluded it in the kitchen, she was out of breath and ready to get started on the first thing she wanted to change—her shoes. The house had *four* flights of stairs.

Leo leaned a hip against the granite island in the center of the kitchen and picked up a cell phone from the counter. "For you. The number is written here, along with the alarm system security codes and the code for wireless internet access."

She took the phone with numb fingers and stared at the glossy screen. Her current cell phone was of the make-a-call-only variety. It would take hours to figure out how this one worked. "Thank you. Is your phone number written down, too?"

"I programmed it into your phone. Here's the user manual." He slid it across the counter and stuck a hand in his pocket, casually, as though they were a normal married couple chatting in the kitchen. "This model has great planning features. Feel free to add things to my schedule as needed. My admin's phone number is programmed in, as well. Mrs. Gordon. She's eager to meet you."

He had an admin, one who knew him far better than Dannie did, like how to make his coffee and whether he paced while on the phone or sat at his desk.

Suddenly, she felt completely out of her depth. "Oh. All right. I'll contact her right away."

"The car and driver will be on call for as long as you like," he continued, and his mellow voice soothed her nerves as he ticked off the items on his mental list. His confidence and self-assurance were potent. "But please, take some time to visit a dealership and buy yourself a car. Whatever kind you like. You'll want the independence."

A *car*. Any car she wanted. She'd been hopping public

transportation for so long, she nearly swooned at the idea. Was there anything he hadn't thought of? "That's very nice. Thank you."

But he wasn't finished waving his benevolence around. "I opened a bank account for you. It will be replenished regularly, but if you find yourself low, let me know. Spend it like it's your money, not mine." From his pocket, he produced a shiny black credit card and handed it to her. "No limit."

"Leo." He'd spun her around so many times now, she could hardly keep her balance. The phone and credit card in her hands blurred as she blinked back overwhelmed, appreciative tears. "This is all very generous. I'm sorry if this is too forward, but I have to ask. Why would you do all this and expect nothing in return?"

His dark eyebrows drew together in confusion. "I expect quite a bit in return, actually."

"I meant in the bedroom."

Leo went still.

Yeah, far too forward. But jeez, really? A no-limit credit card and he didn't even want one conjugal visit a month? There was a punch line here she didn't get and she'd prefer not to have it smack her in the face later.

"Daniella…" Leo swallowed and she realized he was at a loss for words.

Why couldn't she keep her big mouth closed? She should have stuck to *yes* and *thank you*.

"I'm sorry," she said in a rush. "Forgive me. You've been nothing but kind and I have no right to question your motives."

The lines of his handsome face smoothed out and he held up a hand. "No apology needed. I want to have a good relationship, where you feel like we're equals. The best way to achieve that is to give you your own money and the power to do as you like with it."

She stared at him. *Power*. He'd been granting her power with these gestures. The man she'd married was thoughtful, generous and very insightful. This whole experience could have gone very differently. Gratitude welled in her chest. "I don't know what to say."

"You don't have to say anything." He smiled and it was as powerful as it was comforting. "Remember, I'm going to be at the office a lot. You should find a hobby or volunteer work to keep you busy. A car will come in handy."

Implausibly, he was giving her the ability to entertain herself, when her sole focus should be on him and his needs. "Won't I be busy with all your social obligations?"

He waved it off. "That won't take one hundred percent of your time. You're building a life here and when our paths cross, we should enjoy each other's company. You can regale me with stories of the things you're involved in."

Elise had coached her on this extensively. It was part of her role to provide stimulating conversation for Leo's business associates. Who better to practice with than her husband? After all, they *were* a married couple having a chat in the kitchen. "That makes sense."

"Good." His eyes warmed, transforming him from movie-star handsome into something else entirely. Her breath caught.

If that's what happened to his eyes when he was pleased, she *really* wanted to see them stormy with desire.

She shook her head. They were talking about *hobbies*.

Leo took her hand, casually, as if he'd done it a thousand times. "I don't want you to be disappointed by our marriage. In the past, it's been a struggle to balance work and a relationship because the expectations weren't clear from the beginning. Women in my circles tend to demand attention I can't give them and I'm grateful we won't have that issue."

The feel of her hand in his sparked all the way up her arm, unsettling her. It was the only plausible excuse for why she blurted out, "You couldn't find one woman besides me who was willing to forgive your absence in exchange for a life of luxury?"

Her mother would have a coronary if she could hear Dannie being so outspoken. But he'd said in the car they could discuss anything. She hoped he meant it.

"Sure. But I wanted the right woman."

All at once, the reason he'd gone to a matchmaker seemed painfully obvious. He'd tried to buy his way out of putting any effort into a relationship and his previous girlfriends had told him to take a hike. So to avoid a repetition, he bought a wife.

Her.

No wonder he'd been so adamant about honoring commitments. He didn't want her to bail when she figured out she'd be all alone in this big house from now on.

· *Gothic indeed.*

"I see."

"Daniella." His gaze bored into hers, pleading with her to believe…something. But what? "Neither of us have any illusions about this marriage, and that's why it will work. I understand the drive for security. I'm happy to provide it for you because it's a drive we share."

She nodded and excused herself to unpack—and get some breathing room. Security *was* important and she'd married a good, solid man who'd never leave her like her father had. She just hadn't expected gratefulness for that security to blossom into unexpected warmth toward the husband who'd provided it. And who promised to never be around.

As she climbed the stairs to her room, she realized what his unspoken plea had been meant to communicate.

He needed her as much as she needed him.

Three

The scraps of silk had definitely not been in Dannie's suit-case when she packed it.

She fingered the baby-doll lingerie set and noticed the note: "For a red-hot wedding night. —Elise."

Dannie held up the top. Such as it was. Black lace cups overlaid red silk triangles, which tied around the neck halter-style. Red silk draped from the bust, allowing a flirty peek at the tiny G-string panties beneath. Or it would if she was insane enough to actually wear something so blatantly sexy for her husband.

This lingerie was definitely the ticket to a red-hot wedding night. For some other woman, not Daniella Reynolds. Dannie had married a workaholic. With her eyes wide-open.

She tucked the sexy lingerie into the very back of the drawer she'd designated for sleepwear. Ha. There'd be no sleeping going on if she wore *that* outfit. She sighed. Well, it would be the case if her husband pried his eyes off his bottom line. And was attracted to her. And they shared a bedroom.

And what exactly had she expected? That Leo would take one look at his new wife and fall madly in love? She needed to get over herself and stop acting as though Leo had taken away something that she'd never planned on having in the first place.

Elise, the eternal optimist despite being perfectly aware Dannie and Leo had only met that same day, couldn't have known how things would shake out. It was still depressing to be so soundly rejected. How would there be a possibility of children if they didn't share a bedroom?

Dannie slammed the drawer a little harder than an adult probably should have and stomped to the bed to finish unpacking her meager wardrobe.

If she was going to be alone, this was certainly the place to do it. Her bedroom rivaled the finest luxury suite she'd ever seen featured in a movie. She didn't have to leave. Ever. There was a minibar with a small refrigerator, fully stocked. An electronic tablet lay on the bedside table and she suspected Leo had already downloaded hundreds of books since her profile had said she liked to read.

The entertainment center came equipped with a fifty-inch flat-screen TV, cable, a DVD player, a sound system worthy of a nightclub and a fancy touch-screen remote. The owners' manuals lay on the raw silk comforter. Of course. Leo never missed a trick.

She wondered where he kept the owner's manual for Leo Reynolds. That was something she'd gladly read from cover to cover. A forty-seven-point profile only went so far into understanding the man.

There had to be more to Leo than met the eye, because no one voluntarily cut themselves off from people without a reason.

By the time she folded the last pair of socks, the hour had grown late. Leo's parents were due in thirty minutes. She called her mother to see how she was getting along with the nurse and smiled at the effusive recounting of how her mother's new caregiver played a serious game of gin rummy. Her mother sounded happy.

Relieved, Dannie went into the bathroom, where she had left half a cosmetic counter's inventory strewn across the marble vanity. She took a few minutes to organize it in the drawers, which had built-in compartments of different sizes. The bathroom alone was bigger than her entire apartment.

Dannie agonized over what to wear and finally selected a simple pale lavender skirt and dove-gray button-up shirt. Her small wardrobe of coordinated pieces had been another gift from Elise. She was between sizes so everything had to be altered, adding yet more cost to the already expensive clothes. Shoes, however, posed no problems whatsoever. She stepped into a pair of calfskin sling backs that fit as if they'd been custom-made for her foot, then redid her chignon and makeup.

Who *was* that woman in the mirror?

"Daniella Reynolds," she whispered to her reflection, then said it louder to get used to the sound of it. Only telemarketers and her grandmother called her Daniella. She liked the way Leo said it, though.

Since it was far past time to assume her duties as hostess to Leo's parents, she navigated downstairs with only one wrong turn.

Leo was not in the lavishly appointed living room. Or the kitchen, or any of the other maze of rooms on the first floor. Finally she spied his dark head bent over the desk in his study, where he was clearly engrossed in the dollar signs marching across his laptop screen.

Leo was working. Gee. What a shock. Why hadn't she thought to check his study first? Wishful thinking?

For a moment, she watched him, curious to see her husband unguarded. Towering bookshelves lined the room and should have dwarfed the man in it. They didn't. Leo's persona dominated the room. He'd shed his suit jacket and rolled up his shirtsleeves to midforearm. With his hair slightly rumpled, he was kind of adorable.

He glanced up with a distracted, lopsided half smile and her stomach flipped with a long, feminine pull. Okay, he was more than adorable. He was quite delicious and thoroughly untouchable, a combination she suddenly found irresistible. Her inner Scarlett conjured up a naughty mental scenario involving that red-hot lingerie and Leo's desk. *Hey, here's a bottom line you can check out.*

"Busy?" she croaked and cleared her throat. Duh. Of course he was.

"I'm, uh, just finishing up." He shot a furtive glance at his laptop as if the screen contained something shamefully un-work-related.

"What are you doing? Watching YouTube videos?" *Shut up, Scarlett.* It was none of her business whether he was monitoring stock prices or carousing in a role-playing-game forum. "I mean…"

Well, there was really no recovery for that slip.

"No." He shut the lid and she thought that would be the end of it. But then his mouth twitched. "I mentor college students online. I was walking through a business plan with one. Via chat."

"That's wonderful." What in the world was shameful about that? "They must really pay close attention when they see your name pop up. That's like winning the mentor lottery."

Her new husband was so generous and kind. Of course he was. Elise wouldn't have matched her with this man otherwise.

"I mentor anonymously."

"Oh. Why?"

"The business world is—" Flustered, he threaded fingers through his already slightly rumpled hair and she itched to smooth it back for him. "Let's just say my competitors won't hesitate to pounce on weakness. I don't present them with any."

Mentoring the next generation of businessmen could be perceived as a weakness? "Richard Branson mentors young kids. I don't see why he can do it, but you can't."

"He's considered successful." The unspoken *I'm not* hung in the air, but Leo stood and rolled his sleeves down, then rounded the desk, clearly signaling the end of the conversation. "Shall we?"

Her mouth fell open and she clamped it closed, swallowing the dozens of questions that sprang to her lips. His expression had closed off and even she could read the tread-with-caution sign. "Of course."

The doorbell rang and she trailed Leo to the foyer to meet Mr. and Mrs. Reynolds. Leo introduced his parents and Dannie shook hands with smiling, silver-haired Mr. Reynolds.

The spritely woman with Leo's dark hair bounded into the house and swept Dannie up in a fierce hug. "I'm so happy to meet you!"

"I'm happy to meet you, too, Mrs. Reynolds." Dannie breathed in her new mother-in-law's perfume, which reminded her of vanilla cookies.

"Oh, please. I'm Susan."

"I'm sorry, but I was expecting someone..." *Cold. Unforgiving. Judgmental.* "...older."

Susan laughed. "Aren't you sweet? Come with me to the kitchen and let Leo talk to his father while we fetch drinks."

After a glance at Leo to gauge the appropriateness, Dannie followed Susan into the kitchen and proceeded to watch while Leo's mother bustled around gathering glasses and chattering as if they were old friends. Obviously Susan felt comfortable in her son's house. Unlike her son's wife. Dannie wouldn't have known which cabinet contained glasses.

"I apologize for missing the ceremony, Daniella." Susan handed her a glass of tea and touched her shoulder. "It was a stupid, useless protest. But I'm mad at Leo, not you."

"Oh." She had to find a new response. That one was wearing thin. But it had been so appropriate. All day.

"He's just so...*Leo*. You know?" Susan sighed dramatically and Dannie nodded, though she didn't know. But she'd like to. "Too focused. Too intense. Too everything but what matters."

No way was she letting that pass. "What matters?"

"Life. Love. Grandchildren." With narrow eyes, Susan peered at Dannie. "Did he tell you that he draws?"

The tea she'd just sipped almost went down the wrong pipe. "Draws what?"

Susan snorted. "That's what I thought. Leo would rather die than let anyone know he does something frivolous. He can draw anything. Animals. Landscapes. Bridges and buildings. He's very talented. Like his namesake."

"Leo was named after someone who draws?" She envisioned a stooped grandfather doodling cartoon characters on the back of a grocery list.

"Leonardo da Vinci."

Dannie nearly dropped her tea. Leo's full name was Leonardo? Not Leonard? She'd noticed the little extra squiggle at the end of his name on the marriage license but had been so fixated on signing her own name she hadn't thought anything of it.

It shouldn't matter. But it did.

She'd married a man with a romantic name who created art from nothing more than pen and paper. She wanted to see something he'd drawn. Better yet, she wanted him to voluntarily show it to her. To share a deep-seated piece of himself. To connect with his wife.

Leo's mother had torn open a tiny corner of her son's personality and it whipped up a fervor to tear away more. They'd been *matched* and Dannie hungered to learn what they might share beyond a love of books, family and commitment.

"Daniella." Susan crooked her finger and Dannie leaned in. "I get that your marriage to my son is some kind of arrangement and presumably, that's all right with you. I won't pry. But Leo needs someone to love him, someone he can love in return, and neither will come easy. If it's not going to be you, please step aside."

Her pulse hammered in her throat. This marriage was

nothing more than a means to an end. An arrangement between two people based on compatibility, not love—exactly what she'd signed up for. But nothing close to what she wanted, what she dreamed could be possible.

Leo had asked for a wife to run his household, organize his parties and charm his business associates. Most important, his wife should give him what he needed, which wasn't necessarily the same as what he *professed* to need.

The woman behind the man had to be smart about how best to do her job.

Her inner Scarlett snickered and said *new plan*.

"What if it *is* going to be me?"

Leo had such a generous heart, but he cut himself off from people. He needed Dannie's help to understand why. If she could figure him out, it could lead to so much more than an arrangement. It could lead to the enduring love story she'd dreamed of.

Susan's smile could have powered every light in Paris. "Then I say welcome to the family."

Leo shut the door behind his parents and paused a moment before turning. For fortification. It did nothing to ease the screaming awareness of his vibrant wife. Sure enough, when he spun, there she was. Watching him with those keen eyes, chest rising and falling slightly, straining against her soft gray shirt.

He was noticing the way she *breathed*.

Clearly, he needed to go bury himself in a spreadsheet for a couple of hours.

His parents had liked Daniella, fortunately, because their lively discussion covered the fact that Leo hadn't contributed much. He'd been too busy pretending not to be preoccupied by his wife. But she'd been so amazing. A good conversationalist. A good hostess. Warm, friendly. Sexy.

It was just the two of them now. Talking was unavoidable.

"Thank you for entertaining my parents."

She shot him a perplexed look. "You're welcome. That's what I'm here for. Right?"

Since she was gazing at him expectantly, he answered her, though the question should have been rhetorical. "Yes, and I appreciate it."

"I enjoyed meeting your parents. Your mother is very interesting."

That sounded like a lead-up if he'd ever heard one. "What did she say to you in the kitchen?"

"Nothing of consequence." The smile on his wife's face was gracious and innocent. Too much so.

"Don't listen to anything my mother says, Daniella. She suffers from a terrible affliction with no cure—overt romanticism."

"Dannie."

"What?"

She'd inched forward until they were breathing the same air. And her chest nearly touched his with each small inhalation. "Daniella is too formal and stuck-up, don't you think? Call me Dannie."

He shook his head. The more formality the better for his peace of mind. "There's nothing wrong with the name *Daniella*. It's unusual. Beautiful. It suits you."

Her eyes lit up and suddenly, she was the only one breathing because all the organs in his chest stopped functioning. Nothing to the south suffered from the same problem. Everything there hummed on high alert.

"You think I'm beautiful?"

Had he said that? His brain was not refreshing fast enough. "Your name. I said your name is beautiful." Her expression fell and he cursed. If only he could converse with his wife exclusively by email, then maybe he could avoid hurting her feelings. "Of course you are, too. Very lovely."

Nice save, he thought sarcastically. *Lovely.* That described a winter snowscape. From the perspective of an eighty-year-old woman. This was the point where he usually escaped to go do something where he possessed proficiency—work.

Without looking at her again, he muttered, "Good night."

"Leo." A firm hand on his arm stopped him before he'd taken two steps past her. "I asked you to call me Dannie because that's what my friends call me. We're friends, aren't we?"

The warmth in her voice washed over him, settling inside with a slow burn. He didn't turn, didn't dare face her.

Something fundamental had changed in her demeanor—the leash she'd kept on her energy had snapped and yeah, he needed to look out. It leached into the air, electrifying it. She certainly wasn't afraid to speak to him any longer. "I... Yes. Of course."

She brushed against his arm as she rounded it, apparently not content to talk to his back. Her shirt gaped slightly, revealing a tantalizing peek at her cleavage. The slow burn blazed faster. They were talking about being friends, not lovers. What was wrong with him?

Dannie. No, too intimate. *Daniella* was too intriguing. What was he supposed to call her, *hey, you?*

He couldn't compartmentalize his wife. That was bad.

"Friends," he rasped because he had to say something.

Okay, good. Daniella could go into the friends box. It could work. He'd envisioned having a companion to fill a hole in his life. Now he had one.

"Friends." Without breaking eye contact, she reached up and loosened his tie, leaning into it, fingers lingering far too long for the simple task. "Who help each other relax."

Relax? Every nerve in his body skated along a razor's edge, desperately seeking release from the power of his wife's touch. The faint scent of strawberries wafted from her glossy lips and he wanted to taste it. "What makes you think I need to relax?"

"I can feel the tension from here, Leo."

Was that what they were calling it these days? Felt like a good, old-fashioned hard-on to him.

As if pulled by imperceptible threads, his body circled closer to hers and the promise of heat turned into a reality as their lower halves brushed once, twice. His hand flew to the small of her back to clamp her tight against him.

Fingers still tangled in his loosened tie, she tugged slightly. Her face tipped up, lips primed to be taken in another kiss, but this time nothing prevented him from finishing it. From dragging his lips down the length of his wife's torso, straight to...

He cursed—they'd agreed to be platonic only a few hours ago and they were in the middle of an innocuous conversation about being *friends*. Yet he was salivating at the thought of kissing her, of laughing together over a joke, of being so much more than a convenience to each other.

He took a deliberate step backward and her hand dropped from his tie.

If she had this strong an effect on him, he was in hotter water than he'd realized. He did *not* want to be so obsessed with his wife.

"I'm tense because I have a lot of work to do." He willed his body and his bothersome loneliness back into submission. Or tried to. Seemed as though it was destined to be a losing battle. Since she was clearly no longer too scared to talk, he'd have to put space between them another way. "We'll spend time together, but this will not be a conventional relationship. If that's not going to work for you, we should get an annulment."

A hint of hurt crept into her expression. His chest panged. She'd just asked to be friends and loosened his tie. Why was he turning it into a cardinal offense? Wasn't this part of letting their relationship grow more intimate naturally?

"What happened to make you so jaded?" she asked quietly, not the slightest bit cowed by his speech. He liked it better when she said nothing more than *yes* and *thank you*.

"I'm not jaded. I don't have anything against relationships or love in general. Without it, I wouldn't be here. My
parents still make googly eyes at each other across the table.
Didn't you notice?"

"Of course. They're a very happy couple. Why don't you
want the same?"

There was the reason he'd nipped the tie loosening in the
bud. They were married and might even become friends,
but they were never going to be anything more, and it was
a disservice to Daniella to let her have the smallest hope
otherwise.

He was already doing himself a disservice by even contemplating "otherwise."

"Oh, they're happy, all right." He rolled his eyes. "At the
expense of everything else. My parents have no money. No
savings."

And they refused to accept what they called handouts
from Leo. He'd like nothing more than to take care of them,
had offered a house, cars, even vacations, to no avail. Apparently, they enjoyed the gangs and graffiti spray-painted
on the front sidewalk. Their memories appeared to be short,
but Leo could never forget the gun-wielding thief who'd broken into their house when he was six. The terror had fueled
his drive to escape and kept him on the straight and narrow.

"You fault your parents for being happy over making
money?"

"No, I don't blame my father for working a low-paying
job so he could be home with my mom and me. I choose to
live my life differently. I'll never force my child to be grateful for one gift under the Christmas tree. To stay home from
school on the days when the rest of the class goes on field
trips to the zoo because I can't afford for my kid to go."

"Oh, Leo."

The compassion shining in her eyes unearthed something
poignant inside. That had to go. This wasn't about feeling
sorry for poor, little Leo Reynolds from the section of east

Dallas where even the churches had bars on the windows. It was about making a point.

"See all this?" He cut a hand through the air to indicate the house at large. "I worked for every dime. I held three jobs in college so I could graduate with no debt and then put my nose to the grindstone for years to get ahead. I'm still not there. If I take my eye off the prize for even a moment, poof. It all vanishes."

His wife gazed at him without speaking, lips pursed in a plump bow. Firm breasts strained against her blouse, inviting him to spread the fabric wide and—maybe he needed to internalize which prize he wasn't supposed to take his eyes off of.

Other venture capital companies were unearthing the next Google or staking start-ups that sold to competitors for billions of dollars. Reynolds Capital would be there soon if he kept on course. All he had to do was resist temptation. He'd married a woman who would help him avoid the dangers of giving in.

If she'd just stay in her box, that is.

He breathed in the scent of strawberries and the sizzling energy of his wife. "I work, Daniella. All the time. I can't invest in a relationship. It wouldn't be fair if I let you believe in that possibility."

He couldn't let himself dwell on the possibilities, either. No weakness. Indulgence led to immersion and immersion led to ruin. Carmen had proved that, nearly derailing his entire senior year and subsequently, his life. It was easier to never start down that path and the last thing he wanted was to hurt Daniella.

Four

Dannie slept poorly that night. The bed was comfortable, but she wasn't. Leo had her tied up in knots.

Now that she knew how truly earthshaking his eyes looked when they were hot with passion, she didn't know if she'd ever be comfortable again. The spike of awareness inside—deep, *deep* inside—had peaked the second he touched her and then died a miserable death during the "I'm a workaholic, deal with it" conversation.

He was definitely attracted to her. And perfectly willing to ignore it in favor of his bottom line. How exactly did he envision them moving past being polite strangers?

Her new plan might need some refining. Just because she and Leo's mother thought he might benefit from a woman's tender affections didn't mean Leo thought that. And if Dannie irritated him any further with unwanted advances, he might seek that annulment on his own. At which point she'd get nothing and she'd let her mother and Elise down. Plus herself.

But as far she was concerned, they were married for life, and she wanted to eventually be friends *and* lovers. Despite Leo's impassioned speech, she really didn't understand why he didn't want that, too.

Hence the sleepless night.

She woke in the morning, groggy but determined to be a better wife to Leo Reynolds than he could ever dream. Rob had wanted a fade-into-the-background woman and she'd messed up. Elise's training had taught her how to beat back that strong-willed inner Scarlett.

Leo was going to get what he'd asked for.

If she addressed his needs—especially the unrealized ones—maybe *that* would lead them into a deeper relationship.

After she dressed and arrived downstairs, one of the maids informed her Leo had already left for the day. Instead of wallowing in disappointment she had no business feeling, she familiarized herself with the kitchen as she toasted bread and scrambled eggs. Tomorrow morning, she'd set an alarm and be up early to make Leo coffee or breakfast or whatever he preferred, which she needed to learn pronto if she hoped to see him in the morning.

Dannie spent the rest of the morning in an endless parade of tasks: learning the ins and outs of a difficult phone that she refused to believe was smarter than she was, memorizing the brands of Leo's clothes, determining how he preferred his closet to be organized, researching the recommended care of all the fabrics. As mistress of the household, it was her responsibility to ensure the servants did their jobs well and correct poor performance as necessary. By lunch, her brain hurt.

And she hadn't even started on Leo's social calendar.

Once she tapped into the wealth of information named Mrs. Gordon, Dannie breathed a little easier. Leo's admin talked for a solid hour and then sent a dozen emails full of links and instructions about the care and feeding of a venture capitalist.

Dannie read everything twice as she absently shoved a sandwich in her mouth.

Mrs. Gordon wrapped up the exchange with a tip about an invitation to an alumni event from Leo's college, which was that very night. She kindly agreed to delete the reminder entry she'd already set up so Dannie could practice scheduling.

Perfect. Dannie plunked the stupid phone into her palm and eyed it. "I'm the boss. You better cooperate," she told it, and proceeded to manhandle the appointment onto Leo's calendar.

When his acceptance appeared, she nearly broke into an impromptu dance. Until she noticed she'd scheduled it for tomorrow night. Grimly, she rescheduled and got it right the second time. Leo was probably sitting in his office shaking his head as he accepted the updated request.

Enough of that job. Dannie went to agonize over her meager wardrobe in anticipation of her first social appearance as Mrs. Leo Reynolds. This she'd have to get right on the first shot. She couldn't carry a second outfit in her clutch in case of dress remorse.

Leo walked through the door at precisely six o'clock. Dannie was ready and waiting for him in the kitchen, the closest room to the detached garage. The salmon-colored dress she wore accentuated her figure but had tasteful, elegant lines. Elise had taught her to pick flattering clothes and it looked fantastic on her, especially coupled with strappy Jimmy Choos heels. Would Leo notice?

"How was your day?" she asked politely while taking in the stress lines and shadows around his eyes that said he'd slept poorly, as well.

Something unfolded in her chest, urging her to smooth back the dark hair from his forehead and lightly massage his temples. Or whatever would soothe him. She wanted to know what to do for him, what he'd appreciate.

He set a brown leather messenger bag on the island in the kitchen. "Fine. And yours?"

"Wonderful." Except for the part where he hadn't kissed her goodbye. Or hello. *Shut up, Scarlett.* "The alumni gala is at the Renaissance Hotel. My driver will take us as soon as we're ready."

He hadn't said a word about her dress. Perhaps she'd take that as a sign he wouldn't be ashamed to be seen with her and not dwell on whether it got a response or not. Compliments weren't the reason she'd married Leo.

"That's fine. Let me change and we'll go." Leo set off for the stairs, fingers already working on his tie, which she'd have gladly taken off for him, if he'd let her. "They're giving an award to a friend of mine, and we should take him to dinner afterward."

Reservations. Where? For how many? But Leo was gone before she could ask.

Totally winging it, she called the most expensive restaurant she'd heard of and booked a table for four in Leo's name. If nothing else, the restaurant might be willing to add a few more to the party for a distinguished guest like Leo Reynolds.

Leo returned to the kitchen a short time later and she forgot all about a little thing like reservations. In black tie, Leo simply stole her breath.

"Ready?" he asked with raised eyebrows, likely because her fish-mouth impersonation amused him.

He was so delicious with his dark hair and dark suit, all crisp and masculine with a slight sensuous edge that set off something sharp and hot inside her. Last night, she'd felt just enough of the body he carried under that suit and the memory reintroduced itself as she let her eyes travel the entire length of her husband.

He cleared his throat and her gaze snapped to his. He was still waiting on her response.

"Ready," she squeaked and grabbed her clutch.

Leo kept up the conversation as they rode to the hotel with his confident, steady presence. She suspected—and appreciated—it was a ploy to dispel her nervousness, but it didn't work.

Leo escorted her through the lobby of the hotel with a hand at the small of her back. She liked the way his hand fit there. It served a dual purpose of providing support and showing everyone they were together.

And boy, did people notice. Heads swiveled as they entered the crush in the Renaissance ballroom. A string quartet played Strauss on a small platform in the corner, but the music couldn't cover the rush of whispers that surely were about the woman with Leo.

One flawless society wife in progress. Who hadn't gone to college but was going to be brilliant or die trying. Dannie squared her shoulders.

The neckline of her dress slipped, revealing a healthy slice of breast. Surreptitiously, she fingered it back into place. The deep vee over her cleavage wasn't terribly daring, but it was low-cut and the spaghetti straps were too long for her torso. Since the svelte salmon-colored dress had cost Elise seven hundred dollars, paying to have it altered felt like a sin.

It slipped down again as Leo steered her toward the far corner. As she walked, she lowered one shoulder, Quasimodo-style, hoping to nudge the neckline back where it belonged through a combination of shifting her balance and sheer will.

"Are you okay?" Leo whispered.

She should have worn the dress all day and practiced walking in it. Hindsight. Double-sided tape could have fixed the problem in a jiffy.

"Of course." She pasted on a serene smile as they halted before a group of men and women Leo clearly knew. Nodding, she greeted people and used all her tricks to remember names. Constantly being fired from a variety of jobs had an upside—few situations or people intimidated her.

"And this is Jenna Crisp," Leo concluded, indicating a gorgeous redhead on the arm of Leo's friend Dax Wakefield, who was receiving the alumni award that evening. "Jenna, this is my wife, Daniella Reynolds."

Dannie shook the woman's hand but Jenna wasn't looking at her. The redhead's attention was on Leo. Hmm. Dannie glanced at him. He didn't notice Jenna's scrutiny. Too busy discussing a patent infringement case with Dax. "I'm happy to meet you, Jenna. Have you known Leo long?"

Jenna focused on Dannie, and her expression noticeably cooled. "Long enough. How did you two meet, again?"

The redhead's tone oozed with challenge, as if there might be something tawdry to the story.

That was one area they'd definitely not covered. Did his friends know he'd gone to a matchmaker? She'd have to settle for a half-truth lest she embarrass Leo. "A mutual acquaintance introduced us."

"Interesting." The other woman nodded, sweeping long locks over her bare shoulders. She curled her lips in a semblance of a smile, which didn't fool Dannie for a second. Jenna did not like her.

"That's how Dax and I met, too. Leo introduced us."

"Oh?" Leo—a matchmaker himself? That *was* interesting. "I'm sure he was happy to help his friends find each other."

"You think so? Considering the fact that Leo and I were dating at the time, I wasn't sure what to make of it."

Oh, dear. No wonder the daggers in Jenna's eyes were so sharp. Dannie groaned inwardly. The dinner reservations had just gotten a whole lot more complicated than whether the table would be big enough.

"I'm sorry. I can't speak for Leo. If you're curious about his motives, you'd best ask him. Champagne?" she offered brightly, intending to put some distance between herself and Leo's ex-girlfriend. At least until she figured out how to navigate the bloody water full of sharks her husband had dropped her into.

"That would be lovely," Jenna said just as brightly and took Leo's arm to join in his conversation with Dax, physically blocking Dannie from the group.

In historical novels, they called that the cut direct. In real life, Dannie called it something else entirely, and if she said that many four-letter words out loud, Leo would have a heart attack.

Instead, she went to get Jenna and Leo a glass of champagne.

Really, she understood Jenna's animosity. She'd be confused, too, if Leo had shuffled her off on a friend and then promptly married someone else. Dannie also had the superior position between them, a point Jenna likely hadn't missed. At the end of the day, Dannie's last name was Reynolds and Jenna's wasn't.

Now she wondered what had really happened between Jenna and Leo. It was a little uncivilized of Leo not to have warned her. Men. Didn't he realize what he'd dragged Dannie into?

In reality, he probably hadn't considered it a problem. And it wasn't. Their marriage was an arrangement and her emotions weren't Leo's primary concern. That put a little steel in her spine. She had a job to do.

When she rejoined the group, Leo shot her a sidelong smile in gratitude for the glass of champagne. The flutters his very private grin set off were enough to forgive him. Almost.

A good wife might choose to forget the whole conversation. She bit her lip.

Then again, a good wife who paid attention to unspoken nuances might also ensure she didn't mistakenly cause her husband embarrassment. Forewarned was forearmed, and if Leo expected her to chat up his associates, she should know exactly what that association was. Right?

"You used to date Jenna?" she murmured in his ear as Dax engaged his date in their own conversation.

"Briefly." Leo's gaze sought out the woman in question, his eyes narrowing and growing a tad frigid. "She told you? I'm surprised she'd be so tactless. And I apologize if I put you in an uncomfortable position."

He'd leaned in, breath teasing along her cheek as he

spoke, and she caught a whiff of something fresh and maybe a little wintry but definitely all male. His hip brushed hers. Heat pooled at the contact and spread, giving a whole new meaning to an uncomfortable position.

She waved off his apology. "Nothing I can't handle. I'm sure you didn't do it on purpose."

He'd apologized instead of calling her out for sticking her nose in his business. That was a relief. Walking that line between being a complement to Leo and fading into the background was harder than she'd anticipated. Regardless, she was going to be a star wife. No compromise.

Leo frowned. "We only went out for a little while and obviously it didn't work out, or I wouldn't have introduced her to a friend. Jenna wanted more than I could give and Dax pays attention to her. It seemed perfect."

Oh. Of course. Jenna was the reason Leo needed a wife who wouldn't expect him to be around—she'd presumed to spend time with a man she liked and grew weary of the "I'm a workaholic, deal with it" speech.

The longing glances Jenna kept throwing Leo's way made a heck of a lot more sense now. Despite most likely being told in no uncertain terms not to get emotionally involved, Jenna had done it anyway. Only to be cast aside.

It was a sobering reminder. Dannie had a lot to lose if she made the same mistake.

Sobering. But ineffective.

As her husband's hand came to rest against the small of her back, she couldn't help but be tremendously encouraged that Leo had cared enough about Jenna to help her find happiness with someone better suited for her. In the kitchen yesterday, he'd expressed genuine interest in ensuring Dannie wasn't disappointed with their marriage.

Small gestures, but in Dannie's mind, they added up to something much larger. He had a good heart underneath all that business acumen. And despite his determination to keep her at arm's length, he needed her to break through the shell he kept around himself.

But how?

The champagne left a bitter taste in Leo's mouth.

If he'd known Jenna would deliberately upset Daniella, he'd never have brought his wife within a mile of her.

He should be having a conversation with Miles Bennett, who was about to launch a software product with some good buzz around it. John Hu was on his radar to speak to as well, and there John was by the bar, talking to Gene Ross's ancient wife. That conversation couldn't be about anything other than Mrs. Ross's show poodle or Miami this time of year, and Leo had no qualms about interrupting either.

Several recent investments hadn't panned out the way he'd hoped. He needed new blood now. Yesterday would have been better.

Instead of the dozen other things he should be doing, he was watching his wife. Out of the corner of his eye, no less, while he pretended to talk to Dax, who pretended he didn't notice Leo's fixation.

Daniella dazzled everyone, despite Jenna's mean-spirited disclosure.

The mechanics of marriage were still new and he hadn't fully considered the potential ramifications of introducing the two women. A wife was supposed to be *less* complicated than regular females, not more. Was Daniella uncomfortable being in the same room with Jenna? Or was she taking it in stride like everything else?

Daniella didn't *look* upset. She looked like a gift-wrapped present he'd put on his list a month ago and Christmas was still a week away.

That dress. It dipped against her breasts, revealing just enough to be interesting but not enough to be labeled indecent. The zipper in the back called his name. One tug and the wrapping would peel away, revealing a very nice gift indeed. The delicate shoes she wore emphasized her shapely legs and he liked that far more than he wanted to.

Daniella was the most gorgeous woman in the room. And the most interesting, the most poised and the most vivacious. Bar none. And he wasn't the only one who thought so, instilling in him a quiet sense of pride with every appreciative glance she earned.

In case she was more upset about Jenna than she let on, he kept a close eye on her as she talked to a couple of Reynolds Capital's partners. No hardship on his part to watch her graceful hands gesture and her pink-stained lips form words. Then she laughed and the dress slipped a tantalizing inch farther down her breasts. And then another inch.

A flash of heat tensed his entire body and tightened his pants uncomfortably.

He swore and Dax stared at him as if he'd lost his mind. Which didn't appear to be as far out of the realm of possibility as it should.

"I need a refill," Leo explained and waved his empty champagne flute at a passing waiter.

When the waiter returned, he downed the glass in two gulps. It didn't cool him down. Something needed to change, very quickly.

He glanced at Daniella. She didn't turn her head, but her eyes swiveled and she met his gaze with a secret smile, as if to say, *later*.

Or maybe that was his lower half projecting her meaning. The upper half refused to entertain even one little fantasy about later. Intimacy was supposed to be a progression, and abandoning that idea on day two didn't bode well for Leo's state of mind.

They hadn't developed a *friendship* yet and he was fantasizing about skipping right over that.

The music swelled, signaling the start of the awards ceremony. Daniella moved toward him at the same moment he stepped forward to grasp her arm. They bumped hips and somehow, the button on his jacket caught her dress.

One of Daniella's nipples popped free of the fabric, searing his vision and sending a surge straight to his groin. She gasped with a feminine squeal of humiliation, hands flying to her chest.

Instantly, Leo whirled her into a snug embrace, hiding her from view. And oh, dear God. His wife's body aligned with his like flowing honey, clinging sweetly to every groove.

"No one saw," he murmured into her hair and prayed she wouldn't take offense to the obvious erection pushing into her abdomen. It wasn't as though he could step away and compose himself.

The sight of that bare, rosy nipple was emblazoned on his brain and worse, both of her nipples pressed against his chest, raising the temperature in the stuffy ballroom about a hundred degrees.

"Are you all...arranged?" he asked hoarsely.

She was shaking. Or was that him?

"I can't," she whispered and her hand worked between their bodies, brushing his erection an ungodly number of times. "The button won't come loose."

He nearly groaned. "We'll have to get to the hall. Somehow. Can you turn?"

"Yes. If you keep your arm around me."

They did a fair impression of Siamese twins, shuffling as one toward the back of the ballroom, Daniella clutching Leo with one hand and her dress with the other. Which meant her hands were nowhere near his erection—and that was good. One more brush of those manicured nails against him would have produced fireworks better left unlit in public.

Miraculously, the crowd had thinned. The awards presenter droned from the next room. Leo was missing the ceremony but Dax would have to understand.

An eternity later, they reached the hall and Leo hustled

Daniella into a deep alcove housing a giant sculpture of a mermaid.

"We're totally hidden from view. It's okay," he said.

She took a half step backward, as far as their tangled clothes would allow.

"My definition of okay and yours must be different." Head bent, she studiously fingered the threads holding his button hostage until they finally came apart. "I'm sorry, Leo. You must be mortified."

Her head was still down, as if she didn't want to look at him.

"Me?" He tipped her chin up with a loosely fisted hand. Her cheeks were on fire. "You're the one who has a reason to be mortified. I can't imagine how you must feel. First I force you to make nice to Jenna and then almost rip off your dress. I'm the one who's sorry."

"It's not *your* fault," she countered fiercely. "This dress doesn't fit quite right. I shouldn't have worn it."

Five minutes ago, he'd have agreed. If she'd dressed a little more matronly, he might be having that conversation with John Hu right now. Except the alternative—being wedged into a secluded alcove with his wife—suddenly didn't seem so terrible. "That dress fits you perfectly."

She shook her head as she twisted the waistline back into place. "All my clothes have to be altered. I know that. But I didn't have this one done. Stupid. I should have thought about the consequences. My job is to make you look good, not embarrass you in public. I'm sorry. I'm not making a very good first impression."

That's what she was worried about? That she'd messed up and displeased him? A weight settled onto his chest. Did she think he was that concerned about their agreement? Obviously so.

"On the contrary, you've made a great impression. Exactly as I expected. I watched you with my business associates. They liked you." She'd charmed them easily and he could already envision her doing the same at future events. Daniella was amazing, through and through.

"Really?" The disbelief in her voice settled that weight a little deeper. She seemed so disheartened by what was such a small blip in the evening.

Daniella was his wife, not a casual date he might or might not see again. The very act of making her his wife changed everything. He wanted her to be happy, which he hadn't planned, could never have predicted. Not only did he want her to be happy, he'd discovered a healthy drive to care for her and ensure her security. He wanted her to know she could depend on him, always.

Problem being, of course, that his experience with serious relationships started and ended with the woman in front of him.

He nodded, scouting for a way to put a smile back on her face. "If nothing else, you can take solace in the fact that your wardrobe malfunction didn't take place on national TV."

She laughed, as he'd intended. The resurrection of his hard-on, he hadn't. But who could blame him? Her laugh curled through him like fine wine and came coupled with the distinct memory of her beautiful breast.

The secluded alcove grew close and heavy with awareness as she locked on to his gaze. Her irises warmed. "Thank you for rescuing me. It was very chivalrous."

The back of his neck heated at the adoration in her eyes. He felt like a fake. There wasn't a romantic bone in his body. "I wouldn't have abandoned you."

"Your button." Without breaking eye contact, she touched it with her fingertips. "It's loose."

"No problem." He swallowed and his throat was on fire. Everything was on fire. "I have another one."

Slim eyebrows arched as she cocked her head. Loose tendrils of dark brown hair fell against her cheeks and he barely resisted an urge to tuck them back for her. And as a treat for himself. The shiny, slightly wavy locks would be soft against his fingers.

"Should we rejoin the party?" she asked in an incredible show of courage. Not many people would walk back into a room where they'd performed a free peep show. His admiration for her swelled. "As long as I don't move around too much, I should stay tucked away."

His gaze dropped to her cleavage automatically. She was quite tucked away, but the promise of what he knew lay beneath the fabric teased him. How easily he could thumb down that dress and run the pads across those taut nipples. No effort required at all. No one could see them back here behind the sculpture.

He sucked in a hot breath.

"Leo," she murmured and slid lithe fingers along his lapels, straightening them as she traveled south.

"Hmm?" She was so close he could see golden flecks in her eyes. Raw energy radiated from her, wrapping around him in a heated veil.

"The party?" Her lips met on the last syllable and he recalled how they'd sparked against his when he'd kissed her at their wedding ceremony.

This was like a first date, wasn't it? He'd kissed women on dates, lots of times. It might even be considered expected. A major disappointment if he didn't do it.

Would kissing her be as hot the second time? Hotter?

His curiosity would only be satisfied one way.

"We should go back. Shouldn't we?" she asked. But she stood there, frozen, peeking up from beneath her lashes coyly, as if she could read the intent in his eyes.

Yes. They should go back. His body strained toward her, desperate to be closer.

The scent of strawberries wafted to him on a sensuous cloud as she swayed into his space. Or maybe he was the one who moved.

Like honey, he thought as their bodies met. Their lips

touched hesitantly, then firmly, deliberately, and his mind pushed out everything except the sizzle of flesh on flesh.

His wife's mouth opened under his and he swept her deep into his embrace as he kissed her. His back hit the wall but he scarcely noticed as Daniella came alive, hands in his hair, her mouth strong and ferocious against his.

Hunger thundered through his veins. His hips circled against hers involuntarily, uncontrollably as he sought to ease the ache she'd inflamed. With one hand, he enveloped her neck and pushed, tipping her head back so he could open her wider, then tentatively stroked her tongue with his.

She stroked him back, deeper, harder. Leo groaned against her mouth. She kissed like a horny teenager's fantasy. Deep. Wet. Carnal.

Those perfect breasts haunted him. *Touch them,* his libido begged. The temptation was almost too much to bear, but he feared if he gave in to it, he might never surface.

Home. They could go home. Right now. They lived together, after all.

If he took her home, he could strip that dress away to taste every peak and valley of his wife's body. Especially the parts he hadn't yet seen but could feel easily through the silky drape of cloth over her luscious skin.

The kiss deepened, heating further, enflaming his skin. Desire screamed through his body. He'd never kissed a woman on a date quite like this. Hell, he'd never kissed a woman like this *ever,* not even in bed.

She was luring him into a dark pit of need and surfacing suddenly wasn't so appealing.

He trailed openmouthed kisses along her throat and palmed her sexy rear again. Unbelievably, this incredible, stimulating woman was *his.* She moaned under his touch and her head fell back.

"Leo," she murmured as he slipped a pin from her fancy done-up hair. "Don't you need to go back?"

As if she'd thrown a bucket of water over him, his lust-hazed bubble burst. They were in the hallway of a hotel and his wife was reminding *him* of the importance of circulating at the alumni ceremony.

He pulled back to breathe the cool air of sanity. "I do."

Her face remained composed, but a storm of desire brewed in her gaze, one he suspected would easily explode again with his touch. She'd been just as turned on as he had.

"Till later, then?" she asked.

Oh, no. That wouldn't do at all. *Focus, Reynolds.*

At least four people he must speak with mingled in the ballroom less than a hundred yards away and his wife's mussed hair and plump, kiss-stung lips alone threatened to steal his composure. If he had to suffer through the rest of the night while anticipating *later,* nothing of consequence would be accomplished.

You're weak, the nasty voice of his conscience whispered. And that was the real reason he couldn't lose his single-mindedness.

If he let himself indulge—in drawing, in a woman, in *anything* other than the goal—he'd be lost. Look what had just happened with a simple kiss.

He released her and his body cooled a degree or two. It wasn't enough to erase the imprint of her in his senses. "I apologize. That was inappropriate. Please, take a few moments in the ladies' room and meet me back in the ballroom. We'll act as if that never happened."

Disappointment replaced the desire in her expression and made him feel like a world-class jerk.

"If that's what you want."

It was absolutely not what he wanted. But distance was what he needed in order to get a measure of control.

This marriage should be the perfect blend of necessity and convenience. *Should be.* But the possibility of being friends was already out the window due to the curse of his weaknesses, and it would only get worse the further under his skin she dug.

"This is a business event and I haven't been treating it like one."

"Of course." Her tone had become professional, as it should. Even in this, she remained poised, doing her duty as expected, because *she* wasn't weak. She was thoroughly brilliant.

He hated putting up a barrier, but she'd become exactly what he'd suspected she would—a disturbance he couldn't afford.

But she was also proving to be exactly what he'd hoped. The perfect complement of a wife. She deserved happiness and he'd provide no assurance of security—for either of them—if he took his eye off the success of Reynolds Capital Management for even a moment. His wife would not be forced into the poorhouse because of him, like his father had done to Leo's mother.

No more digressions. It was too dangerous to kiss her. Or think about her as a friend.

Daniella was back in the employee box. She had to stay there.

How in the world was he going to forget what those strawberry-scented lips could do?

Five

Leo was already gone by the time Dannie emerged from her bedroom the next morning. Even though she'd set an alarm, he still beat her.

She'd screwed up at the alumni gala. Leo had been kissing her—*oh, my God,* had he been kissing her—and then he hit the brakes. Of course work came first, and the woman behind the man should never forget that. But to pretend *that kiss* hadn't happened? It was impossible. She wasn't naive enough to believe she'd break through his shell in one evening, but she thought she'd lifted it a little at least.

At home, his obsession with work shouldn't be a factor, especially before he left for the office. Tomorrow morning, she'd shove the alarm back thirty minutes. If she beat him to the kitchen, they'd have a chance to talk and maybe share a laugh. Then think about each other fondly over the course of the day.

All good elements of both friendship and marriage.

The next morning she missed him again, and continued to miss him for a week.

Four declined event appointments should have clued her in, but it wasn't until she caught the startled look on his face when he came out of his bedroom one morning that she realized he'd been avoiding her.

"Good morning." She smiled despite his wary expression and the fact that she'd been awake since five hoping to catch him.

"Morning." He nodded and brushed past without another word.

Stung, she watched him retreat down the stairs and vowed not to think about Leo Reynolds the rest of the day. She had a job to do here.

Dannie spent an hour with the staff going over weekly household accounts, then interviewed a prospective maid to replace one who had given notice. She enjoyed organizing Leo's life. At the alumni gala, she'd navigated Leo's social circles, recovered from a humiliating dress fail and smiled through dinner with her husband's ex-girlfriend.

What more could Leo possibly want in a wife?

At four o'clock, Leo texted her with a short message she'd come to expect: I'll be home late. Make dinner plans on your own.

As she'd been doing for a week. Leo clearly planned to keep her at arm's length, despite *that kiss*.

Fuming, she called her mother and invited her over for dinner. Might as well take advantage of the cook Leo kept on staff. She and her mother ate prime rib and lobster bisque, both wonderfully prepared, but neither could keep her attention. Her mother raved about the food, about Dannie's marriage, about how much she liked her new nurse. Dannie smiled but nothing penetrated the cloud of frustration cloaking what should have been a nice evening with her mom.

As far back as Dannie could remember, her mother had constantly passed on relationship advice: *Men don't stick around. Don't listen to their pretty words and promises.* And variations aplenty espousing the evils of falling in love. The whole point of this arranged marriage was so Dannie wouldn't end up alone and miserable like her mother. And despite her mother's best attempts to squash Dannie's romanticism, it was still there, buried underneath reality.

All men couldn't be like her father. Leo didn't flatter her with slick charm, and he'd been nothing but honest with her.

Furthermore, her husband had kissed her passionately,

madly, more completely than Dannie had ever been kissed in her life. She couldn't pretend it hadn't happened or that she didn't want more than an occasional text message out of her marriage.

They'd never get past being virtual strangers at this rate. Maybe it was for the best, if Jenna's fate bore any credence to what might become Dannie's story. But she couldn't accept that she and Leo would *never* see each other. Surely they could spend a little time together. An hour. Thirty minutes.

How was she supposed to handle his social commitments and take care of his every need if he kept avoiding her?

After she saw her mother off in the chauffeured car that Dannie couldn't quite give up yet, she parked on the couch nearest the stairs, determined to wait for Leo until the cows came home, if necessary. They needed to talk.

An hour later, Dannie started to wonder if Leo intended to sleep at the office. He wouldn't. Would he? Had she screwed up so badly that he couldn't even stand to be in the same house with her?

She flung her head back on a cushion and stared at the ceiling. He certainly hadn't lied to her. He did work all the time and she had done nothing to find her own amusements. Because she didn't want to. She wanted to be Leo's wife in every sense of the word, or at least she thought she did, despite being given little opportunity to find out.

Another hour passed. This was ridiculous. Not only was he hindering her ability to take care of him, but he'd agreed they could be friends. How did he think friendship developed?

New tactics were in order. Before she could remind herself of all the reasons she shouldn't, she sent Leo a text message: I heard a noise. I think someone is in the house. Can you come home?

Immediately, he responded: Call the police and hit the intruder alarm.

She rolled her eyes and texted him back: I'm scared. I'd like you to come home.

Leo: Be there as soon as I can.

Bingo. She huffed out a relieved breath. It had been a gamble, but only a small one. Leo had a good heart, which wouldn't have allowed him to do anything else but come home to his wife.

Twenty minutes later, Leo pulled into the drive at the front of the house. Dannie flicked on the enormous carriage lights flanking the entrance arch, illuminating the wide porch, and met him on the steps.

"Are you okay?" he asked, his hard gaze sweeping the shadows behind her.

His frame bristled with tension, saying in no uncertain terms he'd protect her from any threat imaginable, and it pulled a long, liquid flash from her core that sizzled. An intruder wouldn't stand a chance against so much coiled intensity.

"I'm fine." In a manner of speaking.

Leo's dark suit looked as superb on him as a tuxedo did. More so, because he was at full alert inside it, his body all hard and masculine. Warrior Leo made her mouth water. She might have to fan herself.

"Did you call the police?" He ushered her inside quickly, one hand steady at her back.

"No. I didn't hear the noise again and I didn't want to waste anyone's time." Especially since the noise was entirely fictional. Hopefully, once she hashed things out with Leo, an excuse wouldn't be necessary to get his attention.

He shot off a series of questions and she answered until he was satisfied there was no imminent danger. "Next time, push the panic button. That's what the security alarm is for."

"Did I interrupt something important at work?"

Lines deepened around his eyes as his carriage relaxed and he smiled. "It's all important. But it's okay. It'll still be there in the morning."

Relaxed Leo was nice, too. So much more approachable. She returned his smile and tugged on his arm. "Then sit down for a minute. Tell me about your day."

He didn't budge from his statue impression in the foyer. "Not much to tell. Why don't you go on up to bed? I'll hang out downstairs and make sure there's really nothing to worry about."

Oh, no, you don't. "I'm not tired. You're here. I'm here. Come talk to me for a minute."

He hefted the messenger bag in his hand a little higher in emphasis with an apologetic shrug. "I have some work to finish up."

"That'll be there in the morning, too." Gently, she took the bag from him and laid it on the Hepplewhite table against the wall, a little surprised he'd let her. "We haven't talked since the alumni gala."

The mere mention of it laced the atmosphere with a heaviness that prickled her skin. Leo's gaze fell on hers and silence stretched between them. Was he remembering the kiss? Or was he still determined to forget about it? If so, she'd like to learn that trick.

"There's a reason for that," he finally said.

Her stomach tumbled at his frank admission that he'd been avoiding her. She nodded. "I suspected as much. That's why I want to talk."

His gaze swept over her face. "I thought you wanted me to tell you about my day."

"I do." She started to reach out but stopped as she took in the firm line of his mouth. "But we need to talk regardless. I was hoping to be a little more civil about it, though."

"Maybe we can catch up tomorrow." He picked up the messenger bag from the table, but before he could stride from the foyer, she stepped in front of him, blocking his path.

Arms crossed, she stared him down. "Be straight with

me. I can handle it. Are you regretting your choice in wives? Maybe you're wishing you'd picked Jenna after all?"

The bag slipped from Leo's hand and thunked to the floor. "Not now, Daniella."

"You mean *not now,* and by the way, *not ever?* When will we have this conversation if not now?" Too annoyed to check her action, she poked a finger in his chest. Being demure had gotten her exactly nowhere. "You've been avoiding me. I want to know why. Am I not performing up to your expectations?"

"I'm not avoiding you." Guilt flitted through his expression, contradicting the statement. "I've got three proposals out, the shareholder value on one of my major investments took a forty percent loss over the last week and a start-up I staked declared bankruptcy today. Is that enough truth for you? The reason we haven't talked is because I'm extremely busy keeping my company afloat."

The Monet on the wall opposite her swirled into a mess of colors as she shared some of that guilt. "I'm sorry. I shouldn't have bothered you about the noise. I just wanted to…" *See you. Talk to you. Find out if you've been thinking of me.* "Not be scared."

Leo's expression softened and he reached out to grip her shoulder protectively. "You shouldn't have been. I had the security system installed as soon as you agreed to marry me and it's top-of-the-line. It would take a SWAT team to breach it. You're safe here. Do you not feel like you are?"

She stared up into his worried blue eyes and her insides liquefied. He genuinely cared about the answer. "I do."

It dawned on her then that Leo did a lot behind the scenes—far more than she'd realized. Almost as if he preferred for no one to know about all the wonderful gestures he made or that he was such a kind person underneath. Was he afraid she'd figure out he cared about her more than he let on?

"Good." The worry slipped from his expression and was

replaced with something that looked an awful lot like affection. "The last thing I want is for you to feel anxious or insecure."

Perfect segue. They shared a drive for security. Surely he'd understand her need to settle things. "You know what would make me feel a lot less anxious? If I knew what was going on between us." Emboldened by the fact that Leo had cared enough to rush home for her, she went on. "We're supposed to enjoy each other's company when we cross paths, but we never cross paths."

"We just went out a week ago," he protested with a glint in his eye that warned her to tread carefully.

She wasn't going to. If Leo pulled another disappearing act, this might be her only chance to make her case. Besides, he said they could talk about anything.

"Exactly. A whole week ago and we haven't spoken since then, other than a terse 'Good morning.' I can't handle your life if I'm not in it. Besides, our relationship won't ever develop without deliberate interaction. On both our parts."

"Daniella." He put a thumb to his temple. Great, now she was giving him a headache. "What are you asking of me?"

He said it as if she hoped he'd blow through the door and ravish her, when all she really wanted was a conversation over a nice glass of wine. "For starters, call me Dannie. I want to be friends. Don't you?"

Wariness sprang into his stance. "Depends on your definition of friends. The last time you brought that up, I got the distinct impression it was a euphemism for something else."

"You mean sex?" Oh, Scarlett had just been chomping at the bit to get in the middle of this conversation, hadn't she?

Leo gave a short nod. "Well, to be blunt."

Oh, no. There was that word again. Her last fight with Rob flashed through her mind and she swallowed. Was she trying to ruin everything?

But Leo wasn't a spineless, insecure guy like Rob who

couldn't handle a woman's honest opinion. Besides, this was her marriage and she was prepared to go to the mat for it.

"Our marriage apparently calls for blunt. Since I might not get another opportunity to speak to you this century, here it is, spelled out for you. My offer of friendship is not a veiled invitation to jump me."

His brows rose. "Then what is it?"

Laughter bubbled from her mouth. "Guess I don't spell as well as I think I do. Didn't we decide our relationship would eventually be intimate?" *Not blunt enough.* "Sorry, I mean, that we'd eventually have sex?"

To Leo's credit, he didn't flinch. "We did decide that. I envision it happening very far in the future."

Gee, that made her feel all warm and fuzzy. "Great. Except intimacy is about so much more than shedding clothes, Leo. Did you think we'd wake up one day and just hop into bed? It doesn't work like that. There's an intellectual side to intimacy that evolves through spending time together. By becoming *friends.* I want to know you. Your thoughts. Dreams. Sex starts in here." She tapped her forehead. "At least it does for me."

"You want to be romanced," he said flatly.

"I'm female. The math shouldn't be that hard to do."

"Math is one of my best skills."

What was that supposed to mean? That he'd done the math and knew that's what she wanted—but didn't care? She stumbled back a step.

With her new distance, the colors of the Monet swirled again, turning from a picture of a girl back into a jumble of blotches.

She and Leo needed to get on the same page. She took a deep breath. "How did *you* think we were going to get from point A to point B?"

"I never seemed to have any trouble getting a woman interested before," he grumbled without any real heat. "Usually it's getting them uninterested that's the problem."

Ah, so she'd guessed correctly from the very beginning. "You've never had to invest any energy in a relationship before, have you?"

Gorgeous, well-spoken, rich men probably never did as often as women surely threw themselves at them. He'd probably gone through a series of meaningless encounters with interchangeable women.

"I don't have time for a relationship, Daniella," he said quietly, which only emphasized his deliberate use of her full name all the more. "That's why I married you."

Blunt. And devastating. She nearly reeled from it.

This was what he'd been telling her since the beginning, but she'd been determined to connect the dots in a whole new way, creating a mess of an Impressionist painting that looked like *nothing* when she stepped back to view the whole. The spectacular kiss, the security system, the gentle concern—none of it had signaled anything special.

He'd meant what he said. He didn't *want* to invest energy in a relationship. That's why he cut himself off from people. Too much effort. Too much trouble. Too much fill-in-the-blank.

There was no friendship on the horizon, no tenderness, no progression toward intimacy. He expected her to get naked, get pleasure and get out. Eventually.

She nodded. "I see. We'll enjoy each other's company when we cross paths and then go our separate ways." *He'd* been the one euphemizing sex and she'd missed it.

Her heart twisted painfully. But this wasn't news. She just hadn't realized that being in a marriage that wasn't a marriage was worse than being alone.

How could Elise's computer have matched her with Leo? Oh, sure, neither of them had professed an interest in a love match, which was more of a tiny white lie in her case, but to not even be *friends?* It was depressing.

Leo looked relieved. "I'm glad we talked, then. To answer

your earlier question, you're everything I'd hoped. I'm very happy with my choice of wife. Jenna wasn't right at all."

Because she'd inadvisably bucked the rule: don't ask Leo for more than he chooses to give.

"Speaking of which," he continued, "I'd like you to plan a dinner party for twenty guests in about two weeks. Does that give you enough time?"

"Of course."

Two weeks?

Panic flipped her stomach inside out. How would she organize an entire party in two weeks? Well, she'd just have to.

This was why Elise matched her with Leo, and running his personal life was what she'd signed up for. She couldn't lose sight of that. "I'd be happy to handle that for you. Can you email me the guest list?"

He nodded. "Tommy Garrett is the guest of honor. Make sure you pick a date he's available. No point in having the party if he can't be there. Any questions?"

A million and five. "Not right now. I'll start on it immediately."

That was the key to enduring a marriage that wasn't a marriage. Jump into her job with both feet and keep so busy she didn't have time to castigate herself. After all, if she'd begun to believe this marriage might become more than an arrangement because of a few sparks, it was her fault. Not Leo's.

Her mother was being taken care of. Dannie was, too. Furthermore, she'd spoken her mind with as much blunt opinion as she could muster and Leo hadn't kicked her out. What else could she possibly want? This was real life, not a fairy tale, and she had work to do.

She bid Leo good-night, her head full of party plans. It wasn't until her cheek hit the pillow that she remembered the total discomfort on Leo's face when he thought friendship had been code for sex.

If he expected her to get naked, get pleasured and get out, why wouldn't he take immediate advantage of what he assumed she was offering?

Leo's forehead thunked onto his desk, right in the middle of the clause outlining the expiration date for his proposal to finance Miles Bennett's software company.

That woke him up in a hurry.

Why didn't he go upstairs to bed? It was 3:00 a.m. Normal people slept at this time of night, but not him. No—Leo Reynolds had superpowers, granting him the ability to go days without sleep, because otherwise he'd get behind. John Hu had slipped through his fingers at the alumni gala and was even now working with another backer. It should have been Leo. Could have been Leo, if he'd been on his game.

And not spending a good portion of his energy recalling his wife's soft and gorgeous smile. Or how much he enjoyed seeing her on the porch waiting for him, the way she had been tonight.

Sleep was for weaker men.

Younger men.

He banished that thought. Thirty-five—thirty-six in two months—wasn't old. But lately he felt every day of his age. Ten years ago he could have read contracts and proposals until dawn and then inhaled a couple of espressos to face the day with enthusiasm.

Now? Not so much. And it would only get worse as he approached forty. He had to make every day count while he could. No distractions. No seductive, tantalizing friendships that would certainly turn into more than he could allow.

Maybe he should up his workout regimen from forty-five minutes a day to an hour. Eat a little better instead of shoveling takeout into his mouth while he hunched over his desk at the office.

Gentle hands on his shoulders woke him.

"Leo," Daniella murmured as she pressed against his arm. "You fell asleep at your desk."

He bolted upright. Blearily, he glanced up at Daniella and then at his watch. Six-thirty. Normally he was already at work by now.

"Thanks for waking me up," he croaked and cleared his throat. "I don't know how that happened."

She lifted a brow. "Because you were tired?"

Her stylish dress was flowery and flirty, but clearly altered to fit perfectly, and her hair hung loose down her back. Flawlessly applied makeup accentuated her face and plumped her lips and he tore his gaze away from them.

"Besides that." He shuffled the Miles Bennett proposal back into some semblance of order without another glance at his wife. Though he wanted to soak in the sight of her. How did she look so amazing this early in the morning?

"Let me make you a cup of coffee," she offered and perched a hip on his desk as if she planned to stay awhile.

"I have to go. I'm late."

She stopped him with a warm hand on his bare forearm, below his rolled-up sleeve. "It's Saturday. Take ten minutes for coffee. I'd like to make it for you. Indulge me."

The plea in her eyes unhitched something inside. After he'd thrown up barrier upon barrier, she still wanted to make him coffee. How could he gracefully refuse? "Thanks. Let me take a quick a shower and I'll meet you in the kitchen."

The shower cleared the mist of sleep from his mind. He dressed in freshly pressed khakis and a button-down shirt instead of a suit since it was Saturday. A concession he couldn't recall making before. What had possessed him to do it today?

When he walked into the kitchen, the rich, roasted smell of coffee greeted him only a moment before his wife did.

She smiled and handed him a steaming mug. "Perfect timing."

He took a seat at the inlaid bistro table off the kitchen

and sipped. Liquid heaven slid down his throat. He wasn't surprised she'd somehow mastered brewing a cup of coffee to his tastes. "You even got the half-and-half right."

"Practice makes perfect." She slid into the opposite seat and folded her hands into her lap serenely.

Something in her tone piqued his interest. "How long have you been practicing?"

"Since the wedding." She shrugged, and her smile made light of the admission. "I've been trying to get up before you every morning so I could make you coffee. Today's the first day I succeeded."

The coffee didn't go down as smoothly on the next sip. Why had she put so much effort into something so meaningless? "That wasn't part of our agreement. You should sleep as late as you want."

"Our agreement includes making sure your life runs fluidly, especially at home. If you want coffee in the morning, it's my job to ensure you get it."

My job.

Daniella was in the employee box in his head, but he'd never expected her to view herself that way. Of course, why would she view herself any differently when all he talked about was their arrangement?

The cup of coffee—and the ironed clothes, ready at a moment's notice—took on implications of vast proportions. Everything EA International promised, he'd received. Daniella had slipped into her role as if she'd always been his wife. The staff liked her and already deferred to her judgment, which freed him from having to deal with the cook's grocery account or the gardener's questions about seasonal plants.

She was incredible.

If only he'd gotten the wife he really meant for EA International to match him with—one he could ignore—his life would be perfect.

It wasn't Daniella's fault he suffered from all-or-nothing syndrome. Intensity was the major backbone of his temperament. That's why he didn't draw anymore. Once he started, he could fill an entire notebook with landscapes, people's faces—Carmen's beautiful form—and then scout around for a blank book to begin filling that one, too.

If it hadn't been for his calculus teacher's timely intervention, Leo would probably be a starving artist right now, doodling in the margins of take-out menus and cursing the woman who'd been his first model. And his first lover. He'd been infatuated with capturing her shape on the paper, infatuated with her. His teacher had opened his eyes to his slipping grades, the upcoming SATs and a potentially bleak future mirroring his parents' if he didn't stop skipping school to draw Carmen. Fortunately, he'd listened and turned his intensity toward his education, then Reynolds Capital Management, vowing to never again let his obsessive personality loose on anything other than success.

He knew it the way he knew the sky was blue: the second he let himself taste Daniella again, that would be it. He wouldn't stop until he'd filled them both. And once wouldn't be enough. He'd be too weak to focus on anything except her.

"Thanks for the coffee. I should go." Leo shoved away from the table.

Her warm almond-colored eyes sought his. "Before you do, I have a couple of questions about the party for Tommy Garrett."

He settled back into the uncomfortable wrought-iron chair. "Sure."

It was the only subject that could have gotten him to stay. The party was critically important since Garrett had narrowed down the field to two firms. Leo didn't intend to lose out to the other guy.

She leaned forward on her forearms with all the attentiveness of someone about to leap into a negotiation. "What does Garrett Engineering make?"

Not *What china should I use?* or *What hors d'oeuvres should I serve?* "Why does that matter?"

"I'm curious. But also because I'd like to know more about the guest of honor. From you. I'll call his admin but I want your opinion. It will help me plan the menu and the decorations."

There was something hypnotic about Daniella's voice that pulled at him. He could listen to her recite the phone book. "I wouldn't have thought of that."

Her mouth tipped up in a smile that was so sweet, it pulled one from him. "That's why I'm here. Tell me."

"Tommy's a bit of a whiz kid." Leo pursed his lips as he contemplated the most relevant facets of the man—and he used the term *man* in the loosest sense—he wanted to do business with. "One of those geniuses who wears Converse sneakers and hoodies to work. He's just as likely to spout Xbox stats as engineering principles and no one cares because he graduated summa cum laude from Yale. He designed a modification to the way gasoline is consumed in a car that will increase gas mileage by almost double. It's revolutionary."

"You like him."

"Yes." The admission surprised him.

He hadn't thought one way or another about whether he *liked* Tommy Garrett. Leo liked the instant profitability of Garrett's design. He liked the idea of orchestrating the financing and letting Tommy be the face of the venture. Tommy had a lot of spirit, a quick wit and, despite the hoodies, he also had a work ethic Leo respected. It wasn't unusual to have a conversation at eleven o'clock on a Saturday night to brainstorm ideas.

Impressed, he cocked his head at his wife. "How did you ferret that out from what I said?"

"Because I listened with my eyes." Her smile widened as he snorted. "I could see it in your expression."

Leo tried to scowl but he was enjoying the back-and-forth just as much as the sound of Daniella's voice.

"It doesn't matter whether I like him. We stand to make a lot of money together and that's the key to our association. The party is paramount. He's got another potential partner on the hook and I need to convince him to go with Reynolds."

"What percentage stake in his company did you offer in the proposal?" He did a double take and she laughed. "I read up on how venture capital works. How can I help you land the deal if I don't know what I'm talking about?"

Perhaps he should have had a cup of coffee with his wife long before now. "I guess I thought you'd handle the party details and I'd handle Garrett. But I'm reconsidering that plan."

If he unleashed the formidable force of Daniella on Tommy Garrett, the poor guy probably wouldn't even know what hit him.

"You do that. Tell me more."

Her smile relaxed him. She had the best smile, easily given, genuine. He liked seeing it on her, but liked being the one to put it there even more. Making women smile wasn't a skill he felt particular proficient at, though. Maybe he should take a cue from his wife and practice.

"Not only will his design fit new engines, it retrofits to existing engines so it can be sold to both consumers and automobile manufacturers. It's almost miraculous. He might as well have designed a way to print money."

"Sounds like you really believe in the product. I can't imagine why Mr. Garrett would choose another venture capital firm."

"Because it's business. Not personal. And actually, I couldn't care less what the product is as long as the entrepreneur comes to me with a solid business plan and proven commitment."

"All business is personal, Leo," she said quietly. "If you

didn't spend so much time behind the scenes, you might discover that for yourself."

"Behind the scenes is where I function best." Ensuring the players never had to worry about money as they took center stage—that was his comfort zone. He couldn't afford to get truly involved or he'd bury himself.

Her expression softened, drawing him in. "But in the middle of things is where the best experiences are."

He had the distinct impression they weren't talking about Tommy Garrett anymore and had moved on to something he did not want to acknowledge in any way, shape or form.

"Thanks for the coffee. I'm going to head in to the office." He glanced at his watch. Almost seven-thirty, but there was no rush hour on Saturday, so he hadn't lost too much time. "If you have any more questions about the party, don't hesitate to call me."

"Have a good day." She covered his hand with hers and squeezed. "Don't look now, Leo, but I think we just had a friendly conversation. Are you shocked it didn't kill you?"

No, the shock happened when he laughed.

Her return smile stayed with him as he climbed into his car. The gas gauge needle pointed to full. When was the last time he'd even glanced at it? He drove to the office and instead of thinking about whatever else should be on his mind, he thought about Daniella.

Dannie. Maybe she could be Dannie and that wouldn't kill him, either.

No way. He couldn't imagine allowing it to roll from his tongue.

As much as he wished he could ignore his wife, he was painfully aware she conversely wished he wouldn't. They had an agreement, but it didn't seem to be sticking and she was flesh and blood, not a piece of paper. Or an employee.

And agreements could be terminated.

He was getting what he hoped from this marriage. She wasn't, not fully. If he wanted her to be happy, he had to give a little. Otherwise she might walk. A sick worm of insecurity wiggled into his stomach at the idea of losing a woman who fit into his life so well. And who, against all odds, he liked.

Friends. It didn't sound so terrible. Surely he could handle a friendship with his wife.

Six

Dannie hummed as she drew up proposed menus. She hummed as she perused the guest list Leo emailed her and savored the little thrill she got from the short message at the bottom.

You make a great cup of coffee.

She hummed as she waited on hold to speak with Tommy Garrett's admin and later as she checked off several more things on her to-do list. The tune was aimless. Happy. Half of it was due to finally connecting with Leo on some small level, especially after he'd made it clear he wasn't interested in developing their relationship.

The other half had to do with finding her niche. Growing up, her chief source of entertainment had been old movies and TV shows on the free channels, and she'd always wanted to have her own household like the glamorous women of the '50s. It was everything she'd expected. Being in charge of her domain gave her a heady sense of accomplishment and purpose, which popped out of her mouth in song.

When Leo strode through the door at six o'clock that evening with a small, lopsided grin, her throat seized up and quit working entirely.

"I thought we'd have dinner together," he said as she stared at him, wordless. "If you don't have other plans."

Dinner? *Together?* Why?

"Oh," she squeaked and sucked in a couple of lungfuls

of oxygen in hopes it might jar everything else into functioning. "No plans. I'll let the cook know."

Clothes, she thought as she flew to alert the staff Leo would be dining in. She should change clothes. And open a bottle of wine. Her foot tangled on the edge of the Persian runner lining the stairs to the second floor. *And slow down.* A broken leg wouldn't do her any favors.

This was the first time she'd dine alone with Leo since they'd gotten married. It was practically like a date. Better than a date, because it had been his idea and totally a surprise. She wanted it to be flawless and so enjoyable he couldn't wait to do it again.

In spite of a triple-digit pulse and feeling as though her tongue was too big for her mouth, she could get used to that kind of surprise.

Dannie opened her closet and surveyed her small but lovely wardrobe. She'd never owned such amazing clothes and shoes before and never got tired of dressing up. She slipped into a casual black cocktail dress that veed over her breasts, buckled her feet into the sexiest Louboutins she owned and curled her lip at the state of her hair. Quickly she brushed it out and twisted it up into a sleek chignon.

Done. That was as close as she could get to looking like the kind of wife a man would enjoy coming home to. She took her time descending the stairs in her five-inch heels and spent a few minutes in the wine cellar glancing at labels until she put her hand on a sauvignon blanc *Wine Spectator* had talked up. A perfect date-night wine.

She stuck the bottle in a bucket of ice and left it on the formal dining room sideboard to chill until dinner, which the cook informed her would be a few minutes yet. At loose ends, she tormented the place settings until the silverware was either perfectly placed or exactly where it'd been when she started. She couldn't tell, which meant *stop obsessing.*

The cook announced dinner at last. She went to fetch Leo and found him in his study, of course, attention decisively on his laptop. His suit jacket hung on the back of the leather chair. His shirtsleeves were rolled up on his forearms and he'd already removed his tie. Rumpled Leo might be her favorite.

Leaning on the doorjamb, she watched him type in efficient strokes, pause and type again. Mentoring anonymously via chat again, most likely. She hated to interrupt. But not really.

"Dinner's ready."

He glanced up without lifting his head and the way he peeked out from under his lashes was so sexy, it sent a spiral of heat through her tummy.

"Right now?" he asked.

"Um, yeah." She cleared the multitude of frogs camping out on her vocal cords. "We don't want it to get cold."

He typed for another couple of seconds and then closed the laptop's lid with a snick as he stood. "That would be a shame."

Boldly, she watched him approach, aware her body blocked the doorway and curious what he'd do about it. "I'm a believer in hot food, myself."

He stopped a healthy distance away when he apparently realized she wasn't budging. "I'm looking forward to a home-cooked meal. Thought I should start eating better. I've had too much takeout lately."

Whose fault is that? "Just the food, then? The company wasn't a draw?"

"Of course the company was a factor." Something flickered in the depths of his blue eyes and heat climbed all over her.

Oh, that had all sorts of interesting possibilities locked inside. They gazed at each other for a long, delicious moment, and he didn't look away. Or back up.

Then he gestured to the hall. "Shall we, Mrs. Reynolds?"

And somehow, that was far more intimate than calling her Dannie. Deliberate? Oh, goodness, she hoped so.

Leo's capable palm settled into the small of her back as they walked and she felt the contact all the way to the soles of her feet. Something had changed. Hadn't it? Was her coffee *that* good?

In the dining room, Leo drew back the heavy chair and allowed her to sit on the brocade cushion before pushing it in for her. Then he expertly poured the wine to exactly the same level in both glasses on the first try—impressive evidence of how good Leo was with both detail and his hands.

Not that she'd needed additional clues the man hid amazing things under his workaholic shell. Were they at a point where she could admit how outrageously attracted to Leo she was? Or was that going past blunt into another realm entirely?

Placing her glass on the table before her, he took the seat catercorner to hers instead of across the table. "So we can talk without shouting," he said when she raised her eyebrows.

All small, small gestures, but so huge to her romance-starved soul. Flutters spread from her stomach to every organ in her body. Especially her heart.

For whatever reason, he was trying, really *trying,* to give her some of his time. But what was his intent? The friendship she'd hoped for or merely a small gesture toward crossing her path?

She'd keep her wits about her and under no circumstances would she read anything into what was essentially just dinner. As they dug into Greek salads served with crusty bread, she stuck to discussing her progress on the party. The more the wine flowed, the more relaxed they both became.

About halfway through her swordfish, she brought up the one thing she'd been dying to ask since the night of their marriage. "Do you still draw?"

Leo's fork froze over a piece of grilled zucchini. "How did you know about that?"

"Your mother told me."

He grimaced. "I should have guessed. She still has every piece of paper I've ever touched with a pencil."

Which was no answer at all. "Is it a sensitive subject?"

"No." Carefully, he cut a hunk of fish and chewed it in a spectacular stall tactic she recognized a mile away. He didn't want to discuss his art, that much was clear.

"So, never mind then. It's not important," she lied. His reaction said there was more to the story and it was very important, but she didn't want to alienate him. "Tell me something else instead. Why venture capital?"

His expression warmed. "If you're good, you can make a lot of money. You just have to recognize the right opportunities."

"Are you good?"

She already knew the answer but was curious what he thought about the empire he'd built. Most of her research into the complexities of venture capital had been conducted by reading articles about her husband's successful company before she'd even spoken to him on the phone for the first time.

"I'm competent. But I've made my share of mistakes."

As if that was something to be ashamed of. He seemed determined to downplay all his positives. "Everyone makes mistakes. You've recovered from yours quite well. The reputation of Reynolds Capital Management is unparalleled."

He inclined his head with a pleased smile. "It's a work in progress."

Fascinated with the way his eyes turned deeper blue when he engaged, she drained her wineglass and propped her chin on a curled hand. This was exactly what she'd envisioned their friendship would look like. "So how do you recognize the right opportunity?"

The cook bustled in and cleared their empty dinner plates, replacing them with bananas Foster for dessert. She lit the rum and blew it out in an impressive culinary display, then efficiently disappeared.

Leo spooned the dessert into his mouth and murmured appreciatively before answering Dannie's question. "Experience. Gut instinct. A large percentage of success is simply showing up. I create the remaining percentage by getting there first and staying until everyone else has gone home."

"Do you see your job as creative?" Dannie took a small bite of banana, gratified Leo liked the dessert as much as she did, but determined to keep him engaged in conversation. A full mouth wouldn't lend itself well to that.

He pursed his lips. "In a way, I suppose. Without backing, a lot of entrepreneurs' ideas would never see the light of day. I provide the platform for other people to tap into their creativity."

Which was what he'd done for her—given her the opportunity and the means to be exactly what she wanted to be. A wife. If tonight was any indication, Leo had changed his mind about spending time getting to know each other. Maybe she'd get the relationship—in some form or fashion—she craved out of it, too.

"You're the puppet master, then," she said.

"Not at all. I never stick my fingers in the pie. Micromanagement is not the most effective way to do business. I'm the money, not the talent."

"But you have talent," she protested.

His expression dimmed. "You've never seen one of my drawings."

"I meant you have a talent for recognizing the right opportunity." She smiled in hopes of keeping things friendly. "But I have a feeling you've got artistic talent, too. Draw me something and I'll let you know."

She was pushing him, she knew she was. But she wanted to know him, and his mysterious artistic side intrigued her.

"I don't draw anymore," he said, the syllables so clipped they nearly drew blood.

Message received. They hadn't connected nearly as deeply as she'd hoped, but they'd only just begun. One day, maybe he'd open up that part to her. "You've moved on to bigger and better canvases. Now you're creating your art with completely different tools."

Leo pushed his chair back. "Maybe. I've got some work to finish up. Thanks for dinner."

He escaped, leaving her to contemplate whether to open another bottle of wine in celebration of a successful dinner or to drown her disappointment since Leo had abandoned her once again.

Drown her disappointment. Definitely.

She located a bottle of pinot that went better with her mood than white wine and filled her glass almost to the rim. Then she called her mother to talk to someone uncomplicated and who she knew loved her always and forever, no matter what.

"Dannie," her mother cried when she answered. "Louise just told me. Thank you!"

Dannie grinned. Her mother's caregiver had turned into a friend almost instantly, and the two were constantly chattering. "Thanks for what?"

"The cruise, silly. The Bahamas! I'm so excited, I can hardly stand it." Her mother clucked. "I can't believe you kept this a secret, you bad girl."

The wineglass was somehow already half-empty again, but she didn't think she'd drunk enough to be *that* confused. "I didn't know. What cruise?"

"Oh. You don't? Louise said Leo booked us on a seven-day cruise, leaving out of Galveston. Next week. I thought for sure you suggested it. Well, thank him for us. For me, especially."

A steamroller flattened her heart. Her husband was a startling, deeply nuanced man underneath it all.

Dannie listened to her mother gush for several more minutes and managed to get a couple of sentences in sideways in spite of the question marks shooting from her brain. Were Leo's nice gestures indicative of deeper feelings he didn't want to admit for some reason? No man did a complete about-face without a motive. Had he come home for dinner in hopes of developing a friendship—or more?

Regardless, *something* had changed, all right, and her husband owed her a straight answer about what.

Sometimes talking to Leo was worse than pulling teeth, like their conversation after her text about the fake noise. Her marriage didn't just call for blunt—if she wanted to get answers, it apparently called for Scarlett, as well. And Scarlett had been squashed up inside for a really long time.

Three glasses of wine put a good dose of liquid courage in Dannie's blood. She ended the call and cornered Mr. Behind the Scenes in his office.

She barged into the study. Leo glanced up, clearly startled. She rounded the desk to pierce him with the evil eye, not the slightest bit concerned about the scattered paperwork under his fingers.

"About this cruise." Bumping a hip against the back of his chair, she swiveled it so he faced her, swinging his knees to either side of hers.

Not the slightest bit intimidated, he locked gazes with her. "What about it?"

Good gravy, when he was this close to her, the man practically dripped some sort of special brand of masculinity that tightened her thighs and put a tingle between them.

"Are you going to deny you did something nice for my mother?"

"No?" He lifted his brows. "Or yes, depending on whether *you* thought it was nice, I suppose."

His voice hitched so slightly, she almost didn't notice it until she registered the rising heat in his expression. *Oh, my.* That was lovely. Her proximity was putting a tingle in his parts, too.

"It was nice. She's very excited. Thank you."

He sat back in his chair, as if trying to distance himself

from the sizzling electricity. "Why do you seem a little, ah, agitated?"

"Agitated." She inched forward, not about to give up any ground, and her knees grazed the insides of his thighs. "I *am* agitated. Because I don't get why you won't ever acknowledge the wonderful things you do."

His gaze flicked down the length of her body and back up again slowly. "What would be the point of that?"

Her husband was nuanced all right...and also incredibly frustrating. He likely refused to take credit for his actions because that would require too much of an *investment* from him. Someone might want to reciprocate and make him feel good, too, and then there'd be a whole cycle of emotions. *That* would never do.

She huffed out a noise of disgust and poked him in the chest, leaning into it as her temper rose. "You do these things and it's almost like you'd prefer I didn't find out you've got a kind streak. Jig's up, Leo."

He removed her finger from his rib cage, curling it between his and holding it away from his body instead of releasing it. Probably so she wouldn't wound him, but his skin sparked against hers and nearly buckled her knees.

The memory of *that kiss* exploded in her mind and heightened the gathering heat at her core.

But she still didn't know what was happening between them—friends, lovers, more? Maybe it was actually none of the above. If she gave in to the passion licking through her, would he disappear afterward until the next time he wanted sex? Or could this be the start of something special?

"You have an active imagination," he said.

She rolled her eyes to hide the yearning he'd surely see in them. "Yeah, I get it. You're a ruthless, cold-blooded businessman who'd rather be caught dead than disclosing your real name to a couple of students. What's it going to take to get you off the sidelines and into the middle of your own life?"

That was the key to unlocking his no-emotional-investment stance on marriage. It had to be. If he'd only wade into the thick of things and stop cutting himself off, he'd see how wonderful a real relationship could be. How satisfying. Fulfilling. Surely their marriage could be more than an occasional crossing of paths. He needed her to help him see that.

Leo's frame tensed and slowly he rose from the chair, pushing into her space. "I like the sidelines."

Toe-to-toe, they eyed each other, the impasse almost as palpable in the atmosphere as the swirl of awareness. "Why did you book my mother on a cruise?"

He shrugged, lashes low, shuttering his thoughts from her. "I thought she would like it."

"That's only half the truth. You did it for me." A huge leap. But she didn't think she was wrong.

Their gazes locked and the intensity shafted through her. "What if I did?"

Her pulse stuttered. Coffee, then dinner. Now this. What was he trying to accomplish? "Well, I'm shocked you'd admit that. Before you know it, we'll be buying each other birthday cards and taking vacations together. Like real couples."

Like the marriage of her dreams. Just because neither of them had expressed an interest in a love match didn't mean it was completely impossible to have found one. What better security was there between two people than that of knowing someone would love you forever?

He threw up a palm. "Let's don't get out of hand now."

She advanced, pushing his palm into her cleavage, burning her skin with his touch and backing him against the desk. She wanted to bond with her husband in the most elemental way possible. To complete the journey from A to B and see what they really could have together.

"I like getting out of hand."

"Do you have a response for everything?" His fingertips curled, nipping into her skin.

"If you don't like what I have to say, then shut me up."

His expression turned carnal. He watched her as he slid an index finger down the valley between her breasts and hooked the neckline of her dress. In a flash, he hauled her forward, capturing her lips in a searing kiss.

On legs turned to jelly, she melted into it, into him as he wrapped his arms around her, finally giving her what she'd been after since she walked in. Maybe since before that.

Greedy for all of him, she settled for the small, hot taste of Leo against her mouth. With a moan, she tilted her head and parted his lips with hers. She plunged into the heat, seeking his tongue with hers, and he obliged her with strong, heated licks.

His arms tightened, crushing her against his torso, aligning their hips. Need soaked her senses as his hard ridge nudged her. She cupped the back of his neck as his hand snaked under her dress to caress the back of her thigh.

Yes. As seduction techniques went, he could teach a class.

Soft cotton skimmed under her fingers as she explored the angles and muscles of his back. Delicious. Her husband's body was hard and strong, exactly as she liked, exactly perfect to keep her safe and satisfied at the same time.

The kiss deepened and the hand on her thigh inched higher, trailing sparkling warmth along with it. She tilted her hips in silent invitation, begging him to take those fingers wherever he so desired.

But then he pulled away, chest heaving, and spun her to face the wall, his torso hot against her spine.

"Daniella," he murmured in her ear, and his fingertip traced the line of her dress where it met the flesh of her back, toying with the zipper. "I'm about to pull this down and taste every inch of you until we're both mindless. Is that what you want?"

Damp heat flooded her and she shuddered. "Only if you call me Dannie while you do it."

He strangled over a groan and moved her forward a confusing foot, then two. "I can't do this."

"Don't say you don't want me." *So close. Don't back off now.* She whirled and tilted her chin at the bulge in his pants she'd felt branding her bottom. "I already know that's not true. You don't kiss someone like that unless you mean it."

"That's the problem." Breath rattled in his throat on a raw exhale. "You want me to mean it in a very different way than I do mean it. I'd rather not disappoint you and that's where this is headed. Making love will not change the fact that tomorrow I'm still going to work a sixteen-hour day, leaving little time for you. Until both of us can live with that, I need you to *walk away.*"

He was blocking himself off from her again, but for a very good reason. The rejection didn't even bother her. How could it? He was telling her he didn't want to treat her like a one-night stand.

That set off a whole different sort of flutter.

"I'm walking." *For now.* She needed a cooler head— among other parts—to navigate this unexpected twist to their marriage.

She skirted the desk, putting much-needed distance between them.

Raking a hand through his hair, he sank into the chair with a pained grimace. "Good night."

"This was the best date I've ever been on."

With that parting shot, she left him to his paperwork, already plotting how to crack that shell open a little wider and find the strong, amazing heart she knew beat beneath. He thought they were holding off until she was okay with no-emotional-investment sex, but he was already so emotionally invested, he was afraid of hurting her.

That's what had changed. Somehow, she had to help him see what he truly needed from her.

If a large percentage of success happened by showing up and then outwaiting the competition, she could do that. Yes, her competition was an intangible, unfathomable challenge called *work,* but the reward compensated for the effort.

Time for a little relocation project.

Seven

The silky feel of Daniella's thigh haunted Leo for days. And if he managed to block it from his mind, her fiery responses when he kissed her replaced that memory immediately.

It didn't seem to matter how many spreadsheets he opened on his laptop. Or how many proposals for new ventures he heard. Or whether he slept at the office because he lacked the strength to be in the same house with Daniella. Sleeping as a whole didn't work so well when his wife invaded his unconscious state to star in erotic dreams.

There was no neat, predefined box for her. For any of this. It was messing him up.

He hadn't seen Daniella in four days and the scent of strawberries still lingered in his nose.

Fingers snapped before his eyes and Leo blinked. Mrs. Gordon was at his desk, peering at him over her reading glasses. "I called your name four times."

"Sorry. Long night."

Mrs. Gordon's gaze flicked to the other end of Leo's office, where a sitting area overlooked downtown Dallas. "Because that couch is too short for a big, strapping young man like you."

He grinned in spite of being caught daydreaming, a mortifying situation if it had been anyone other than his admin. "Are you flirting with me?"

"Depends. How much trouble are you in at home?" Her

raised eyebrows wiped the smile off his face. "Enough that an old woman looks pretty good right about now?"

"I'm not in trouble at home. What does that even mean? You think I got kicked out?" He frowned.

It bothered him because deep down, he knew he'd taken the coward's way out. Being friends with his wife hadn't worked out so well. She was too sexy, too insightful.

"Au contraire. You're in trouble. It's all over your face."

"That's ridiculous." Leo scrubbed his jaw, not that he believed for a second he could erase whatever she thought she saw there, and fingered a spot he'd missed shaving that morning. The executive bathroom off his office left nothing to be desired, but two hours of sleep had affected his razor hand, apparently.

"Forget her birthday, did you?" Mrs. Gordon nodded sagely.

Soon we'll be buying each other birthday cards, Daniella had said, but he didn't even know when her birthday was. "Our marriage isn't like that."

Mrs. Gordon's mouth flattened. Her favorite way to remind him she had his number. "Why do I get the feeling you and your wife have differing opinions about that?"

He sighed and the hollow feeling in his stomach grew worse because she was right. "Did you hear from Tommy Garrett's people yet?"

"Don't change the subject. I'd have told you if I heard from Garrett and you know it. Just like you know you've got a problem at home that you better address sooner rather than later. I've been married for thirty years. I know things." She clucked. "Take my advice. Buy her flowers and sleep in your own bed tonight."

He had the distinct impression Mrs. Gordon believed his wife would be in the bed, as well. He didn't correct her.

After all, what sort of weakness did *that* reveal?

He couldn't have sex with his own wife because he'd backed himself into an impossible corner. She wanted some kind of intimacy, which he couldn't give her, and he didn't want to hurt her. He'd thought friendship might be enough, but friends apparently talked about aspects of themselves that he just couldn't share. Especially not drawing. It was tied to his obsessive side, which he kept under wraps.

How long would Dannie remain patient before finding someone who *would* give her what she wanted? Women in his life usually lasted about two months before bailing.

He'd never cared before. Never dreamed he'd experience moments of pure panic at the thought of Daniella going the way of previous companions. They had a convenient marriage, but that meant it would be easy to dissolve when it was no longer convenient for her.

By 9:00 p.m., Leo couldn't argue with his admin's logic any longer. His body screamed to collapse in a dead sleep, but he couldn't physically make himself lie down on that couch.

What was he really accomplishing by avoiding his wife? When he'd told her to walk after nearly stripping her bare right there in his study, she had. No questions, no hysterics, no accusations. She was fine with holding off on advancing their relationship.

Daniella wasn't the problem. He was.

He was a weak daydreamer who'd rather scratch a pencil over pieces of paper all day and then spend several hours exploring his wife's naked body that night. And do it again the next day, abandoning all his goals with Reynolds Capital Management in a heartbeat for incredible sex and a few pictures. He'd done exactly that before, and he feared the consequences would be far worse if he did it with Daniella.

If he could resist the lure of drawing, he could resist the Helen of Troy he'd married. As long as he didn't kiss her again, he had a good shot at controlling himself. Of course, the real problem was that deep down, he was pretty sure he didn't want to.

He drove to the house he'd bought with his own money,

where he'd created a safe, secure home that no one could take away. The lights always shone brightly and the boiler always heated water. And Leo would die before allowing that to change.

Daniella wasn't downstairs. Good. Hopefully she was already asleep in her room. If so, he could get all the way to his bedroom without running into her.

As he passed the study, his neck heated as the dream from last night roared into his mind—the one where he finished that kiss from the other night by spinning Daniella facedown onto the desk, pushing up that sexy dress and plunging into her wet heat again and again until she convulsed around him with a cry.

That room was off-limits from now on. He'd buy a new desk and have it moved into his bedroom.

So exhausted he could hardly breathe, he climbed the stairs and stumbled to his bedroom. No lights. Too bright for his weary eyes.

His shin cracked against something heavy and knocked him off balance. He cursed as his hand shot out to break his fall and scraped across…whatever he'd tripped over.

Snick. Light flooded the dark room via the lamp on his bedside table.

"Are you okay?" Daniella asked.

His head snapped up in shock. "What are you doing here? Why are you in my bed?"

His wife, hair swept back in a ponytail and heavy lidded with sleep, regarded him calmly from beneath the covers of *his bed.* "It's my bed, too, now. I moved into your room. If you'd come home occasionally, you might have known I rearranged the furniture."

The throb in his shin rivaled the sudden throb in his temples. "I didn't… You ca—" He sucked in a fortifying breath. "You had no right to do that."

She studied him for a moment, her face contemplative and breathtakingly beautiful in its devoid-of-makeup state.

"You said I should think of this as my home. Anything I wanted to change, you'd be willing to discuss."

"Exactly. *Discuss.*"

The firm cross of her arms said she'd gladly have done so, if he hadn't been hiding out at the office.

"You're bleeding." She threw the covers back, slipped out of bed and crossed the room to take his hand, murmuring over the shallow cut.

As she was wearing a pair of plaid pants cinched low on her slim hips and a skintight tank top that left her midriff bare, a little blood was the least of his problems.

"And you're cold," he muttered and tore his gaze from the hard peaks beneath the tank top, which scarcely contained dark, delicious-looking nipples.

Too late. Heat shuddered through his groin, tightening his pants uncomfortably. Couldn't she find some clothes that she wasn't in danger of bursting out of? Like a suit of armor, perhaps?

"I'll be fine." She tugged on his hand, flipping the long ponytail over her shoulder. "Come into the bathroom. Let me put a bandage on this cut."

"It's not that bad. Go back to bed. I'll sleep somewhere else." As if he had a prayer of sleep tonight.

Adrenaline coursed through his veins. Muscles strained to reach for her, to yank on the bow under her navel and let those plaid pants pool around her ankles. One tiny step and he could have her in his arms.

He tried to pull away but she clamped down on his hand, surprisingly strong for someone so sensuously built.

"Leo." Her breasts rose on a long sigh and under her breath she muttered something about him that sounded suspiciously uncomplimentary. "Please let me help you. It's my fault you're hurt."

It was her fault he had a hard-on the size of Dallas. But it was not her fault that he'd been avoiding her and thus didn't know the layout of his own bedroom any longer. "Fine."

He followed her into the bathroom, noting the addition of a multitude of mysterious girly accoutrements, and decided he preferred remaining ignorant of their purposes.

Daniella fussed over him, washing his cut and patting it dry. In bare feet, she was shorter than he was used to. Normally she had no trouble looking him in the eye when she wore her architecturally impossible and undeniably sexy heels. He hadn't realized how much he liked that.

Or how much he'd also like this slighter, attentive Daniella who took care of him. Fatigue washed over him, muddling his thoughts, and he forgot for a second why it wasn't a good idea to share a bed with her.

"All better." She patted his hand and bent to put the box of bandages under the sink, pulling her pajama pants tight across her rear, four inches from his blistering erection. He closed his eyes.

"About the room sharing," he began.

She brushed his sensitive flesh and his lids flew up. He'd swayed toward her, inadvertently. She glanced up to meet his gaze in the mirror. The incongruity between her state of undress and his buttoned-up suit shouldn't have been so erotic. But it was.

"Are you going to read me the riot act?" she asked, her eyes enormous and guileless and soft. "Or consider the possibilities?"

"Which are?" The second it was out of his mouth, he wished he could take it back. Foggy brain and half-dressed wife did not make for good conversation elements.

"You work a hundred hours a week. Our paths will never cross unless we do it here." She gestured toward the bedroom. "This way, we'll both get what we want."

In the bright bathroom light, the semitransparent tank top left nothing to the imagination. Of course, he already knew what her bare breast looked like and the longer she stood there with the dark circles of her nipples straining against the fabric, the more he wanted to see them both, but this time with no interruptions.

"What do you think I want?"

"You want me." She turned to face him. "All the benefits without the effort, or so you say. I don't believe you. If you wanted that, my dress wouldn't have stayed zipped for longer than five seconds after dinner. Sharing a bedroom offers you a chance to figure out why you let me walk away. It won't infringe on your work hours and it gives me a chance to forge the friendship I want. Before we become physically involved."

That cleared the fog in a hurry. "What are you saying, that you'll be like a *roommate?*"

"You sound disappointed." Her eyebrows rose in challenge. "Would you like to make me a better offer?"

Oh, dear God. She should be negotiating his contracts, not his lawyer.

"You're driving me bananas. No. Worse than that." He squeezed the top of his head but his brain still felt as though she'd twirled it with a spaghetti fork. "What's worse than bananas?"

"Pomegranates," she said decisively. "They're harder to eat and don't taste as good."

He bit back a laugh. Yes, exactly. His incredibly perceptive wife drove him pomegranates. "That about covers it."

"Will you try it my way? Give it a week. Then if you still think sex will complicate our marriage too much, I'll move back to my bedroom. I promise I'll keep my hands to myself." To demonstrate, she laced her fingers over her sexy rear and he swore. She'd done that exact thing in one of his dreams. "If you'll promise the same."

His shin didn't hurt nearly as badly as his aching groin. "Are you seriously suggesting we share a bed platonically?"

"Seriously. Show me you think our marriage is worth it. Sharing a room is the only way we'll figure this out, unless you plan to work less. It's unorthodox, but being married to a workaholic has forced my creative hand, so to speak."

It was definitely creative, he'd give her that, and hit him where it hurt—right where all the guilt lived. If he wanted her to be happy in this marriage and stick with him, he had to prove it.

Her logic left him no good reason not to say yes. Except for the fact that it was insane.

Her seductive brown eyes sucked him in. "What are you going to do, Leo?"

Somehow, she made it sound as if he held all the cards. As if all he had to do was whisper a few romantic phrases in her ear and she'd be putty in his hands. If only it was that easy.

And then she shoved the knife in a little further. "Try it. What's the worst that can happen?"

He groaned as several sleepless nights in a row hit him like a freight train. "I'm certain we're about to find out."

Fatigue and a strong desire to avoid his wife's backup plan if he said no—that was his excuse for stripping down to a T-shirt and boxer shorts and getting into bed next to a woman who blinded him with lust by simply breathing. Whom he'd agreed not to touch.

Just to make her happy. Just for a few days. Just to prove he wasn't weak.

He fell into instant sleep.

Dannie woke in the morning quite pleased but quite uncomfortable from a night of clinging to the edge of the bed so she didn't accidentally roll over into Leo's half. Or into Leo.

She'd probably tortured him enough.

But her will wasn't as strong as she thought, not when her husband lay mere feet away, within touching distance, breathing deeply in sleep. The alarm on his phone had beeped, like, an hour ago, but hadn't produced so much as a twitch out of Leo. Who was she to wake him when he obviously needed to sleep? A good wife ensured her husband was well rested.

The view factored pretty high in the decision, too.

Goodness. He was so gorgeous, dark lashes frozen above his cheekbones, hair tousled against the pillow.

How in the world had she convinced him to sleep in the same bed with her *and* agree to hold off on intimacy? She'd thought for sure they'd have a knock-down-drag-out and then he'd toss her out—bound and determined to ignore his own needs, needs he likely didn't even recognize. But instead of cutting himself off from her again, he'd waded right into the middle of things like she'd asked, bless him.

Because his actions spoke louder than words, and his wife was an ace at interpreting what lay beneath.

If this bedroom sharing worked out the way she hoped, they'd actually talk. Laugh over a sitcom. Wake up together. Then maybe he'd figure out he was lying to himself about what he really wanted from this marriage and realize just how deeply involved he already was.

They'd have intimacy—physically and mentally. She couldn't wait.

She eased from the bed and took a long shower, where she fantasized about all the delicious things Leo would do when he finally seduced her. It was coming. She could feel it.

And no matter how much she wanted it, anticipated it, she sensed she could never fully prepare for how earthshaking their ultimate union would truly be.

When she emerged from the bathroom, Leo was sitting up, rubbing the back of his neck, and her mouth went dry. Even in a T-shirt, he radiated masculinity.

"Good morning," she called cheerfully.

"What happened to my alarm?" He did not look pleased.

"I turned it off after listening to it chirp for ten minutes."

"Why didn't you wake me up?"

"I tried," she lied and fluttered her lashes. "Next time would you like me to be a little more inventive?"

"No." He scowled, clearly interpreting her question to mean she'd do it in the dirtiest, sexiest way she could envision.

"I meant with a glass of water in your face. What did you think I meant?"

He rolled his eyes. "So this is what roommates do?"

"Yes. Until you want to be something else."

With that, she flounced out the door to check off the last few items on the list for Tommy Garrett's party. It was tomorrow night and it was going to be spectacular if she had to sacrifice her Louboutins to the gods of party planning to ensure it.

Leo came downstairs a short while later, actually said goodbye and went to work.

When he strolled into the bedroom that evening, the hooded, watchful gaze he shot her said he'd bided his time all day, primed for the showdown about to play out.

"Busy?" he asked nonchalantly.

Dannie carefully placed the e-reader in her hand on the bedside table and crossed her arms over her tank top. What was it about that look on his face that made her feel as if she'd put on Elise's red-hot wedding night set? "Not at all. By the way, I picked up your dry cl—"

"Good." He threw his messenger bag onto the Victorian settee in the corner and raked piercing blue eyes over her, all the way to her toes tucked beneath a layer of Egyptian cotton. They heated, despite the flimsy barrier, and the flush spread upward at an alarming rate to spark at her core.

What had she been talking about?

He shed his gray pin-striped suit jacket and then his tie. "You caught me at a disadvantage last night. I had a few other things on my mind, so I missed a couple of really important points about this new sleeping arrangement."

Her relocation project had just blown up in her face. He was good and worked up over it.

"Oh? Which ones?" The last syllable squeaked out more like a dolphin mating call than English as he dropped his pants, then slowly unbuttoned his crisp white shirt. What had she done to earn her very own male stripper? Because she'd gladly do it fourteen more times in a row.

"For starters, what happens if I don't keep my hands to myself?"

The shirt hit the floor and her jaw almost followed. Her husband had quite the physique hidden under his worka-holic shell.

So maybe he wasn't mad. But what was he?

Clad in only a pair of briefs, Leo yanked the covers back and slid into his side of the bed. She peeled her gaze from his well-defined chest and refixed it on his face, which was drawn up in a slight smirk, as if he'd guessed the direction of her thoughts. Her cheeks flamed.

"I'll scold you?" She swallowed as he casually lounged on his pillow, head propped on his hand as if settling in for a nice, long chat instead of using those hands to do some-thing far more...intimate. "I mean, it wouldn't be very sport-ing of you."

"Noted." He stretched a little and the covers slipped down his torso. "What happens if *you* don't keep your hands to yourself?"

He was toying with her, seeing if he could get her to break her own vow of chastity. In his thoroughly male mind, he'd be in the clear if *she* made the move. His eyelids dropped to a very sexy half-mast and sizzled her to the core.

"And Daniella? Be sure you spell really well so it's all very clear for those of us who didn't barge into someone else's bed and start slinging rules around."

Actually, the relocation project might be working bet-ter than she'd assumed. At least they were talking. Now to get him to understand this wasn't a contest. Their relation-

ship was at a crossroads and he had to choose which fork
he wanted to take.

"There are no rules," she corrected. "I don't have a list
of punishments drawn up if you decide you're not on board
with being roommates, whether you want to go back to separate bedrooms or strip me naked right now. You're calling
the shots. You're the one who shut it down after dinner the
other night. *Walk away,* you said, and I did, but that's not
what either of us wanted."

"Yeah?" Lazily, he traced the outline of her shoulder
against the propped-up pillow at her back, carefully not
touching her skin but skating so close the heat from his finger raised every hair on her body. "What would you rather
I have told you to do?"

"No games, Leo." She met his gaze squarely. "I'm giving
us an opportunity to develop a friendship. But I also readily
admit I want you. I want your mouth on me. Here." Just as
lazily, she traced a line over her breast and circled the nipple,
arching a little. "I want it so badly, I can hardly stand it."

She watched him, and went liquid as his expression darkened sinfully.

"No games?" he asked and cleared the rasp from his
throat. "Then what is this?"

"A spelling lesson." And she obviously had to really lay
it out for him. She dropped her hand. "You want me, then
come and get me. Be as emotionally naked as you are physically. Strip yourself as bare as your body and let's see how
fantastic it can be between us."

Stiffening, he closed off, his expression shuttering and
his body angling away. "That's all? You don't ask for much."

"Then forget I mentioned it. We don't have to hold out
for a connection that may not ever happen. If either of us
becomes uninterested in the hands-to-yourself proposition
I laid out, it's off." She flung herself back against the pillow, arms splayed wide. "Take me now. I won't complain.
We'll have sex, it'll be great and then we'll go to sleep."

He didn't move.

"What's the matter?" she taunted, glancing at him sideways. "It's just sex. Surely you've had just sex before. No brain required. I have no doubt a man with your obvious, um...*talent* can make me come in no time at all. In fact, I'm looking forward to it. I'm hot for you, Leo. Don't make me wait a second longer."

"That's not funny. Stop being ridiculous." Translation: he didn't like being thoroughly trounced at his own game.

She widened her eyes. "Did you think I was joking? I'm not. We're married. We're consenting adults. Both of us have demonstrated a healthy interest in getting the other naked. We'll eventually go all the way. It's your choice what sort of experience that will be."

This had never been about withholding sex. She'd be naked in a heartbeat as soon as he made a move. All the power was in his hands and when that move came, it would be monumental. And he'd be so very, very aware of exactly what it meant.

He shoved both hands through his hair. "Why is it my choice?"

Poor, poor man. If he was too clueless to know she didn't have a choice, far be it from her to fill him in. This was something he had to figure out on his own. Besides, he was the one with the crisis of conscience that prevented him from making love to her until something he probably couldn't even articulate happened.

But she knew exactly what he needed—to let himself go. She'd exploit this situation gladly in order to get the marriage she desperately wanted and help him find the affection and affinity he so clearly yearned for.

She smiled. "Because. I'm—" *Already emotionally invested.* "—generous that way."

She was going to drag Leo off the sidelines kicking and screaming if that's what it took to have the love match she sensed in her soul Elise had actually orchestrated.

Eight

By nine o'clock, the party hummed along in full swing, a success by anyone's account. Except perhaps Leo's. In the past hour, he'd said no more than two words to Dannie.

She tried not to let it bother her as she flitted from group to group, ensuring everyone had a full glass of champagne and plenty to talk about. The final guest list had topped out at twenty-five and no one sent their regrets. Chinese box kites hung from the ceiling, artfully strung by the crew she'd hired. Their interesting geometric shapes and whimsical tails provided a splash of color in the otherwise severe living room. A papier-mâché dragon lounged on the buffet table, breathing fire under the fondue pot in carefully timed intervals.

Tommy's admin had mentioned his love of the Orient and the decorations sprang easily from that. More than one guest had commented how unusual and eye-catching the theme was, but Tommy's signature on the dotted line was the only praise she needed.

Well, she'd have taken a "You look nice" from Leo. The ankle-length black sequined dress had taken three shopping trips to find and a white-knuckle twenty-four hours to alter. She'd only gotten it back this morning and it looked great on her.

Not that anyone else had noticed.

She threw her shoulders back and smiled at the knot of

guests surrounding her, determined to be the hostess Leo expected.

Hyperawareness burned her back on more than one occasion, and she always turned to see Leo's piercing blue eyes on her and his expression laced with something dangerous.

The bedroom-sharing plan was a disaster. He hated it. That had to be his problem—not that she'd know for sure, because he'd clammed up. Was he waiting until the party was over to give her her walking papers?

Turning her back on Leo and the cryptic bug up his butt, she came face-to-face with Leo's friend Dax Wakefield. "Enjoying the party?" she asked him brightly.

Not one person in this room was going to guess she had a mess of uncertainty swirling in her stomach.

"Yes, thank you." Unfailingly polite, Dax nodded, but his tone carried a hint of frost. "The buffet is wonderful."

Her radar blipped as she took note of the distinct lack of a female on Dax's arm. A good-looking guy like Dax—if you liked your men slick and polished—was obviously alone by choice. Was he no longer dating Jenna? Or had Leo asked him not to bring her in some misguided protective notion?

"I'm so glad." She curved her lips graciously and got nothing in response. Maybe he was aloof with everyone. "Congratulations again on the distinguished alumni award. Leo assures me it was well deserved."

"Thank you." Not one hair on his perfectly coiffed head moved when he granted her a small nod. "Took me a little longer to achieve than Leo. But our industries are so different."

What did that mean? There was an undercurrent here she couldn't put her finger on, but Dax definitely wasn't warming up to her. *Problem alert.* Dax and Leo were old friends and a wife was a second-class citizen next to that. Was Dax the genesis of Leo's silent treatment?

"Well, your media empire is impressive nonetheless. We watch your news channel regularly." It wasn't a total lic—

Leo had scrutinized stock prices as they scrolled across the bottom of the screen last night as she pretended to sleep after the spelling lesson.

Dax smiled and a chill rocked her shoulders. If Leo wanted people to believe he was a ruthless, cold-blooded businessman, he should take lessons from his friend. That guy exuded *take no prisoners.*

One of the servers discreetly signaled to get her attention and she pounced on the opportunity to escape. "Will you excuse me? Duty calls."

"Of course." Dax immediately turned to one of Leo's new partners, Miles Bennett, and launched into an impassioned speech about the Cowboys roster and whether they could make it to the Super Bowl this time around.

The server detailed a problem in the kitchen with several broken champagne bottles, which Dannie solved by pulling out Leo's reserve stash of Meunier & Cie. It was a rosé, but very good and would have to do in a pinch. Most of the guests were men and such a girly drink had definite potential to go over like a lead balloon.

Mental note—next time, buy extra champagne in case of nervous, butterfingered staff.

She poured two glasses of the pink champagne and sought out Tommy Garrett. Something told her he'd take to both an out-of-the-norm drink and being roped into a coconspiracy.

Maybe because of the purple canvas high-tops he'd worn with his tuxedo.

"Tommy." Grateful she'd caught him alone by the stairs, she handed him a champagne flute. When Leo had introduced them earlier, they'd chatted for a while and she'd immediately seen why her husband liked him. "You look thirsty. Humor me and drink this. Pretend it's beer."

A brewery in the Czech Republic exported Tommy's vice of choice, which she'd gleaned from his admin. But he'd already had two pints and hopefully wouldn't balk at her plea.

The young man flipped chin-length hair, bleached almost white by the sun, out of his face. "You read my mind. Talking to all these suits has parched me fiercely."

Half the champagne disappeared into Tommy's mouth in one round and he didn't gag. A glance around the room showed her that others weren't tossing the rosé into the potted plants. Crisis averted.

"Thanks, Mrs. Reynolds." She shot him a withering glare and he winked. "I mean Dannie. Sorry, I forgot. Beautiful women get me all tongue-tied."

She laughed. "Does that geek approach actually work?"

"More often than I would have ever imagined. Yet I find myself devoid of promising action this evening." Tommy sighed dramatically and waggled his brows, leaning in to murmur in her ear. "Wanna see my set of protractors sometime?"

Her grin widened. She really liked him, too, and was almost disappointed he hadn't worn a hoodie to her fancy party. "Why, Thomas Garrett, you should be ashamed of yourself. Hitting on a married lady."

"I should be, but I'm totally not. Anyway, I couldn't pry you away from Leo with a crowbar and my own private island. Could I?" he asked hopefully with a practiced once-over she suspected the coeds fell for hook, line and sinker.

"Not a chance," she assured him. "I like my men all grown-up. But feel free to keep trying your moves on me. Eventually you'll become passable at flirting with a woman."

Tommy clutched his heart in mock pain. "Harsh. I think there might be blood."

That prickly, hot flash traveled down her back an instant before Leo materialized at her elbow. His palm settled with familiarity into the groove at her waist and she clamped down on the shiver before it tipped him off that such a simple touch could be so affecting. *Why* had she worn a backless dress?

"Hey, Leo." Tommy lifted his nearly empty glass in a toast. "Great party. Dannie was telling me how much she likes protractors."

"Was she, now?" Leo said easily, his voice mellower than the scotch in his highball.

Uh-oh. She'd never heard him speak like that.

Swiping at Tommy with a flustered hand, she glanced up at Leo and nearly flinched at the lethal glint in her husband's eyes. Directed at her or Tommy? "Protractors. Yes. They get the job done, don't they? Just like Leo. Think of him as a protractor and Reynolds's competitor, Moreno Partners, as a ruler. Why not use the right tool for the job from the very beginning?"

Tommy eyed her. "Moreno is pretty straight and narrow in their approach. Maybe that's what I need."

Good, he'd picked up on her desperate subject change.

"Oh, no." Dannie shook her head and prayed Leo's stiff carriage wasn't because he didn't like the way she was sticking her nose in his business with Tommy. This was absolutely what she was here for and she absolutely didn't want to blow it, especially with Leo in such a strange, unpredictable mood. "Reynolds can help you. Leo's been doing this far longer than Moreno. He has connections. Expertise. You know Leo has a degree in engineering, too, right?"

Leo's hand drifted a little lower. His pinky dipped inside her dress and grazed the top edge of her panties. Her brain liquefied into the soles of her sparkly Manolos and she forgot to mention he'd actually double majored in engineering and business.

"Daniella," Leo murmured. "Perhaps you'd see to Mrs. Ross? She's wandering around by the double glass doors and I'm afraid she might end up in the pool."

"Of course." She smiled at Tommy, then at Leo and went on the trumped-up errand Leo had devised, likely to avoid saying outright in front of a prospective partner that he could handle his own public relations. Which she appreciated.

As she guided Mrs. Ross toward the buffet, she laughed at the sweet old lady's jokes, but kept an eye on Leo and Tommy. They were still talking near the stairs and Leo's expression had finally lost that edge she so desperately wanted to understand.

If she'd gone too far with the bedroom-sharing idea, why didn't he just tell her?

This party was a measure of how effectively she could do her job as Leo's wife and how well she contributed to his success. Coupled with the high-level tension constantly pulsing between them, her nerves had stretched about as tight as they could without snapping.

Dannie showed the last guest to the door and spent a long thirty minutes with the auxiliary staff wrapping up postparty details.

Leo was nowhere to be seen.

Around midnight, she finally stumbled to their bedroom with the last bottle of champagne, uncorked, intending to split it with him in celebration of a successful party. Surely Leo shared that opinion. If he didn't, she really should be told why.

Darkness shrouded the bedroom.

She set the champagne bottle and two glasses on the dresser and crossed to the freestanding Tiffany torchiere lamp in the corner. She snapped it on and bracing against the wall, fingered apart the buckle on one shoe.

"Oh, you should leave those on." Leo tsked, his voice silky as scotch again.

She whirled. He was lounging on the settee, tie loose and shirt unbuttoned three down. Not that she was counting. "What are you doing sitting here in the dark?"

"Seemed appropriate for my mood."

That sounded like a warning. She thumbed off the other shoe in case she had to make a run for the door. "Would you like me to turn off the light?"

He contemplated her for a long moment. "Would darkness make it easier for you to pretend I was Tommy Garrett?"

She couldn't help it. The laugh bubbled out.

It was a straight-from-the-bottle kind of night. Retrieving the champagne from the dresser, she gulped a healthy dose before wiping her mouth with the back of one hand. "Jealousy? That's so…" *Cliché.* Well, it seemed like a tell-it-like-it-is night, too. "…cliché, Leo."

His gaze scraped her from head to toe, darkening as he lingered at the vee of her cleavage. "What should I feel while watching my wife flirt with another man?"

"Gratitude?" she offered. "I was working him for you."

Leo barked out a laugh. "Shall I call him back, then? See if he's up for a threesome?"

This was going downhill fast. Not only was he not thrilled with her party, he'd transformed into a possessive husband. "Are you drunk?"

Maybe she should catch up. If she downed the entire bottle of champagne, her husband might make a lot more sense. Or it would dull the coming rejection—which this time would no doubt include an annulment. Alcohol had the potential to make either one more bearable.

"Not nearly drunk enough," he muttered. Louder, he said, "Since you're so free with your favors this evening, perhaps you'd do me another one."

Her eyes narrowed. "Like what?"

"Show me what's under that dress."

Okay, *not* the direction she'd anticipated him going. *More champagne, STAT.* She swigged another heady gulp and set the bottle on the dresser. "Why? So you can stake your claim? Jealousy is not a good enough reason to strip for you."

His mouth quirked. "What would be?"

"Diamonds. A trip to Bora-Bora. A Jaguar." She ticked

them off on her fingers airily. If he was going to be cliché, she could, too. "The typical kept woman baubles."

"What if I called you…Dannie?" He drew it out and in that silky voice, it swept down her spine and coalesced in her core with heat. "It's the key to intimacy, isn't it? You let Tommy call you that. The two of you were very cozy."

She cursed under her breath. How dare he turn her on while accusing her of dallying with Tommy? "He's twenty-four, Leo. I'm old enough to be his…older sister. Stop being such a Neanderthal."

"So that's your objection to Tommy? His age?" Leo slid off the settee and advanced on her, slowly enough to trip her pulse. "What about Dax? He's my age. Maybe you'd like him better."

"What's this really about?" Boldly, she stared him down as he approached, determined to get past this barrier she sensed he'd thrown up to avoid the real issue—she'd failed at being the wife he needed, on all levels. Somehow. "You're not threatened by Tommy. Or Dax. You've been weird all evening. If you've got a problem with me, lay it out. No more smoke and mirrors."

Only a breath away, he halted, towering over her. Without heels, she wasn't that much shorter than he was, but his presence—and his dark, intense mood—overwhelmed her.

"You know, I do have a problem with you." His gaze traveled over her and that's when she saw the vulnerability he'd hidden behind a mask of false allegations. "You're still dressed."

Baffled, she cocked her head and studied him. Hints of what he was so carefully not telling her filtered through. All at once, she realized. He *was* threatened by other men and conversely paralyzed by his conscience, which had dictated that he wouldn't touch her until she was okay with what he could give.

His body language was equally conflicted. His fingers

curled and uncurled repeatedly, as if he wanted to reach for her but couldn't.

She was his wife. But not his wife, in the truest sense.

Her heart softened. He wanted something he had no experience with, no vocabulary to define. And she'd been trying to force him into admitting his needs by sharing his bed and denying him the only outlet for his emotions that he understood, assuming her way was best.

Well, this was all new to her, too, but she wasn't above changing course to give him what he needed.

Their connection was already there. Instead of waiting on some murky criteria she doubted either of them could verbalize, she'd just show him.

That was a good enough reason to strip for him.

Dannie locked her gaze on his and reached up to her nape to unclasp her dress.

Leo was acting like an ass.

Knowing it didn't give him any better ability to control it, or to eliminate the constant spike of lust when he caught sight of his wife. Seeing her laugh with another man had generated something ugly and primal inside.

He didn't like it.

He didn't like how he'd focused so much energy and attention on this deal with Tommy Garrett and then spent the night sulking in the corner instead of using the opportunity to do his job. His wife had picked up the slack. *His wife.* Once again, she'd kept the importance of the evening front and center while he wallowed in jealousy.

How dare she be so perfect and imperfect at the same time?

A few more fingers of scotch might have dulled the scent of strawberries. But he doubted it. When he was this close to his wife, nothing could dilute the crushing awareness.

Daniella's fingers danced across the back of her neck. His gut clenched as he realized what she was doing, but the protest died in his throat as her glittery dress waterfalled off her body, catching at the tips of her breasts for one breathless second. Then it puddled on the floor, baring her to his greedy gaze.

A beautiful, half-nude vision stood before him. Daniella, in all her glory. Fire raged south, ravaging everything in its path to his center, numbing his extremities and nearly bringing him to his knees.

It would be fitting to kneel before a goddess.

"Daniella." His raw voice scraped at his throat and he cleared it. "What are you doing?"

He knew. She was doing what he'd been pushing her to do. But she was supposed to slap him. Or storm out. Or push him in kind, the way she always did. As long as she punished him for being an ass, any response would have been fine.

Except this. And it was a far more suitable penance to get exactly what he asked for.

"I'm eliminating the problems," she said, head held high. "*All* the problems."

That was impossible, let alone this way. "Put your clothes back on. I'm—"

Actually, he had no clue what he was. Nothing could have prepared him to feel so…ill equipped to be in the same room with a woman who radiated power and sensual energy.

He shut his eyes.

Strip yourself as bare as your body, she'd suggested. But his wife's simple act of disrobing, of making herself vulnerable, had accomplished that for him, even while he was still fully dressed.

Everything about her touched him in places no one had ever dared tread.

This night was not going to end well. She wanted something he couldn't allow himself to give her. Once that bottle was uncorked, he'd focus on nothing but Daniella and lose his drive to succeed. Then he'd fail her—and himself—on a whole different level, which he could not accept.

"Leo." The softness in her voice nearly shattered him. "Open your eyes. Look at me."

He did. God help him, but he couldn't resist. His gaze sought hers, not the gorgeous bare breasts there for his viewing pleasure. His eyes burned with effort to keep them trained straight ahead.

"I would never—" she emphasized the word with a slash of her hand "—dishonor you with anyone else, let alone a friend or a business partner. I respect you too much. I'm sorry if I behaved in a way that made you question that."

Her words, sweetly issued and completely sincere, wrenched that hollow place inside. He'd been treating her horribly all night for who knew what reason and she was apologizing. "You didn't. You were just being a good hostess."

A very poor depiction of how absolutely stellar a party she'd thrown. She deserved far more than degradation at the hands of her husband. Far more than the absent, unavailable man she'd cleaved to.

"I really hope you think so." Her expression warmed. "You're the only man I want. Forever. That's why I married you."

The sentiment flowed like warm honey through his chest. This was the kind of romantic nonsense he'd gone to EA International to avoid. But then, wasn't she describing exactly what he'd asked for? Fidelity and commitment? It just sounded like so much *more* than that from her mouth, so deep and profound.

What was he supposed to do with that? With her?

"Don't you want me, too?" she asked, her voice dropping into a seductive whisper that funneled straight to his erection.

"So much more than I should," he muttered and regretted saying it out loud.

"Then come over here and show me."

His feet were rooted to the carpet. It wasn't going to be just sex. Maybe just sex wasn't possible with someone he'd made his wife.

Regardless, he'd married Daniella, and consummating their relationship meant they were embarking on forever at this very moment.

Part of him strained to dash for the door, to down the rest of the scotch until the unquenchable thirst for Daniella faded from memory. Then he wouldn't have to deal with the other part that compelled him to accept everything she was offering him, even the alarming nebulous nonphysical things.

"So the touching moratorium is lifted?" he asked. "Or is this the precursor to another round of rules?"

Apparently he wasn't finished lashing out at her. If he infuriated her enough to leave, they could go back to circling each other and he'd put off finding out exactly how weak he was.

He didn't want her to leave.

"This is about nothing more than being together. Do whatever feels right to you." She spread her arms, jutting out her perfectly mounded breasts. His mouth tingled and he imagined he could taste one. "Standing here in nothing other than a tiny thong is turning me into Jell-O. I'd really like it if you'd kiss me now."

"A thong?" He'd been so focused on her front, the back hadn't even registered. The feel of silk beneath his pinky when he'd pushed past the fabric at her waist during the party rushed back and he groaned.

Slowly, she half turned and cocked a hip, bare cheek thrust out. "I wore it for you. Hoping you'd pick tonight to make me your wife in more than name only."

He was so hard he couldn't breathe. Let alone walk. Or kiss. Neither was he ready to cross that line, to find out how far she'd suck him down the rabbit hole if he gave in to the maelstrom of need.

Her lips curved up in a secret, naughty smile. Palms flat against her waist, she smoothed them downward over the curve of her rear, down her thighs. "If you're not going to touch me, I'll just do it myself."

Provocatively, she teased one of her nipples with an index finger. Her eyes fluttered halfway closed in apparent pleasure and he swore. Enough was enough.

She was serious. No more choices, rules, games or guidelines. She wanted him.

It was too late to address all the lingering questions about the status of their relationship or how this would change it. It was too late to imagine he'd escape, and far too late to pretend he wanted to.

Daniella was going in the lover box. Now.

In one stride, he crossed the space between them and swept her up in his arms. He swallowed her gasp a moment before his lips captured hers. Crushing her against him, he leaped into the carnal desire she'd incited all night. Actually, since that first glimpse of her on the stairs at their wedding. Every moment in between.

Their mouths aligned, opened, fed. Eagerly, she slid her tongue along his, inviting him deeper. He delved willingly, exploring leisurely because this time there'd be no interruptions.

He was going to make Daniella his, once and for all. Then he'd recover his singular concentration and no more deals would slip away as he daydreamed.

The taste of her sang through his veins and instead of weakening him, she gave him strength. Enough strength to pleasure this woman until she cried out with it. Enough to grant her what she'd been begging for. Enough to make love to her all night long.

He'd hold on to that strength, because he'd need it to walk away again in the morning. It was the only outcome he'd allow, to delve into the physical realm without losing himself in it. Just tonight, just once.

Leo broke the kiss long enough to pick her up in his arms. Carefully, he laid her out on the bed and spent a long moment drinking in the panorama of his wife's gorgeous body. All that divine skin pleaded for his touch, so he indulged himself, running fingertips down her arms, over the peaks and valleys of her torso and all the way down to her siren-red toenails.

He glanced at her face. She was so sensuously lost in pleasure, his pulse nearly doubled instantly.

She shivered.

"Cold?" he asked.

Shaking her head, she got up on her knees and pulled his tie free. "Hot. For you."

Then she slid off his jacket and went to work on the buttons of his shirt, watching him as she slipped them free.

Finally, she'd completely undressed him. Taking her in his arms, he rolled with her to the middle of the bed and picked up the kiss where they'd left off.

Her lips molded to his and his mind drained as her warm body snugged up against him. They were naked together, finally. Physically, at least.

Almost naked. He skimmed a hand down her spine and fingered the thong. Silky. Sexy. She'd worn it for him. If he'd known that, the party would have been over at about seven-thirty.

Her palm raced across his skin in kind and her touch ignited an urgency he couldn't allow. He'd take as little pleasure from this as possible. Otherwise he'd never leave the bed. It was a delicate balance, made more complicated by the fact that no matter what she'd said, she still wished for something cataclysmic out of this.

He'd make it as physically cataclysmic as he could. That was the best he could do.

Still deep in her mouth, he yanked off the thong and then explored her torso with tiny openmouthed kisses until he reached her core. There, he licked her with the very tip of his tongue.

"Leo," she gasped, which only drove his urgency higher.

"You taste like heaven." He wanted more and took her nub in his mouth to nibble it gently, then harder, laving his tongue against it until she writhed beneath his onslaught.

Mewls deep in her throat attested to her mindless pleasure and then she cried, "More. I'm about to come," which was so hot it shoved him to the brink.

His erection pulsed and he clamped down, aching with the effort to keep from exploding. He drove a finger into her wet core, then two, and tongued her and she arched up as she clinched around him, shattering into a beautiful climax.

He rose up and tilted her chin to soak up the sated, satisfied glint in her eyes as he gave her a minute to recover. But not too long. When her breathing slowed a bit, he guided her hands upward and curled them around the top edge of the headboard.

If she touched him, he'd lose all his hard-won control.

"Hold on," he murmured, and she did, so trusting, so eager.

He parted her thighs and slowly pushed into her. Rapture stole across her face, thrilling him. She enveloped him like a vise, squeezing tight. She was amazing, open, wet.

His vision flickered as Daniella swamped his senses.

More. He thrust into her. *Again.*

Desire built, heavy and thick, and he thumbed her nub, circling it. Heat broke over him and he ached to come but needed her to come first. To prove he wasn't weak, and that he could still resist her.

"Daniella," he ground out hoarsely, and she captured his gaze.

He couldn't break free.

Everything shrank down to this one suspended moment and her bottomless, tender irises ensnared him, encouraging him to just feel. And he did feel it, against his will, but heaviness spread alarmingly fast through his chest, displacing what should be there. Against all odds, she'd wrenched something foreign and indefinable and magnificent from his very depths.

Only one thing could encapsulate it, one word. "Dannie."

It left his mouth on a broken plea and she answered with a cry, convulsing around him, triggering his release. He poured all his desire, all his confusion—and what he feared might be part of his soul—into her, groaning with sensual gratification he'd never meant to experience.

Daniella had taken his name, taken his body. Taken something primal and physical and turned it into poetry. The awe of it engulfed him, washing through his chest. He wanted to mark every page of her again and again and never stop. And let her do the same to him.

Intellectually, he'd realized long ago that one small taste of her would never be enough. But the actual experience had burst from its neat little box, crushing the sides, eclipsing even his wildest fantasies.

He couldn't allow himself to indulge like that again. Otherwise his wife would swallow him whole and take every bit of his ambition with her.

Nine

Dannie awoke at dawn tangled with Leo. Her husband, in every sense.

Muscles ached and begged to be stretched so beautifully again. Above all, her heart longed to hear him say "Dannie" with such raw yearning as they joined. Like he had last night, in that smoking-hot voice.

The bedroom-sharing plan deserved an award.

Leo was still asleep, but holding her tightly against him with his strong forearms, her back against his firm front. The position seemed incongruous for someone so determined to remain distanced. But in sleep, his body told her what he couldn't say with his mouth.

He craved a relationship with her, too. The yearning bled from him in waves every moment she spent in his company. It was all over the good deeds he did behind the scenes, which she no longer believed were designed to avoid emotional investment.

He just didn't know how to reach out. And she'd gladly taken on the job of teaching him.

As he guided her toward her full potential as his wife, she'd done the same, pushing him to keep opening up, giving him what he needed. She'd keep on doing it until he embraced everything this marriage could be. The rewards of being the woman behind the man were priceless.

She hated to disturb him, but his front was growing

firmer by the moment and it pressed hot and hard against her suddenly sensitized flesh.

Heat gathered at the center of her universe and her breath caught.

Involuntarily, her back arched, pushing her sex against his erection. She rubbed back and forth experimentally. Hunger shafted through her. Oh, *yes*.

Then his whole body stiffened and his hands curled against her hips, forcing her to be still. Awake, and obviously not on board with a round of morning love.

Wiggling backward, she deliberately teased him without words.

"Daniella," he murmured thickly. "Stop. I forgot to set my alarm. I have to go to work."

"Yes, you do." She wiggled again, harder, and he sucked in a ragged breath. "Ten minutes. I'm so turned on, I'm almost there already."

Cool air rushed against her back as he rolled away and left the bed without another word.

Her heart crashed against her ribs as he disappeared into the bathroom. The shower hummed through the walls.

Nothing had changed between them.

Last night had meant everything to her. But she'd vastly overplayed her hand. Instead of viewing it as a precious stepping-stone toward a fulfilling marriage, Leo seemed perfectly content to sleep with her at night and ignore her the rest of the day.

Exactly what he'd warned her would happen.

She had no call to be disappointed. She'd given him what he needed and hoped it would be the beginning of their grand, sweeping love affair. It obviously wasn't. She'd dropped her dress, pushed him into making that final move and, for her effort, got a round of admittedly earth-shattering sex. She'd even given him permission to do whatever felt right.

At what point had she asked for anything more?

Since the *I do*s, she'd put considerable effort into preventing screwups, convinced each successful event or household task solidified her role as Mrs. Reynolds.

It never occurred to her the real screwup would happen when she invented a fictional future where Leo became the husband of her dreams.

Flinging the covers up over her shoulder, she buried herself in the bed, dry-eyed, until Leo left the bedroom without saying goodbye.

Then she let her eyes burn for an eternity, refusing to let the tears fall.

Her stupid phone's musical ringtone split the air. *Leo.*

Bolting upright, she bobbled the phone into her hands. He was calling to apologize. Tell her good morning. That it had been a great party. Something.

A bitter taste rose at the back of her throat when she saw *Mom* on the caller ID. She swallowed and answered.

"Hi," she said and her voice broke in half.

"What's wrong, baby?"

Great, now her mother was concerned. Worrying her mother was the last thing Dannie wanted.

"Nothing," she lied brightly. "I'm still in bed. Haven't woken up yet. How are you?"

"Fine." A round of coughing negated that. "Do you want to have lunch today?"

Oh, that would never do. Her mother would instantly see the hurt in her heart blossoming on Dannie's face. She had to get over the disenchantment first. "I've got a few things to do. Maybe tomorrow?"

"I'm leaving on the cruise tomorrow. Did you forget? I wanted to see you before I go."

Yes, she had forgotten and it was a brutal reminder about what was important—her mother. Not Dannie's bruised feelings.

Suck it up, honey. "I can rearrange my appointments. I'll pick you up around eleven, okay?"

"Yes! I'll see you then."

Dannie hung up, heaved a deep shuddery breath and hit the shower to wash away every trace of Leo from her body. If only she could wipe him from her mind as easily, but his invisible presence stained the atmosphere of the entire house.

She fought tears for twenty excruciating minutes as the car sped toward her mother's.

The driver paused at the curb outside her mother's apartment and Dannie frowned. Paint peeled from the wood siding and weeds choked the grass surrounding the front walk. The shabbiness had never bothered her before. How was it fair that Dannie got to live in the lap of luxury but her mother suffered both pulmonary fibrosis and near poverty?

But what could Dannie do about it? She didn't have any money of her own—everything was Leo's. A nasty voice inside suggested he could pony up alternative living space for her mother in reciprocation for last night.

She hushed up that thought immediately. Leo hadn't treated her like that. He'd told her what would happen on more than one occasion and she'd chosen to create a fairy tale in her head where love conquered all.

Her mom slid into the car and beamed at Dannie. The nurse had done wonders to improve her mother's quality of life with daily pulmonary therapy and equally important emotional support.

"I'm so glad to see you, baby," her mom gushed.

The driver raised the glass panel between the front seat and the back, then pulled out into the flow of traffic to ferry them to the restaurant. Dannie leaned into her mother's cheek buss and smiled. "Glad to see you, too."

What ills could she possibly have that Mom couldn't make all better? The pricking at her eyelids grew worse.

Her mother's hands on her jaw firmed. "Uh, oh. What happened?"

She should have known better—sonar had nothing on a

mom's ability to see beneath the surface. Dannie pulled her face from her mother's grasp and looked out the window in the opposite direction. "Nothing. Leo and I had a little… misunderstanding. I'll get over it."

Probing silence settled on her chest and she risked a glance at her mother. She was watching her with an unreadable expression. "Nothing serious, I hope."

Dannie half laughed. "Not in his opinion."

With a sigh of relief, her mother settled back against the seat. "That's good."

"Well, I don't think he's planning to divorce me, if that's what you're worried about."

At least not yet. By all rights, her desperate mental reorganization of their arrangement should have resulted in a firm boot to the backside long before now. Yet, he hadn't breathed a word about divorce, so apparently he still needed her for reasons of his own.

"Of course that's a concern." Her mother's warm hand found Dannie's elbow. "Fortunately, you married a solid, respectable man who believes in commitment. A very wise choice. You'll never end up brokenhearted and alone like I did."

Yes. That was the purpose of this marriage. Not grand, sweeping passion and a timeless love. This was a job. Wife was her career. Hardening her heart against the tiny tendrils of feelings she'd allowed to bloom last night in Leo's arms, Dannie nodded. "You're right. Leo is a good man."

The muted sound of sirens filtered through the car's interior a moment before an ambulance whizzed by in the opposite direction. She'd ridden in an ambulance for the first time not too long ago, on the way to the hospital, with her mother strapped to a gurney and fighting to breathe. When the bill came, she'd gone to the library that same day seeking a way to pay it.

And now she was riding in the modern-day equivalent

of a horse-drawn carriage, but better because it had air-conditioning and leather seats.

Leo had saved them both, providing security for her and for her mother. She couldn't lose sight of that again. He'd held up his end of the bargain honestly. It was time for her to do the same and stop wallowing in the mire of lost romance that she'd never been promised in the first place.

Love didn't work out for other people. Why would it be any different for her?

"The misunderstanding wasn't over the possibility of children, was it?" her mother asked.

Hesitantly, Dannie shook her head.

They hadn't used protection. Actually, she could be pregnant right now. Warmth soaked through her chilled soul. If Leo gave her a child, his absence would be notably less difficult. Her mother had raised her single-handedly. Dannie could do that, too.

Funny how she hadn't thought about procreation once last night. Yet children had been foremost on her mind when she'd agreed to marry Leo. Back when she assumed there was no possibility of more between them than an arrangement. Now she knew for a fact there was no possibility.

Suck it up. She pasted on a smile for her mother. "Tell me more about the cruise."

Her mother chatted all through lunch and Dannie responded, but couldn't have repeated the content of their discussion for a million dollars. Fortunately, Leo didn't come up again. That she would have remembered.

Leo didn't call and didn't join her for dinner. She got ready for bed, resigned to sleeping alone.

At ten o'clock, he strolled into the bedroom.

Her gaze flicked over him hungrily, searching for small clues to the state of mind of the man who'd put his lips on her body in very inventive ways not twenty-four hours ago.

"Hi," she said politely and flicked off the TV she'd been

staring at for who knew how long with no idea what was on. "How was your day?"

"Fine," he said. "I got you something."

Her eyebrows rose. "Like a present?"

Lifting the small silver gift bag clutched in his fingers, he nodded and crossed to the bed to hand it to her. She spilled out the contents and opened the square box. Diamond earrings sparkled against royal-blue velvet.

The box burned her hand and she threw it on the bedside table. "Thank Mrs. Gordon for me. She has lovely taste."

His face instantly turned into a brick wall. "I spent an hour picking them out myself. To thank you for the party. You were amazing. I should have told you before now."

"I'm sorry." Remorse clogged her throat. What had happened to the quiet, demure girl Elise created? Lately, Dannie rarely thought twice about what came out of her mouth. "That was obnoxious."

"And well earned." He cleared his throat and sought her gaze, his blue eyes liquid. "I'm sorry I left the way I did this morning. That was *far* more obnoxious. And undeserved."

"Oh." He'd robbed her of speech. Which was probably fortunate, since the question on the tip of her tongue was, *Why* did *you leave that way, then?* She didn't ask. If he'd intended for her to know, he'd have told her.

Regardless, he'd apologized. *Apologized.* And bought her a present.

Leo retrieved the box and handed it to her. "Will you wear the earrings? I'll take them back if you don't like them."

A touch of the vulnerability she'd witnessed last night darted across his expression. The earrings represented both a thank-you and an apology and he wanted her to like them. Just when she thought she had the dynamic between them straight in her head, he flipped it upside down.

"I love them." She unscrewed the backs and stuck them in her ears, then struck a pose. "How do they look?"

"Beautiful." His gaze skittered down her body and back up again. He wasn't even looking at her ears.

A wealth of undisclosed desire crackled below the surface. Some of it was physical. But not all. He'd picked out the earrings himself. What did that mean? She'd lay odds *he* didn't even know what the significance of that was.

Last night, she'd learned one surefire way to communicate with him.

She flung back the covers and crawled to him. He watched her, his body poised to flee, but she snagged his lapels before he could. Without speaking, she peeled his jacket from his shoulders and teased his lips with hers as she unknotted his tie.

"Daniella." He groaned against her lips and pulled back a fraction. "The earrings weren't... I'm not—"

"Shh. It's okay." The tie came apart in her hands and she leaned into him, rubbing his chest in small circles with her pebbled nipples.

Almost imperceptibly, he shook his head. "I don't expect sex in exchange for jewelry."

How could such a simple statement sink hooks so deeply into her heart? He was trying so hard to be honorable, so hard to keep from hurting her at great expense to himself. "And I don't expect jewelry in exchange for sex. Now that's out of the way. Shut up and put your hands on me."

His eyelids flew closed and he swallowed. That was close enough to a yes for her. She bridged the gap and claimed his lips with hers.

Winding the ends of his tie around her hands, she pulled him closer and deepened the kiss. A firestorm swept outward from their joined lips, incinerating her control.

Urgently, wordlessly, she undressed him, desperate to bare Leo in the only way he'd allow. He ripped off her pajamas and they fell to the bed already intertwined.

Leo kissed her and it was long and thorough. *This* was the man who'd held her in his sleep. The man who'd whispered

her name with gut-wrenching openness. As she'd known beyond a shadow of a doubt, this joining of bodies spoke vol-
umes beyond the scope of mere words. And it said Leo had
far more going on beneath the surface than he dared let on.

As she cradled her husband's beautiful body and stared
into the depths of his hot-with-passion blue eyes, something
blossomed inside. Something huge and reckless, and she
tamped it down with no small effort. But it rose up again,
laced with images of Leo's child growing in her womb. She
imagined the tenderness of his gaze as he looked down on
their newborn child and the back of her throat heated.

Suddenly, the fear of Leo tiring of her romantic foolishness wasn't her only problem anymore.

She'd traded it for the painful, diametrically opposite
problem of what was going to happen if she fell in love
with him and doomed herself to a lifetime of marriage to a
man who would forever keep his kind heart buried beneath
a workaholic shell.

Tap. Tap. Tap.

Leo blinked and glanced up. Dax tapped his pen a few
more times, his face expressionless as he nodded to the
laptop screen filled with verbiage regarding the proposed
joint venture to finance a start-up company called Mastermind Media.

"Clause two?" Dax prompted and lowered a brow. "They
agreed to extend the deadline to midnight. We don't have
long. You were supposed to be telling me why you don't
like it."

*I don't like it because it's standing between me and a
bed with my wife in it.*

Theoretically, that applied to the entire proposal he and
Dax had been tearing apart since four-thirty with only a
short break for General Tso's chicken in bad sauce from
Jade Dragon.

Leo stole a peek at his watch. Nine o'clock on a Friday night.

If he left the office now, he could be home in twenty minutes. Sixteen if he ignored the speed limit. He might even text Daniella as he drove to let her know he'd be there soon. Maybe she'd greet him wearing nothing but the diamonds he'd given her.

What started as a simple thank-you gift had somehow transformed into something else. Hell if he knew what. He hadn't intended to make love to her again. At least not this soon, not while he was still struggling to maintain some semblance of control around her.

But one minute Daniella was threading the diamonds through her ears, and the next...

The memory of last night and his sexy wife invaded his mind. Again. The way she'd been doing all day.

"The clause is fine." *No.* It wasn't. Leo shook his head and tried to focus. "It will be fine. With a minor tweak to the marketing expectations."

More tapping. Then Dax tossed down his pen with a sense of finality.

"Leo." Dax shrank down in the high-backed chair and laced his hands over one knee, contemplating the ebony conference table. Lines appeared across his forehead. "I'm starting to get the impression you don't think we should do this deal."

"What?" Leo flinched. *No more daydreaming.* What was wrong with him? "I've put in sixty hours on this. It's a solid proposal."

"Then what's up?" His friend eyed him, concern evident in his expression. "We've been looking at Mastermind Media for months. If you're worried about you and me doing business together, you should have spoken up long before now."

Hesitating, Leo rolled his neck. They'd known each other

more than fifteen years—since college. Dax was the one person who'd call him on it if Leo zoned out. "That's not it."

"Is the financing sticky?" Dax frowned, wrinkling his pretty-boy face. "You're not using your own money on this because of our relationship, are you?"

"Of course not." Venture capital relied on other people's money. Leo never risked anything he didn't have to.

"I've run out of teeth to pull. Spill. Or I'm walking."

Walking. As in, he'd purposefully let the deal expire because Leo wanted to go home and sleep with his wife. He sighed. Apparently losing John Hu hadn't been enough of a wake-up call.

"I'm distracted. Sorry. It's not the proposal. Something else."

Something that needed to stop. Leo's will was ironclad and had been since he was seventeen. How had Daniella destroyed it so easily?

Dax smirked. "I should have known. You've been different since you married that woman."

He wasn't the slightest bit different. Was he?

"Watch your tone."

Friendship or not, Dax had no call to refer to Daniella as "that woman," as if Leo had hooked up with a chain-smoker in a tube top, straight from the trailer park. He'd deliberately chosen a classy, elegant woman. Not one who mirrored his childhood neighbors in the near ghetto.

Throwing up his hands dramatically, Dax flipped his gaze heavenward. "It begins. We've been through a lot of women together, my friend. What's so special about this one?"

The answer should be nothing. But it wasn't.

"I married her."

And now he was lying to his best friend. Not only was that just part of the answer, it was the tip of the iceberg. He couldn't stop thinking about her. About how beautifully she'd handled the party. Her laugh. The way she took care of things, especially him, with some kind of extrasensory perception.

When he was inside her, his world shifted. He'd never realized his world *could* be shifted. Or that he'd like its new tilt so much. That he'd willingly slide down Daniella's slippery incline.

Snorting, Dax glanced at the laptop screen positioned between their chairs and tapped on the keyboard. "So? It's not like you have feelings for her. She's a means to an end."

A vehement protest almost left his mouth unchecked. But Dax was right. Why would he protest? Daniella *was* a means to an end, like Leo had told him. It just sounded so cold from his friend's perspective. "Feelings aside, she's my wife. Not a casual date. It's important for her to be happy."

"Why? Because she might leave you? Think again. Gold diggers don't bite the hand that feeds them."

Quick-burning anger sliced through Leo's gut. "She's not a gold digger. Our marriage is beneficial to us both. You know that. Surely you don't believe it's acceptable for me to treat my wife like a dog and expect her to put up with it because I have money."

Dax quirked one eyebrow. "Like I said. This one is special."

Leo rolled his eyes. Dax saw meaning where there was none. Except they knew each other well. The Chinese food churned through Leo's stomach greasily. Or maybe that was a smear of guilt.

His track record with women spoke for itself—he wouldn't win any awards for tenderness, attentiveness or commitment. And maybe he did buy expensive presents to apologize for all of the above.

"Let's have this conversation again when *you* get married."

"Ha. That's a good one. There's no *when* in that statement. There's hardly an *if.* Women are good for one thing." Dax flashed his teeth. "They give you a reason to drink."

Perfect subject-change material. "Things not going well with Jenna?"

Too bad. Dax obviously needed someone in his life who could knock down all his commitment and trust issues. Jenna wasn't the right woman for that anyway.

"What are you talking about? She's great. The sex is fantastic." Waggling his brows, Dax leaned back in his chair. "Well, you know."

Leo's already unsettled stomach turned inside out at Dax's smarmy reference to the fact that she'd been Leo's lover first. Had Leo always treated women so casually, blowing it off as a necessary evil of success?

No. Not always. Daniella *was* special, but not the way Dax implied. Leo had treated her differently from the beginning, demonstrating a healthy respect for the institution of marriage. That's all. He was making an iceberg out of an ice cube.

Dax sat up to type out a few more corrections to the proposal. "Judging by the way you couldn't keep your eyes off Daniella at the party the other night, she must be a wildcat. Let me know if you get tired of her."

The chair's wheels squealed as Leo launched to his feet. Staring down at Dax, he crossed his arms so he didn't punch his oldest friend. "I strongly suggest you close your trap before I do it for you."

"Jeez, Leo. Calm down. She's just a woman."

"And you're just a friend." When Dax glanced up, surprise evident, Leo skewered him with a glare that couldn't possibly be misinterpreted. "Things change. Get over it."

Slowly, Dax rose to his feet. Eye to eye, they faced off and Leo didn't like the glint flashing in his friend's gaze as Dax gave Leo's stiff carriage a once-over.

"I can't believe you'd let a chick come between us. Especially not one you found through a matchmaker." Dax nearly spat the word. "Let the deal with Mastermind expire. When you come back from la-la land and realize you've lost your edge over an admittedly nice pair of boobs, I'll be around to help you pick up the pieces. We've been friends too long."

Dax stepped back and Leo let him, though his fingers were still curled into a nice, fat fist that ached to rearrange that pretty-boy face. "I agree. It's best not to go into business together right now."

"Go home to your wife," Dax called over his shoulder as he gathered his bag, phone and travel coffee mug. "I hope she's good enough in bed to help you forget how much money we just lost."

He strode out the door of Leo's conference room without a backward glance.

Sinking into the nearest chair, Leo stared out the window at the green argon lights lining the Bank of America Plaza skyscraper. Since the building housed the headquarters of Dax's far-flung media empire, the familiar outline drove the barb further into Leo's gut.

Yeah, they'd lost a lot of money. And a friendship.

He didn't imagine for a second this rift would be easily repaired. Not because of the sense of betrayal Leo felt, and not because Dax had said reprehensible things about Leo's wife.

But because Dax was right. Leo had changed since marrying Daniella. No longer could he stomach being that guy Dax described, who treated women horribly but rationalized it away and bought them shiny presents to make up for it. Or that guy who wasn't bothered by introducing an ex-girlfriend to Dax because she hadn't meant anything to him.

Dax didn't see a problem with either. Leo couldn't continue to be friends with someone who held such a low opinion of women. Why hadn't he seen that long before now? And what would it take to get Dax to recognize the problem? Maybe Dax should visit a matchmaker himself. If Elise could find the perfect woman for Leo, she could do it for anyone.

Losing the friendship hurt. Letting the deadline expire

for their proposal to Mastermind Media hurt worse. In his entire professional career, he'd never willfully given up. And one thing hadn't changed, would never change—Leo also didn't want to be that guy who lost deals or worse, lost his edge. For any reason. Let alone over a woman who drove him to distraction.

He'd lost John Hu. Now this deal. Was Tommy Garrett next?

He refused to allow that to happen. Daniella's invisible, ill-defined hold on him had to end. Immediately. He'd tried ignoring her. He'd tried sleeping at the office. He'd even tried going in the opposite direction and allowing himself small tastes of her. None of that had worked to exorcise his wife from his consciousness.

So he'd have to try the only thing left. He was going to spend the weekend in bed with Daniella in full-on immersion. By Monday, she would be out of his system and he'd have his focus back. He could share a house with her at night and forget about her during the day, like he'd planned all along.

It had to work. He'd toiled so hard to build a secure company and he owed it to everyone to maintain it. Especially Daniella. He'd vowed to care for her and he'd scrub floors at a state prison before he'd allow his wife to live next door to a meth lab like his own father had.

Ten

The book Dannie was reading held her interest about as well as the last one. Which was to say not at all. She'd parked on the settee to wait in hopes that Leo might come home soon, but it was already almost ten o'clock.

One more page. The story had to get better at some point. If it didn't, she'd get ready for bed. Leo's alarm went off before dawn and she was still adjusting to his routine.

The atmosphere shifted and she glanced up from her e-reader. Leo stood in the open doorway, one hand on the frame and the other clutching a bouquet of red roses. And he was watching her with undisguised, delicious hunger.

Heat erupted at her center and radiated outward, flushing her whole body. The e-reader fell to the carpet with a thunk, released by her suddenly nerveless fingers.

"Roses? For me?" Her voice trembled, and he didn't miss it. Her temperature rose as his expression darkened.

"In a manner of speaking." Striding to the settee, he held out his free hand and when she took it, he pulled her to her feet. His torso brushed hers and her nipples hardened. "Follow me."

Anywhere.

Mystified, she trailed him into the bathroom, where he flicked on the lights to one-quarter brightness and began filling the bathtub. Over his shoulder, he called, "It probably hasn't escaped your notice that I work a lot. I have very little opportunity to indulge in simple pleasures. So I'm correcting that oversight right now. I have this fantasy involving you, me and rose petals. This time of night, I had to buy them still attached."

He gathered the petals in one hand and wrenched them from the stalks, then released them into the water.

As the red circles floated down to rest on the surface, her heart tumbled along with them. "You have fantasies about me?"

The look on his face shot her temperature up another four thousand notches.

"Constantly."

"What am I doing in these fantasies?" she asked, her tongue nearly tripping over the words.

"Driving me pomegranates, mostly." He grinned and it was so un-Leo-like she did a double take. "By the way, I'm taking the weekend off. If you don't have other plans, I'd like to spend it with you. Maybe we could consider it a delayed honeymoon."

Honeymoon? *Weekend off?* She jammed her hands down on her hips and stared at him. "Who are you and what have you done with Leonardo Reynolds?"

His expression turned sheepish and he shrugged. "Let's say I had a revelation. We're married. I have to do things differently than I've done in the past. I *want* to do things differently," he stressed. "For you. Because you deserve it. You're a great wife."

A hard, painful lump slammed into her throat. He wanted to spend time with her. Romance her, as she'd asked. The roses were reciprocation—one great husband, coming up.

Little stabs at the corners of her eyes warned of an imminent deluge. What was he trying to do to her? She'd just become good and convinced their marriage was enough as it was. Now this.

I will not cry. I will not cry.

"You ain't seen nothing yet."

"Yeah?" He twisted the faucet handle and shut off the water. "You've been holding out on me?"

"Maybe. Talk to me about these fantasies." A good, strong dose of Leo's potent masculinity—that was what she needed to keep the emotion where it belonged. Inside. At least until she figured out where all this was coming from. Her husband had done so many about-faces she couldn't help but be slightly wary. "Have you really had a lot about me? Like what?"

"Oh, I've been so remiss, haven't I?" He tsked and sat on the edge of the garden tub, feet on the lowest step leading up to the rim. "Come here."

Her toes curled against the cold travertine as she approached and then she forgot all about a small thing like bare feet as Leo drew her between his split legs, his gaze heavy lidded with sensuous promise.

"I've been a very bad husband," he told her. "You clearly have no idea how wickedly sexy I find you. Let's correct that oversight, too, while we're at it."

Her insides disintegrated and she had no idea how she was still standing with no bones.

Slowly, he loosened each button on her blouse, widening the vee over her bra until he'd bared it entirely. The shirt slipped from her shoulders and Leo reeled in the fabric, pulling her forward.

"My fantasies are no match for the real thing." His open mouth settled onto the curve of her breast where the edge of her bra met skin. His tongue darted inside, circling her nipple. Pure, unaltered desire flared from her center, engulfing her senses.

Clutching at his shoulders, she moaned his name as he unzipped her skirt, still suckling her, wetting her bra with his ministrations. Impatiently, he peeled the cup from her breast and sucked the nipple between his teeth to scrape it lightly.

She pushed farther into his mouth and drowned in sensation as he lit her up expertly with a combination of hard teeth and magic hands against her bottom.

"Daniella," he murmured against her flesh, abrading it with slight five-o'clock shadow, which felt so amazing she shuddered.

Leo lifted his mouth and she nearly sobbed as it left her skin. He licked his lips in a slow, achingly obvious gesture designed to communicate how delicious he found her. Drinking in the sight of her pale pink bra-and-panty set, he reached around to unhook her bra, letting her breasts fall free.

He cursed, almost reverently. "Beautiful. You're the most beautiful woman I've ever seen. And you're all mine."

Her knees went numb, but his sure hands held her upright as he leaned down to kiss her waist, openmouthed, drawing her panties down simultaneously. His fingers trailed between her legs up the backside, wandering unchecked in some unknown pattern and thoroughly driving her insane.

"Leo," she choked out.

"Right here," he murmured and captured her hand. "In you go."

He led her up the stairs and into the tub, helping her lie back against the incline of the oval. She peeked up at him as he snagged a rose petal, swishing it through the water, through the valley of her breasts, around her already sensitized nipples. The motion shafted biting desire through her flesh.

When he rubbed the petal between her legs, a moan rumbled in her throat.

"Playtime is over." She yanked on his tie. "I want you in here with me."

His irises flared with dark heat.

Clothes began hitting the floor and she shamelessly watched as he revealed his taut body inch by maddeningly slow inch. A smattering of dark hair covered his chest, screaming his masculinity, and hard thighs perfectly showcased the prominent erection she wanted inside her with every shuddering breath.

He splashed into the water. The giant garden tub shrank as gorgeous, vibrant male filled it.

Leo grasped her arms and settled her into place against his chest spoon-style and immediately covered her breasts with his hands, kneading them. She gasped as his thick flesh ground hard against her rear.

Rose petals floated in the water, catching on wet skin, filling the air with their warm floral scent. He murmured wicked things in her ear as he touched her, and in combination with the warm water, his hands felt like silk against her skin, in her core, against her sensitive nub.

She reached behind her to grasp his erection. It filled her palm, hard and hot, and she caressed the slick tip. A groan ripped from deep in his chest.

He tore her hand away and clasped her hips, repositioned her and drove home in one swift stroke.

"Dannie," he whispered, his voice guttural, raw. Beautiful. It crawled inside her, filling her as surely as he filled her body. Clasping her close, he held her, torso heaving against her back as they lay joined in the water. Completed perfectly by the other.

After an eternity, he lifted her hips high enough to yank a long slice of heat from her center and eased her down again. They shuddered in pleasure together.

This *was* different. Leo was different. More focused. Drawing it out, allowing her to revel in the sensations, to feel so much more than the physical. It was a slow ride with plenty of mental scenery along the way.

Intense Leo was her new favorite and his brand of romance stole her breath.

"Dannie," he said again and increased the rhythm, hypnotically, sensuously.

He repeated her name over and over as he completed her. A dense torrent of heat gathered at the source and she split apart with a sob, not the slightest bit surprised he'd made her cry after all. She'd given him what he needed and it had been returned, tenfold.

What he'd started with the diamonds, he ended with the rose petals. She wasn't in the process of falling in love with him. It was done. Irrevocably. Wholly.

Her heart belonged to her husband.

"Leo, I…" What would he say if she told him? Surely he was in the throes, too. That's what this was all about, wasn't it? Their marriage looked different than what they'd originally thought. He wanted it to be different.

"Speechless? You?" He chuckled. "I'm incredibly flattered."

It took every ounce of Elise's personality-makeover training to bite back the words as he drained the tub and helped her out, then dried her with slow, tender swipes of a soft towel. This was too important to let Scarlett off the leash. Too important to screw up.

He'd never said he loved her. Only that he wanted to do things differently. Maybe this pseudohoneymoon was simply about sex. Goodness knew she'd given him permission to make it so often enough.

But honestly. If he didn't want her to fall in love with him, he should stop being so wonderful.

Leo threw on a robe and returned with flutes and a bottle of champagne. They drank it in bed while they talked about nothing and everything.

She kept looking for the right opening to blurt it all out. Shouldn't he know that he'd made her wildly happy? That their marriage was everything she'd ever dreamed of? Her feelings for Leo far eclipsed anything she'd ever felt for Rob. She'd found purpose and meaning in being a wife; she'd married a man who made her body and soul sing in perfect harmony and her mother was being taken care of. Leo was a sexy genie in a bottle, granting all her wishes effortlessly. She wanted to tell him.

The right moment never came.

He didn't shoot her long, lingering glances with his gaze full of love. When he took her glass and set it on the bedside table, then thoroughly ravished her, he didn't whisper the things in his heart while holding her.

Instead, he fell into a dead sleep. She lay awake, but he didn't murmur secret confessions into the darkness. Though he did seek her out while unconscious, sliding his solid thigh between hers and wrapping her up in a cloak of Leo. That part she had no difficulty understanding. He enjoyed having her in his bed. Enjoyed the closeness without the requirement of having to expose himself emotionally.

The feelings, the rush of love and tenderness, were strictly one-sided. For now.

Her marriage was *almost* everything she'd yearned for since she was a little girl. She had forty-eight hours to entice Leo that last few feet to the finish line.

When the early light of dawn through the triple bay window of the bedroom woke Leo, he didn't hesitate to indulge in another fantasy—the one he'd denied himself thus far.

He gripped Daniella's hips and wedged that sweet rear against his instant erection. His fingers trailed over her breasts and she sighed and it was sleepy. Erotic.

"Leo. It's—" One of her eyes popped open and immediately shut. "Six twenty-three. In the *morning.*"

"I know." He nuzzled her neck and she arched sensuously against him. "I slept sinfully late. It's refreshing."

"Thought you were taking the weekend off," she muttered and rolled her hips expertly. The cleft between her bare cheeks sandwiched his raging erection. His eyes crossed.

"Taking the weekend off to—" She did it again. Deliberately.

"Talk a lot?" she suggested sweetly and choked on the words as he skimmed a finger through the swollen folds of her center.

Closing his eyes, he breathed in the scent of crushed roses and the musk of Daniella's arousal. "Not hardly."

He sank into her and it was amazing. There was something about spooning with her that just killed him. They fit together this way, moving in perfect cadence as they had last night, and he savored it.

All her beauty was within easy reach and he made full use of the access, tweaking her gorgeous breasts and circling her nub as he sheathed himself from behind again and again. Hot friction sparked, driving them both faster.

She climaxed with a sexy moan and he followed in a brilliant chain reaction of sensation that didn't quit.

Playing hooky from work had a lot going for it. He was slightly ashamed at how much he was enjoying his weekend off, especially given that it had essentially just started. There was a lot more indulgence to be had. A lot more fantasies to enact. A lot more dread at the imminent reel back Monday morning.

How was he going to forget Daniella and concentrate on work? It was like ordering your heart not to beat so your lungs could function.

Eventually, they rolled out of bed and he let his wife make him pancakes. It beat an energy bar by quadruple. Her coffee, as always, was amazing. He hadn't enjoyed it with her since the first time she'd made it after he fell asleep at his desk. But he never left the house without a full travel mug. Somehow it had become part of his routine to drink it on the way to work. The empty mug sat on his desk all day and the sight of it made him smile.

"What should we do with all this borrowed time?" he asked her and forked another bite into his mouth as they sat at the bistro table in the breakfast nook.

Daniella peered at him over her coffee mug. "Is that what it is? Borrowed?"

"Well...yeah." Something in her frozen posture tipped him off that he might have stumbled into quicksand. "The initiatives I have going on at the office didn't magically disappear. I'm putting them off until Monday."

"I see."

"You sound disappointed." The next bite didn't go down so well. He could stand a lot of things, but Daniella's disappointment was not one of them.

She shook her head, long brown hair rippling the way it had this morning over his shoulder. "Just trying to interpret your phrasing. *Borrowed* implies you'll have to pay it back at some point. I don't want you to have to do that."

"I made the decision to spend the weekend with you. I wanted to. Don't feel guilty."

Her eyebrows lifted. "I don't. I mean I wish you didn't have to choose. Like you've got a lot of balls to juggle and I'm the one you happened to grab."

"What other choice do I have, Daniella?" Suddenly frustrated, he dropped his fork into the middle of his half-eaten pancakes. "I have a company to run. But I'm here with you now, aren't I? I'm juggling the best I can."

It was the voice of his worst fears—that he would drop a ball. Or all of them. He was horrible at juggling.

She laughed. "Yes, you're here, but it doesn't seem like either of us are fond of the juggling. Isn't there a way to whittle down the number of balls until you can hold them all in your hand? Maybe you can hire some additional staff members or change your focus."

"You're telling me to scale back my involvement in Reynolds Capital. Take on fewer partners."

His gut clenched at the mere thought of how quickly the company would dissolve if he did what she suggested. Venture capital was a carefully constructed illusion of leveraged moving parts. Like a Jenga puzzle. Move one piece the wrong way and the whole thing crashed into an ugly pile.

"I don't know what would work best. But you do." Casually, she sipped her coffee. "Why don't you try it? Then you don't have to borrow time from work to spend it with me."

Really? She'd morphed into the opposite of an under-standing wife who forgave her workaholic husband's sched-ule. He'd married her specifically to avoid this issue. Now she'd joined the ranks of every other woman he'd ever dated.

"*I'm* the Reynolds in Reynolds Capital. I spent a decade building the company from nothing and—" Quickly, he squashed his temper. *Give a woman an inch and forget a mile—she'll take the circumference of the Earth instead.*

"Forgive me if I overstepped. You were the one who said you wanted to do things differently and I was offering a solution. Less juggling would be different." She had the grace to smile as she covered his hand with her more deli-cate one. But he wasn't fooled. She had more strength in one pinky than most men did in their whole bodies. "I only meant to point out we all have choices and you make yours every day. That's all."

"Uh…" His temper fizzled. She'd only been trying to solve a problem *he'd* expressed. "Fair enough."

"Let's forget this conversation and enjoy our weekend."

Somehow, he had a feeling it wasn't going to be that simple. The die had been cast and she'd made a point with logic and style. Much to his discomfort.

True to his word, Leo didn't so much as glance at his phone or boot up his laptop once. He kept waiting for jitters to set in, like an addict deprived of his fix. The absence of being plugged in should be taking a toll. It wasn't.

He wrote it off as a keen awareness that he owed Dani-ella his attention until Monday morning. And then there was her gift for distraction. By midafternoon, they were naked in the warmed spa adjacent to the pool. He easily for-got about the blinking message light on his phone as they christened the spa.

He'd immersed himself in his wife's deep water and sur-facing was the last thing on his mind.

So it was a bit of a shock to join Daniella in the media

room for a late movie and have her announce with no fan-
fare, "You need to call Tommy Garrett."

"Tommy? Why? How do you know?" Leo set down the
bottle of wine and stemware he'd gone to the cellar to re-
trieve and pulled the corkscrew from his pocket.

"He's been trying to reach you all day. He called my cell
phone, wondering if you'd been rushed to the hospital."

About a hundred things careened through his head, but
first things first. "How does Tommy have your cell phone
number?"

Anger flared from his gut, as shocking as it was powerful.

"Don't wave all that testosterone in my face. How do
you imagine he RSVP'd for your party if he didn't have my
cell phone number?" She arched a brow. "Pony Express?"

His stomach settled. Slightly. He eased the cork from
the bottle and poured two glasses. Wine scraped down his
throat, burning against the shame already coating it. "I'm
sorry. I don't know where that comes from."

"It's okay. It makes me all gushy inside to know you
care." She giggled at his expression. "The movie can wait.
Call Tommy. It seemed rather urgent."

Grumbling, he went in search of his phone and found it
on the counter in the kitchen. Yeah, Tommy had called a
time or twelve. Four text messages, one in all caps.

He hit Callback and shook his head. Kids.

"Leo. Finally," Tommy exclaimed when the call connected. "My lawyers got all their crap straightened out.
I'm going with you, man. Let's get started taking the world
by storm."

Leo blindly searched for a seat. His hand hit a bar stool
at the kitchen island. Good enough. "You're accepting my
proposal?"

"That's what I said, isn't it? Why didn't you answer
your phone, by the way?" Munching sounds filled a sudden pause. Tommy lived on Doritos and Red Bull, which

Leo always kept on hand at the office in case of impromptu meetings. Thankfully, there'd be a lot more of those in the future. "Took me forever to find Dannie's number again. I didn't save it to my contacts."

"I'm taking some…" Leo's mouth dried up and he had to force the rest. "Time off."

This was it—the Holy Grail of everything he'd worked for. Now Leo would find out if he was as good as he thought he was at selecting a winner. But not today. He'd have to sit on his hands for the rest of the weekend.

"That's cool. We can talk mañana."

It was physically painful for Leo to open his mouth and say, "It'll have to be Monday."

"Seriously?" Tommy huffed out a noise of disgust that crawled up Leo's spine. "Well, I gotta say. I'd tell you to piss off, too, if I had a woman at home like Dannie. They sure don't make many of 'em like that. I'll be by on Monday."

Leo bit his tongue. Hard. Because what could he say to refute that? Daniella *was* the reason Leo couldn't talk shop on a Sunday when normally no hour of the day or night was too sacred to pour more cement in the foundation of Reynolds Capital Management's success.

But dear God, it was difficult to swallow.

Even harder was the task of sitting next to his wife on the plush couch in the media room and *not* asking her for leeway on his promise to spend the weekend with her. He did it. Barely. And insisted Tommy's call was unimportant when she asked.

Why had he told her he was taking the whole weekend off? She would have been happy with just Saturday. It was too late now. After her speech about choices, he couldn't imagine coming right out and saying he was picking work over her.

While the movie played, Daniella emptied almost an entire bottle of wine by herself and then expressed her appreciation for the rose-petal bath the night before with a grcat deal of creativity. By the time the credits rolled, Leo couldn't have stated his own name under oath.

The whirlpool of Daniella had well and truly sucked him under and he could no longer pretend he was taking the weekend off for any other reason than because he physically ached when he wasn't with her.

He didn't want to pick work over her. Or vice versa. If thcrc was a morc difficult placc to bc than bctwccn a woman and ambition, Leo didn't want to know about it. Not just any woman, but one who tilted his world and righted it in the same breath. And not just ambition, but the culmination of banishing childhood fears and achieving adult aspirations.

Sunday, after the last round of sleepy morning indulgence Leo would permit himself to experience for a long, long time, Daniella kissed him soundly and retrieved a flat package from under the bed.

"For me?" An odd ping of pleasure pierced his chest as she nodded, handing it to him.

He tore off the plain brown wrapping to reveal a framed sepia-toned drawing.

"It's one of da Vinci's," Daniella explained quietly. "You probably know that."

IIc did. Revcrently, hc tiltcd thc framc away from thc light to reduce the glare. It was one of his favorites, a reproduction of da Vinci's earliest drawing of the Arno Valley. "The original hangs in the Uffizi. Thank you. What made you think of this?"

"Da Vinci was more than a painter. He invented. He drew. He was a sculptor and a mathematician. And, like, four other things I've forgotten." With a small laugh, she tugged the frame from his grasp and laid it on the bed, then took his hand. "He was so much more than the *Mona Lisa*. Like you're more than Reynolds Capital Management. I wanted you to know I see that."

The gift suddenly took on meaning of exponential proportions. And he wasn't sure he liked it. "Are you angling for me to show you something I drew?"

The exposure of such a thing was inconceivable. Drawing was for him alone. No one else. It would be like slicing open his brain and allowing his deepest secrets to flow out, then trying to stitch the gray matter back together. It would never heal quite right. There'd always be a scar and the secrets would be out there in the world, unprotected.

"I would have asked if that's what I was after."

"What are you after, then?"

Her expression softened. "No nefarious motives. All my motives are right here." Crossing her heart with an index finger, she sought his gaze, her irises as deep and rich as melted chocolate.

"What does that mean?"

"What do you think it means, Leo?" She smiled. "I gave you the picture because I love you and want to express that in tangible ways."

His insides shuddered to an icy halt.

I love you.

It echoed in his head, pounding at the base of his skull. Where had that *come* from? No one had ever said that to him before. Well, except his mom.

Oh, dear God. His overtly romantic mother would have a field day with this. Leo's arranged marriage had just blown up in his face. His wife had *fallen in love with him*.

What was he supposed to say in response?

"You can't drop something like that on me out of the blue."

"I can't?" She sat up, covers—and her state of undress—forgotten. "How should I have led up to it, then?"

He unstuck his tongue from the desert the roof of his mouth had turned into. "I mean, you didn't have to say it at all. That's... We're not—" He pinched the bridge of his nose and tried to corral his spooked wits before he told her the truth. That he'd liked the sound of those words far more than he would have expected. "That's not the kind of marriage we agreed to."

She recoiled and quickly composed her expression, but not before he saw the flicker of hurt. "I know that. It doesn't erase my feelings. You're a kind, generous man who makes me happy. We spent a romantic weekend together and you kind of pushed me over the edge after Tommy called and you blew him off. Wouldn't you rather I be honest with you?"

Not really, no. Not when it involved sticky emotions he couldn't fathom. Dangerous emotions. Wonderful, terrible emotions that quaked through him. Love was a hell of an indulgence and he could hardly comprehend the ramifications of her blithe announcement.

But it was out there and he couldn't ignore it. Like he couldn't ignore the corkscrew through his gut over what he had to do next. "Since you're such an advocate of honesty, I lost a couple of deals over those fantasies I couldn't get out of my head. I spent the weekend with you so I could go back to work on Monday and finally concentrate."

The pain radiating from her gaze sliced through his chest like a meat cleaver.

Get some distance before you hurt her even worse.

He couldn't reach for her. He wanted to. Wanted to tell her it was all a big lie and *I love you* was the sweetest phrase in the English language. It almost made the Tommy-free weekend worth it and that scared him the most. Because he might do it again.

Curling his fingers under, he said the most horrible thing he could think of.

"The rose petals weren't intended to seduce you into falling in love. It was an exorcism."

One that had just failed miserably. His wife had fallen in love with him. It was all over her face, in her touch. Had been for some time and he'd only just realized how much he liked it on her.

Worse, he had to pretend that her words hadn't lodged in his heart. That his soul wasn't turning them over, examining them from all angles and contemplating grabbing on with all its might. Whispering seductive ideas.

It could be like it was this weekend forever. Forget about work, not your wife. You don't have to surface. Not really.

Said Satan about the apple.

Love was the decisive destroyer of security, the ultimate quicksand that led to the ghetto, and he would not fall prey to the temptations of his weaknesses. He would not become his father. No matter how hard it was to force out the words.

"We have a marriage of convenience, Daniella. That's all."

"I understand," she whispered, and nodded once without looking up from her folded hands.

She wasn't going to slap him and storm out. The relief he'd expected to feel didn't materialize. Instead, the juggling act had grown exponentially harder. Now he had the Herculean task of continuing to push her away so she didn't utter *I love you* in his presence again. He couldn't take that raw devastation on her face, knowing that he was hurting her, knowing that he'd hurt her even more later if he slipped and said it back.

And neither would Leo allow Dax to be right. He still had his edge and that wasn't ever changing.

Eleven

The pill was so tiny. How could such small packaging prevent such a huge thing like pregnancy?

Dannie stuck the birth control pill in her mouth and swallowed, the action serving the dual purpose of getting it down her throat and keeping the tears at bay. The pill was both functional and symbolic. Not only was she preventing pregnancy, but she was giving up on grand, sweeping passion and love. Forever.

Her heart was too bruised to imagine having a baby with Leo. Not now. Maybe at some point in the future she'd get those images of him smiling tenderly at their child out of her head. Leo didn't have an ounce of tenderness in him.

Okay, that wasn't true. He had it, he just used a great deal of judiciousness in how and when he allowed it to surface. She couldn't willingly give birth to a child who would one day want his or her daddy's attention. No child deserved to be fathered by a man who refused to participate in his own life.

Scratch a baby off the list. Yet another sacrifice she'd make. She understood people didn't always get their heart's desire. But she'd about run out of dreams for her non-fairy-tale real life to strip away.

She'd had an entire weekend to show Leo how wonderful their marriage could be. And she'd failed. He didn't find the idea of opening his heart to her the least bit appealing. In her most spectacular screwup to date, she'd assumed they'd grow to care for each other. Maybe not at the same rate, but they'd eventually catch up, right? It had never occurred to her he'd refuse to show even a tiny bit of affection for his wife.

She was simply a convenience. Exactly as he'd always said. Reading unmet needs into his actions and pushing him into intimacy hadn't gotten her anywhere but brokenhearted.

Wife was her identity, her essence. Work was his. Cliché indeed.

So he went back to his sixteen-hour days and she made a doctor's appointment. After three days of falling asleep before Leo came home, the pills were unnecessary insurance thus far. Apparently telling her husband she loved him was birth control in and of itself.

The music of her stupid phone's ringtone cut the silence in the bathroom.

She glanced at it. Elise's name flashed from the screen. What in the world?

"Hello?"

"It's Elise. I'm sorry to bother you, but I'm in a bind and I need your help."

"Of course. Whatever you need, it's yours."

There was very little Dannie wouldn't do for the woman who had changed her life, broken heart notwithstanding. Elise had helped her find a secure marriage. This was the "for worse" part—so much worse than she'd predicted, and she'd expected it to *suck* if she fell in love with Leo and he didn't return her feelings.

"Thank you. So much. I've got a new applicant for the program and I'm totally booked. But I can't turn her away. Will you go through the preliminary stages with her?"

"You want *me* to teach someone else how to do her hair and makeup?"

Elise chuckled. "Don't sound so surprised. You're highly qualified."

That was only because her fairy godmother had no idea

how solidly catastrophic Dannie's match had become. "As long as it's just preliminaries. I couldn't do any of the rest."

"Oh, I'll pay you."

"I wasn't talking about that." But now she was thinking about how it was almost like a short part-time job. Good timing. That might get her mind off the empty house. "I'd do it for free."

"I insist. Can you help me out or am I imposing on your new marriage?"

Dannie bit back maniacal laughter. "I can do it. Be there in thirty minutes."

She ended the call and finished getting ready for the day. She'd stopped rolling out of bed before dawn and making Leo's coffee. What would be the point? He probably hadn't even noticed.

Elise's elegant two-story town house in uptown brought back bittersweet memories. Inside these walls, Dannie had transformed from an outspoken, penniless—and hopeless—woman into a demure, suitable wife for the man Elise's computer had matched her with.

Well, not so demure. Scarlett sometimes took over, especially when Dannie's clothes came off. And when Leo made her mad, or smiled at her or—okay, Scarlett was here to stay. Dannie sighed. The suitable part was still true. She'd orchestrated a heck of a party and Tommy had signed with Reynolds Capital. Clearly, *some* of Elise's training had taken root.

Elise answered the door and threw her arms around Dannie in an exuberant hug that knocked her off balance, despite the fact that Dannie had six inches on Elise in height. But what she lacked vertically, Elise more than made up for in personality and heart.

"Look at you," Elise gushed. "So gorgeous and sophisticated. Thanks, by the way. Come meet Juliet."

Dannie followed Elise into the living room where she'd married Leo. It seemed like aeons ago that she'd stood at that fireplace, so nervous about entering an arranged marriage she could barely speak. Never had she imagined as she slipped that ring on Leo's finger that she'd fall in love and when she told him, he'd so thoroughly reject it.

Not just reject it. He'd *exorcised* her. As if she'd been haunting Leo and he hoped to banish the grim specter of his wife from the attic in his head.

If she had known, would she have still married him? Her mother's face swam into her mind. Yeah. She would have. Her mother was too important to balk at a little thing like a broken heart.

Dannie turned her back on the fireplace.

The woman huddled on the couch unfolded and stood to greet her.

"Juliet Villere," she said and held out a hand.

Even without the slight accent, her European descent was obvious. She had that quality inherent in people from another country—it was in the style of her shoes, the foreign cut of her clothing and light brown hair, and in the set of her aquiline features.

Dannie introduced herself and smiled at the other woman. Curiosity was killing her. As Dannie did, surely Juliet had a story behind why she'd answered Elise's ad. "You're here to let Elise sprinkle some magic dust over you?"

"Magic would help."

She returned Dannie's smile, but it didn't reach her eyes and Dannie was sold. No wonder Elise hadn't turned her away. The woman radiated a forlorn aura that made Dannie want to cover her with a warm quilt and ply her with hot chocolate. And it was eighty-five degrees outside.

Elise nodded. "Juliet is a self-described tomboy. I couldn't think of anyone more ladylike than Dannie and I've already taken on more candidates than I can handle. It's a perfect match."

Heat climbed into Dannie's cheeks. She *was* ladylike when it counted. What had happened between her and Leo in the media room after he ignored Tommy's call was nobody's business but hers. Besides, he liked it when she put on her brazen side.

At least she excelled in that area of her marriage.

"Thank you for helping me, Ms. Arundel. I had nowhere else to turn." Juliet bobbed her head first at Elise and then at Dannie. "I would be grateful to find an American husband."

"Did your computer already spit out some possibles?" Dannie asked Elise.

Elise shook her head. "She's not entered yet. Makeover first, then I do the match. The computer doesn't care what you look like, but I find that the makeover gives women the confidence to answer the profile questions from the heart instead of their head. Then the algorithm matches based on personality."

"Wait." Dannie went a little faint. "External characteristics aren't part of the profile process?"

"Of course not. Love isn't based on looks."

"But…" Dannie sank onto the couch. "You matched me with Leo because he was looking for certain qualities in a wife. Organized. Sophisticated. Able to host parties and mingle with the upper crust."

Which had everything to do with external qualities. Not internal.

"Yes. That covers about four of the profile points. The rest are all related to your views on relationships. Love. Family. How you feel about sex. Conflict. You and Leo fit on all forty-seven."

"That's impossible," she countered flatly.

"Name one area where that's not true and I'll refund Leo's money right now."

"Love. I believe in it. He doesn't." Saying it out loud made it real all of a sudden and a breakdown threatened Dannie's immediate future.

"That's totally false." Elise's brow puckered as she paused. "Unless he lied on his profile. Which I suppose is possible but highly improbable."

"It can't be that foolproof."

Why was she arguing about this? The computer had matched her with Leo because they'd both agreed a marriage based on mutual goals made sense. Neither of them had expressed an interest in love from the outset and Elise was absolutely correct—Dannie had answered the profile questions from her heart. She loved her mother and marrying Leo had saved her. End of story.

"It's not. But I am." The flash of Elise's smile did not temper her self-assurance. "I administer the profile test myself and I wrote it."

Juliet watched the exchange as though it was a tennis match, eyelids shielding her thoughts. "But something is amiss or you would not be having this discussion, right?" she suggested.

Something as in Dannie had created this mess by forgetting love didn't create security, but honoring your word did. Her mother's stance on relationships had never steered her wrong before, and if she'd tried a little harder to embrace the idea of a loveless marriage, she could have avoided all this.

Elise deflated a little. "Yes, of course you're right. I'm sorry. I have to shut down my analytical side or it takes over."

Yeah, Dannie knew all about shutting down inappropriate emotional outbursts. "I'm just disappointed and mad at myself for thinking I could entice him away from his dollar signs with promises of fulfillment. It's not your fault."

Elise put a comforting hand on Dannie's arm. "My point is that you totally can. I'm sorry he's being difficult about accepting all that you have to offer beyond the ability to schedule personal appointments. But you've got what he needs emotionally, too."

Did she?

And did she have what he really needed or only what he thought he needed? For a long time, she'd smugly believed she knew the difference and her job was to guide him into understanding how to express his true desires. But really, her own pent-up needs had messed that up. And how.

Dannie took Juliet upstairs to Elise's war room, complete with a long lighted mirror and counter, racks of clothing and more hairstyling and makeup tools than a Vegas show-girl dressing room.

"All this is necessary?" Juliet's gaze darted around the room, her nostrils flaring. "What is *that?* Will it hurt?"

The panicked questions lightened Dannie's mood. "It's a straightening iron. For your hair. We don't stick your fingers between the plates unless you fail at balancing a book on your head." The other woman's cheeks blanched and Dannie laughed. "I'm kidding. Sit down in that chair and let's get started. Drink?"

Dannie crossed to the small refrigerator stocked with water, lemons, cucumbers and ice packs, the best beauty accoutrements on the planet behind a good night's sleep.

"Thank you. I'm not thirsty."

"You need to drink plenty of water. It's good for your skin and helps you stay full so you don't feel as hungry." Elise's lessons rolled out of Dannie's brain effortlessly. "Lemon gives a little bit of taste, if you prefer."

"I prefer to be sailing or swimming." The frown had no trouble reaching Juliet's eyes, unlike her smile. "I miss the water."

"Where are you from?" Dannie asked as she plugged in the hair dryer, straightening iron, curling iron and hot rollers. She hadn't decided yet how Juliet's long hair would best be styled, though it would surely benefit from a more elegant cut. And she'd definitely need a facial. Dannie mentally ticked off a few more details and realized she was humming.

It was the happiest she'd felt all week.

"South of France. Delamer." Juliet spat out the country's name as if it had the reputation of being a leper's colony instead of a Mediterranean playground for the rich and beautiful.

"That's a lovely place. And you've got those two gorgeous princes. I read that Prince Alain is getting married soon. I hope they televise it." Dannie sighed a little in what she assumed would be mutual appreciation for a dreamy, out-of-reach public figure and his royal romance.

Juliet instead burst into tears.

Dannie gathered the other woman into a wet embrace and patted her back. "Oh, honey. What's wrong?"

Juliet snuffled against her shoulder. "Matters of the heart. They can undo us like no other."

She had that right. "Is that why you left Delamer? Someone broke your heart at home?"

With one last sniff, Juliet pulled out of Dannie's arms and dragged the back of a hand under both newly steeled eyes. "I want to forget that man exists. In Delamer, it's impossible. They splash his picture on everything. If I marry an American husband, I don't have to return and watch him with his perfect princess."

Dannie finally caught up and sank into the second director's chair. "Prince Alain broke your heart?"

This story called for chocolate and lots of red wine. Unfortunately, it wasn't even lunchtime and Elise kept neither in the house.

With a nod, Juliet twirled a brush absently, her thoughts clearly thousands of miles away. "There was a scandal. It's history. I can't change it and now I have to move on. What should we do first to transform me into a woman who will attract an American husband?"

Dannie let her change the subject and spent the next two hours teaching Juliet the basics of makeup and hair. It was a challenge, as the woman had never learned an iota about either.

"If you line only the bottom lip with a pencil that's a shade darker than your lipstick, it'll create an illusion of fuller lips." Dannie demonstrated on Juliet's mouth.

"Why would I want to do that? I can't sleep in lipstick. In

the morning, my husband will realize I'm not pouty lipped, won't he?" Juliet pursed her newly painted lips and scowled at her reflection in the mirror.

"Well, figure out a way to distract him before he notices," Dannie suggested and moved on to eye-shadow techniques. There was no polite way to say Juliet needed some style.

Tomboy she was, down to her bitten-off fingernails, Mediterranean sailor's tan and split ends. The tears had unlocked something in Juliet and she talked endlessly with Dannie about her life in Delamer, minus any details about the prince.

Dannie bit back her questions, but she'd love to know how such a down-to-earth woman without an ounce of polish had gotten within five feet of royalty, let alone long enough to develop a relationship with a prince. Then there was the briefly mentioned scandal.

She didn't ask. The internet would give up the rest of the tale soon enough.

Elise checked in and offered to have lunch delivered. Since Dannie had nowhere else to be, she stayed the rest of the day. She took Juliet shopping at the Galleria in North Dallas and by the time they returned to Elise's house, Dannie had made a friend. Which, she suspected, they both desperately needed.

Before Dannie left to go back to her empty house, Elise pulled her aside. "You did a fantastic job with Juliet. If you're in the market for a permanent job, I would hire you in a second."

Dannie stared at the matchmaker. "Are you serious?"

"Totally." Elise flipped her pageboy-cut hair back. "It takes time to groom these women, and I've got more men in the computer than I ever thought possible. Successful men don't have a lot of patience for sorting out good women from bad and I provide a valuable service to them. Business is booming, in short. If you've got spare time, it would be a huge help to me."

Elise named a salary that nearly popped Dannie's eyes from their sockets. "Let me think about it."

Her job was Leo Reynolds's Wife. But suddenly, it didn't have to be. She could make money working for Elise and take care of her mother.

Leo was married to his company, first and foremost. He made that choice every day. And now, Dannie had choices, too.

She didn't want a divorce. She wanted to be Leo's wife and have the marriage of her dreams, but Leo was half of that equation. Before she made a final decision about how she'd spend the next fifty years, he should have the opportunity to fully understand what her choices were. And how they'd affect him. He might give her the final piece she needed to make up her mind.

Maybe she'd get an exorcism of her own out of it.

The exorcism was not only a colossal failure, but Leo had also learned the very uncomfortable lesson that he couldn't find a method to erase the scent of strawberries from his skin.

He'd tried four different kinds of soap. Then something called a loofah. In one of his less sane moments, sandpaper started looking very attractive. It was totally irrational. The scent couldn't actually still be there after so many days, but he sniffed and there it was. Essence of Daniella.

Leo clenched the pencil in his hand and pulled his gaze from the Dallas skyline outside his office window. The garbage can by his desk overflowed with crumpled paper. He balled the sheet on his desk and threw the latest in another round of useless brainstorming on top. It bounced out to roll under his chair. Of course. Nothing was happening as it should. Normally, paper and pencil was his go-to method when he needed to unblock.

Surprise. It wasn't working.

Tommy Garrett was very shortly going to be furious that

he'd signed with Leo instead of Moreno Partners. This deal represented the pinnacle of venture capital success and Leo's brain was fried. He had nothing to show for his half of the partnership. He was supposed to provide business expertise. Connections in manufacturing. Marketing. Ideas.

Instead he'd spent the past few days mentally embroiled in about a million more fantasies starring his wife, whom he'd deliberately driven away. For all the good it had done.

His pencil trailed across the paper and in seconds, graphite lines appeared in the form of a woman. He groaned and shut his eyes. Then opened them. What the hell. Nothing else was coming out of his brain.

As his long-suppressed muse whispered halting, undisciplined inspiration, his hand captured it, transforming the vision into the concrete. Details of Daniella's shape flowed onto the paper. Glorious. Ethereal. So beautiful his chest ached. The ache spread, squeezing his lungs and biting through muscle painfully.

Sweat broke out across the back of his neck and his hand cramped but he didn't stop. He yanked more minutiae, more emotion, from a place deep inside until he was nearly spent.

Another. More paper. Draw.

As if the drawing conjured the woman, Leo glanced up to see his wife standing in the doorway of his office. In the flesh. Dear God, Daniella was luminous in a blue dress and sky-high heels that emphasized the delicate arch to her feet.

Heart pounding, he slipped a blank sheet over the drawing and shoved everything he'd just freed back into its box. He glanced at the clock. It was eight-thirty. And dark. When had that happened?

"What are you doing here?" he asked her and stood. *Nice greeting for your wife, moron.*

"I came to see you. Do you have a few minutes?" She waltzed in as if he'd said yes.

He hadn't seen her awake since Sunday, but his body reacted as if she'd slid up against him into that niche where she fit like clinging honey instead of taking a seat on the couch in his sitting area.

"Would you like to sit down?" she offered politely, every bit the queen of the manor despite the fact that his business acumen paid the rent on this office space. Or it used to. He was this close to selling caricatures on the street if something didn't change ASAP.

He sat on the other couch. Good. Distance was good. Kept their interaction impersonal. "How are you?"

"Fine. Elise offered me a job today."

She smoothed her skirt and crossed her legs, which he watched from the corner of his eye. It was so much more powerful a blow to witness those legs sliding together when he knew what they felt like against his. What he felt like when she was near him, even when they weren't touching.

"A job? As a matchmaker?"

"As a tutor. She asked me to help her polish the women she accepts into her program. Hair, makeup. That sort of thing."

"You'd be a natural. Are you here to ask my permission? I certainly don't mind if you—"

"I'm here to ask if there's the smallest possibility you could ever love me."

A knot the size of a Buick hardened in his chest. All his carefully constructed arguments regarding the status of their relationship had ended up forming a bridge to nowhere. Probably because he could hardly convince her of it when he'd failed to convince himself.

"Daniella, we've been over this."

"No, we haven't." She clasped her hands together so tightly one of her knuckles cracked. "I told you I loved you and you freaked."

That was a pretty accurate assessment. "Well, I don't want to rehash it. We have an arranged marriage with a useful design. Let's stick with it."

"Sorry. We're rehashing it right now. Extenuating circumstances caused me to give up what I really want in a marriage. And extenuating circumstances have caused me to reevaluate. I love you and want you to love me. I need to know if we can have a marriage based on that."

I love you. Why did that settle into so many tender places inside all at once?

"You make it sound simple. It's not," he said, his voice inexplicably gruff. All the emotions drawing had dredged up weren't so easily controlled as they would have been if he'd resisted the temptation in the first place.

"Explain to me what's complicated about it."

Everything.

"You want me to choose you over my company and that's an impossible place to be."

"I'm not asking you to do that. I would never presume to take away something so important to you. Why can't you have both?"

It was the juggling-act conversation all over again. As if it was simple to just choose to have both. This would always be a problem—he saw that now. And now was the time to get her crystal clear on the subject. Get them both clear.

"I'm not built that way. I don't do anything halfway, something you might better appreciate after this past weekend. Surely you recall how thoroughly I threw myself into pleasuring you." He raked his gaze over her deliberately to make the point and a gorgeous blush rose up in her cheeks. Which made him feel worse for God knew what reason. "I went to a matchmaker to find a wife who would be happy with what I could provide financially and overlook the number of hours I put into my company. Because I don't do that halfway, either. One side is going to suffer."

All or nothing. And when it came to Daniella, he was so far away from nothing, he couldn't even *see* nothing.

Her keen gaze flitted over his expression and it wasn't difficult to pinpoint the exact instant she gleaned more than he'd intended. "But that doesn't mean you don't have feelings for me, just that you're too afraid to admit something unexpected happened between us."

"What do you want me to say, Daniella?" His voice dipped uncontrollably as he fought to keep those feelings under wraps. "That you're right? That of all the things I expected to happen in our marriage, this conversation was so far down the list it was nearly invisible?"

Her bottom lip trembled. "I want you to say what's in your heart. Or are you too afraid?"

She didn't get it. He wasn't afraid of what was in his heart; he just couldn't give in to it. The cost of loving her was too high.

"My heart is not up for discussion."

Nodding, she stood up. "Security is vitally important to me and I married you to get it. It was the only way I could guarantee my mother would be taken care of. Elise changed that today. I can support my mother on the salary she'll pay me."

An arctic chill bit into his skin, creeping through the pores to flash freeze his whole body. "Are you asking me for a divorce?"

Please, God, no.

If he lost her, it was what he deserved.

She shook her head. "I'm telling you I have a choice. And I'm making it. I took lifetime vows I plan to honor. Now I'm giving you a chance to make a choice as well as to how that marriage will look. Get off the sidelines, love me and live happily ever after. Or we'll remain married, I'll manage your personal life but I'll move back into my own room. Separate hearts, separate bedrooms. What are you going to do?"

Panic clawed at his insides, a living thing desperate to get out and not particular about how many internal organs it destroyed in its quest. She wanted something worse than a divorce. The one thing money couldn't buy—him. His time. His attention. His love.

"That's ridiculous," he burst out and clamped his mouth closed until he could control what came out of it. "I told you what I need, which is for you to be happy with what I can give. Like I've told you from the very beginning. You're throwing that back at me, drawing a line. You or Reynolds Capital Management."

A tear tracked down her cheek. "Don't you see, Leo? *You* drew that line. Not me."

"My mistake. The line you drew is the one where you said I can't sleep with you anymore unless I'm in love with you."

"Yes. That is my fault." Her head dropped and it took an enormous amount of will to keep from enfolding her in his arms. But he was the source of her pain, not the solution. "My mother...she's an amazing woman, but she has a very jaded view of marriage and I let it fool me into believing I could be happy with a loveless arrangement. And I probably would have been if you were someone different. Someone I couldn't love. Be the husband I need, Leo."

She raised her head and what he saw in the depths of her shiny eyes nearly put him on his knees, prostrate before her in desperate apology, babbling, "Yes, I will be that husband," or worse, telling her he'd do anything as long as she'd look at him like that forever: as though he was worthy of being loved, even though he'd rejected her over and over again.

The overflowing trash can taunted him.

Lack of focus is what happens when you let your wife swallow you. Other venture capital firms have fewer dominoes, more liquid assets, less leveraged cash. One push and it'll all vanish.

He could never do what she was asking.

Once and for all, he could resolve it. Right here, right now, give her that final push away before he gave in to the emotions and forgot all the reasons he couldn't have his company *and* love Daniella.

"I stay on the sidelines for a reason. It's how I balance my obsessive personality." His heart thumped painfully. This was the right thing, for him and Reynolds Capital. Why didn't it feel like it? "I need you to be the wife I thought I was getting from EA International."

Which was impossible. Daniella could never be the out-of-sight, out-of-mind wife he'd envisioned. He'd given up on categorizing her and forcing her into a box when she insisted on being in all the boxes simultaneously. His multi-talented wife was the only woman alive who could do that.

Her expression went as stiff as her spine. "Then that's what you'll get. I'll schedule your appointments and host your parties and make you look good to your associates. I won't be in your bed at night, but I'll give you a hundred percent during the day and never mention how many hours you work."

It was everything he'd asked for. And the polar opposite of what he wanted. He vised his throbbing temples between his middle finger and his thumb but his brain still felt as though it was about to explode. How had she managed to twist this around so that they were back to their original agreement but it felt as if she'd kicked him in the stomach?

"I wish…" She crossed her arms as if holding herself in. "Love creates security, too. I wish you could see that. But if it's your choice for me to be nothing more than a glorified personal assistant, I hope it makes you happy. Just keep in mind that your company *and* your wife bear your name. You will always be a part of both."

And then she walked out, heels clicking on the stained concrete in perfect rhythm to the sound of his soul splitting in two.

Twelve

"Dorito?" Tommy offered and stuck out the bag.

Leo shook his head. Doritos didn't sit well on an empty stomach. Nothing sat well on an empty stomach, especially not the dreck in his coffee cup. Mrs. Gordon had remade it four times already and the look on her face said he'd better be happy with this round.

He shoved the half-full mug to the far end of the conference table, wished it was a travel mug filled by his wife and scrubbed his jaw. Rough stubble stabbed his fingers. *Forgot to shave. Again.*

"So, amigo." Tommy crunched absently and nodded to the TV on the wall, where Leo's laptop screen was displayed. "I've redone this schematic twice. The prototype passed the CAD analysis. What's it going to take to get you happy with it?"

Hell would probably freeze over before Leo was happy about anything. He'd officially labeled this funk Daniella's Curse, because until she'd said she hoped his choice made him happy, he'd never given a thought to whether he was or not. And this funk was the opposite of happy.

He missed his wife. Her invisible presence invaded every last area of his life, including his car, which never dipped below half a tank of gas. And smelled like strawberries.

"The schematic is still wrong. That's why I keep telling you to redo it." Leo flipped the drawing vertically inside the CAD program and glanced up at the TV. "Look, you can't take this to manufacturing as is. We have to shave another two cubic centimeters somewhere to meet the price point. Otherwise the markup will be too high and the distribution deals will fall through."

Leo's phone beeped. Daniella's picture flashed and he snatched it up. Text message. He frowned at the concisely worded reminder of his appointment for a haircut that afternoon. Of course she hadn't called to talk to him.

"Why does this have to be so complicated?" Tommy complained. "I designed the thing. That should be enough. Why don't *you* figure out where to shave off whatever you think makes sense?"

Leo fiddled with the pencil in his fingers, weaving it through them like a baton, and counted all the way to fifteen for good measure. It did not calm him. "You're the designer. You have to redesign when it's not ready." His fingers sought the leather portfolio on the table. The picture he'd drawn of Daniella was inside. It equaled serenity in the midst of turmoil. Oddly enough. "I help you on the back end. We've been over this."

Shades of the last real conversation he'd had with Daniella filtered through his mind. Why did he have to constantly remind people of things they should already know? Leo had a specific role to fill—in the background. Always. Nobody remembered that he stayed out of the middle, except him.

"I don't know how to get it to your specifications!" Tommy burst out in recalcitrant five-year-old fashion, complete with a scowl and crossed arms. "I've tried. I need help. That's why I signed with you."

"I'm your financial backer. I'm only talking to you about the schematic now because we're behind schedule and I need a good design today." With a short laugh, Leo shook his head. "Why would you assume I could do anything to help?"

Tommy flipped hair out of his face. "Dannie. She believes in you. She totally convinced me you walk on water daily and in your spare time you invest in people's potential. As far as she's concerned, you're the messiah of everything."

His gut spasmed. What exactly had his wife told Tommy to give him such a ridiculous picture of Leo? "That's entirely too fanciful for what I do."

Entirely too fanciful for a mortal man who'd made plenty of mistakes. But it didn't stop the low hum of pleasure behind his rib cage. Did Daniella really think of him like that, as someone heroic and unfailing? Or had she said those things for Tommy's benefit, playing her part as a dutiful wife?

Leo had the distinct, uncomfortable realization it was probably both. And he didn't deserve either.

Eyebrows raised, Tommy crossed his feet casually. "Yeah? If you tell me you don't know exactly what needs to happen with that schematic, I'll call you a dirty liar. You've been trying to lead me to it for an hour and I can't see it."

Leo sighed and thought seriously about driving the pencil through the table, but it would only break the wood, not solve his mounting frustration. Before he could count the reasons why it was a stupid, ridiculous path, he centered a piece of paper under the graphite and drew the first line.

Tommy's purple high-tops hit the floor as he leaned forward to peer over Leo's shoulder. The fuel-converter schematic took shape on the paper. With each new line, he explained to Tommy where he varied from the original design, why the modification was necessary, what the downstream manufacturing effect would be.

Occasionally Tommy interjected questions, objections and once, a really heartfelt "Dude. That's righteous."

One of Tommy's objections was sound and Leo reconsidered his stance on it. He erased that part of the drawing and incorporated Tommy's suggestion. Mrs. Gordon left for the day, shaking her head and mumbling about creative minds. After several hours, many heated exchanges and a few moments of near-poetic collaboration, they had a design they could both live with.

The last time Leo could honestly say he'd had that much fun was during the weekend he'd spent with Daniella. Before that—never.

Once Leo had scanned the finished product into his laptop and displayed it on the TV, Tommy whistled. "A work of art. I have to use every tool known to designers to put something that beautiful together. I can't believe you free-handed that. With a pencil, no less."

"A pencil gets the shading right," Leo muttered with a shrug. "I guess you could say it's a talent."

"I knew you had it in you," Tommy said smugly. "If I'd gone with Moreno Partners, I'd be screwed right now. Kiss your wife for me. She knows her stuff."

If only. Ironically, his current interaction with Daniella wasn't too different from how their marriage had started out, before they'd begun sharing a bedroom. If she hadn't barged in and demanded he start sleeping with her, would they still be exchanging text messages with no clue how much more there could be between them?

"She does have some kind of extrasensory perception," Leo said. "I'm afraid she's the one who walks on water."

No, *he'd* be clueless. She wouldn't. From the beginning, she'd seen possibilities, pushing their relationship into realms deeper and stronger than he'd ever imagined could be between any two people, let alone when one of them was Leo Reynolds.

How had that happened when he wasn't looking? And why did the loss of something he'd never asked for haunt him?

He'd done everything he could to drive her away so she wouldn't be hurt and instead of leaving him, his wife had stayed. Why didn't she get the message already?

With a grin, Tommy nodded vigorously. "Dannie's awesome."

His wife's nickname lodged in his gut, spreading nasty poison.

Leo liked Tommy. He was enthusiastic, tireless, brilliant. So what was it about Tommy simply saying his wife's name that burned Leo up? It was more than jealousy, more than a fear either Tommy or Daniella had less than pure intentions toward each other.

It was because Tommy held up a mirror and Leo hated his reflection.

This Dorito-crunching, Red Bull–slurping wonder kid was a younger, unrestricted, better version of Leo. Tommy could call a woman Dannie and think nothing of it, whereas Leo couldn't descend into that kind of intimacy unless he was drunk on Daniella's powerful chemistry.

And he wished he could be more like Tommy.

Tommy polished off the bag of Doritos. "You're awesome, too. I'm over here soaking it all up like SpongeBob."

A cleansing laugh burst out of Leo's mouth, unchecked. "Thanks. It's nice to have an appreciative audience."

"Dude, you talk and I'll listen, no matter what you say. I'm in awe of you right now. I think I learned more today than I did in four years at Yale. What else can you teach me?"

Oh, no. That was beyond the realm of his role. He and Tommy were financial partners, with a carefully constructed agreement separating their interests into neat boxes. That should be the extent of their relationship.

Should be. Everything should fit into a neat box. And nothing did, despite all of Leo's efforts.

"What do you want to know?"

With a lusty sigh, Tommy grinned. "Everything. Lay it on me."

And that was it. For the first time in his life, Leo had become an in-the-flesh mentor and for whatever reason, it felt right. It was a connection with his profit margin, one he'd never explored but suddenly wanted to.

All business is personal.

His wife had pointed that out long ago and he'd brushed it off as foolish sentiment. But it suddenly made brilliant sense. He hadn't lost the deal for Mastermind Media because he'd lost his edge, but because he'd willfully chosen not to enter into a partnership with Dax, for whom he'd lost a great deal of respect. His relationship with Daniella merely highlighted it, but hadn't caused it.

Leo's relationship with Daniella shone into all of his corners and scared away the excuses, the fears. She hadn't left him because she'd already figured out what Leo should have seen long ago.

Their arrangement was dead. Now they had an opportunity to make their marriage something else.

Instead of being like Tommy, maybe Leo should be a better version of himself. One that could be worthy of a woman like Daniella Reynolds.

Leo's morose mood lightened. After setting aside two afternoons a week for Tommy to bring his best SpongeBob absorption skills, Leo kicked his new disciple out of his office so he could leave.

When he got home, Leo paused outside Daniella's closed bedroom door and placed his palm flat against it, as he did every night. Sometimes he imagined he could feel her breathing through the door. The scent of strawberries lingered in the hall, wrapping around him.

He'd built this home as a fortress, a place that represented all the stability he'd never had as a child. Daniella had become an inseparable part of that. How could he ever have lived here without her? How could he explain to her what value she'd brought to his life?

Guilt gnawed a new hole in his gut. She deserved so much more than what he'd given her.

She should have left him.

The main goal of marriage was security. Odd how he

felt as though the ground was disappearing beneath him at an alarming pace the longer he had a wife in name only.

Instead of standing there like a stalker, he knocked and shifted the bulky package in his hand before him like a peace offering. He prayed it might change things but he had no clue how, or what that change might look like.

He just knew he couldn't do marriage like this anymore. The ball was in his court. Had been the entire time. Hopefully he'd picked up the proper racket.

Daniella opened the door, shiny hair down around her face and clad in a skintight tank top and loose pajama bottoms with her flat midriff peeking through. The swift, hard punch to his solar plexus nearly rendered him speechless.

Somehow he managed to choke out, "Hi."

Her luminous brown eyes sought his and a wealth of unexpressed things poured from them. "Hi."

"A gift. For you." He handed her the wrapped package and laced his fingers behind his back before he pulled her into an embrace she probably wouldn't welcome. But oh, dear God, did he want to touch her. "You gave me one. I'm returning the favor."

She ripped it open and his thudding heart deafened him as he waited.

Silently, she evaluated the basket of pomegranates. "What does this mean?"

She tilted the basket as if to show him, which was unnecessary. He'd placed each one in the basket himself, positioning it just so to interlock with the others. "You're still driving me pomegranates. Sleeping in separate bedrooms hasn't changed that."

The tension spiraled between them, squeezing his lungs, and he smiled in hopes of loosening it.

"I got that part. *Why* are you giving them to me?" Her gaze probed his, challenging him and killing his smile. She wasn't going to make this easy. She always had before, using her special powers to figure out exactly how to help him navigate.

Not this time. He shifted from foot to foot but couldn't find a comfortable stance. "Because I wanted to give you something that had special significance."

Her expression didn't change. "So it's nothing more than a gift designed to buy your way out of giving me anything emotional."

What did she want from him? A pound of flesh? She held in her hands one of the most emotional things he'd ever done. Somehow he had to make her see that.

"It's not just a gift, like jewelry. It's better than that."

Frozen, she stared at him for an eternity, long enough for him to realize he'd devalued the diamonds he'd given her for the party. Which were in her earlobes at this moment.

This was not going at all how he'd envisioned. She was supposed to make the first move. Fall into his arms and tell him this separation was killing her, too.

At the very least, she should be giving him a choice between two impossible options and then pretending it was okay when he picked the wrong one. The way she always did.

Floundering, he cast about for a lifeboat. "I'm sorry. I didn't mean it that way."

"How did you mean it? Or do you even know?"

"I do know!" At her raised eyebrows, he faltered. It had been an off-the-cuff protest. And a lie. Nothing between them was tangible. Or quantifiable. Which made it impossible to define the bottom line.

This was like a bad joke. What did the guy who had never hung on to a woman longer than a few weeks say to his wife? If only she'd tell him the punch line, they could move past this.

"What do you want me to say?"

"That's for you to figure out. I'll be here when you do. Thank you for the pomegranates."

With that, she closed the door in his face. Because at the end of the day, she knew the truth as well as he did. Jewelry. Pomegranates. Same difference. He still hadn't given her the one thing she really wanted—everything.

If he truly hoped to change their marriage, he had to dig much deeper. And it was going to hurt.

Dannie slid to the ground, the wood of her door biting into her back, and muffled a sob against the heel of her hand. *Pomegranates.*

Why did this have to be so hard?

Her mother was right: love was the stupidest thing of all to base a marriage on. It hurt too much. All Leo had to do was say, "I brought you a gift because I love you."

If his inability to do so wasn't bad enough, she had the awful feeling that the basket was indeed symbolic of his inner turmoil. Only supreme will suppressed her desire to knuckle under.

He'd tried. He really had. It just wasn't good enough, not anymore. Once upon a time, she'd believed they were a good match because they both valued security. It was how they went about achieving it where they differed.

Leo was an intense, focused man who cut himself off from people not because he didn't want to invest emotionally, but as some kind of compensation for what he viewed as a shortcoming of his personality. She couldn't spend a lifetime pretending it was okay that he refused to dive headlong into the game. She'd already compromised to the point of pain.

His mother had warned her how challenging Leo would be to love. Dannie should get a medal. So should Leo's mother.

Sleep did not come easily. She glanced at the time, convinced she'd been lying there for an hour but in reality, only four minutes had passed since the last clock check. She gave up at quarter past two and flipped on the TV to watch a fascinating documentary about the Civil War.

Her favorite historical time period unfolded on the screen. Women in lush hoopskirts danced a quadrille in the Old South before everything fell apart at the hands of General Sherman cutting a swath through Georgia on his way to the sea.

Dannie's heart felt as if it had taken a few rounds from a Yankee musket, too.

But where Scarlett O'Hara had raised a fist to the sky and vowed to persevere, Dannie felt like giving up.

A divorce would be easier. She could take care of her mother, live with Elise and try to forget about the man she'd married who refused to get out from behind the scenes.

But she'd taken vows. Her stomach ached at the thought of going back on her word. Her heart ached over the idea of staying. Which was worse?

All she knew was that she couldn't do this anymore.

In the morning, she took a bleary-eyed shower and spent the day at Elise's working with Juliet. They were both subdued and honestly, Dannie didn't see the point in giving Juliet a makeover when the woman was already beautiful. Besides, it wasn't as though a manicure and hot rollers would give Juliet what she most desired.

Or would it?

"What if your match is someone you can't fall in love with? Would you still marry him?" Dannie asked Juliet as she showed her how to pin the hot roller in place against her scalp. Some people didn't care about love. Some people found happiness and fulfillment in their own pursuits instead of through their husbands.

But Dannie wasn't some people, and she'd lied to herself about which side of the fence she was on, embracing her mother's philosophy as if it were her own.

Juliet made a face. "I would marry a warthog if he had

the means to keep me in America. Arranged marriages are common in Europe. You learn to coexist."

"But is it worth it to become someone else in order to have that means?"

The other woman shot her puzzled glance in the mirror. "I'm still me. With fingernails." She stuck out a hand, where a nail technician had created works of art with acrylic extensions.

Dannie glanced at her own reflection in the mirror. She'd been polished for so long, it was no longer a shock to see the elegant, sophisticated Mrs. Reynolds in the glass instead of Dannie White. Except they were one and the same, with a dash of Scarlett.

Elise had done the makeover first, but the computer had matched her to Leo because she was perfect for him. As she was. Not because Elise had infused Dannie with some special magic and transformed her into someone Leo would like.

I'm still me, too, but better.

Leo provided the foundation for her to excel as his wife and let her be as brazen, outspoken and blunt as she wanted. He was okay with Dannie being herself.

Their personalities were the match. She'd heard it over and over but today, it clicked.

She'd been so focused on whether Leo would kick her out if she screwed up it had blinded her to the real problem. They both had come into this marriage seeking security, but struggled with what they said they wanted versus what they'd actually gotten. And they were *both* trying to balance aspects of their incredibly strong personalities *for no reason*.

They wanted the same thing deep in their hearts—the security of an unending bond so strong it could never be broken.

The open-heart lavaliere around her neck caught the light as she leaned over Juliet's shoulder to arrange her hair. Elise had given Dannie the necklace when she'd agreed to marry Leo, as a gift between friends, she'd assumed.

Now she saw it as a reminder that marriage required exactly that—*two* open hearts.

Had she been too harsh with Leo about the pomegranates? Maybe she should find a way to coexist that didn't involve such absolutes. Security was enough for Juliet. A fulfilling partnership had been enough for Dannie once.

She'd pushed intimacy in an attempt to fulfill Leo's unvoiced needs and ignored the need he'd actually voiced— a wife he could depend on, who would stick with him, no matter what. Even through the pain of a one-sided grand, sweeping love affair.

One thing was for sure. Real life wasn't a fairy tale, but Dannie wanted her happily ever after anyway. Cinderella might have had some help from her fairy godmother, but in the end, she'd walked into that ball with only her brain and a strong drive to make her life better. What was a fairy tale but a story of perseverance, courage and choices?

It was time to be the wife Leo said he needed, not the one she assumed he needed.

Leo's car was in the garage when Dannie got home. She eyed it warily and glanced at her watch. It was three o'clock on a Tuesday. Someone had died. Someone *had* to have died.

Dannie dashed into the house, a lump in her throat as she triple checked her phone. She'd have a call if it was her mother. Wouldn't she?

"Leo!" Her shout echoed in the foyer but he didn't answer.

The study was empty. Her stomach flipped. Now she was really scared.

Neither was he in the pool, the kitchen, the media room, the servants' quarters around the back side of the garage or the workout room over the garage.

Dannie tore off two nails in her haste to turn the knob on

his bedroom door, the last threshold she should ever cross, but he could be lying a pool of his own blood and need help.

Curtains blocked the outside sunlight and the room was dark but for the lone lamp on Leo's dresser. It shone down on him. He sat on the carpet, hunched over a long piece of paper resting on a length of cardboard. Clawlike, he gripped a pencil in his hand, stroking it over the paper swiftly.

"Leo?" She paused just inside the door frame. "Are you okay?"

He glanced up. The light threw his ravaged face into relief, shadowing half of it. "I don't know when to stop. I tried to tell you."

"Tell me what? What are you talking about? What do you need to stop?"

"Drawing." He flipped a limp hand toward the room at large and that's when she realized white papers covered nearly every surface.

"How long have you been in here?" There were hundreds of drawings, slashes and fine lines filling the pages with a mess of shapes she couldn't make out in the semidark. *Hundreds.* Apparently she'd massively misconstrued what he meant by not doing things halfway.

"Since the pomegranates." His voice trembled with what had to be fatigue. He'd been holed up in here since last night?

"But your car was gone this morning."

"Needed a pencil sharpener. Is it enough? Look at the pictures, Daniella. Tell me if it's enough."

Her heart fluttered into her throat. "You want me to see your drawings?"

In response, he gathered a handful and clambered to his feet to bring them to her. The half light glinted off the short stubble lining his jaw and dark hair swept his collar. Not only had he skipped the haircut she'd scheduled, but he'd obviously not shaved in several days. His shirt was untucked and unbuttoned and this undone version of Leo had a devastating, intense edge.

As if presenting a broken baby bird, he gingerly handed off the drawings and waited silently.

She glanced at the first one and every ounce of oxygen in the room vanished.

"It's you," she whispered. She flipped through the pages. "They're all of you."

Gorgeously rendered. Drawn by the hand of a master who knew himself intimately and who was unashamed to show the world all the glorious details of what made up Leonardo Reynolds.

And he was completely naked in every single one.

He shut his eyes. "I stripped myself bare. Emotionally, physically, spiritually. For you. I cannot possibly explain what it cost me to put all of it on the paper. But it's there. Tell me it's enough."

Oh, my God.

"Leo," she croaked through a throat suddenly tight with unshed tears. This had all been for her. "Yes. *Yes.* It's enough."

More than enough. She clutched the pages to her abdomen. It was the deepest expression of his love she could possibly imagine and these pictures were worth far more than a thousand words. They told the story she'd yearned to hear, lifting his shell once and for all, revealing everything important about the man she loved.

Artist Leo touched her deep in her soul with invisible, precious fingers.

He deflated, almost collapsing. But then he opened his eyes and caught her in his arms, binding her to his strong, solid body. Her knees weren't too steady either as she let the drawings flutter to the floor and burrowed up against him.

Warm. Beautiful. Hers.

Her brain was having trouble spitting out anything coherent. And then he kissed her and she stopped thinking at all.

It was hungry, openmouthed, sloppy and so powerful. As he kissed her, he mouthed words she couldn't understand.

He broke away and murmured into her hair. And the phrase crystallized. "I want to be the husband you need."

"Oh, darling, you are." In every sense. He had been from the first moment, providing a safe, secure place for her to bloom into his wife. He was her match every bit as much as she was his.

He shook his head. "I haven't been. I don't deserve you. But I want you. So much."

"You have me. Forever. We're married, remember?" She smiled but he didn't return it.

"Not like this. No more agreement. No separate bedrooms. No separate hearts." He put his palm flat against his breastbone like a pledge. "I could've hired a personal assistant. But I didn't. I went looking for a wife because I needed one. I need a wife who sees past all my faults and loves me anyway. It's not too late, is it?"

She placed her palm on top of his. "Never. But, Leo, you didn't go to work today. You're not throwing away your company's success for me. I won't let you."

"I can't—so tired." His knees buckled and he fell to the carpet, taking her with him. He pulled her into his lap and cupped her jaw in his strong hands, fiercely, passionately, as if he'd never let go. "Like you said. You didn't draw the line. I did. It's what I do."

With a lopsided half smile, he jerked his head at the hundreds of drawings decorating the bedroom behind him. "You weren't trying to force me to make impossible choices. The choices weren't yours to present. You were simply helping me see what options had been there all along. Reynolds Capital Management is a part of me I can't give up. So are you."

"You want both? Me and your company?" Hope warred with reality. The drawings were a big, flashing exhibit A of what happened when Leo focused on something. His preferred spot on the sidelines made troubling sense.

"I want it all." His eyes closed for a beat, a habit she'd noticed he fell into when he struggled with what was going on inside. "I don't know how to balance. But I want to. I have to try."

His voice broke, carving indelible lines in her heart.

This was the open, raw, amazing man she'd fallen in love with. But she and Leo were the same, with facets of their personality that weren't always easy to manage.

"You can do it. We'll do it together." Who better to help him figure it out than the woman standing behind him, supporting him? "I love your intensity and I don't ever want you to feel like you can't be you. If you want to hole up on a Saturday because you've got a hot new investment opportunity to work, do it. Just don't expect to get much sleep that night. Don't ever deny any piece of yourself. I need all of you. As long as we both shall live."

Her job as Mrs. Reynolds was so simple: provide a foundation for him to blossom, the way he'd done for her.

"That sounds promising. If I have to work on a Saturday, will you still make me coffee?" he asked hopefully.

She smiled. "Every time. We'll both give a little and balance will come."

Nodding slowly, he cleared his throat. "I think it must be like when you have children. You love one with all your heart. Then another one comes along. Somehow you make room. Because it's worth it."

Children. Leo was talking about having children in the same breath with trying to balance.

The tears gathered in earnest this time. He'd transformed before her very eyes, but instead of a pirate or Rhett Butler or even a battered Mr. Fourpaws before her, he was wholly Leonardo and 100 percent the love of her life. "Yeah. I think it must be like that. We have stretchy hearts."

"Mine's pretty full. Of you." He was kissing her again

like a starving man, murmuring, but this time, she had no trouble deciphering what he was saying—*I love you.*

Then he said, "My hand hurts."

She laughed as she kissed it. "Wait right here. I have pills to throw in the trash and a red-hot wedding night outfit to wear for you. I guarantee you'll forget all about your sore hand."

Technically, it wasn't her wedding night. But in her book, every night was her wedding night when she was married to a man who loved her as much as Leo.

Epilogue

Leo Reynolds wished he could marry his wife, but they were already married and Daniella refused to divorce him just so he could have the fun of proposing to her in some elaborate fashion.

"Come on, you can't fool me," Leo teased her as they gripped the railing of the observation deck on the third level of the Eiffel Tower. Nine hundred feet below, the city of Paris spread as far as the eye could see. "You missed out on the proposal *and* the wedding of your dreams. You wouldn't like to do it all over again?"

Daniella kissed his cheek with a saucy smile, throwing her loose brown hair over her shoulder. "I'm getting the honeymoon of my dreams. And the husband. All that other stuff pales in comparison."

Sure it did. His wife suffered from an affliction with no cure—overt romanticism. Since he loved her beyond measure, he took personal responsibility for ensuring she never lost it. "Then you'll have to forgive me when I do something pale and lackluster like…this."

He slipped the ring box from his pocket and popped it open to reveal the rare red diamond ring inside. "Daniella Reynolds, I love you. Will you promise to be my wife the rest of our days, always wear that sexy lingerie set and let me make you as happy as you've made me?"

Daniella gasped. "Oh, Leo. I love you, too, and of course I promise that, with or without a ring. But it's beautiful."

"It's one of a kind. Like you. This ring is symbolic of a different sort of marriage, one based on love. The one I want with you. Every time I see it on you, I'll think about how love is the best security and how easily I could have lost it." He pulled the ring from its nest of velvet and gripped his wife's hand, slipping it on her third finger to rest against her wedding ring. And then he grinned. "Plus, the stone is the same color as pomegranates."

A tear slipped down her cheek at the same moment she laughed. "Thank you. Paris was enough but this…" She stuck her hand out and tilted it to admire the ring. "This is amazing. When in the world did you find time to shop for jewelry? You've been cramming for Tommy's product launch for weeks so you could squeeze in this trip."

"Tommy came with me and we strategized in between." Leo rolled his eyes. "Trust me, he was thrilled to be involved. I never imagined when he said he wanted to learn everything that would include how to pick out a diamond for a woman."

Daniella giggled. "With you as his mentor, I'm sure he'll make the future love of his life very happy."

Tommy had trashed Leo's original proposal. Garrett-Reynolds Engineering opened its doors that same week and the payoff for becoming full partners had been immeasurable. Not only did Leo have a lot of fun, but for the first time, his profit flowed directly from his hand instead of via carefully constructed financing agreements. Leo was right in the middle of every aspect of the business and it fulfilled him in ways he could never completely comprehend.

Without Daniella, he never would have taken that step. She'd invested in his potential and given him a makeover from the inside out. He'd gladly spend the rest of his life loving her for it.

"How're things going in there?" Leo spread his hand across Daniella's abdomen and the thought of their child eventually being inside tightened his throat with awe and tenderness.

"Not pregnant yet. Though certainly not from lack of trying." Her grin warmed his heart. Everything about her warmed his heart, touching him in places he didn't even know existed. "It's only a matter of time."

"We must try harder. I insist."

A baby was one of many possibilities he eagerly anticipated, owing to his new perspective on marriage. And life in general.

Leo kissed his wife and it felt like the beginning of something that would take a very long time to finish—forever.

* * * * *

A BUSINESS
ENGAGEMENT

MERLINE LOVELACE

To Susan and Monroe and Debbie and Scott
and most especially, le beau Monsieur Al.
Thanks for those magical days in Paris.
Next time, I promise not to break
a foot—or anything else!

Prologue

Ah, the joys of having two such beautiful, loving granddaughters. And the worries! Eugenia, my joyful Eugenia, is like a playful kitten. She gets into such mischief but always seems to land on her feet. It's Sarah I worry about. So quiet, so elegant and so determined to shoulder the burdens of our small family. She's only two years older than her sister but has been Eugenia's champion and protector since the day those darling girls came to live with me.

Now Sarah worries about *me*. I admit to a touch of arthritis and have one annoying bout of angina, but she insists on fussing over me like a mother hen. I've told her repeatedly I won't have her putting her life on hold because of me, but she won't listen. It's time, I think, to take more direct action. I'm not quite certain at this point just what action, but something will come to me. It must.

From the diary of Charlotte,
Grand Duchess of Karlenburgh

One

Sarah heard the low buzz but didn't pay any attention to it. She was on deadline and only had until noon to finish the layout for *Beguile*'s feature on the best new ski resorts for the young and ultrastylish. She wanted to finish the mockup in time for the senior staff's weekly working lunch. If she didn't have it ready, Alexis Danvers, the magazine's executive editor, would skewer her with one of the basilisk-like stares that had made her a legend in the world of glossy women's magazines.

Not that her boss's stony stares particularly bothered Sarah. They might put the rest of the staff in a flophouse sweat, but she and her sister had been raised by a grandmother who could reduce pompous officials or supercilious headwaiters to a quivering bundle of nerves with the lift of a single brow. Charlotte St. Sebastian had once moved in the same circles as Princess Grace and Jackie O. Those days were long gone, Sarah acknowledged, as she switched the headline font from Futura to Trajan, but Grandmama still adhered to the unshakable belief that good breeding and quiet elegance could see a woman through anything life might throw at her.

Sarah agreed completely. Which was one of the reasons she'd refined her own understated style during her three years as layout editor for a magazine aimed at thirtysome-things determined to be chic to the death. Her vintage Chanel suits and Dior gowns might come from Grandmama's closet, but she teamed the gowns with funky costume jewelry and the suit jackets with slacks or jeans and boots. The result was a stylishly retro look that even Alexis approved of.

The primary reason Sarah stuck to her own style, of course, was that she couldn't afford the designer shoes and bags and clothing featured in *Beguile*. Not with Grandmama's medical bills. Some of her hand-me-downs were starting to show their wear, though, and...

The buzz cut into her thoughts. Gaining volume, it rolled in her direction. Sarah was used to frequent choruses of oohs and aahs. Alexis often had models parade through the art and production departments to field test their hair or makeup or outfits on *Beguile*'s predominantly female staff.

Whatever was causing this chorus had to be special. Excitement crackled in the air like summer lightning. Wondering what new Jimmy Choo beaded boots or Atelier Versace gown was creating such a stir, Sarah swung her chair around. To her utter astonishment, she found herself looking up into the face of Sexy Single Number Three.

"Ms. St. Sebastian?"

The voice was cold, but the electric-blue eyes, black hair and rugged features telegraphed hot, hot, hot. Alexis had missed the mark with last month's issue, Sarah thought wildly. This man should have *topped* the magazine's annual Ten Sexiest Single Men in the World list instead of taking third place.

The artist in her could appreciate six-feet-plus of hard, muscled masculinity cloaked in the civilized veneer of a hand-tailored suit and Italian-silk tie. The professional in her responded to the coldness in his voice with equally cool civility.

"Yes?"

"I want to talk to you." Those devastating blue eyes cut to the side. "Alone."

Sarah followed his searing gaze. An entire gallery of female faces peered over, around and between the production department's chin-high partitions. A few of those faces were merely curious. Most appeared a half breath away from drooling.

She turned back to Number Three. Too bad his manners didn't live up to his looks. The aggressiveness in both his tone and his stance were irritating and uncalled for, to say the least.

"What do you want to talk to me about, Mr. Hunter?"

He didn't appear surprised that she knew his name. She did, after all, work at the magazine that had made hunky Devon Hunter the object of desire by a good portion of the female population at home and abroad.

"Your sister, Ms. St. Sebastian."

Oh, no! A sinking sensation hit Sarah in the pit of her stomach. What had Gina gotten into now?

Her glance slid to the silver-framed photo on the credenza beside her workstation. There was Sarah, dark-haired, green-eyed, serious as always, protective as always. And Gina. Blonde, bubbly, affectionate, completely irresponsible.

Two years younger than Sarah, Gina tended to change careers with the same dizzying frequency she tumbled in and out of love. She'd texted just a few days ago, gushing about the studly tycoon she'd hooked up with. Omitting, Gina style, to mention such minor details as his name or how they'd met.

Sarah had no trouble filling in the blanks now. Devon Hunter was founder and CEO of a Fortune 500 aerospace corporation headquartered in Los Angeles. Gina was in

L.A. chasing yet another career opportunity, this time as a party planner for the rich and famous.

"I think it best if we make this discussion private, Ms. St. Sebastian."

Resigned to the inevitable, Sarah nodded. Her sister's flings tended to be short and intense. Most ended amicably, but on several occasions Sarah had been forced to soothe some distinctly ruffled male feathers. This, apparently, was one of those occasions.

"Come with me, Mr. Hunter."

She led the way to a glass-walled conference room with angled windows that gave a view of Times Square. Framed prominently in one of the windows was the towering Condé Nast Building, the center of the universe for fashion publications. The building was home to *Vogue, Vanity Fair, Glamour* and *Allure.* Alexis often brought advertisers to the conference room to impress them with *Beguile*'s proximity to those icons in the world of women's glossies.

The caterers hadn't begun setting up for the working lunch yet but the conference room was always kept ready for visitors. The fridge discreetly hidden behind oak panels held a half-dozen varieties of bottled water, sparkling and plain, as well as juices and energy drinks. The gleaming silver coffee urns were replenished several times a day.

Sarah gestured to the urns on their marble counter. "Would you care for some coffee? Or some sparkling water, perhaps?"

"No. Thanks."

The curt reply decided her against inviting the man to sit. Crossing her arms, she leaned a hip against the conference table and assumed a look of polite inquiry.

"You wanted to talk about Gina?"

He took his time responding. Sarah refused to bristle as his killer blue eyes made an assessing trip from her face to her Chanel suit jacket with its black-and-white checks and signature logo to her black boots and back up again.

"You don't look much like your sister."

"No, I don't."

She was comfortable with her slender build and what her grandmother insisted were classic features, but she knew she didn't come close to Gina's stunning looks.

"My sister's the only beauty in the family."

Politeness dictated that he at least make a show of disputing the calm assertion. Instead, he delivered a completely unexpected bombshell.

"Is she also the only thief?"

Her arms dropped. Her jaw dropped with them. "I beg your pardon?"

"You can do more than beg my pardon, Ms. St. Sebastian. You can contact your sister and tell her to return the artifact she stole from my house."

The charge took Sarah's breath away. It came back on a hot rush. "How dare you make such a ridiculous, slanderous accusation?"

"It's neither ridiculous nor slanderous. It's fact."

"You're crazy!"

She was in full tigress mode now. Years of rushing to her younger sibling's defense spurred both fury and passion.

"Gina may be flighty and a little careless at times, but she would never take anything that didn't belong to her!"

Not intentionally, that is. There was that nasty little Pomeranian she'd brought home when she was eight or nine. She'd found it leashed to a sign outside a restaurant in one-hundred-degree heat and "rescued" it. And it was true Gina and her teenaged friends used to borrow clothes from each other constantly, then could never remember what belonged to whom. And, yes, she'd been known to overdraw her checking account when she was strapped for cash, which happened a little too frequently for Sarah's peace of mind.

But she would never commit theft, as this...this boor was suggesting. Sarah was about to call security to have the man escorted from the building when he reached into his suit pocket and palmed an iPhone.

"Maybe this clip from my home surveillance system will change your mind."

He tapped the screen, then angled it for Sarah to view. She saw a still image of what looked like a library or study, with the focus of the camera on an arrangement of glass shelves. The objects on the shelves were spaced and spot lighted for maximum dramatic effect. They appeared to be an eclectic mix. Sarah noted an African buffalo mask, a small cloisonné disk on a black lacquer stand and what looked like a statue of a pre-Columbian fertility goddess.

Hunter tapped the screen again and the still segued into a video. While Sarah watched, a tumble of platinum-blond curls came into view. Her heart began to thump painfully even before the owner of those curls moved toward the shelving. It picked up more speed when the owner showed her profile. That was her sister. Sarah couldn't even pretend to deny it.

Gina glanced over her shoulder, all casual nonchalance, all smiling innocence. When she moved out of view again, the cloisonné medallion no longer sat on its stand. Hunter froze the frame again, and Sarah stared at the empty stand as though it was a bad dream.

"It's Byzantine," he said drily. "Early twelfth century, in case you're interested. One very similar to it sold recently at Sotheby's in London for just over a hundred thousand."

She swallowed. Hard. "Dollars?"

"Pounds."

"Oh, God."

She'd rescued Gina from more scrapes than she could count. But this… She almost yanked out one of the chairs and collapsed in a boneless heap. The iron will she'd inherited from Grandmama kept her spine straight and her chin up.

"There's obviously a logical explanation for this, Mr. Hunter."

"I very much hope so, Ms. St. Sebastian."

She wanted to smack him. Calm, refined, always polite Sarah had to curl her hands into fists to keep from slapping that sneer off his too-handsome face.

He must have guessed her savagely suppressed urge. His jaw squared and his blue eyes took on a challenging glint, as if daring her to give it her best shot. When she didn't, he picked up where they'd left off.

"I'm very interested in hearing that explanation before I refer the matter to the police."

The police! Sarah felt a chill wash through her. Whatever predicament Gina had landed herself in suddenly assumed a very ominous tone. She struggled to keep the shock and worry out of her voice.

"Let me get in touch with my sister, Mr. Hunter. It may... it may take a while. She's not always prompt about returning calls or answering emails right away."

"Yeah, I found that out. I've been trying to reach her for several days."

He shot back a cuff and glanced at his watch.

"I've got meetings scheduled that will keep me tied up for the rest of this afternoon and well into the night. I'll make dinner reservations for tomorrow evening. Seven o'clock. Avery's, Upper West Side." He turned that hard blue gaze on her. "I assume you know the address. It's only a few blocks from the Dakota."

Still stunned by what she'd seen in the surveillance clip, Sarah almost missed his last comment. When it penetrated, her eyes widened in shock. "You know where I live?"

"Yes, Lady Sarah, I do." He tipped two fingers to his brow in a mock salute and strode for the door. "I'll see you tomorrow."

* * *

Lady Sarah.

Coming on top of everything else, the use of her empty title shouldn't have bothered her. Her boss trotted it out frequently at cocktail parties and business meetings. Sarah had stopped being embarrassed by Alexis's shameless peddling of a royal title that had long since ceased to have any relevance.

Unfortunately, Alexis wanted to do more than peddle the heritage associated with the St. Sebastian name. Sarah had threatened to quit—twice!—if her boss went ahead with the feature she wanted to on *Beguile*'s own Lady Sarah Elizabeth Marie-Adele St. Sebastian, granddaughter to Charlotte, the Destitute Duchess.

God! Sarah shuddered every time she remembered the slant Alexis had wanted to give the story. That destitute tag, as accurate as it was, would have shattered Grandmama's pride.

Having her younger granddaughter arrested for grand larceny wouldn't do a whole lot for it, either.

Jolted back to the issue at hand, Sarah rushed out of the conference room. She had to get hold of Gina. Find out if she'd really lifted that medallion. She was making a dash for her workstation when she saw her boss striding toward her.

"What's this I just heard?"

Alexis's deep, guttural smoker's rasp was always a shock to people meeting her for the first time. *Beguile*'s executive editor was paper-clip thin and always gorgeously dressed. But she would rather take her chances with cancer than quit smoking and risk ballooning up to a size four.

"Is it true?" she growled. "Devon Hunter was here?"

"Yes, he…"

"Why didn't you buzz me?"

"I didn't have time."

"What did he want? He's not going to sue us, is he?

Dammit, I told you to crop that locker-room shot above the waist."

"No, Alexis. You told me to make sure it showed his butt crack. And I told *you* I didn't think we should pay some smarmy gym employee to sneak pictures of the man without his knowledge or consent."

The executive editor waved that minor difference of editorial opinion aside. "So what did he want?"

"He's, uh, a friend of Gina's."

Or was, Sarah thought grimly, until the small matter of a twelfth-century medallion had come between them. She had to get to a phone. Had to call Gina.

"Another one of your sister's trophies?" Alexis asked sarcastically.

"I didn't have time to get all the details. Just that he's in town for some business meetings and wants to get together for dinner tomorrow."

The executive editor cocked her head. An all-too-familiar gleam entered her eyes, one that made Sarah swallow a groan. Pit bulls had nothing on Alexis when she locked her jaws on a story.

"We could do a follow-up," she said. "How making *Beguile*'s Top Ten list has impacted our sexy single's life. Hunter's pretty much a workaholic, isn't he?"

Frantic to get to the phone, Sarah gave a distracted nod. "That's how we portrayed him."

"I'm guessing he can't take a step now without tripping over a half-dozen panting females. Gina certainly smoked him out fast enough. I want details, Sarah. Details!"

She did her best to hide her agitation behind her usual calm facade. "Let me talk to my sister first. See what's going on."

"Do that. And get me details!"

Alexis strode off and Sarah barely reached the chair at her worktable before her knees gave out. She snatched up her iPhone and hit the speed-dial number for her sister. Of course, the call went to voice mail.

"Gina! I need to talk to you! Call me."

She also tapped out a text message and zinged off an email. None of which would do any good if her sister had forgotten to turn on her phone. Again. Knowing the odds of that were better than fifty-fifty, she tried Gina's current place of employment. She was put through to her sister's distinctly irate boss, who informed her that Gina hadn't shown up for work. Again.

"She called in yesterday morning. We'd catered a business dinner at the home of one our most important clients the night before. She said she was tired and was taking the day off. I haven't heard from her since."

Sarah had to ask. "Was that client Devon Hunter, by any chance?"

"Yes, it was. Look, Ms. St. Sebastian, your sister has a flair for presentation but she's completely unreliable. If you speak to her before I do, tell her not to bother coming in at all."

Despite the other, far more pressing problem that needed to be dealt with, Sarah hated that Gina had lost yet another job. She'd really seemed to enjoy this one.

"I'll tell her," she promised the irate supervisor. "And if she contacts you first, please tell her to call me."

She got through the working lunch somehow. Alexis, of course, demanded a laundry list of changes to the ski-resort layout. Drop shadows on the headline font. Less white space between the photos. Ascenders, not descenders, for the first letter of each lead paragraph.

Sarah made the fixes and shot the new layout from her computer to Alexis's for review. She then tried to frame another article describing the latest body-toning techniques. In between, she made repeated calls to Gina. They went unanswered, as did her emails and text messages.

Her concentration in shreds, she quit earlier than usual and hurried out into the April evening. A half block away, Times Square glowed in a rainbow of white, blue and brilliant-red lights. Tourists were out in full force, crowding the sidewalks and snapping pictures. Ordinarily Sarah took the subway to and from work, but a driving sense of urgency made her decide to splurge on a cab. Unbelievably, one cruised up just when she hit the curb. She slid in as soon as the previous passenger climbed out.

"The Dakota, please."

The turbaned driver nodded and gave her an assessing glance in the rearview mirror. Whatever their nationality, New York cabbies were every bit as savvy as any of *Beguile*'s fashion-conscious editors. This one might not get the label on Sarah's suit jacket exactly right but he knew quality when he saw it. He also knew a drop-off at one of New York City's most famous landmarks spelled big tips.

Usually. Sarah tried not to think how little of this month's check would be left after paying the utilities and maintenance fees for the seven-room apartment she shared with her grandmother. She also tried not to cringe when the cabbie scowled at the tip she gave him. Muttering something in his native language, he shoved his cab in gear.

Sarah hurried toward the entrance to the domed and turreted apartment building constructed in the 1880s and nodded to the doorman who stepped out of his niche to greet her.

"Good evening, Jerome."

"Good evening, Lady Sarah."

She'd long ago given up trying to get him to drop the empty title. Jerome felt it added to the luster of "his" building.

Not that the Dakota needed additional burnishing. Now a National Historic Landmark, its ornate exterior had been featured in dozens of films. Fictional characters in a host of novels claimed the Dakota as home. Real-life celebritics like Judy Garland, Lauren Bacall and Leonard Bernstein had lived there. And, sadly, John Lennon. He'd been shot just a short distance away. His widow, Yoko Ono, still owned several apartments in the building.

"The Duchess returned from her afternoon constitutional about an hour ago," Jerome volunteered. The merest hint of a shadow crossed his lean face. "She was leaning rather heavily on her cane."

Sharp, swift fear pushed aside Sarah's worry about her sister. "She didn't overdo it, did she?"

"She said not. But then, she wouldn't say otherwise, would she?"

"No," Sarah agreed in a hollow voice, "she wouldn't.

Charlotte St. Sebastian had witnessed the brutal execution of her husband and endured near-starvation before she'd escaped her war-ravaged country with her baby in her arms and a king's ransom in jewels hidden inside her daughter's teddy bear. She'd fled first to Vienna, then New York, where she'd slipped easily into the city's intellectual and social elite. The discreet, carefully timed sale of her jewels had allowed her to purchase an apartment at the Dakota and maintain a gracious lifestyle.

Tragedy struck again when she lost both her daughter and son-in-law in a boating accident. Sarah was just four and Gina still in diapers at the time. Not long after that, an unscrupulous Wall Street type sank the savings the duchess had managed to accrue into a Ponzi scheme that blew up in his and his clients' faces.

Those horrific events might have crushed a lesser woman. With two small girls to raise, Charlotte St. Sebastian wasted little time on self-pity. Once again she was forced to sell her heritage. The remaining jewels were discreetly disposed of over the years to provide her granddaughters with the education and lifestyle she insisted was their birthright. Private schools. Music tutors. Coming-out balls at the Waldorf. Smith College and a year at the Sorbonne for Sarah, Barnard for Gina.

Neither sister had a clue how desperate the financial situation had become, however, until Grandmama's heart attack. It was a mild one, quickly dismissed by the iron-spined duchess as a trifling bout of angina. The hospital charges weren't trifling, though. Nor was the stack of bills Sarah had found stuffed in Grandmama's desk when she sat down to pay what she'd thought were merely recurring monthly expenses. She'd nearly had a heart attack herself when she'd totaled up the amount.

Sarah had depleted her own savings account to pay that daunting stack of bills. Most of them, anyway. She still had to settle the charges for Grandmama's last echocardiogram. In the meantime, her single most important goal in life was to avoid stressing out the woman she loved with all her heart.

She let herself into their fifth-floor apartment, as shaken by Jerome's disclosure as by her earlier meeting with Devon Hunter. The comfortably padded Ecuadoran who served as maid, companion to Charlotte and friend to both Sarah and her sister for more than a decade was just preparing to leave.

"*Hola,* Sarah."

"*Hola,* Maria. How was your day?"

"Good. We walked, *la duquesa* and me, and shopped a little." She shouldered her hefty tote bag. "I go to catch my bus now. I'll see you tomorrow."

"Good night."

When the door closed behind her, a rich soprano voice only slightly dimmed by age called out, "Sarah? Is that you?"

"Yes, Grandmama."

She deposited her purse on the gilt-edged rococo sideboard gracing the entryway and made her way down a hall tiled in pale pink Carrara marble. The duchess hadn't been reduced to selling the furniture and artwork she'd acquired when she'd first arrived in New York, although Sarah now knew how desperately close she'd come to it.

"You're home early."

Charlotte sat in her favorite chair, the single aperitif she allowed herself despite the doctor's warning close at hand. The sight of her faded blue eyes and aristocratic nose brought a rush of emotion so strong Sarah had to swallow before she could a reply past the lump in her throat.

"Yes, I am."

She should have known Charlotte would pick up on the slightest nuance in her granddaughter's voice.

"You sound upset," she said with a small frown. "Did something happen at work?"

"Nothing more than the usual." Sarah forced a wry smile and went to pour herself a glass of white wine. "Alexis was on a tear about the ski-resort mock-up. I had to rework everything but the page count."

The duchess sniffed. "I don't know why you work for that woman."

"Mostly because she was the only one who would hire me."

"She didn't hire you. She hired your title."

Sarah winced, knowing it was true, and her grandmother instantly shifted gears.

"Lucky for Alexis the title came with an unerring eye for form, shape and spatial dimension," she huffed.

"Lucky for *me*," Sarah countered with a laugh. "Not everyone can parlay a degree in Renaissance-era art into a job at one of the country's leading fashion magazines."

"Or work her way from junior assistant to senior editor in just three years," Charlotte retorted. Her face softened into an expression that played on Sarah's heartstrings like a finely tuned Stradivarius. "Have I told you how proud I am of you?"

"Only about a thousand times, Grandmama."

They spent another half hour together before Charlotte decided she would rest a little before dinner. Sarah knew better than to offer to help her out of her chair, but she wanted to. God, she wanted to! When her grandmother's cane had thumped slowly down the hall to her bedroom, Sarah fixed a spinach salad and added a bit more liquid to the chicken Maria had begun baking in the oven. Then she washed her hands, detoured into the cavernous sitting room that served as a study and booted up her laptop.

She remembered the basics from the article *Beguile* had run on Devon Hunter. She wanted to dig deeper, uncover every minute detail she could about the man before she crossed swords with him again tomorrow evening.

Two

Seated at a linen-draped table by the window, Dev watched Sarah St. Sebastian approach the restaurant's entrance. Tall and slender, she moved with restrained grace. No swinging hips, no ground-eating strides, just a smooth symmetry of motion and dignity.

She wore her hair down tonight. He liked the way the mink-dark waves framed her face and brushed the shoulders of her suit jacket. The boxy jacket was a sort of pale purple. His sisters would probably call that color lilac or heliotrope or something equally girlie. The skirt was black and just swished her boot tops as she walked.

Despite growing up with four sisters, Dev's fashion sense could be summed up in a single word. A woman either looked good, or she didn't. This one looked good. *Very* good.

He wasn't the only one who thought so. When she entered the restaurant and the greeter escorted her to the table by the window, every head in the room turned. Males without female companions were openly admiring. Those with women at their tables were more discreet but no less appreciative. Many of the women, too, slanted those seemingly casual, careless glances that instantly catalogued every detail of hair, dress, jewelry and shoes.

How the hell did they do that? Dev could walk into the belly of a plane and tell in a single glance if the struts were buckling or the rivets starting to rust. As he'd discovered since that damned magazine article came out, however, his powers of observation paled beside those of the female of the species.

He'd treated the Ten Sexiest Singles list as a joke at first. He could hardly do otherwise, with his sisters, brothers-in-law and assorted nieces and nephews ragging him about it nonstop. And okay, being named one of the world's top ten hunks did kind of puff up his ego.

That was before women began stopping him on the street to let him know they were available. Before waitresses started hustling over to take his order and make the same pronouncement. Before the cocktail parties he was forced to attend as the price of doing business became a total embarrassment.

Dev had been able to shrug off most of it. He couldn't shrug off the wife of the French CEO he was trying to close a multibillion dollar deal with. The last time Dev was in Paris, Elise Girault had draped herself all over him. He knew then he had to put a stop to what had become more than just a nuisance.

He'd thought he'd found the perfect tool in Lady Eugenia Amalia Therése St. Sebastian. The blonde was gorgeous, vivacious and so photogenic that the vultures otherwise known as paparazzi wouldn't even glance at Dev if she was anywhere in the vicinity.

Thirty minutes in Gina St. Sebastian's company had deep-sixed that idea. Despite her pedigree, the woman was as bubbleheaded as she was sumptuous. Then she'd lifted the Byzantine medallion and the game plan had changed completely. For the better, Dev decided as he rose to greet the slender brunette being escorted to his table.

Chin high, shoulders back, Sarah St. Sebastian carried herself like the royalty she was. Or would have been, if her grandmother's small Eastern European country hadn't dispensed with royal titles about the same time Soviet tanks had rumbled across its border. The tanks had rumbled out again four decades later. By that time the borders of Eastern Europe had been redrawn several times and the duchy that had been home to the St. Sebastians for several centuries had completely disappeared.

Bad break for Charlotte St. Sebastian and her granddaughters. Lucky break for Dev. Lady Sarah didn't know it yet, but she was going to extract him from the mess she and her magazine had created.

"Good evening, Mr. Hunter."

The voice was cool, the green eyes cold.

"Good evening, Ms. St. Sebastian."

Dev stood patiently while the greeter seated her. A server materialized instantly.

"A cocktail or glass of wine before dinner, madam?"

"No, thank you. And no dinner." She waved aside the gilt-edged menu he offered and locked those forest-glade eyes on Dev. "I'll just be here a few minutes, then I'll leave Mr. Hunter to enjoy his meal."

The server departed, and Dev reclaimed his seat. "Are you sure you don't want dinner?"

"I'm sure." She placed loosely clasped hands on the table and launched an immediate offensive. "We're not here to exchange pleasantries, Mr. Hunter."

Dev sat back against his chair, his long legs outstretched beneath the starched tablecloth and his gaze steady on her face. Framed by those dark, glossy waves, her features fascinated him. The slight widow's peak, the high cheekbones, the aquiline nose—all refined and remote and in seeming contrast to those full, sensual lips. She might have modeled for some famous fifteenth- or sixteenth-century sculptor. Dev was damned if he knew which.

"No, we're not," he agreed, still intrigued by that face. "Have you talked to your sister?"

The clasped hands tightened. Only a fraction, but that small jerk was a dead giveaway.

"I haven't been able to reach her."

"Neither have I. So what do you propose we do now?"

"I propose you wait." She drew in a breath and forced a small smile. "Give me more time to track Gina down before you report your medallion missing or...or..."

"Or stolen?"

The smile evaporated. "Gina didn't steal that piece, Mr. Hunter. I admit it appears she took it for some reason, but I'm sure...I *know* she'll return it. Eventually."

Dev played with the tumbler containing his scotch, circling it almost a full turn before baiting the trap.

"The longer I wait to file a police report, Ms. St. Sebastian, the more my insurance company is going to question why. A delay reporting the loss could void the coverage."

"Give me another twenty-four hours, Mr. Hunter. Please."

She hated to beg. He heard it in her voice, saw it in the way her hands were knotted together now, the knuckles white.

"All right, Ms. St. Sebastian. Twenty-four hours. If your sister hasn't returned the medallion by then, however, I..."

"She will. I'm sure she will."

"And if she doesn't?"

She drew in another breath: longer, shakier. "I'll pay you the appraised value."

"How?"

Her chin came up. Her jaws went tight. "It will take some time," she admitted. "We'll have to work out a payment schedule."

Dev didn't like himself much at the moment. If he didn't have a multibillion-dollar deal hanging fire, he'd call this farce off right now. Setting aside the crystal tumbler, he leaned forward.

"Let's cut to the chase here, Ms. St. Sebastian. I had my people run an in-depth background check on your feather-headed sister. On you, too. I know you've bailed Gina out of one mess after another. I know you're currently providing your grandmother's sole support. I also know you barely make enough to cover her medical co-pays, let alone reimburse me for a near-priceless artifact."

Every vestige of color had drained from her face, but pride sparked in those mesmerizing eyes. Before she could tell him where to go and how to get there, Dev sprang the trap.

"I have an alternate proposal, Ms. St. Sebastian."

Her brows snapped together. "What kind of a proposal?"

"I need a fiancée."

For the second time in as many days Dev saw her composure crumble. Her jaw dropping, she treated him to a disbelieving stare.

"Excuse me?"

"I need a fiancée," he repeated. "I was considering Gina for the position. I axed that idea after thirty minutes in her company. Becoming engaged to your sister," he drawled, "is not for the faint of heart."

He might have stunned her with his proposition. That didn't prevent her from leaping to the defense. Dev suspected it came as natural to her as breathing.

"My sister, Mr. Hunter, is warm and generous and open-hearted and…"

"Gone to ground." He drove the point home with the same swift lethality he brought to the negotiating table. "You, on the other hand, are available. And you owe me."

"*I* owe you?"

"You and that magazine you work for." Despite his best efforts to keep his irritation contained, it leaked into his voice. "Do you have any idea how many women have accosted me since that damned article came out? I can't even grab a meatball sub at my favorite deli without some female writing her number on a napkin and trying to stuff it into my pants pocket."

Her shock faded. Derision replaced it. She sat back in her chair with her lips pooched in false sympathy.

"Ooh. You poor, poor sex object."

"You may think it's funny," he growled. "I don't. Not with a multibillion-dollar deal hanging in the balance."

That wiped the smirk off her face. "Putting you on our Ten Sexiest Singles list has impacted your business? How?"

Enlightenment dawned in almost the next breath. The smirk returned. "Oh! Wait! I've got it. You have so many women throwing themselves at you that you can't concentrate."

"You're partially correct. But it's not a matter of not being able to concentrate. It's more that I don't want to jeopardize the deal by telling the wife of the man I'm negotiating with to keep her hands to herself."

"So instead of confronting the woman, you want to hide behind a fiancée."

The disdain was cool and well-bred, but it was there. Dev was feeling the sting when he caught a flutter of movement from the corner of one eye. A second later the flutter evolved into a tall, sleek redhead being shown to an empty table a little way from theirs. She caught Dev's glance, arched a penciled brow and came to a full stop beside their table.

"I know you." She tilted her head and put a finger to her chin. "Remind me. Where have we met?"

"We haven't," Dev replied, courteous outside, bracing inside.

"Are you sure? I never forget a face. Or," she added as her lips curved in a slow, feline smile, "a truly excellent butt."

The grimace that crossed Hunter's face gave Sarah a jolt

of fierce satisfaction. Let him squirm, she thought gleefully. Let him writhe like a specimen under a microscope.
He deserved the embarrassment.

Except…

He didn't. Not really. *Beguile* had put him under the microscope. *Beguile* had also run a locker-room photo with
the face angled away from the camera just enough to keep
them from getting sued. And as much as Sarah hated to
admit it, the man had shown a remarkable degree of re-
straint by not reporting his missing artifact to the police
immediately.

Still, she didn't want to come to his rescue. She *really*
didn't. It was an innate and very grudging sense of fair
play that compelled her to mimic her grandmother in one
of Charlotte's more imperial moods.

"I beg your pardon," she said with icy hauteur. "I believe my fiancé has already stated he doesn't know you.
Now, if you don't mind, we would like to continue our
conversation."

The woman's cheeks flushed almost the same color as
her hair. "Yes, of course. Sorry for interrupting."

She hurried to her table, leaving Hunter staring after her
while Sarah took an unhurried sip from her water goblet.

"That's it." He turned back to her, amusement slashing
across his face. "That's exactly what I want from you."

Whoa! Sarah gripped the goblet's stem and tried to blunt
the impact of the grin aimed in her direction. Devon Hunter
all cold and intimidating she could handle. Devon Hunter
with crinkly squint lines at the corners of those killer blue
eyes and his mouth tipped into a rakish smile was something else again.

The smile made him look so different. That, and the
more casual attire he wore tonight. He was in a suit again,
but he'd dispensed with a tie and his pale blue shirt was
open at the neck. This late in the evening, a five-o'clock
shadow darkened his cheeks and chin, giving him the so-

phisticated bad-boy look so many of *Beguile*'s male models tried for but could never quite pull off.

The research Sarah had done on the man put him in a different light, too. She'd had to dig hard for details. Hunter was notorious about protecting his privacy, which was why *Beguile* had been forced to go with a fluff piece instead of the in-depth interview Alexis had wanted. And no doubt why he resented the article so much, Sarah acknowledged with a twinge of guilt.

The few additional details she'd managed to dig up had contributed to an intriguing picture. She'd already known that Devon Hunter had enlisted in the Air Force right out of high school and trained as a loadmaster on big cargo jets. She hadn't known he'd completed a bachelor's *and* a master's during his eight years in uniform, despite spending most of those years flying into combat zones or disaster areas.

On one of those combat missions his aircraft had come under intense enemy fire. Hunter had jerry-rigged some kind of emergency fix to its damaged cargo ramp that had allowed them to take on hundreds of frantic Somalian refugees attempting to escape certain death. He'd left the Air Force a short time later and patented the modification he'd devised. From what Sarah could gather, it was now used on military and civilian aircraft worldwide.

That enterprise had earned Hunter his first million. The rest, as they say, was history. She hadn't found a precise estimate of the man's net worth, but it was obviously enough to allow him to collect hundred-thousand-pound museum pieces. Which brought her back to the problem at hand.

"Look, Mr. Hunter, this whole…"

"Dev," he interrupted, the grin still in place. "Now that we're engaged, we should dispense with the formalities. I know you have a half-dozen names. Do you go by Sarah or Elizabeth or Marie-Adele?"

"Sarah," she conceded, "but we are *not* engaged."

He tipped his chin toward the woman several tables away, her nose now buried in a menu. "Red there thinks we are."

"I simply didn't care for her attitude."

"Me, either." The amusement left his eyes. "That's why I offered you a choice. Let me spell out the basic terms so there's no misunderstanding. You agree to an engagement. Six months max. Less, if I close the deal currently on the table. In return, I destroy the surveillance tape and don't report the loss."

"But the medallion! You said it was worth a hundred thousand pounds or more."

"I'm willing to accept your assurances that Gina will return it. Eventually. In the meantime…" He lifted his tumbler in a mock salute. "To us, Sarah."

Feeling much like the proverbial mouse backed into a corner, she snatched at her last lifeline. "You promised me another twenty-four hours. The deal doesn't go into effect until then. Agreed?"

He hesitated, then lifted his shoulders in a shrug. "Agreed."

Surely Gina would return her calls before then and this whole, ridiculous situation would be resolved. Sarah clung to that hope as she pushed away from the table.

"Until tomorrow, Mr. Hunter."

"Dev," he corrected, rising, as well.

"No need for you to walk me out. Please stay and enjoy your dinner."

"Actually, I got hungry earlier and grabbed a Korean taco from a street stand. Funny," he commented as he tossed some bills on the table, "I've been in and out of Korea a dozen times. Don't remember ever having tacos there."

He took her elbow in a courteous gesture Grandmama would approve of. Very correct, very polite, not really possessive but edging too close to it for Sarah's comfort. Walking beside him only reinforced the impression she'd gained yesterday of his height and strength.

They passed the redhead's table on the way to the door. She glanced up, caught Sarah's dismissive stare and stuck her nose back in the menu.

"I'll hail you a cab," Hunter said as they exited the restaurant.

"It's only a few blocks."

"It's also getting dark. I know this is your town, but I'll feel better sending you home in a cab."

Sarah didn't argue further, mostly because dusk had started to descend and the air had taken on a distinct chill. Across the street, the lanterns in Central Park shed their golden glow. She turned in a half circle, her artist's eye delighting in the dots of gold punctuating the deep purple of the park.

Unfortunately, the turn brought the redhead into view again. The picture there wasn't as delightful. She was squinting at them through the restaurant's window, a phone jammed to her ear. Whoever she was talking to was obviously getting an earful.

Sarah guessed instantly she was spreading the word about Sexy Single Number Three and his fiancée. The realization gave her a sudden, queasy feeling. New York City lived and breathed celebrities. They were the stuff of life on *Good Morning America,* were courted by Tyra Banks and the women of *The View,* appeared regularly on *Late Show with David Letterman.* The tabloids, the glossies, even the so-called "literary" publications paid major bucks for inside scoops.

And Sarah had just handed them one. Thoroughly disgusted with herself for yielding to impulse, she smothered a curse that would have earned a sharp reprimand from Grandmama. Hunter followed her line of sight and spotted the woman staring at them through the restaurant window, the phone still jammed to her ear. He shared Sarah's pessimistic view of the matter but didn't bother to swallow his curse. It singed the night air.

"This is going turn up in another rag like *Beguile,* isn't it?"

Sarah stiffened. True, she'd privately cringed at some of the articles Alexis had insisted on putting in print. But that didn't mean she would stand by and let an outsider disparage her magazine.

"*Beguile* is hardly a rag. We're one of the leading fashion publications for women in the twenty to thirty-five age range, here and abroad."

"If you say so."

"I do," she ground out.

The misguided sympathy she'd felt for the man earlier had gone as dry and stale as yesterday's bagel. It went even staler when he turned to face her. Devon Hunter of the crinkly squint lines and heart-stuttering grin was gone. His intimidating alter ego was back.

"I guess if we're going to show up in some pulp press, we might as well give the story a little juice."

She saw the intent in his face and put up a warning palm. "Let's not do anything rash here, Mr. Hunter."

"Dev," he corrected, his eyes drilling into hers. "Say it, Sarah. Dev."

"All right! Dev. Are you satisfied?"

"Not quite."

His arm went around her waist. One swift tug brought them hip to hip. His hold was an iron band, but he gave her a second, maybe two, to protest.

Afterward Sarah could list in precise order the reasons she should have done exactly that. She didn't like the man. He was flat-out blackmailing her with Gina's rash act. He was too arrogant, and too damned sexy, for his own good.

But right then, right there, she looked up into those

dangerous blue eyes and gave in to the combustible mix of guilt, nagging worry and Devon Hunter's potent masculinity.

Three

Sarah had been kissed before. A decent number of times, as a matter of fact. She hadn't racked up as many admirers as Gina, certainly, but she'd dated steadily all through high school and college. She'd also teetered dangerously close to falling in love at least twice. Once with the sexy Italian she'd met at the famed Uffizi Gallery and spent a dizzying week exploring Florence with. Most recently with a charismatic young lawyer who had his eye set on a career in politics. That relationship had died a rather painful death when she discovered he was more in love with her background and empty title than he was with her.

Even with the Italian, however, she'd never indulged in embarrassingly public displays of affection. In addition to Grandmama's black-and-white views of correct behavior, Sarah's inbred reserve shied away from the kind of exuberant joie de vivre that characterized her sister. Yet here she was, locked in the arms of a near stranger on the sidewalk of one of New York's busiest avenues. Her oh-so-proper self shouted that she was providing a sideshow for everyone in and outside the restaurant. Her other self, the one she let off its leash only on rare occasions, leaped to life.

If *Beguile* ever ran a list of the World's Ten Best Kissers, she thought wildly, she would personally nominate Devon Hunter for the top slot. His mouth fit over hers as though it was made to. His lips demanded a response.

Sarah gave it. Angling her head, she planted both palms on his chest. The hard muscles under his shirt and suit coat provided a feast of tactile sensations. The fine bristles scraping her chin added more. She could taste the faint, smoky hint of scotch on his lips, feel the heat that rose in his skin.

There was nothing hidden in Hunter's kiss. No attempt to impress or connect or score a victory in the battle of the sexes. His mouth moved easily over hers. Confidently. Hungrily.

Her breath came hard and fast when he raised his head. So did his. Sarah took immense satisfaction in that—and the fact that he looked as surprised and disconcerted as she felt at the moment. When his expression switched to a frown, though, she half expected a cutting remark. What she got was a curt apology.

"I'm sorry." He dropped his hold on her waist and stepped back a pace. "That was uncalled for."

Sarah wasn't about to point out that she hadn't exactly resisted. While she struggled to right her rioting senses, she caught a glimpse of a very interested audience backlit inside the restaurant. Among them was the redhead, still watching avidly, only this time she had her phone aimed in their direction.

"Uncalled for or not," Sarah said with a small groan, "be prepared for the possibility that kiss might make its way into print. I suspect your friend's phone is camera equipped."

He shot a glance over his shoulder and blew out a disgusted breath. "I'm sure it is."

"What a mess," she murmured half under her breath. "My boss will *not* be happy."

Hunter picked up on the ramifications of the comment instantly. "Is this going to cause a problem for you at work? You and me, our engagement, getting scooped by some other rag, uh, magazine?"

"First, we're not engaged. Yet. Second, you don't need to worry about my work."

Mostly because he wouldn't be on scene when the storm hit. If *Beguile*'s executive editor learned from another source that Sarah had locked lips with Number Three on busy Central Park West, she'd make a force-five hurricane seem like a spring shower.

Then there was the duchess.

"I'm more concerned about my grandmother," Sarah admitted reluctantly. "If she should see or hear something before I get this mess straightened out…"

She gnawed on her lower lip, trying to find a way out of what was looking more and more like the kind of dark, tangly thing you find at the bottom of a pond. To her surprise, Hunter offered a solution to at least one of her problems.

"Tell you what," he said slowly. "Why don't I take you home tonight? You can introduce me to your grandmother. That way, whatever happens next won't come as such a bolt from the blue."

It was a measure of how desperate Sarah was feeling that she actually considered the idea.

"I don't think so," she said after a moment. "I don't want to complicate the situation any more at this point."

"All right. I'm staying at the Waldorf. Call me when you've had time to consider my proposal. If I don't hear from you within twenty-four hours, I'll assume your tacit agreement."

With that parting shot, he stepped to the curb and flagged down a cab for her. Sarah slid inside, collapsed against the seat and spent the short ride to the Dakota alternately feeling the aftereffects of that kiss, worrying about her sister and cursing the mess Gina had landed her in.

When she let herself in to the apartment, Maria was emptying the dishwasher just prior to leaving.

"*Hola,* Sarah."

"*Hola,* Maria. How did it go today?"

"Well. We walk in the park this afternoon."

She tucked the last plate in the cupboard and let the dishwasher close with a quiet whoosh. The marble counter got a final swipe.

"We didn't expect you home until late," the housekeeper commented as she reached for the coat she'd draped over a kitchen chair. "*La duquesa* ate an early dinner and retired to her room. She dozed when I checked a few minutes ago."

"Okay, Maria. Thanks."

"You're welcome, *chica.*" The Ecuadoran shrugged into her coat and hefted her suitcase-size purse. Halfway to the hall, she turned back. "I almost forgot. Gina called."

"When!"

"About a half hour ago. She said you texted her a couple times."

"A couple? Try ten or twenty."

"Ah, well." A fond smile creased the maid's plump cheeks. "That's Gina."

"Yes, it is," Sarah agreed grimly. "Did she mention where she was?"

"At the airport in Los Angeles. She said she just wanted to make sure everything was all right before she got on the plane."

"What plane? Where was she going?"

Maria's face screwed up in concentration. "Switzerland, I think she said. Or maybe…Swaziland?"

Knowing Gina, it could be either. Although, Sarah thought on a sudden choke of panic, Europe probably boasted better markets for twelfth-century Byzantine artifacts.

She said a hurried good-night to Maria and rummaged

frantically in her purse for her phone. She had to catch her sister before her plane took off.

When she got the phone out, the little green text icon indicated she had a text message. And she'd missed hearing the alert. Probably because she was too busy letting Devon Hunter kiss her all the way into next week.

The message was brief and typical Gina.

Met the cuddliest ski instructor.
Off to Switzerland. Later.

Hoping against hope it wasn't too late, Sarah hit speed dial. The call went immediately to voice mail. She tried texting and stood beside the massive marble counter, scowling at the screen, willing the little icon to pop back a response.

No luck. Gina had obviously powered down her phone. If she ran true to form, she would forget to power the damned thing back up for hours—maybe days—after she landed in Switzerland.

Sarah could almost hear a loud, obnoxious clock ticking inside her head as she went to check on her grandmother. Hunter had given her an additional twenty-four hours. Twenty-three now, and counting.

She knocked lightly on the door, then opened it as quietly as she could. The duchess sat propped against a bank of pillows. Her eyes were closed and an open book lay in her lap.

The anxiety gnawing at Sarah's insides receded for a moment, edged aside by the love that filled her like liquid warmth. She didn't see her grandmother's thin, creased cheeks or the liver spots sprinkled across the back of her hands. She saw the woman who'd opened her heart and her arms to two scared little girls. Charlotte St. Sebastian had nourished and educated them. She'd also shielded them from as much of the world's ugliness as she could. Now it was Sarah's turn to do the same.

She tried to ease the book out of the duchess's lax fingers without waking her. She didn't succeed. Charlotte's papery eyelids fluttered up. She blinked a couple of times to focus and smiled.

"How was your dinner?"

Sarah couldn't lie, but she could dodge a bit. "The restaurant was definitely up to your standards. We'll have to go there for your birthday."

"Never mind my birthday." She patted the side of the bed. "Sit down and tell me about this friend of Eugenia's. Do you think there's anything serious between them?"

Hunter was serious, all right. Just not in any way Charlotte would approve of.

"They're not more than casual acquaintances. In fact, Gina sent me a text earlier this evening. She's off to Switzerland with the cuddliest ski instructor. Her words, not mine."

"That girl," Charlotte huffed. "She'll be the death of me yet."

Not if Sarah could help it. The clock was pounding away inside her head, though. In desperation, she took Hunter's advice and decided to lay some tentative groundwork for whatever might come tomorrow.

"I actually know him better than Gina does, Grandmama."

"The ski instructor?"

"The man I met at the restaurant this evening. Devon Hunter." Despite everything, she had to smile. "You know him, too. He came in at Number Three on our Ten Sexiest Singles list."

"Oh, for heaven's sake, Sarah. You know I only peruse *Beguile* to gain an appreciation for your work. I don't pay any attention to the content."

"I guess it must have been Maria who dog-eared that particular section," she teased.

Charlotte tipped her aristocratic nose. The gesture was

instinctive and inbred and usually preceded a withering set-down. To Sarah's relief, the nose lowered a moment later and a smile tugged at her grandmother's lips.

"Is he as hot in real life as he is in print?"

"Hotter." She drew a deep mental breath. "Which is why I kissed him outside the restaurant."

"You kissed him? In public?" Charlotte *tch-tched*, but it was a halfhearted effort. Her face had come alive with interest. "That's so déclassé, dearest."

"Yes, I know. Even worse, there was a totally obnoxious woman inside the restaurant. She recognized Devon and made a rather rude comment. I suspect she may have snapped a picture or two. The kiss may well show up in some tabloid."

"I should hope not!"

Her lips thinning, the duchess contemplated that distasteful prospect for a moment before making a shrewd observation.

"Alexis will throw a world-class tantrum if something like this appears in any magazine but hers. You'd best forewarn her."

"I intend to." She glanced at the pillbox and crystal water decanter on the marble-topped nightstand. "Did you take your medicine?"

"Yes, I did."

"Are you sure? Sometimes you doze off and forget."

"I took it, Sarah. Don't fuss at me."

"It's my job to fuss." She leaned forward and kissed a soft, lily-of-the-valley-scented cheek. "Good night, Grand-mama."

"Good night."

She got as far as the bedroom door. Close, so close, to making an escape. She had one hand on the latch when the duchess issued an imperial edict.

"Bring this Mr. Hunter by for drinks tomorrow evening, Sarah. I would like to meet him."

"I'm not certain what his plans are."

"Whatever they are," Charlotte said loftily, "I'm sure he can work in a brief visit."

Sarah went to sleep trying to decide which would be worse: entering into a fake engagement, informing Alexis that a tabloid might beat *Beguile* to a juicy story involving one of its own editors or continuing to feed her grandmother half-truths.

The first thing she did when she woke up the next morning was grab her cell phone. No text from Gina. No email. No voice message.

"You're a dead woman," she snarled at her absent sibling. "Dead!"

Throwing back the covers, she stomped to the bathroom. Like the rest of the rooms in the apartment, it was high ceilinged and trimmed with elaborate crown molding. Most of the fixtures had been updated over the years, but the tub was big and claw-footed and original. Sarah indulged in long, decadent soaks whenever she could. This morning she was too keyed up and in too much of a hurry for anything more than a quick shower.

Showered and blow-dried, she chose one of her grandmama's former favorites—a slate-gray Pierre Balmain minidress in a classic A-line. According to Charlotte, some women used to pair these thigh-skimming dresses with white plastic go-go boots. *She* never did, of course. Far too gauche. She'd gone with tasteful white stockings and Ferragamo pumps. Sarah opted for black tights, a pair of Giuseppi Zanottis she'd snatched up at a secondhand shoe store and multiple strands of fat faux pearls.

Thankfully, the duchess preferred a late, leisurely breakfast with Maria, so Sarah downed her usual bagel and black coffee and left for work with only a quick goodbye.

She got another reprieve at work. Alexis had called in to say she was hopping an early shuttle to Chicago for a short-notice meeting with the head of their publishing group. And to Sarah's infinite relief, a computer search of stories in print for the day didn't pop with either her name or a lurid blowup of her wrapped in Devon Hunter's arms.

That left the rest of the day to try to rationalize her unexpected reaction to his kiss and make a half-dozen futile attempts to reach Gina. All the while the clock marched steadily, inexorably toward her deadline.

Dev shot a glance at the bank of clocks lining one wall of the conference room. Four-fifteen. A little less than four hours to the go/no-go point.

He tuned out the tanned-and-toned executive at the head of the gleaming mahogany conference table. The man had been droning on for almost forty minutes now. His equally slick associates had nodded and ahemed and interjected several editorial asides about the fat military contract they were confident their company would win.

Dev knew better. They'd understated their start-up costs so blatantly the Pentagon procurement folks would laugh these guys out of the competition. Dev might have chalked this trip to NYC as a total waste of time if not for his meeting with Sarah St. Sebastian.

Based on the profile he'd had compiled on her, he'd expected someone cool, confident, levelheaded and fiercely loyal to both the woman who'd raised her and the sibling who gave her such grief. What he hadn't expected was her inbred elegance. Or the kick to his gut when she'd walked into the restaurant last night. Or the hours he'd spent afterward remembering her taste and her scent and the press of her body against his.

His visceral reaction to the woman could be a potential glitch in his plan. He needed a decoy. A temporary fiancée to blunt the effect of that ridiculous article. Someone to act as a buffer between him and the total strangers hitting on him everywhere he went—and the French CEO's wife who'd whispered such suggestive obscenities in his ear.

Sarah St. Sebastian was the perfect solution to those embarrassments. She'd proved as much last night when she'd cut Red off at the knees. Problem was the feel of her, the taste of her, had damned near done the same to Dev. The delectable Sarah could well prove more of a distraction than the rest of the bunch rolled up together.

So what the hell should he do now? Call her and tell her the deal he'd offered was no longer on the table? Write off the loss of the medallion? Track Gina down and recover the piece himself?

The artifact itself wasn't the issue, of course. Dev had lost more in the stock market in a single day than that bit of gold and enamel was worth. The only reason he'd pursued it this far was that he didn't like getting ripped off any more than the next guy. That, and the damned Ten Sexiest Singles article. He'd figured he could leverage the theft of the medallion into a temporary fiancée.

Which brought him full circle. What should he do about Sarah? His conscience had pinged at him last night. It was lobbing 50mm mortar shells now.

Dev had gained a rep in the multibillion-dollar world of aerospace manufacturing for being as tough as boot leather, but honest. He'd never lied to a competitor or grossly underestimated a bid like these jokers were doing now. Nor had he ever resorted to blackmail. Dev shifted uncomfortably, feeling as prickly about the one-sided deal he'd offered Sarah as by the patently false estimates Mr. Smooth kept flashing up on the screen.

To hell with it. He could take care of at least one of those itches right now.

"Excuse me, Jim."

Tanned-and-toned broke off in midspiel. He and his associates turned eager faces to Dev.

"We'll have to cut this short," he said without a trace of

apology. "I've got something hanging fire that I thought could wait. I need to take care of it now."

Jim and company concealed their disappointment behind shark-toothed smiles. Professional courtesy dictated that Devon offer a palliative.

"Why don't you email me the rest of your presentation? I'll study it on the flight home."

Tanned-and-toned picked up an in-house line and murmured an order to his AV folks. When he replaced the receiver, his smile sat just a few degrees off center.

"It's done, Dev."

"Thanks, Jimmy. I'll get back to you when I've had a chance to review your numbers in a little more depth."

Ole Jim's smile slipped another couple of degrees but he managed to hang on to its remnants as he came around the table to pump Devon's hand.

"I'll look forward to hearing from you. Soon, I hope."

"By the end of the week," Devon promised, although he knew Mr. Smooth wouldn't like what he had to say.

He decided to wait until he was in the limo and headed back to his hotel to contact Sarah. As the elevator whisked him down fifty stories, he tried to formulate exactly what he'd say to her.

His cell phone buzzed about twenty stories into the descent. Dev answered with his customary curt response, blissfully unaware a certain green-eyed brunette was just seconds away from knocking his world off its axis.

"Hunter."

"Mr. Hunter... Dev... It's Sarah St. Sebastian."

"Hello, Sarah. Have you heard from Gina?"

"Yes. Well, sort of."

Hell! So much for his nagging guilt over coercing this woman into a fake engagement. All Devon felt now was a searing disappointment that it might not take place. The feeling was so sharp and surprisingly painful he almost missed her next comment.

"Gina's on her way to Switzerland. Or she was when she texted me last night."

"What's in…?"

He broke off, knowing the answer before he asked the question. Bankers in Switzerland would commit hara-kiri before violating the confidentiality of deals brokered under their auspices. What better place to sell—and deposit the proceeds of—a near-priceless piece of antiquity?

"So where does that leave us?"

It came out stiffer than he'd intended. She responded in the same vein.

"I'm still trying to reach Gina. If I can't…"

The elevator reached the lobby. Dev stepped out, the phone to his ear and his adrenaline pumping the way it did when his engineers were close to some innovative new concept or major modification to the business of hauling cargo.

"If you can't?" he echoed.

"I don't see I have any choice but to agree to your preposterous offer."

She spelled it out. Slowly. Tightly. As if he'd forgotten the conditions he'd laid down last night.

"Six months as your fiancée. Less if you complete the negotiations you're working on. In return, you don't press charges against my sister. Correct?"

"Correct." Crushing his earlier doubts, he pounced. "So we have a deal?"

"On one condition."

A dozen different contingency clauses flashed through his mind. "And that is?" he said cautiously.

"You have to come for cocktails this evening. Seven o'clock. My grandmother wants to meet you."

Four

Dev frowned at his image in the elevator's ornate mirror and adjusted his tie. He was damned if he knew why he was so nervous about meeting Charlotte St. Sebastian.

He'd flown into combat zones more times than he could count, for God's sake. He'd also participated in relief missions to countries devastated by fires, tsunamis, earthquakes, horrific droughts and bloody civil wars. More than once his aircraft had come under enemy fire. And he still carried the scar from the hit he'd taken while racing through a barrage of bullets to get a sobbing, desperate mother and her wounded child aboard before murderous rebels overran the airport.

Those experiences had certainly shaped Dev's sense of self. Building an aerospace design-and-manufacturing empire from the ground up only solidified that self-confidence. He now rubbed elbows with top-level executives and power brokers around the world. Charlotte St. Sebastian wouldn't be the first royal he'd met, or even the highest ranking.

Yet the facts Dev had gathered about the St. Sebastian family painted one hell of an intimidating picture of its matriarch. The woman had once stood next in line to rule a duchy with a history that spanned some seven hundred years. She'd been forced to witness her husband's execution by firing squad. Most of her remaining family had disappeared forever in the notorious gulags. Charlotte herself had gone into hiding with her infant daughter and endured untold hardships before escaping to the West.

That would be heartbreak enough for anyone. Yet the duchess had also been slammed with the tragic death of her daughter and son-in-law, then had raised her two young granddaughters alone. Few, if any, of her friends and acquaintances were aware that she maintained only the facade of what appeared to be a luxurious lifestyle. Dev knew because he'd made it his business to learn everything he could about the St. Sebastians after beautiful, bubbly Lady Eugenia had lifted the Byzantine medallion.

He could have tracked Gina down. Hell, anyone with a modicum of computer smarts could track a GPS-equipped cell phone these days. Dev had considered doing just that until he'd realized her elder sister was better suited for his purposes. Plus, there was the bonus factor of where Sarah St. Sebastian worked. It had seemed only fair that he get a little revenge for the annoyance caused by that article.

Except, he thought as he exited the elevator, revenge had a way of coming back to bite you in the ass. What had seemed like a solid plan when he'd first devised it was now generating some serious doubts. Could he keep his hands off the elegant elder sister and stick to the strict terms of their agreement? Did he want to?

The doubts dogged him right up until he pressed the button for the doorbell. He heard a set of melodic chimes, and his soon-to-be fiancée opened the door to him.

"Hello, Mr.… Dev."

She was wearing chunky pearls, a thigh-skimming little dress and black tights tonight. The pearls and gray dress gave her a personal brand of sophistication, but the tights showcased her legs in a way that made Dev's throat go bone-dry. He managed to untangle his tongue long enough to return her greeting.

"Hello, Sarah."

"Please, come in."

She stood aside to give him access to a foyer longer than the belly of a C-17 and almost as cavernous. Marble tiles, ornate wall sconces, a gilt-edged side table and a crystal bowl filled with something orange blossomy. Dev absorbed the details along with the warning in Sarah's green eyes.

"I've told my grandmother that you and Gina are no more than casual acquaintances," she confided in a low voice.

"That's true enough."

"Yes, well…" She drew in a breath and squared shoulders molded by gray silk. "Let's get this over with."

She led the way down the hall. Dev followed and decided the rear view was as great as the front. The dress hem swayed just enough to tease and tantalize. The tights clung faithfully to the curve of her calves.

He was still appreciating the view when she showed him into a high-ceilinged room furnished with a mix of antiques and a few pieces of modern technology. The floor here was parquet; the wood was beautifully inlaid, but cried for the cushioning of a soft, handwoven carpet to blunt some of its echo. Windows curtained in pale blue velvet took up most of two walls and gave what Dev guessed was one hell of a view of Central Park. Flames danced in the massive fireplace fronted in black marble that dominated a third wall.

A sofa was angled to catch the glow from the fire. Two high-backed armchairs faced the sofa across a monster coffee table inset with more marble. The woman on one of those chairs sat ramrod straight, with both palms resting on the handle of an ebony cane. Her gray hair was swept up into a curly crown and anchored by ivory combs. Lace wrapped her throat like a muffler and was anchored by a cameo brooch. Her hawk's eyes skewered Dev as he crossed the room.

Sarah summoned a bright smile and performed the introductions. "Grandmama, this is Devon Hunter."

"How do you do, Mr. Hunter?"

The duchess held out a veined hand. Dev suspected that courtiers had once dropped to a knee and kissed it reverently. He settled for taking it gently in his.

"It's a pleasure to meet you, ma'am. Gina told me she'd inherited her stunning looks from her grandmother. She obviously had that right."

"Indeed?" Her chin lifted. Her nose angled up a few degrees. "You know Eugenia well, then?"

"She coordinated a party for me. We spoke on a number of occasions."

"Do sit down, Mr. Hunter." She waved him to the chair across from hers. "Sarah, dearest, please pour Mr. Hunter a drink."

"Certainly. What would you like, Dev?"

"Whatever you and your grandmother are having is fine."

"I'm having white wine." Her smile tipped into one of genuine affection as she moved to a side table containing an opened bottle of wine nested in a crystal ice bucket and an array of decanters. "Grandmama, however, is ignoring her doctor's orders and sipping an abominable brew concocted by our ancestors back in the sixteenth century."

"*Žuta Osa* is hardly abominable, Sarah," the duchess countered. She lifted a tiny liqueur glass and swirled its amber-colored contents before treating her guest to a bland look. "It simply requires a strong constitution."

Dev recognized a challenge when one smacked him in the face. "I'll give it a try."

"Are you sure?" Sarah shot him a warning glance from behind the drinks table. "The name translates roughly to yellow wasp. That might give you an idea of what it tastes like."

"Really, Sarah! You must allow Mr. Hunter to form his own opinion of what was once our national drink."

Dev was already regretting his choice but concealed it behind a polite request. "Please call me Dev, ma'am."

He didn't presume to address the duchess by name or by rank. Mostly because he wasn't sure which came first. European titles were a mystery wrapped up in an enigma to most Americans. Defunct Eastern European titles were even harder to decipher. Dev had read somewhere that the form of address depended on whether the rank was inherited or bestowed, but that didn't help him a whole lot in this instance.

The duchess solved his dilemma when she responded to his request with a gracious nod. "Very well. And you may call me Charlotte."

Sarah paused with the stopper to one of the decanters in hand. Her look of surprise told Dev he'd just been granted a major concession. She recovered a moment later and filled one of the thimble-size liqueur glasses. Passing it to Dev, she refilled her wineglass and took a seat beside her grandmother.

As he lifted the glass in salute to his hostess, he told himself a half ounce of yellow wasp couldn't do much damage. One sip showed just how wrong he was. The fiery, plum-based liquid exploded in his mouth and damned near burned a hole in his esophagus.

"Holy sh…!"

He caught himself in time. Eyes watering, he held the glass at arm's length and gave the liqueur the respect it deserved. When he could breathe again, he met the duchess's amused eyes.

"This puts the stuff we used to brew in our helmets in Iraq to shame."

"You were in Iraq?" With an impatient shake of her

head, Charlotte answered her own question. "Yes, of course you were. Afghanistan, too, if I remember correctly from the article in *Beguile*."

Okay, now he was embarrassed. The idea of this gray-haired matriarch reading all that nonsense—and perusing the picture of his butt crack!—went down even rougher than the liqueur.

To cover his embarrassment, Dev took another sip. The second was a little easier than the first but still left scorch marks all the way to his gullet.

"So tell me," Charlotte was saying politely, "how long will you be in New York?"

"That depends," he got out.

"Indeed?"

The duchess did the nose-up thing again. She was good at it, Dev thought as he waited for the fire in his stomach to subside.

"On what, if I may be so bold to ask?"

"On whether you and your granddaughter will have dinner with me this evening. Or tomorrow evening."

His glance shifted to Sarah. The memory of how she'd fit against him, how her mouth had opened under his, hit with almost the same sucker punch as the *Žuta Osa*.

"Or any evening," he added, holding her gaze.

Sarah gripped her wineglass. She didn't have any trouble reading the message in his eyes. It was a personal challenge. A not-so-private caress. Her grandmother would have to be blind to miss either.

Okay. All right. She'd hoped this meeting would blunt the surprise of a sudden engagement. Dev had done his part. The ball was now in her court.

"I can't speak for Grandmama, but I'm free tomorrow evening. Or any evening," she added with what felt like a silly, simpering smile.

She thought she'd overplayed her hand. Was sure of it when the duchess speared her with a sharp glance.

The question in her grandmother's eyes ballooned Sarah's guilt and worry to epic proportions. She couldn't do this. She couldn't deceive the woman who'd sold every precious family heirloom she owned to provide for her granddaughters. A confession trembled on her lips. The duchess forestalled it by turning back Devon Hunter.

"I'm afraid I have another engagement tomorrow evening."

Both women knew that to be a blatant lie. Too caught up in her own web of deceit to challenge her grandmother, Sarah tried not to squirm as the duchess slipped into the role of royal matchmaker.

"But I insist you take my granddaughter to dinner tomorrow. Or any evening," she added drily. "Right now, however, I'd like to know a little more about you."

Sarah braced herself. The duchess didn't attack with the same snarling belligerence as Alexis, but she was every bit as skilled and tenacious when it came to extracting information. Dev didn't stand a chance.

She had to admit he took the interrogation with good grace. Still, her nerves were stretched taunt when she went to bed some hours later. At least she'd mitigated the fallout from one potentially disastrous situation. If—*when*—she and Devon broke the news of their engagement, it wouldn't come as a complete shock to Grandmama.

She woke up the next morning knowing she had to defuse another potentially explosive situation. A quick scan of her phone showed no return call or text from Gina. An equally quick scan of electronic, TV and print media showed the story hadn't broken yet about Sarah and Number Three. It would, though. She sensed it with every instinct she'd developed after three years in the dog-eat-dog publishing business.

Alexis. She had to tell Alexis some version of her involvement with Devon Hunter. She tried out different slants as she hung from a handrail on the subway. Several more in the elevator that zoomed her up to *Beguile*'s offices. Every possible construction but one crumbled when Alexis summoned her into her corner office. Pacing like a caged tiger, the executive editor unleashed her claws.

"Jesus, Sarah!" Anger lowered Alexis's smoker's rasp to a frog-like croak. "You want to tell me why I have to hear secondhand that one of my editors swapped saliva with Sexy Single Number Three? On the street. In full view of every cabbie with a camera phone and an itch to sell a sensational story."

"Come on, Alexis. How many New York cabbies read *Beguile* enough to recognize Number Three?"

"At least one, apparently."

She flung the sheet of paper she was holding onto the slab of Lucite that was her desk. Sarah's heart tripped as she skimmed the contents. It was a printed email, and below the printed message was a grainy color photo of a couple locked in each other's arms. Sarah barely had time for a mental apology to Red for thinking she'd be the one to peddle the story before Alexis pounced.

"This joker wants five thousand for the picture."

"You're kidding!"

"See this face?" The executive editor stabbed a finger at her nose. "Does it look like I'm kidding?"

"This…this isn't what you think, Alexis."

"So maybe you'll tell me what the hell it is, Lady Sarah."

It might have been the biting sarcasm. Or the deliberate reference to her title. Or the worry about Gina or the guilt over lying to her grandmother or the pressure Devon Hunter had laid on her. Whatever caused Sarah's sudden meltdown, the sudden burst of tears shocked her as much as it did Alexis.

"Oh, Christ!" Her boss flapped her hands like a PMS-ing

hen. "I'm sorry. I didn't mean to come at you so hard. Well, maybe I did. But you don't have to cry about it."

"Yes," Sarah sobbed, "I do!"

The truth was she couldn't have stopped if she wanted to. All the stress, all the strain, seemed to boil out of her. Not just the problems that had piled up in the past few days. The months of worrying about Grandmama's health. The years of standing between Gina and the rest of the world. Everything just seemed to come to a head. Dropping into a chair, she crossed her arms on the half acre of unblemished Lucite and buried her face.

"Hey! It's okay." Alexis hovered over her, patting her shoulder, sounding more desperate and bullfroggish by the moment. "I'll sit on this email. Do what I can to kill the story before it leaks."

Sarah raised her head. She'd struck a deal. She'd stand by it. "You don't have to kill it. Hunter... He and I..."

"You and Hunter...?"

She dropped her head back onto her arms and gave a muffled groan. "We're engaged."

"What! When? Where? How?"

Reverting to her natural self, Alexis was relentless. Within moments she'd wormed out every succulent detail. Hunter's shocking accusation. The video with its incontrovertible proof. The outrageous proposal. The call from Gina stating that she was on her way to Switzerland.

"Your sister is a selfish little bitch," Alexis pronounced in disgust. "When are you going to stop protecting her?"

"Never!" Blinking away her tears, Sarah fired back with both barrels. "Gina's all I have. Gina and Grandmama. I'll do whatever's necessary to protect them."

"That's all well and good, but your sister..."

"*Is* my sister."

"Okay, okay." Alexis held up both palms. "She's your sister. And Devon Hunter's your fiancé for the next six months. Unless..."

Her face took on a calculating expression. One Sarah knew all too well. She almost didn't want to ask, but the faint hope that her boss might see a way out of the mess prompted a tentative query.

"Unless what?"

"What if you keep a journal for the next few weeks? Better yet, a photo journal?"

Deep in thought, Alexis tapped a bloodred nail against her lips. Sarah could almost see the layout taking shape in her boss's fertile mind.

"You and Hunter. The whirlwind romance. The surprise proposal. The romantic dinners for two. The long walks in Central Park. Our readers would eat it up."

"Forget it, Alexis. I'm not churning out more juicy gossip for our readers."

"Why not?"

The counter came as swift and as deadly as an adder. In full pursuit of a feature now, Alexis dropped into the chair next to Sarah and pressed her point.

"You and I both know celebrity gossip sells. And this batch comes with great bonus elements. Hunter's not only rich, but handsome as hell. You're a smart, savvy career woman with a connection to royalty."

"A connection to a royal house that doesn't exist anymore!"

"So? We resurrect it. Embellish it. Maybe send a photographer over to shoot some local color from your grandmother's homeland. Didn't you say you still had some cousins there?"

"Three or four times removed, maybe, but Grandmama hasn't heard from anyone there in decades."

"No problem. We'll make it work."

She saw the doubt on Sarah's face and pressed her point with ruthless determination.

"If what you give me is as full of glam and romance as I think it could be, it'll send our circulation through the roof. And that, my sweet, will provide you with enough of a bonus to reimburse Hunter for his lost artifact. *And* pay off the last of your grandmother's medical bills. *And* put a little extra in your bank account for a rainy day or two."

The dazzling prospect hung before Sarah's eyes for a brief, shining moment. She could extricate Gina from her latest mess. Become debt-free for the first time in longer than she could remember. Splurge on some totally unnecessary luxury for the duchess. Buy a new suit instead of retrofitting old classics.

She came within a breath of promising Alexis all the photos and R-rated copy she could print. Then her irritating sense of fair play raised its head.

"I can't do it," she said after a bitter internal struggle. "Hunter promised he wouldn't file charges against Gina if I play the role of adoring fiancée. I'll try to get him to agree to a photo shoot focusing on our—" she stopped, took a breath, continued "—on our engagement. I'm pretty sure he'll agree to that."

Primarily because it would serve his purpose. Once the word hit the street that he was taken, all those women shoving their phone numbers at him would just have to live with their disappointment. So would Alexis.

"That's as far as I'll go," Sarah said firmly.

Her boss frowned and was priming her guns for another salvo when her intercom buzzed. Scowling, she stabbed at the instrument on her desk.

"Didn't I tell you to hold all calls?"

"Yes, but…"

"What part of 'hold' don't you understand?"

"It's…"

"It's what, dammit?"

"Number Three," came the whispered reply. "He's here."

Five

If Dev hadn't just run past a gauntlet of snickering females, he might have been amused by the almost identical expressions of surprise on the faces of his fiancée and her boss. But he had, so he wasn't.

Alexis Danvers didn't help matters by looking him up and down with the same scrutiny an auctioneer might give a prize bull. As thin as baling wire, she sized him up with narrowed, calculating eyes before thrusting out a hand tipped with scarlet talons.

"Mr. Hunter. Good to meet you. Sarah says you and she are engaged."

"Wish I could say the same, Ms. Danvers. And yes, we are."

He shifted his gaze to Sarah, frowning when he noted her reddened eyes and tearstained cheeks. He didn't have to search far for the reason behind them. The grainy color photo on Danvers's desk said it all.

Hell! Sarah had hinted the crap would hit the fan if some magazine other than hers scooped the story. Looked as if it had just hit. He turned back to the senior editor and vectored the woman's anger in his direction.

"I'm guessing you might be a little piqued that Sarah didn't clue you in to our relationship before it became public knowledge."

Danvers dipped her chin in a curt nod. "You guessed right."

"I'm also guessing you understand why I wasn't real anxious for another avalanche of obnoxious publicity."

"If you're referring to the Ten Sexiest Singles article…"

"I am."

"Since you declined to let us interview you for that article, Mr. Hunter, everything we printed was in the public domain. Your military service. That cargo thingamajig you patented. Your corporation's profits last quarter. Your marital status. All we did was collate the facts, glam them up a little, toss in a few pictures and offer you to an admiring audience."

"Any more admiration from that audience and I'll have to hire a bodyguard."

"Or a fiancée?"

She slipped that in with the precision of a surgeon. Dev had to admire her skill even as he acknowledged the hit.

"Or a fiancée," he agreed. "Luckily I found the perfect one right here at *Beguile.*"

Which reminded him of why he'd made a second trek to the magazine's offices.

"Something's come up," he told Sarah. "I was going to explain it to you privately, but…"

"You heard from Gina?"

Her breathless relief had Dev swearing silently. Little Miss Gina deserved a swift kick in the behind for putting her sister through all this worry. And he might just be the one to deliver it.

"No, I haven't."

The relief evaporated. Sarah's shoulders slumped. Only for a moment, though. The St. Sebastian steel reasserted itself almost immediately. Good thing, as she'd need every ounce of it for the sucker punch Dev was about to deliver.

"But I did hear from the CEO I've been negotiating with for the past few months. He's ready to hammer out the final details and asked me to fly over to Paris."

She sensed what was coming. He saw it in the widening of her green eyes, the instinctive shake of her head. Dev ignored both and pressed ahead.

"I told him I would. I also told him I might bring my fiancée. I explained we just got engaged, and that I'm thinking of taking some extra time so we can celebrate the occasion in his beautiful city."

"Excuse me!" Danvers butted in, her expression frigid. "Sarah has an important job here at *Beguile,* with deadlines to meet. She can't just flit off to Paris on your whim."

"I appreciate that. It would only be for a few days. Maybe a week."

Dev turned back to Sarah, holding her gaze, holding her to their bargain at the same time.

"We've been working this deal for months. I need to wrap it up. Monsieur Girault said his wife would be delighted to entertain you while we're tied up in negotiations."

He slipped in that veiled reminder of one of his touchiest problems deliberately. He'd been up front with her. He wanted her to provide cover from Elise Girault. In exchange, he'd let her light-fingered sister off the hook.

Sarah got the message. Her chin inched up. Her shoulders squared. The knowledge she would stick to her side of the bargain gave him a fiercer sense of satisfaction than he had time to analyze right now.

"When are you thinking of going?" she asked.

"My executive assistant has booked us seats on a seven-ten flight out of JFK."

"Tonight?"

"Tonight. You have a current passport, don't you?"

"Yes, but I can't just jet off and leave Grandmama!"

"Not a problem. I also had my assistant check with the top home health-care agencies in the city. A licensed, bonded RN can report for duty this afternoon and stay with your grandmother until you get back."

"Dear God, no!" A shudder shook her. "Grandmama would absolutely hate that invasion of her privacy. I'll ask our housekeeper, Maria, to stay with her."

"You sure?"

"I'm sure."

"Since I'm springing this trip on you with such short notice, please tell your housekeeper I'll recompense her for her time."

"That's not necessary," she said stiffly.

"Of course it is."

She started to protest, but Dev suggested a daily payment for Maria's services that made Sarah blink and her boss hastily intervene.

"The man's right, kiddo. This is his gig. Let him cover the associated costs."

She left unsaid the fact that Dev could well afford the generous compensation. It was right there, though, like the proverbial elephant in the room, and convinced Sarah to reluctantly agree.

"We're good to go, then."

"I...I suppose." She chewed on her lower lip for a moment. "I need to finish the Sizzling Summer Sea-escapes layout, Alexis."

"And the ad for that new lip gloss," her boss put in urgently. "I want it in the June edition."

"I'll take my laptop. I can do both layouts on the plane." She pushed out of her chair and faced Dev. "You understand that my accompanying you on this little jaunt is contingent on Maria's availability."

"I understand. Assuming she's available, can you be ready by three o'clock?"

"Isn't that a little early for a seven-ten flight?"

"It is, but we need to make a stop on the way out to JFK. Or would you rather go to Cartier now?"

"Cartier? Why do we…? Oh." She gave a low groan. "An engagement ring, right?"

"Right."

She shook her head in dismay. "This just keeps getting better and better."

Her boss took an entirely different view. With a hoarse whoop, she reached for the phone on her desk.

"Perfect! We'll send a camera crew to Cartier with you." She paused with the phone halfway to her ear and raked her subordinate with a critical glance. "Swing by makeup on your way out, Sarah. Have them ramp up your color. Wouldn't hurt to hit wardrobe, too. That's one of your grandmother's Dior suits, right? It's great, but it needs something. A belt, maybe. Or…"

Sarah cut in, alarm coloring her voice. "Hold on a minute, Alexis."

"What's to hold? This is exactly what we were talking about before Hunter arrived."

Sarah shot Dev a swift, guilty glance. It didn't take a genius for him to fill in the blanks. Obviously, her boss had been pressing to exploit the supposed whirlwind romance between one of her own and Number Three.

As much as it grated, Dev had to admit a splashy announcement of his engagement to Sarah St. Sebastian fell in with his own plans. If nothing else, it would get the word out that he was off the market and, hopefully, keep Madame Girault's claws sheathed.

"I'll consent to a few pictures, if that's what Sarah wants."

"A few pictures," she agreed with obvious reluctance, leveling a pointed look at her boss. "Just this *one* time."

"Come on, Sarah. How much more romantic can you get than April in Paris? The city of light and love. You and Hunter here strolling hand in hand along the Quai de Conti…"

"No, Alexis."

"Just think about it."

"No, Alexis."

There was something in the brief exchange Dev couldn't quite get a handle on. The communication between the two women was too emphatic, too terse. He didn't have time to decipher it now, however.

"Your people get this one shoot," he told Danvers, putting an end to the discussion. "They can do it at Cartier." He checked his watch. "Why don't you call your housekeeper now, Sarah? Make sure she's available. If she is, we'll put a ring on your finger and get you home to pack."

Sarah battled a headache as the limo cut through the Fifth Avenue traffic. Devon sat beside her on the cloud-soft leather, relaxed and seemingly unperturbed about throwing her life into total chaos. Seething, she threw a resentful glance at his profile.

Was it only two days ago he'd stormed into her life? Three? She felt as though she'd been broadsided by a semi. Okay, so maybe she couldn't lay all the blame for the situation she now found herself in on Dev. Gina had certainly contributed her share. Still…

When the limo pulled up at the front entrance to Cartier's iconic flagship store, the dull throb in her temples took on a sharper edge. With its red awnings and four stories of ultra high-end merchandise, the store was a New York City landmark.

Sarah hadn't discovered until after her grandmother's heart attack that Charlotte had sold a good portion of her jewels to Cartier over the years. According to a recent invoice, the last piece she'd parted with was still on display in their Estate Jewelry room.

Dev had called ahead, so they were greeted at the door

by the manager himself. "Good afternoon, Mr. Hunter. I'm Charles Tipton."

Gray-haired and impeccably attired, he shook Dev's hand before bowing over Sarah's with Old World courtesy.

"It's a pleasure to meet you, Ms. St. Sebastian. I've had the honor of doing business with your grandmother several times in the past."

She smiled her gratitude for his discretion. "Doing business with" stung so much less than "helping her dispose of her heritage."

"May I congratulate you on your engagement?"

She managed not to wince, but couldn't help thinking this lie was fast taking on a life of its own.

"Thank you."

"I'm thrilled, of course, that you came to Cartier to shop for your ring. I've gathered a selection of our finest settings and stones. I'm sure we'll find something exactly to your..."

He broke off as a cab screeched over to the curb and the crew from *Beguile* jumped out. Zach Zimmerman—nicknamed ZZ, of course—hefted his camera bags while his assistant wrestled with lights and reflectors.

"Hey, Sarah!" Dark eyed and completely irreverent about everything except his work, ZZ stomped toward them in his high-top sneakers. "You really engaged to Number Three or has Alexis been hitting the sauce again?"

She hid another wince. "I'm really engaged. ZZ, this is my fiancé, Devon..."

"Hunter. Yeah, I recognize the, uh, face."

He smirked but thankfully refrained from referring to any other part of Dev's anatomy.

"If you'll all please come with me."

Mr. Tipton escorted them through the first-floor showroom with its crystal chandeliers and alcoves framed with white marble arches. Faint strains of classical music floated on the air. The seductive scent of gardenia wafted from strategically positioned bowls of potpourri.

A short elevator ride took them to a private consultation room. Chairs padded in gold velvet were grouped on either side of a gateleg, gilt-trimmed escritoire. Several cases sparkling with diamond engagement sets sat on the desk's burled wood surface.

The manager gestured them to the chairs facing the desk but before taking his own he detoured to a sideboard holding a silver bucket and several Baccarat flutes.

"May I offer you some champagne? To toast your engagement, perhaps?"

Sarah glanced at Dev, saw he'd left the choice up to her, and surrendered to the inevitable.

"Thank you. That would be delightful."

The cork had already been popped. Tipton filled flutes and passed them to Sarah and Dev. She took the delicate crystal, feeling like the biggest fraud on earth. Feeling as well the stupidest urge to indulge in another bout of loud, sloppy tears.

Like many of *Beguile*'s readers, Sarah occasionally got caught up in the whole idea of romance. You could hardly sweat over layouts depicting the perfect engagement or wedding or honeymoon without constructing a few private fantasies. But this was about as far from those fantasies as she could get. A phony engagement. A pretend fiancé. A ring she would return as soon as she fulfilled the terms of her contract.

Then she looked up from the pale gold liquid bubbling in her flute and met Dev's steady gaze. His eyes had gone deep blue, almost cobalt, and something in their depths made her breath snag. When he lifted his flute and tipped it to hers, the fantasies begin to take on vague form and shape.

"To my…" he began.

"Wait!" ZZ pawed through his camera bag. "I need to catch this."

The moment splintered. Like a skater on too-thin ice,

Sarah felt the cracks spidering out beneath her feet. Panic replaced the odd sensation of a moment ago. She had to fight the urge to slam down the flute and get off the ice before she sank below the surface.

She conquered the impulse, but couldn't summon more than a strained smile once ZZ framed the shot.

"Okay," the photographer said from behind a foot-long lens, "go for it!"

Dev's gesture with his flute was the same. So was the caress in his voice. But whatever Sarah had glimpsed in his blue eyes a moment ago was gone.

"To us," he said as crystal clinked delicately against crystal.

"To us," she echoed.

She took one sip, just one, and nixed ZZ's request to repeat the toast so he could shoot it from another angle. She couldn't ignore him or his assistant, however, while she tried on a selection of rings. Between them, they made the process of choosing a diamond feel like torture.

According to Tipton, Dev had requested a sampling of rings as refined and elegant as his fiancée. Unfortunately, none of the glittering solitaires he lifted from the cases appealed to Sarah. With an understanding nod, he sent for cases filled with more elaborate settings.

Once again Sarah could almost hear a clock ticking inside her head. She needed to make a decision, zip home, break the startling news of her engagement to Grandmama, get packed and catch that seven-ten flight. Yet none of the rings showcased on black velvet triggered more than a tepid response.

Like it mattered. Just get this over with, she told herself grimly.

She picked up a square cut surrounded by glittering baguettes. Abruptly, she returned it to the black velvet pad.

"I think I would prefer something unique." She looked Tipton square in the eye. "Something from your estate sales, perhaps. An emerald, for my birth month. Mounted in gold."

Her birthday was in November, and the stone for that month was topaz. She hoped Hunter hadn't assimilated that bit of trivia. The jeweler had, of course, but he once again proved himself the soul of discretion.

"I believe we might have just the ring for you."

He lifted a house phone and issued a brief instruction. Moments later, an assistant appeared and deposited an intricately wrought ring on the display pad.

Thin ropes of gold were interwoven to form a wide band. An opaque Russian emerald nested in the center of the band. The milky green stone was the size and shape of a small gumball. When Sarah turned the ring over, she spotted a rose carved into the stone's flat bottom.

Someone with no knowledge of antique jewelry might scrunch their noses at the overly fussy setting and occluded gemstone. All Sarah knew was that she had to wear Grandmama's last and most precious jewel, if only for a week or so. Her heart aching, she turned to Dev.

"This is the one."

He tried to look pleased with her choice but didn't quite get there. The price the manager quoted only increased his doubts. Even fifteen-karat Russian emeralds didn't come anywhere close to the market value of a flawless three- or four-karat diamond.

"Are you sure this is the ring you want?"

"Yes."

Shrugging, he extracted an American Express card from his wallet. When Tipton disappeared to process the card, he picked up the ring and started to slip it on Sarah's finger.

ZZ stopped him cold. "Hold it!"

Dev's blue eyes went glacial. "Let us know when you're ready."

"Yeah, yeah, just hang on a sec."

ZZ thrust out a light meter, scowled at the reading and

barked orders to his assistant. After a good five minutes spent adjusting reflectors and falloff lights, they were finally ready.

"Go," the photographer ordered.

Dev slipped the ring on Sarah's finger. It slid over her knuckle easily, and the band came to rest at the base of her finger as though it had been sized especially for her.

"Good. Good." ZZ clicked a dozen fast shots. "Look up at him, Sarah. Give him some eye sex."

Heat rushed into her cheeks but she lifted her gaze. Dev wore a cynical expression for a second or two before exchanging it for one more lover-like.

Lights heated the room. Reflectors flashed. The camera shutter snapped and spit.

"Good. Good. Now let's have the big smooch. Make it hot, you two."

Tight lines appeared at the corners of Dev's mouth. For a moment he looked as though he intended to tell ZZ to take his zoom lens and shove it. Then he rose to his feet with lazy grace and held out a hand to Sarah.

"We'll have to try this without an audience sometime," he murmured as she joined him. "For now, though…"

She was better prepared this time. She didn't stiffen when he slid an arm around her waist. Didn't object when he curled his other hand under her chin and tipped her face to his. Yet the feel of his mouth, the taste and the scent of him, sent tiny shock waves rippling through her entire body.

A lyric from an old song darted into her mind. Something about getting lost in his kiss. That was exactly how she felt as his mouth moved over hers.

"Good. Good."

More rapid-fire clicks, more flashes. Finally ZZ was done. He squinted at the digital screen and ran through the entire sequence of images before he gave a thumbs-up.

"Got some great shots here. I'll edit 'em and email you

the best, Sarah. Just be sure to credit me if you use 'em on your bridal website."

Right. Like that was going to happen. Still trying to recover from her second session in Devon Hunter's arms, Sarah merely nodded.

While ZZ and his assistant packed up, Dev checked his watch. "Do you want to grab lunch before I take you home to pack?"

Sarah thought for a moment. Her number-one priority right now was finding some way to break the news to the duchess that her eldest granddaughter had become engaged to a man she'd met only a few days ago. She needed a plausible explanation. One that wouldn't trigger Charlotte's instant suspicion. Or worse, so much worse, make her heart stutter.

Sarah's glance dropped to the emerald. The stone's cloudy beauty gave her the bravado to respond to Dev's question with a completely false sense of confidence.

"Let's have lunch with Grandmama and Maria. We'll make it a small celebration in honor of the occasion, then I'll pack."

Six

Dev had employed a cautious, scope-out-the-territory approach for his first encounter with the duchess. For the second, he decided on a preemptive strike. As soon as he and Sarah were in the limo and headed uptown, he initiated his plan of attack.

"Do you need to call your grandmother and let her know we're coming?"

"Yes, I should." She slipped her phone out of her purse. "And I'll ask Maria to put together a quick lunch."

"No need. I'll take care of that. Does the duchess like caviar?"

"Yes," Sarah replied, a question in her eyes as he palmed his own phone, "but only Caspian Sea osetra. She thinks beluga is too salty and sevruga too fishy."

"What about Maria? Does she have a favorite delicacy?"

She had to think for a moment. "Well, on All Saints Day she always makes *fiambre*."

"What's that?"

"A chilled salad with fifty or so ingredients. Why?" she asked as he hit a speed-dial key. "What are you…?"

He held up a hand, signaling her to wait, and issued a

quick order. "I need a champagne brunch for four, delivered to Ms. St. Sebastian's home address in a half hour. Start with osetra caviar and whatever you can find that's close to… Hang on." He looked to Sarah. "What was that again?"

"Fiambre."

"Fiambre. It's a salad…Hell, I don't know…Right. Right. Half an hour."

Sarah was staring at him when he cut the connection. "Who was that?"

"My executive assistant."

"She's here, in New York?"

"It's a he. Patrick Donovan. We used to fly together. He's back in L.A."

"And he's going to have champagne and caviar delivered to our apartment in half an hour?"

"That's why he gets paid the big bucks." He nodded to the phone she clutched in her hand. "You better call the duchess. With all this traffic, lunch will probably get there before we do."

Despite his advance preparations, Dev had to shake off a serious case of nerves when he and Sarah stepped out of the elevator at the Dakota. His introduction to Charlotte St. Sebastian last night had given him a keen appreciation of both her intellect and her fierce devotion to her granddaughters. He had no idea how she'd react to this sudden engagement, but he suspected she'd make him sweat.

Sarah obviously suspected the same thing. She paused at the door to their apartment, key in hand, and gave him a look that was half challenge, half anxious appeal.

"She…she has a heart condition. We need to be careful how we orchestrate this."

"I'll follow your lead."

Pulling in a deep breath, she squared her shoulders. The key rattled in the lock, and the door opened on a parade of white-jacketed waiters just about to exit the apartment. Their arms full of empty cartons, they stepped aside.

"Your grandmother told us to set up in the dining room," the waiter in charge informed Sarah. "And may I say, ma'am, she has exquisite taste in crystal. Bohemian, isn't it?"

"Yes, it is."

"I thought so. No other lead crystal has that thin, liquid sheen."

Nodding, Sarah hurried down the hall. Dev lingered to add a hefty tip to the service fee he knew Patrick would have already taken care of. Gushing their thanks, the team departed and Dev made his way to the duchess's high-ceilinged dining room.

He paused on the threshold to survey the scene. The mahogany table could easily seat twelve, probably twenty or more with leaves in, but had been set with four places at the far end. Bone-white china gleamed. An impressive array of ruby-red goblets sparkled at each place setting. A sideboard held a row of domed silver serving dishes, and an opened bottle of champagne sat in a silver ice bucket.

Damn! Patrick would insist Dev add another zero to his already astronomical salary for pulling this one off.

"I presume this is your doing, Devon."

His glance zinged to the duchess. She stood ramrod straight at the head of the table, her hands folded one atop the other on the ivory handle of her cane. The housekeeper, Maria, hovered just behind her.

"Yes, ma'am."

"I also presume you're going to tell me the reason for this impromptu celebration."

Having agreed to let Sarah take the lead, Dev merely moved to her side and eased an arm around her waist. She stiffened, caught herself almost instantly and relaxed.

"We have two reasons to celebrate, Grandmama. Dev's asked me to go to Paris with him."

"So I understand. Maria informed me you asked her to stay with me while you're gone."

Her arctic tone left no doubt as to her feelings about the matter.

"It's just for a short while, and more for me than for you. This way I won't feel so bad about rushing off and leaving you on such short notice."

The duchess didn't unbend. If anything, her arthritic fingers clutched the head of her cane more tightly.

"And the second reason for this celebration?"

Sarah braced herself. Dev could feel her body go taut against his while she struggled to frame their agreement in terms her grandmother would accept. It was time for him to step in and draw the duchess's fire.

"My sisters will tell you I'm seriously deficient in the romance department, ma'am. They'll also tell you I tend to bulldoze over any and all obstacles when I set my sights on something. Sarah put up a good fight, but I convinced her we should get engaged before we take off for Paris."

"Madre de Dios!" The exclamation burst from Maria, who gaped at Sarah. "You are *engaged?* To this man?"

When she nodded, the duchess's chin shot up. Her glance skewered Dev where he stood. In contrast to her stark silence, Maria gave quick, joyous thanks to the Virgin Mary while making the sign of the cross three times in rapid succession.

"How I prayed for this, *chica!*"

Tears sparkling in her brown eyes, she rushed over to crush Sarah against her generous bosom. Dev didn't get a hug, but he was hauled down by his lapels and treated to a hearty kiss on both cheeks.

The duchess remained standing where she was. Dev was damned if he could read her expression. When Sarah approached, Charlotte's narrow-eyed stare shifted to her granddaughter.

"We stopped by Cartier on our way here, Grandmama. Dev wanted to buy me an engagement ring."

She raised her left hand, and the effect on the duchess was instant and electric.

"Dear God! Is that...? Is that the Russian Rose?"

"Yes," Sarah said gently.

Charlotte reached out a veined hand and stroked the emerald's rounded surface with a shaking fingertip. Dev felt uncomfortably like a voyeur as he watched a succession of naked emotions cross the older woman's face. For a long moment, she was in another time, another place, reliving memories that obviously brought both great joy and infinite sadness.

With an effort that was almost painful to observe, she returned to the present and smiled at Sarah.

"Your grandfather gave me the Rose for my eighteenth birthday. I always intended you to have it."

Her glance shifted once again to Dev. Something passed between them, but before he could figure out just what the hell it was, the duchess became all brisk efficiency.

"Well, Sarah, since you're traipsing off to Paris on such short notice, I think we should sample this sumptuous feast your...your fiancé has so generously arranged. Then you'll have to pack. Devon, will you pour the champagne?"

"Yes, ma'am."

Dev's misguided belief that he'd escaped unscathed lasted only until they'd finished brunch and Sarah went to pack. He got up to help Maria clear the table. She waved him back to his seat.

"I will do this. You sit and keep *la duquesa* company."

The moment Maria bustled through the door to the kitchen, *la duquesa* let loose with both barrels. Her pale eyes dangerous, she unhooked her cane from her chair arm and stabbed it at Dev like a sword.

"Let's be sure we understand each other, Mr. Hunter. I

may have been forced to sell the Russian Rose, but if you've purchased it with the mistaken idea you can also purchase my granddaughter, you'd best think again. One can't buy class or good genes. One either has both—" she jabbed his chest with the cane for emphasis "—or one doesn't."

Geesh! Good thing he was facing this woman over three feet of ebony and not down the barrel of an M16. Dev didn't doubt she'd pull the trigger if he answered wrong.

"First," he replied, "I had no idea that emerald once belonged to you. Second, I'm perfectly satisfied with my genes. Third…"

He stopped to think about that one. His feelings for Sarah St. Sebastian had become too confused, too fast. The way she moved…. The smile in her green eyes when she let down her guard for a few moments…. Her fierce loyalty to her grandmother and ditz of a sister…. Everything about her seemed to trigger both heat and hunger.

"Third," he finally admitted, "there's no way I'll ever match Sarah's style or elegance. All I can do is appreciate it, which I most certainly do."

The duchess kept her thoughts hidden behind her narrowed eyes for several moments. Then she dropped the tip of the cane and thumped the floor.

"Very well. I'll wait to see how matters develop."

She eased back against her chair and Dev started to breathe again.

"I'm sure you're aware," she said into the tentative truce, "that Paris is one of Sarah's favorite cities?"

"We haven't gotten around to sharing all our favorites yet," he replied with perfect truthfulness. "I do know she attended the Sorbonne for a year as an undergraduate."

That much was in the background dossier, as was the fact she'd majored in art history. Dev planned to use whatever spare time they might have in Paris to hit a few museums with her. He looked forward to exploring the Louvre or the Cluny with someone who shared his burgeoning interest in art. He was certainly no expert, but his appreciation of art in its various forms had grown with each incremental increase in his personal income...as evidenced by the Byzantine medallion.

The belated reminder of why he was here, being poked in the chest by this imperious, indomitable woman, hit with a belated punch. He'd let the side details of his "engagement" momentarily obscure the fact that he'd arm-twisted Sarah into it. He was using her, ruthlessly and with cold deliberation, as a tool to help close an important deal. Once that deal was closed...

To borrow the duchess's own words, Dev decided, they'd just have to wait and see how matters develop. He wouldn't employ the same ruthlessness and calculation to seduce the eminently seductive Lady Sarah as he had to get a ring on her finger. But neither would he pass up the chance to finesse her into bed if the opportunity offered.

The possibility sent a spear of heat into his belly. With a sheer effort of will, he gave the indomitable Charlotte St. Sebastian no sign of the knee-jerk reaction. But he had to admit he was now looking forward to this trip with considerably more anticipation than when Jean-Jacques Girault first requested it.

Seven

Three hours out over the Atlantic Sarah had yet to get past her surprise.

"I still can't believe Grandmama took it so well," she said, her fingers poised over the keyboard of her laptop. "Not just the engagement. This trip to Paris. The hefty bonus you're paying Maria. Everything!"

Dev looked up from the text message he'd just received. Their first-class seat pods were separated by a serving console holding his scotch, her wine and a tray of appetizers, but they were seated close enough for him to see the lingering disbelief in her jade-green eyes.

"Why shouldn't she take it well?" he countered. "She grilled me last night about my parents, my grandparents, my siblings, my education, my health, my club memberships and my bank account. She squeezed everything else she wanted to know out of me today at lunch. It was a close call, but evidently I passed muster."

"I think it was the ring," Sarah murmured, her gaze on the milky stone that crowned her finger. "Her whole attitude changed when she spotted it."

Dev knew damn well it was the ring, and noted with

interest the guilt and embarrassment tinging his fiancée's cheeks.

"I supposed I should have told you at Cartier that the Russian Rose once belonged to Grandmama."

"Not a problem. I'm just glad it was available."

She was quiet for a moment, still pondering the luncheon.

"Do you know what I find so strange? Grandmama didn't once ask how we could have fallen in love so quickly."

"Maybe because she comes from a different era. Plus, she went through some really rough times. Could be your security weighs as heavily in her mind as your happiness."

"That can't be it. She's always told Gina and me that her marriage was a love match. She had to defy her parents to make it happen."

"Yes, but look what came next," Dev said gently. "From what I've read, the Soviet takeover of her country was brutal. She witnessed your grandfather's execution. She barely escaped the same fate and had to make a new life for herself and her baby in a different country."

Sarah fingered the emerald, her profile etched with sadness. "Then she lost my parents and got stuck with Gina and me."

"Why do I think she didn't regard it as getting stuck? I suspect you and your sister went a long way to filling the hole in her heart."

"Gina more than me."

"I doubt that," Dev drawled.

As he'd anticipated, she jumped instantly to her sister's defense.

"I know you think Gina's a total airhead…"

"I do."

"…but she's so full of joy and life that no one—I repeat, *no one*—can be in her company for more than three minutes without cracking a smile."

Her eyes fired lethal darts, daring him to disagree. He didn't have to. He'd achieved his objective and erased the sad memories. Rather than risk alienating her, he changed the subject.

"I just got a text from Monsieur Girault. He says he's delighted you were able to get away and accompany me."

"Really?" Sarah hiked a politely skeptical brow. "What does his wife say?"

To Dev's chagrin, heat crawled up his neck. He'd flown in and out of a dozen different combat zones, for God's sake! Could stare down union presidents and corporate sharks with equal skill. Yet Elise Girault had thrown him completely off stride when he'd bent to give her the obligatory kiss on both cheeks. Her whispered suggestion was so startling—and so erotic—he'd damned near gotten whiplash when he'd jerked his head back. Then she'd let loose with a booming, raucous laugh that invited him to share in their private joke.

"He didn't say," Dev said in answer to Sarah's question, "but he did ask what you would like to do while we're locked up in a conference room. He indicated his wife is a world-class shopper. Apparently she's well-known at most of the high-end boutiques."

He realized his mistake the moment the words were out. He'd run Sarah St. Sebastian's financials. He knew how strapped she was.

"That reminds me," he said with deliberate nonchalance. "I don't intend for you to incur any out-of-pocket expenses as part of our deal. There'll be a credit card waiting for you at the hotel."

"Please tell me you're kidding."

Her reaction shouldn't have surprised him. Regal elegance was only one of the traits Lady Sarah had inherited from her grandmother. Stiff-necked pride had to rank right up near the top of the list.

"Be reasonable, Sarah. You're providing me a personal service."

Which was becoming more personal by the hour. Dev was getting used to her stimulating company. The heat she ignited in him still took him by surprise, though. He hadn't figured that into his plan.

"Of course I'll cover your expenses."

Her expression turned glacial. "The hotel, yes. Any meals we take with Madame and Monsieur Girault, yes. A shopping spree on the rue du Faubourg Saint-Honoré, no."

"Fine. It's your call."

He tried to recover with an admiring survey of her petal-pink dress. The fabric was thick and satiny, the cut sleek. A coat in the same style hung in their cabin's private closet.

"The rue du Whatever has nothing on Fifth Avenue. That classy New York look will have Elise Girault demanding an immediate trip to the States."

She stared at him blankly for a moment, then burst into laughter. "You're not real up on haute couture, are you?"

"Any of my sisters would tell you I don't know haute from hamburger."

"I wouldn't go that far," she said, still chuckling. "Unless I miss my guess, your shoes are Moroccan leather, the suit's hand-tailored and the tie comes from a little shop just off the Grand Canal in Venice."

"Damn, you're good! Although Patrick tells me he orders the ties from Milan, not Venice. So where did that dress come from?"

"It's vintage Balenciaga. Grandmama bought it in Madrid decades ago."

The smile remained, but Dev thought it dimmed a few degrees.

"She disposed of most of her designer originals when… when they went out of style, but she kept enough to provide a treasure trove for me. Thank goodness! Retro is the new 'new,' you know. I'm the envy of everyone at *Beguile*."

Dev could read behind the lines. The duchess must have sold off her wardrobe as well as her jewelry over the years. It was miracle she'd managed to hang on to the apartment at the Dakota. The thought of what the duchess and Sarah had gone through kicked Dev's admiration for them both up another notch. Also, his determination to treat Sarah to something new and obscenely expensive. He knew better than to step on her pride again, though, and said merely, "Retro looks good on you."

"Thank you."

After what passed for the airline's gourmet meal, Dev used his in-flight wireless connection to crunch numbers for his meetings with Girault and company while Sarah went back to work on her laptop. She'd promised Alexis she would finish the layout for the Summer Sea-escapes but the perspectives just wouldn't gel. After juggling Martha's Vineyard with Catalina Island and South Padre Island with South Georgia Island, she decided she would have to swing by *Beguile*'s Paris offices to see how the layout looked on a twenty-five-inch monitor before shooting it off to Alexis for review.

Dev was still crunching numbers when she folded down the lid of her computer. With a polite good-night, she tugged up the airline's fleecy blue blanket and curled into her pod.

A gentle nudge brought her awake some hours later. She blinked gritty eyes and decided reality was more of a fantasy than her dreams. Dev had that bad-boy look again. Tie loosened. Shirt collar open. Dark circles below his blue eyes.

"We'll be landing in less than an hour," he told her.

As if to emphasize the point, a flight attendant appeared with a pot of fresh-brewed coffee. Sarah gulped down a half cup before she took the amenity kit provided to all business- and first-class passengers to the lavatory. She emerged with her face washed, teeth brushed, hair combed and her soul ready for the magic that was springtime in Paris.

Or the magic that might have been.

Spring hadn't yet made it to northern France. The temperature hovered around fifty, and a cold rain was coming down in sheets when Sarah and Dev emerged from the terminal and ducked into a waiting limo. The trees lining the roads from the airport showed only a hint of new green and the fields were brown and sere.

Once inside the city, Paris's customary snarl of traffic engulfed them. Neither the traffic nor the nasty weather could dim the glory of the 7th arrondissement, however. The townhomes and ministries, once the residences of France's wealthiest nobility, displayed their mansard roofs and wrought-iron balconies with haughty disregard for the pelting rain. Sarah caught glimpses of the Eiffel Tower's iron symmetry before the limo rolled to a stop on a quiet side street in the heart of Saint-Germain. Surprise brought her around in her seat to face Dev.

"We're staying at the Hôtel Verneuil?"

"We are."

"Gina and I and Grandmama stayed here years ago, on our last trip abroad together."

"So the duchess informed me." His mouth curved. "She also informed me that I'm to take you to Café Michaud to properly celebrate our engagement," he said with a smile.

Sarah fell a little bit in love with him at that moment. Not because he'd booked them into this small gem of a palace instead of a suite at the much larger and far more expensive Crillon or George V. Because he'd made such an effort with her grandmother.

Surprised and shaken by the warmth that curled around her heart, she tried to recover as they exited the limo. "From what I remember, the Verneuil only has twenty-five or twenty-six rooms. The hotel's usually full. I'm surprised you could get us in with such short notice."

"I didn't. Patrick did. After which he informed me that I'd just doubled his Christmas bonus."

"I have to meet this man."

"That can be arranged."

He said it with a casualness that almost hid the implication behind his promise. Sarah caught it, however. The careless words implied a future beyond Paris.

She wasn't ready to think about that. Instead she looked around the lobby while Dev went to the reception desk. The exposed beams, rich tapestries and heavy furniture covered in red velvet hadn't changed since her last visit ten or twelve years ago. Apparently the management hadn't, either. The receptionist must have buzzed her boss. He emerged from the back office, his shoulders stooped beneath his formal morning coat and a wide smile on his face.

"*Bonjour,* Lady Sarah!"

A quick glance at his name tag provided his name. "*Bonjour,* Monsieur LeBon."

"What a delight to have you stay with us again," he exclaimed in French, the Parisian accent so different from that of the provinces. "How is the duchess?"

"She's very well, thank you."

"I'm told this trip is in honor of a special occasion," the manager beamed. "May I offer you my most sincere congratulations?"

"Thank you," she said again, trying not to cringe at the continuation of their deception.

LeBon switched to English to offer his felicitations to Dev. "If I may be so bold to say it, Monsieur Hunter, you are a very lucky man to have captured the heart of one such as Lady Sarah."

"Extremely lucky," Dev agreed.

"Allow me to show you to your floor."

He pushed the button to summon the elevator, then stood aside for them to enter the brass-bedecked cage. While it lifted them to the upper floors, he apologized profusely for not being able to give them adjoining rooms as had been requested.

"We moved several of our guests as your so very capable assistant suggested, Monsieur Hunter, and have put you and Lady Sarah in chambers only a short distance apart. I hope they will be satisfactory."

Sarah's was more than satisfactory. A mix of antique, marble and modern, it offered a four-poster bed and a lovely sitting area with a working fireplace and a tiny balcony. But it was the view from the balcony that delighted her artist's soul.

The rain had softened to a drizzle. It glistened on the slate-gray rooftops of Paris. Endless rows of chimneys rose from the roofs like sentries standing guard over their city. And in the distance were the twin Gothic towers and flying buttresses of Notre Dame.

"I don't have anything scheduled until three this afternoon," Dev said while Monsieur LeBon waited to escort him to his own room. "Would you like to rest awhile, then go out for lunch?"

The city beckoned, and Sarah ached to answer its call. "I'm not tired. I think I'd like to take a walk."

"In the rain?"

"That's when Paris is at its best. The streets, the cafés, seem to steal the light. Everything shimmers."

"Okay," Dev said, laughing, "you've convinced me. I'll change and rap on your door in, say, fifteen minutes?"

"Oh, but…"

She stopped just short of blurting out that she hadn't intended that as an invitation. She could hardly say she didn't want her fiancé's company with Monsieur LeBon beaming his approval of a romantic stroll.

"…I'll need a bit more time than that," she finished. "Let's say thirty minutes."

"A half hour it is."

As she changed into lightweight wool slacks and a hip-length, cherry-red sweater coat that belted at the waist, Sarah tried to analyze her reluctance to share these first hours in Paris with Dev. She suspected it stemmed from the emotion that had welled up when they'd first pulled up at the Hôtel Verneuil. She knew then that she could fall for him, and fall hard. What worried her was that it wouldn't take very much to push her over the precipice.

True, he'd blackmailed her into this uncomfortable charade. Also true, he'd put a ring on her finger and hustled her onto a plane before she could formulate a coherent protest. In the midst of those autocratic acts, though, he'd shown incredible forbearance and generosity.

Then there were the touches, the kisses, the ridiculous whoosh every time he smiled at her. Devon Hunter had made *Beguile*'s list based on raw sex appeal. Sarah now realized he possessed something far more potent…and more dangerous to her peace of mind.

She had to remember this was a short-term assignment. Dev had stipulated it would last only until he wrapped up negotiations on his big deal. It looked now as though that might happen within the next few days. Then this would all be over.

The thought didn't depress her. Sarah wouldn't let it. But worked hard to keep the thought at bay.

She was ready when Dev knocked. Wrapping on a biscuit-colored rain cape, she tossed one of its flaps over a shoulder on her way to the door. With her hair tucked up under a flat-brimmed Dutch-boy cap, she was rainproof and windproof.

"Nice hat," Dev said when she stepped into the hall.

"Thanks."

"Nice everything, actually."

She could have said the same. This was the first time she'd seen him in anything other than a suit. The man was made for jeans. Or vice versa. Their snug fit emphasized his flat belly and lean flanks. And, she added with a gulp when he turned to press the button for the elevator, his tight, trim butt.

He'd added a cashmere scarf in gray-and-blue plaid to his leather bomber jacket, but hadn't bothered with a hat. Sarah worried that it would be too cold for him, but when they exited the hotel, they found the rain was down to a fine mist and the temperature had climbed a few degrees.

Dev took her arm as they crossed the street, then tucked it in his as they started down the boulevard. Sarah felt awkward with that arrangement at first. Elbow to elbow, shoulder to shoulder, strolling along the rain-washed boulevard, they looked like the couple they weren't.

Gradually, Sarah got used to the feel of him beside her, to the way he matched his stride to hers. And bit by bit, the magic of Paris eased her nagging sense that this was all just a charade.

Even this late in the morning the *boulangeries* still emitted their seductive, tantalizing scent of fresh-baked bread. Baguettes sprouted from tall baskets and the racks were crammed with braided loaves. The pastry shops, too, had set out their day's wares. The exquisitely crafted sweets, tarts, chocolate éclairs, gâteaux, caramel mousse, napoleons, macaroons—all were true works of art, and completely impossible to resist.

"God, these look good," Dev murmured, his gaze on the colorful display. "Are you up for a coffee and an éclair?"

"Always. But my favorite patisserie in all Paris is just a couple of blocks away. Can you hold out a little longer?"

"I'll try," he said, assuming an expression of heroic resolution.

Laughing, Sarah pressed his arm closer to her side and guided him the few blocks. The tiny patisserie was nested between a bookstore and a bank. Three dime-size wrought-iron tables sat under the striped awning out front; three more were wedged inside. Luckily two women were getting up from one of the tables when Dev and Sarah entered.

Sarah ordered an espresso and *tart au citron* for herself, and a café au lait for Dev, then left him debating his choice of pastries while she claimed the table. She loosed the flaps of her cape and let it drift over the back of her chair while she observed the drama taking place at the pastry case.

With no other customers waiting, the young woman behind the counter inspected Dev with wide eyes while he checked out the colorful offerings. When he made his selection, she slid the pastry onto a plate and offered it with a question.

"You are American?"

He flashed her a friendly smile. "I am."

Sarah guessed what was coming even before the woman's face lit up with eager recognition.

"Aah, I knew it. You are Number Three, yes?"

Dev's smile tipped into a groan, but he held his cool as she called excitedly to her coworkers.

"C'est lui! C'est lui! Monsieur Hunter. Numéro trois."

Sarah bit her lip as a small bevy of females in white aprons converged at the counter. Dev took the fuss with good grace and even autographed a couple of paper napkins before retreating to the table with his chocolate éclair.

Sarah felt the urge to apologize but merely nodded when he asked grimly if *Beguile* had a wide circulation in France.

"It's our third-largest market."

"Great."

He stabbed his éclair and had to dig deep for a smile when the server delivered their coffees.

"In fact," Sarah said after the girl giggled and departed,

"*Beguile* has an office here in the city. I was going to swing by there when you go for your meeting."

"I'll arrange a car for you."

The reply was polite, but perfunctory. The enchantment of their stroll through Paris's rain-washed streets had dissipated with the mist.

"No need. I'll take the subway."

"Your call," Dev replied. "I'll contact you later and let you know what time we're meeting the Giraults for dinner tonight."

Eight

The French offices of *Beguile* were located only a few blocks from the Arc de Triomphe, on rue Balzac. Sarah always wondered what that famed French novelist and keen observer of human absurdities would think of a glossy publication that pandered to so many of those absurdities.

The receptionist charged with keeping the masses at bay glanced up from her desk with a polite expression that morphed into a welcoming smile when she spotted Sarah.

"*Bonjour*, Sarah! So good to see you again!"

"*Bonjour*, Madeline. Good to see you, too. How are the twins?"

"Horrors," the receptionist replied with a half laugh, half groan. "Absolute horrors. Here are their latest pictures."

After duly admiring the impish-looking three-year-olds, Sarah rounded the receptionist's desk and walked a corridor lined with framed, poster-size copies of *Beguile* covers. Paul Vincent, the senior editor, was pacing his glass cage of an office and using both hands to emphasize whatever point he was trying to make to the person on the speakerphone. Sarah tipped him a wave and would have proceeded to the production unit, but Paul gestured her inside and abruptly terminated his call.

"Sarah!"

Grasping her hands, he kissed her on both cheeks. She bent just a bit so he could hit the mark. At five-four, Paul tended to be as sensitive about his height as he was about the kidney-shaped birthmark discoloring a good portion of his jaw. Yet despite what he called his little imperfections, his unerring eye for color and style had propelled him from the designers' cutting rooms to his present exalted position.

"Alexis emailed to say you would be in Paris," he informed Sarah. "She's instructed me to put François and his crew at your complete disposal."

"For what?"

"To take photos of you and your fiancé. She wants all candids, no posed shots and plenty of romantic backdrop in both shallow and distant depth of field. François says he'll use wide aperture at the Eiffel Tower, perhaps F2.8 to…"

"No, Paul."

"No F2.8? Well, you'll have to speak with François about that."

"No, Paul. No wide aperture, no candids, no Eiffel Tower, no François!"

"But Alexis…."

"Wants to capitalize on my engagement to Number Three. Yes, I know. My fiancé agreed to a photo shoot in New York, but that's as far as either he or I will go. We told Alexis that before we left."

"Then you had better tell her again."

"I will," she said grimly. "In the meantime, I need to use Production's monitors to take a last look at the layout I've been working on. When I zap it to Alexis, I'll remind her of our agreement."

She turned to leave, but Paul stopped her. "What can you tell me of the Chicago meeting?"

The odd inflection in his voice gave Sarah pause. Wondering what was behind it, she searched her mind. So much had happened in the past few days that she'd forgotten about the shuttle Alexis had jumped for an unscheduled meeting with the head of their publishing group. All she'd thought about her boss's unscheduled absence at the time was that it had provided a short reprieve. Paul's question now brought the Chicago meeting forcibly to mind.

"I can't tell you anything," she said honestly. "I didn't have a chance to talk to Alexis about it before I left. Why, what have you heard?"

He folded his arms, bent an elbow and tapped two fingers against the birthmark on his chin. It was a nervous gesture, one he rarely allowed. That he would give in to it now generated a distinct unease in Sarah.

"I've heard rumors," he admitted. "Only rumors, you understand."

"What rumors?"

The fingers picked up speed, machine-gunning his chin.

"Some say… Not me, I assure you! But some say that Alexis is too old. Too out of touch with our target readership. Some say the romance has gone out of her, and out of our magazine. Before, we used to beguile, to tantalize. Now we titillate."

Much to her chagrin, Sarah couldn't argue the point. The butt shot of Dev that Alexis had insisted on was case in point. In the most secret corners of her heart, she agreed with the ambiguous, unnamed "some" Paul referenced.

Despite her frequent differences of opinion with her boss, however, she owed Alexis her loyalty and support. She'd hired Sarah right out of college, sans experience, sans credentials. Grandmama might insist Sarah's title had influenced that decision. Maybe so, but the title hadn't done more than get a neophyte's foot in the door. She'd sweated blood to work her way up to layout editor. And now, apparently, it was payback time.

Alexis confirmed that some time later in her response to Sarah's email.

Sea-escapes layout looks good. We'll go with it. Please re-think the Paris photo shoot. Chicago feels we need more romance in our mag. You and Hunter personify that, at least as far as our readers are concerned.

The email nagged at Sarah all afternoon. She used the remainder of her private time to wander through her favorite museum, but not even the Musée d'Orsay could resolve her moral dilemma. Questions came at her, dive-bombing like suicidal mosquitoes as she strolled through the converted railroad station that now housed some of the world's most celebrated works of art.

All but oblivious to the Matisses and Rodins, she weighed her options. Should she support her boss or accede to Dev's demand for privacy? What about the mess with Gina? Would Alexis exploit that, too, if pushed to the wall? Would she play up the elder sister's engagement as a desperate attempt to save the younger from a charge of larceny?

She would. Sarah knew damned well she would. The certainty curdled like sour milk in the pit of her stomach. Whom did she most owe her loyalty to? Gina? Dev? Alexis? Herself?

The last thought was so heretical it gnawed at Sarah's insides while she prepped for her first meeting with the Giraults early that evening. Dev had told her this would be an informal dinner at the couple's Paris town house.

"Ha!" she muttered as she added a touch of mascara. "I'll bet it's informal."

Going with instinct, she opted for a hip-length tuxedo jacket that had been one of Grandmama's favorite pieces. Sarah had extracted the jacket from the to-be-sold pile on at least three separate occasions. Vintage was vintage, but

Louis Féraud was art. He'd opened his first house of fashion in Cannes 1950, became one of Brigitte Bardot's favorite designers and grew into a legend in his own lifetime.

This jacket was quintessential Féraud. The contour-hugging design featured wide satin lapels and a double-breasted, two-button front fastening. Sarah paired it with a black, lace-edged chemise and wide-pegged black satin pants. A honey-colored silk handkerchief peeked from the breast pocket. A thin gold bangle circled her wrist. With her hair swept up in a smooth twist, she looked restrained and refined.

For some reason, though, restrained just didn't hack it tonight. Not while she was playing tug-of-war between fiercely conflicting loyalties. She wanted to do right by Dev. And Alexis. And Gina. And herself. Elise Girault could take a flying leap.

Frowning, she unclipped her hair and let the dark mass swirl to her shoulders. Then she slipped out of the jacket and tugged off the chemise. When she pulled the jacket on again, the two-button front dipped dangerously low. Grandmama would have a cow if she saw how much shadowy cleavage her Sarah now displayed. Dev, she suspected, would approve.

He did. Instantly and enthusiastically. Bending an arm against the doorjamb, he gave a long, low whistle.

"You look fantastic."

"Thanks." Honesty compelled her to add, "So do you."

If the afternoon negotiating session with Monsieur Girault had produced any stress, it didn't show in his face. He was clean shaven, clear eyed and smelled so darned good Sarah almost leaned in for a deeper whiff. His black hair still gleamed with damp. From a shower, she wondered as she fought the urged to feather her fingers through it, or the foggy drizzle that had kept up all day?

His suit certainly wasn't vintage, but had obviously been

tailored with the same loving skill as Grandmama's jacket. With it he wore a crisp blue shirt topped by a blue-and-silver-striped tie.

"What was it Oscar Wilde said about ties?" Sarah murmured, eyeing the expensive neckwear.

"Beats me."

"Something about a well-tied tie being the first serious step in a man's life. Of course, that was back when it took them hours to achieve the perfect crease in their cravat."

"Glad those days are gone. Speaking of gone... The car's waiting." He bowed and swept a hand toward the door. "Shall we go, *ma chérie?*"

Her look of surprise brought a smug grin.

"I had some time after my meeting so I pulled up a few phrases on Google Translate. How's the accent?"

"Well..."

"That bad, huh?"

"I've heard worse."

But not much worse. Hiding a smile, she picked up her clutch and led the way to the door.

"How did the meeting go, by the way?"

"We're making progress. Enough that my chief of production and a team of our corporate attorneys are in the air as we speak. We still need to hammer out a few details, but we're close."

"You *must* be making progress if you're bringing in a whole team."

Sarah refused to acknowledge the twinge that gave her. She hadn't really expected to share much of Paris with Dev. He was here on business. And she was here to make sure that business didn't get derailed by the wife of his prospective partner. She reminded herself of that fact as the limo glided through the lamp-lit streets.

Jean-Jacques Girault and his wife greeted them at the door to their magnificent town house. Once inside the palatial foyer, the two couples engaged in the obligatory cheek-kissing. Madame Girault behaved herself as she congratulated her guests on their engagement, but Dev stuck close to his fiancée just in case.

The exchange gave Sarah time to assess her hostess. The blonde had to be in her mid-fifties, but she had the lithe build and graceful carriage of a ballerina...which she used to be, she informed Sarah with a nod toward the portrait holding place of honor in the palatial foyer. The larger-than-life-size oil depicted a much younger Elise Girault costumed as Odile, the evil black swan in Tchaikovsky's *Swan Lake*.

"I loved dancing that part." With a smile as wicked as the one she wore in the portrait, Madame Girault hooked an arm in Sarah's and led her through a set of open double doors into a high-ceilinged salon. "Being bad is so much more fun than being good, yes?"

"Unless, as happens to Odile in some versions of *Swan Lake,* being bad gets you an arrow through the heart."

The older woman's laugh burst out, as loud and booming as a cannon. "Aha! You are warning me, I think, to keep my hands off your so-handsome Devon."

"If the ballet slipper fits..."

Her laugh foghorned again, noisy and raucous and totally infectious. Sarah found herself grinning as Madame Girault spoke over her shoulder.

"I like her, Devon."

She pronounced it Dec-vón, with the accent on the last syllable.

"I was prepared not to, you understand, as I want you for myself. Perhaps we can arrange a ménage à trois, yes?"

With her back to Dev, Sarah missed his reaction to the suggestion. She would have bet it wasn't as benign as Monsieur Girault's.

"Elise, my pet. You'll shock our guests with these little jokes of yours."

The look his wife gave Sarah brimmed with mischief and the unmistakable message that she was *not* joking.

Much to Sarah's surprise, she enjoyed the evening. Elise Girault didn't try to be anything but herself. She was at times sophisticated, at other times outrageous, but she didn't cross the line Sarah had drawn in the sand. Or in this case, in the near-priceless nineteenth-century Aubusson carpet woven in green-and-gold florals.

The Giraults and their guests took cocktails in the salon and dinner in an exquisitely paneled dining room with windows overlooking the Seine. The lively conversation ranged from their hostess's years at the Ballet de l'Opéra de Paris to Sarah's work at *Beguile* to, inevitably, the megabusiness of aircraft manufacturing. The glimpse into a world she'd had no previous exposure to fascinated Sarah, but Elise tolerated it only until the last course was cleared.

"Enough, Jean-Jacques!"

Pushing away from the table, she rose. Her husband and guests followed suit.

"We will take coffee and dessert in the petite salon. And you," she said, claiming Dev's arm, "will tell me what convinced this delightful woman to marry you. It was the story in *Beguile,* yes?" Her wicked smile returning, she threw Sarah an arch look. "The truth, now. Is his derriere as delicious as it looked in your magazine?"

Her husband shook his head. "Be good, Elise."

"I am, *mon cher.* Sooo good."

"I'm good, Dee-vón." Grinning, Sarah batted her lashes as the Hôtel Verneuil's elevator whisked them upward. "Sooo good."

Amused, Dev folded his arms and leaned his shoulders against the cage. She wasn't tipsy—she'd restricted her alcoholic intake to one aperitif, a single glass of wine and a few sips of brandy—but she was looser than he'd yet seen her.

He liked her this way. Her green eyes sparkling. Her hair windblown and brushing her shoulders. Her tuxedo jacket providing intermittent and thoroughly tantalizing glimpses of creamy breasts.

Liked, hell. He wanted to devour her whole.

"You were certainly good tonight," he agreed. "Especially when Elise tried to pump you for details about our sex life. I still don't know how you managed to give the impression of torrid heat when all you did was arch a brow."

"Ah, yes. The regal lift. It's one of Grandmama's best weapons, along with the chin tilt and the small sniff."

She demonstrated all three and had him grinning while he walked her to her door.

"Elise may be harder to fend off when she and I have lunch tomorrow," Sarah warned as she extracted the key card from her purse. "I may need to improvise."

His pulse jumping, Dev took the key and slid it into the electronic lock. The lock snicked, the door opened and he made his move.

"No reason you should have to improvise."

She turned, her expression at once wary and disbelieving. "Are you suggesting we go to bed together to satisfy Elise Girault's prurient curiosity?"

"No, ma'am." He bent and brushed his lips across hers. "I'm suggesting we go to bed together to satisfy ours."

Her jaw sagged. "You're kidding, right?"

"No, ma'am," he said again, half laughing, wholly serious.

She snapped her mouth shut, but the fact that she didn't stalk inside and slam the door in his face set Dev's pulse jumping again.

"Maybe," she said slowly, her eyes locked with his, "we could go a little way down that road. Just far enough to provide Elise with a few juicy details."

That was all the invitation he needed. Scooping her into his arms, he strode into the room and kicked the door shut. The maid had left the lamps on and turned down the duvet on the bed. Much as Dev ached to vector in that direction, he aimed for the sofa instead. He settled on its plush cushions with Sarah in his lap.

Exerting fierce control, he slid a palm under the silky splash of her hair. Her nape was warm, her lips parted, her gaze steady. The thought flashed into Dev's mind that he was already pretty far down the road.

Rock hard and hurting, he bent his head again. No mere brush of lips this time. No tentative exploration. No show for the cameras. This was hunger, raw and hot. He tried to throttle it back, but Sarah sabotaged that effort by matching him kiss for kiss, touch for touch. His fingers speared through her hair. Hers traced the line of his jaw, slipped inside his collar, found the knot of his tie.

"To hell with Oscar Wilde," she muttered after a moment. "The tie has to go."

The tie went. So did the suit coat. When she popped the top two buttons of his dress shirt, he reached for the ones on her jacket. The first one slid through its opening and Dev saw she wasn't wearing a bra. With a fervent prayer of thanks, he fingered the second button.

"I've been fantasizing about doing this from the moment you opened the door to me this evening," he admitted, his voice rough.

"I fantasized about it, too. Must be why I discarded the chemise I usually wear with this outfit."

Her honesty shot straight to his heart. She didn't play games. Didn't tease or go all pouty and coy. She was as hungry as Dev and not ashamed to show it.

Aching with need, he slid the second button through its opening. The satin lapels gaped open, baring her breasts. They were small and proud and tipped with dark rose nipples that Dev couldn't even begin to resist. Hefting her a little higher, he trailed a line of kisses down one slope and caught a nipple between his lips.

Her neck arched. Her head tipped back. With a small groan, Sarah reveled in the sensations that streaked from her breast to her belly. They were so deep, so intense, she purred with pleasure.

It took her a few moments to realize she wasn't actually emitting that low, humming sound. It was coming from the clutch purse she'd dropped on the sofa table.

"That's my cell phone," she panted through waves of pleasure. "I put it on vibrate at the Giraults."

"Ignore it."

Dev turned his attention to her other breast and Sarah was tempted, so tempted, to follow his gruff instruction.

"I can't," she groaned. "It could be Grandmama. Or Maria," she added with a little clutch of panic.

She scrambled upright and grabbed her bag. A glance at the face associated in her address book with the incoming number made her sag with relief.

Only for a moment, however. What could Alexis want, calling this late? Remembering her conversation with Paul Vincent at *Beguile*'s Paris office this afternoon, Sarah once again felt the tug of conflicting loyalties.

"Sarah? Are you there?" Alexis's hoarse rasp rattled through voice mail. "Pick up if you are."

Sarah sent Dev an apologetic glance and hit Answer. "I'm here, Alexis."

"Sorry, kiddo, I didn't think about the time difference. Were you in bed?"

"Almost," Dev muttered.

Sarah made a shushing motion with her free hand but it was too late. Alexis picked up the scent like a bloodhound.

"Is that Hunter? He's with you?"

"Yes. We just got in from a late dinner."

Not a lie, exactly. Not the whole truth, either. There were some things her boss simply didn't need to know.

"Good," Alexis was saying. "He can look over the JPEGs I just emailed you from the photo shoot at Cartier. I marked the one we're going to use with the blurb about your engagement."

"We'll take a look at them and get back to you."

"Tonight, kiddo. I want the story in this month's issue."

"Okay." Sighing, Sarah closed the flaps of her jacket and fastened the top button one-handed. "Shoot me the blurb, too."

"Don't worry about it. It's only a few lines."

The too-bland assurance set off an internal alarm.

"Send it, Alexis."

"All right, all right. But I want it back tonight, too."

She cut the connection, and Sarah sank back onto the cushions. Dev sat in his corner, one arm stretched across the sofa back. His shirttails hung open and his belt had somehow come unbuckled. He looked more than willing to pick up where they'd left off, but Sarah's common sense had kicked in. Or rather her sense of self-preservation.

"Saved by the bell," she said with an attempt at lightness. "At least now I won't have to improvise when Elise starts digging for details."

The phone pinged in her hand, signaling the arrival of a text message.

"That's the blurb Alexis wants to run with the pictures from Cartier. I'll pull it up with the photos so you can review them."

"No need." Dev pushed off the sofa, stuffed in his shirt and buckled his belt. "I trust you on this one."

"I'll make sure there are no naked body parts showing," she promised solemnly.

"You do that, and I'll make sure we're not interrupted next time."

"Next time?"

He dropped a quick kiss on her nose and grabbed his discarded suit coat.

"Oui, ma chérie," he said in his truly execrable French. "Next time."

Nine

Dev had a breakfast meeting with his people, who'd flown in the night before. That gave Sarah the morning to herself. A shame, really, because the day promised glorious sunshine and much warmer temperatures. Perfect for strolling the Left Bank with that special someone.

Which is what most of Paris seemed to be doing, she saw after coffee and a croissant at her favorite patisserie. The sight of so many couples, young, old and in between, rekindled some of the raw emotions Dev had generated last night.

In the bright light of day, Sarah couldn't believe she'd invited him to make love to her. Okay, she'd practically demanded it. Even now, as she meandered over the Pont de l'Archevêché, she felt her breasts tingle at the memory of his hands and mouth on them.

She stopped midway across the bridge. Pont de l'Archevêché translated to the Archbishop's Bridge in English, most likely because it formed a main means of transit for the clerics of Notre Dame. The cathedral's square towers rose on the right. Bookseller stalls and cafés crowded the broad avenue on the left. The Seine flowed dark and silky below. What intrigued her, though, were the padlocks of all shapes and sizes hooked through the bridge's waist-high, iron-mesh scrollwork. Some locks had tags attached, some were decorated with bright ribbons, some included small charms.

She'd noticed other bridges sporting locks, although none as heavily adorned as this one. They'd puzzled her but she hadn't really wondered about their significance. It became apparent a few moments after she spotted a pair of tourists purchasing a padlock from an enterprising lock seller at the far end of the bridge. The couple searched for an empty spot on the fancy grillwork to attach their purchase. Then they threw the key into the Seine and shared a long, passionate kiss.

When they walked off arm in arm, Sarah approached the lock seller. He was perched on an upturned wooden crate beside a pegboard displaying his wares. His hair sprouted like milky-white dandelion tufts from under his rusty-black beret. A cigarette hung from his lower lip.

"I've been away for a while," she said in her fluent Parisian. "When did this business with the locks begin?"

"Three years? Five? Who can remember?" His shoulders lifted in the quintessential Gallic shrug. "At first the locks appeared only at night, and they would be cut off each day. Now they are everywhere."

"So it seems."

Mistaking her for a native, he winked and shared his personal opinion of his enterprise. "The tourists, they eat this silly stuff up. As if they can lock in the feelings they have right now, today, and throw away the key. We French know better, yes?"

His cigarette bobbed. His gestures grew extravagant as he expounded his philosophy.

"To love is to take risks. To be free, not caged. To walk away if what you feel brings hurt to you or to your lover. Who would stay, or want to stay, where there is pain?"

The question was obviously rhetorical, so Sarah merely spread her hands and answered with a shrug.

She was still thinking about the encounter when she met Madame Girault for lunch later that day. She related the lock seller's philosophy to Elise, who belted out a raucous laugh that turned heads throughout the restaurant.

"My darling Sarah, I must beg to disagree!"

With her blond hair drawn into a tight bun that emphasized her high cheekbones and angular chin, Elise looked more like the Black Swan of her portrait. Her sly smile only heightened the resemblance.

"Locks and, yes, a little pain can add a delicious touch to an affair," she said, her eyes dancing. "And speaking of which…"

Her mouth took a sardonic tilt as a dark-haired man some twenty-five or thirty years her junior rose from his table and approached theirs.

"Ah, Elise, only one woman in all Paris has a laugh like yours. How are you, my love?"

"Very well. And you, Henri? Are you still dancing attendance on that rich widow I saw you with at the theater?"

"Sadly, she returned to Argentina before I extracted full payment for services rendered." His dark eyes drifted to Sarah. "But enough of such mundane matters. You must introduce me to your so-lovely companion."

"No, I must not. She's in Paris with her fiancé and has no need of your special skills." Elise flapped a hand and shooed him off. "Be a good boy and go away."

"If you insist…"

He gave a mocking half bow and returned to his table, only to sign the check and leave a few moments later. A fleeting look of regret crossed Elise's face as he wove his way toward the exit. Sighing, she fingered her glass.

"He was so inventive in bed, that one. So *very* inventive. But always in need of money. When I tired of emptying my purse for him, he threatened to sell pictures of me in certain, shall we say, exotic positions."

Sarah winced, but couldn't say anything. Any mention of the paparazzi and sensational photographs struck too close to home.

"Jean-Jacques sent men to convince him that would not be wise," Elise confided. "The poor boy was in a cast for weeks afterward."

The offhand comment doused the enjoyment Sarah had taken in Elise's company up to that point. Madame Girault's concept of love suddenly seemed more tawdry than amusing. Deliberately, Sarah changed the subject.

"I wonder how the negotiations are going? Dev said he thought they were close to a deal."

Clearly disinterested, Elise shrugged and snapped her fingers to summon their waiter.

Halfway across Paris, Dev had to force himself to focus on the columns of figures in the newly restructured agreement. It didn't help that his seat at the conference table offered a panoramic view of the pedestrians-only esplanade and iconic Grande Arche that dominated Paris's financial district. Workers by the hundreds were seated on the steps below the Grande Arche, their faces lifted to the sun while they enjoyed their lunch break.

One couple appeared to be enjoying more than the sun. Dev watched them share a touch, a laugh, a kiss. Abruptly, he pushed away from the table.

"Sorry," he said to the dozen or so startled faces that turned in his direction. "I need to make a call."

Jean-Jacques Girault scooted his chair away from the table, as well. "Let's all take a break. We'll reconvene in thirty minutes, yes? There'll be a catered lunch waiting when we return."

Dev barely waited for Girault to finish his little speech. The urge to talk to Sarah, to hear her voice, drove him through the maze of outer offices and into the elevator. A short while later he'd joined the throng on the steps below the Grande Arche.

It took him a moment to acknowledge the unfamiliar sensation that knifed through him as he dialed Sarah's number. It wasn't just the lust that had damned near choked him last night. It was that amorphous, indefinable feeling immortalized in so many sappy songs. Grimacing, he admitted the inescapable truth. He was in love, or close enough to it to make no difference.

Sarah answered on the second ring. "Hello, Dev. This must be mental telepathy. I was just talking about you."

"You were, huh?"

"How are the negotiations going?"

"They're going."

The sound of her voice did something stupid to his insides. To his head, too. With barely a second thought, he abandoned Girault and company to the team of sharks he'd flown in last night.

"We've been crunching numbers all morning. I'm thinking of letting my people handle the afternoon session. What do you have planned?"

"Nothing special."

"How about I meet you back at the hotel and we'll do nothing special together?"

He didn't intend to say what came next. Didn't have any control over the words. They just happened.

"Or maybe," he said, his voice going husky, "we can work on our next time."

A long silence followed his suggestion. When it stretched for several seconds, Dev kicked himself for his lack of finesse. Then she came back with a low, breathless response that damned near stopped his heart.

"I'll catch a cab and meet you at the hotel."

* * *

Sarah snapped her phone shut and sent Madame Girault a glance that was only a shade apologetic. "That was Dev. I'm sorry, but I have to go."

Elise looked startled for a moment. But only a moment. Then her face folded into envious lines.

"Go," she ordered with a wave of one hand. "Paris is the city of love, after all. And I think yours, *ma petite,* is one that deserves a lock on the Archbishop's Bridge."

Sarah wanted to believe that was what sent her rushing out of the restaurant. Despite the lock seller's philosophical musings, despite hearing the details of Elise's sordid little affair, she wanted desperately to believe that what she felt for Dev could stand the test of time.

That hope took a temporary hit when she caught up with the dark-haired, dark-eyed Henri on the pavement outside of the restaurant. He'd just hailed a cab, but generously offered it to her instead.

Or not so generously. His offer to escort her to her hotel and fill her afternoon hours with unparalleled delight left an unpleasant taste in Sarah's mouth. Unconsciously, she channeled Grandmama.

"I think not, monsieur."

The haughty reply sent him back a pace. The blank surprise on his face allowed Sarah more than enough time to slide into the cab and tell the driver her destination. Then she slammed the door and forgot Henri, forgot Elise, forgot everything but the instant hunger Dev's call had sparked in her.

She wrestled with that hunger all the way back to the hotel. Her cool, rational, practical-by-necessity self kept asserting that her arrangement with Dev Hunter was just that, an arrangement. A negotiated contract that would soon conclude. If she made love with him, as she desperately wanted to do, she'd simply be satisfying a short-term physical need while possibly setting herself up for long-term regrets.

The other side of her, the side she usually kept so sternly repressed, echoed Gina at her giddiest. Why not grab a little pleasure? Taste delight here, now, and let tomorrow take care of itself?

As was happening all too frequently with Dev, giddy and greedy vanquished cool and rational. By the time Sarah burst out of the elevator and headed down the hall toward her room, heat coursed through her, hot and urgent. The sight of Dev leaning against the wall beside the door to her room sent her body temperature soaring up another ten degrees.

"What took you so long?" he demanded.

Snatching the key card from her hand, he shoved it into the lock. Two seconds after the door opened, he had her against the entryway wall.

"I hope you had a good lunch. We won't be coming up for food or drink anytime soon."

The bruising kiss spiked every one of Sarah's senses. She tasted him, drank in his scent, felt his hips slam hers against the wall.

He kicked the door shut. Or did she? She didn't know, didn't care. Dev's hands were all over her at that point. Unbuttoning her blouse. Hiking up her skirt. Shoving down her bikini briefs.

Panting, greedy, wanting him so much she ached with it, she struggled out of her blouse. Kicked her shoes off and the panties free of her ankles. Hooked one leg around his thighs.

"Sarah." It was a groan and a plea. "Let's take this to the bedroom."

Mere moments later she was naked and stretched out on the king-size bed. Her avid gaze devoured Dev as he stood beside the bed and shed his clothing.

She'd seen portions of him last night. Enough to confirm that he ranked much higher than number three on her personal top ten list. Those glimpses didn't even begin to compare with the way he looked now with his black hair catching the afternoon light and his blue eyes fired with need. Every muscle in his long, lean body looked taut and eager. He was hard for her, and hungry, and so ready that Sarah almost yelped when he turned away.

"What are you doing?"

"Making sure you don't regret this."

Her dismay became a wave of relief when she saw him extract a condom from the wallet in his discarded pants. She wasn't on the pill. She'd stopped months ago. Or was it years? Sarah couldn't remember. She suspected her decision to quit birth control had a lot to do with the realization that taking care of Grandmama and keeping a roof over their heads were more important to her than casual sex.

Showed what she knew. There was nothing casual about this sex, however. The need for it, the gnawing hunger for it, consumed her.

No! Her mind screamed the denial even as she opened her arms to Dev. This wasn't just sex. This wasn't just raw need. This was so elemental. So...so French. Making love in the afternoon. With a man who filled her, physically, emotionally, every way that mattered.

His hips braced against hers. His knees pried hers apart. Eagerly, Sarah opened her legs and her arms and her heart to him. When he eased into her, she hooked her calves around his and rose up to meet his first, slow thrusts. Then the pace picked up. In. Out. In again.

Soon, *too* soon, dammit, her vaginal muscles began to quiver and her belly contracted. She tried to suppress the spasms. Tried to force her muscles to ease their greedy grip. She wanted to build to a steady peak, spin the pleasure as long as she could.

Her body refused to listen to her mind. The tight, spiraling sensation built to a wild crescendo. Panting, Sarah arched her neck. A moment later, she was flying, sailing, soaring. Dev surged into her, went taut and rode to the crest with her. Then he gave a strangled grunt and collapsed on top of her.

* * *

Sarah was still shuddering with the aftershocks when he whispered a French phrase into her ear. Her eyes flew open. Her jaw dropped.

"What did you say?"

He levered up on one elbow. A flush rode high in his cheeks and his blue eyes were still fever bright, but he managed a semicoherent reply.

"I was trying to tell you I adore you."

Sarah started giggling and couldn't stop. No easy feat with 180 plus pounds of naked male pinning her to the sheets.

A rueful grin sketched across Dev's face. "Okay, what did I really say?"

"It sounded…it sounded…" Helpless with laughter, she gasped for breath. "It sounded like you want to hang an ornament on me."

"Yeah, well, that, too." His grin widening, he leaned down and dropped a kiss on her left breast. "Here. And here…"

He grazed her right breast, eased down to her belly.

"And here, and…"

"Dev!"

Pleasure rippled in waves across the flat plane of her stomach. She wouldn't have believed she could become so aroused so fast. Particularly after that shattering orgasm. Dev, on the other hand, was lazy and loose and still flaccid.

"Don't you need to, uh, take a little time to recharge?"

"I do." His voice was muffled, his breath hot against her skin. "Doesn't mean you have to. Unless you want to?"

He raised his head and must have seen the answer in her face. Waggling his brows, he lowered his head again. Sarah gasped again when his tongue found her now super-sensitized center.

The climax hit this time without warning. She'd just reached up to grip the headboard and bent a knee to avoid a cramp when everything seemed to shrink to a single, white-hot nova. The next second, the star exploded. Pleasure pulsed through her body. Groaning, she let it flow before it slowly, exquisitely ebbed.

When she opened her eyes again, Dev looked smug and pretty damn pleased with himself. With good reason, she thought, drifting on the last eddies. She sincerely hoped he still needed some time to recharge. She certainly did!

To her relief, he stretched out beside her and seemed content to just laze. She nestled her head on his arm and let her thoughts drift back to his mangled French. He said he'd been trying to tell her that he adored her. What did that mean, exactly?

She was trying to find a way to reintroduce the subject when the phone buzzed. His this time, not hers. With a muffled grunt, Dev reached across her and checked his phone's display.

"Sorry," he said with a grimace. "I told them not to call unless they were about to slam up against our own version of a fiscal cliff. I'd better take this."

"Go ahead. I'll hit the bathroom."

She scooped up the handiest article of clothing, which happened to be Dev's shirt, and padded into the bathroom. The tiles felt cool and smooth against her bare feet. The apparition that appeared in the gilt-edged mirrors made her gasp.

"Good grief!"

Her hair could have provided a home for an entire flock of sparrows. Whatever makeup she'd started out with this morning had long since disappeared. She was also sporting one whisker burn on her chin and another on her neck. Shuddering at the thought of what Elise Girault would say if she saw the telltale marks, Sarah ran the taps and splashed cold water on her face and throat.

That done, she eyed the bidet. So practical for Europeans, so awkward for most Americans. Practical won hands down in this instance. Clean and refreshed, Sarah reentered the bedroom just as Dev was zipping up his pants.

"Uh-oh. Looks like your negotiators ran into that cliff."

"Ran into it, hell. According to my chief of production, they soared right over the damned thing and are now in a free fall."

"That doesn't sound good."

Detouring to her closet, she exchanged Dev's shirt for the thigh-length, peony-decorated silk robe Gina had given her for her birthday last year.

"It's all part of the game," he said as she handed him back his shirt. "Girault's just a little better at it than I gave him credit for."

The comment tripped a reminder of Elise's disclosures at lunch. Sarah debated for a moment over whether she should share them with Dev, then decided he needed to know the kind of man he would be doing business with.

"Elise said something today about her husband that surprised me."

Dev looked up from buttoning his shirt. "What was that?"

"Supposedly, Jean-Jacques sent some goons to rough up one of her former lovers. The guy had threatened to sell pictures of her to the tabloids."

"Interesting. I would have thought Girault man enough to do the job himself. I certainly would have." He scooped up his tie and jacket and gave her a quick kiss. "I'll call as soon as I have a fix on when we'll break for dinner."

Sarah nodded, but his careless remark about going after Elise's lover for trying to sell pictures of her had struck home. The comment underscored his contempt for certain members of her profession. How much would it take, she wondered uneasily, for him to lump her in with the sleaziest among them?

Ten

Still troubled by Dev's parting comment, Sarah knotted the sash to her robe and stepped out onto her little balcony. She'd lost herself in the view before, but this time the seemingly endless vista of chimneys and gray slate roofs didn't hold as much interest as her bird's-eye view of the street four stories below.

The limo Dev had called for idled a few yards from the hotel's entrance. When he strode out of the hotel, the sight of him once again outfitted in his business attire gave Sarah's heart a crazy bump. She couldn't help contrasting that with the image of his sleek, naked body still vivid in her mind.

The uniformed driver jumped out to open the rear passenger door. Dev smiled and said a few words to him, inaudible from Sarah's height, and ducked to enter the car. At the last moment he paused and glanced up. When he spotted her, the friendly smile he'd given the driver warmed into something so private and so sensual that she responded without thinking.

Touching her fingers lightly to her lips, she blew him a kiss—and was immediately embarrassed by the gesture. It was so schmaltzy, and so out of character for her. More like something Gina might do. Yet she remained on the balcony like some lovelorn Juliet long after Dev had driven off.

Even worse, she couldn't summon the least desire to get dressed and meander through the streets. Peering into shop windows or people watching at a café didn't hold as much allure as it had before. She would rather wait until Dev finished with his meeting and they could meander together.

She'd take a long, bubbly bath instead, she decided. But first she had catch up on her email. And call Grandmama. And try Gina again. Maybe this time her sister would answer the damned phone.

Gina didn't, but Sarah caught the duchess before she went out for her morning constitutional. She tried to temper her habitual concern with a teasing note.

"You won't overdo it, will you?"

"My darling Sarah," Charlotte huffed. "If I could walk almost forty miles through a war-torn country with an infant in my arms, I can certainly stroll a few city blocks."

Wisely, Sarah refrained from pointing out that the duchess had made the first walk more than fifty years ago.

"Have you heard from Gina?" she asked instead.

"No, have you?"

"Not since she texted me that she was flitting off to Switzerland."

She'd tried to keep her the response casual, but the duchess knew her too well.

"Listen to me, Sarah Elizabeth Marie-Adele. Your sister may act rashly on occasion, but she's a St. Sebastian. Whatever you think she may be up to, she won't bring shame on her family or her name."

The urge to tell her grandmother about the missing medallion was so strong that Sarah had to bite her lip to keep from blurting it out. That would only lead to a discussion of how she'd become involved with Dev, and she wasn't ready to explain that, either. Thankfully, her grandmother was content to let the subject drop.

"Now tell me about Paris," she commanded. "Has Devon taken you to Café Michaud yet?"

"Not yet, but he said you'd given him strict orders to do so. Oh, and he had his people work minor miracles to get us into the Hôtel Verneuil on such short notice."

"He did? How very interesting."

She sounded so thoughtful—and so much like a cat that had just lapped up a bowl of cream—that Sarah became instantly suspicious.

"What other instructions did you give him?"

"None."

"Come on. Fess up. What other surprises do I have in store?"

A soft sigh came through the phone. "You're in Paris, with a handsome, virile man. One whom I suspect is more than capable of delivering surprises of his own."

Sarah gave a fervent prayer of thanks that the duchess hadn't yet mastered the FaceTime app on her phone. If she had, she would have seen her elder granddaughter's cheeks flame at the thought of how much she'd *already* enjoyed her handsome, virile fiancé.

"I'll talk to you tomorrow, Grandmama. Give Maria my love."

She hung up, marveling again at how readily everyone seemed to have accepted Dev Hunter's sudden appearance in their lives. Grandmama. Maria. Alexis. Sarah herself. Would they accept his abrupt departure as readily?

Would they have to?

Sarah was no fool. Nor was she blind. She could tell Dev felt at least some of the same jumbled emotions she did. Mixed in with the greedy hunger there was the shared laughter, the seduction of this trip, the growing delight in each other's company. Maybe, just maybe, there could be love, too.

She refused to even speculate about anything beyond that. Their evolving relationship was too new, too fragile, to project vary far ahead. Still, she couldn't help humming the melody from Edith Piaf's classic, "La Vie En Rose," as she started for the bathroom and a long, hot soak.

The house phone caught her halfway there. She detoured to the desk and answered. The caller identified himself as Monsieur LeBon, the hotel's manager, and apologized profusely for disturbing her.

"You're not disturbing me, monsieur."

"Good, good." He hesitated, then seemed to be choosing his words carefully. "I saw Monsieur Hunter leave a few moments ago and thought perhaps I might catch you alone."

"Why? Is there a problem?"

"I'm not sure. Do you by chance know a gentleman by the name of Henri Lefèvre?"

"I don't recognize the name."

"Aha! I thought as much." LeBon gave a small sniff. "There was something in his manner…"

"What has this Monsieur Lefèvre to do with me?"

"He approached our receptionist earlier this afternoon and claimed you and he were introduced by a mutual acquaintance. He couldn't remember your name, however. Only that you were a tall, slender American who spoke excellent French. And that you mentioned you were staying at the Hôtel Verneuil."

The light dawned. It had to be Elise's former lover. He must have heard her give the cabdriver instructions to the hotel.

"The receptionist didn't tell him my name, did she?"

"You may rest assured she did not! Our staff is too well trained to disclose information on any of our guests. She referred the man to me, and I sent him on his way."

"Thank you, Monsieur LeBon. Please let me know immediately if anyone else inquires about me."

"Of course, Lady Sarah."

The call from the hotel manager dimmed a good bit of Sarah's enjoyment in her long, bubbly soak. She didn't particularly like the fact that Elise's smarmy ex-lover had tracked her to the hotel.

Dev called just moments after she emerged from the tub. Sounding totally disgusted, he told her he intended to lock everyone in the conference room until they reached a final agreement.

"The way it looks now that might be midnight or later. Sorry, Sarah. I won't be able to keep our dinner date."

"Don't worry about that."

"Yeah, well, I'd much rather be with you than these clowns. I'm about ready to tell Girault and company to shove it."

Sarah didn't comment. She couldn't, given the staggering sums involved in his negotiations. But she thought privately he was taking a risk doing business with someone who hired thugs to pound on his wife's lover.

Briefly, she considered telling Dev that same lover had shown up at the hotel this afternoon but decided against it. He had enough on his mind at the moment and Monsieur LeBon appeared to have taken care of the matter.

She spent what remained of the afternoon and most of the evening on her laptop, with only a short break for soup and a salad ordered from room service. She had plenty of work to keep her busy and was satisfied with the two layouts she'd mocked up when she finally quit. She'd go in to the offices on rue Balzac tomorrow to view the layouts on the twenty-five-inch monitor.

Unless Dev finished negotiations tonight as he swore he would do. Then maybe they'd spend the day together. And the night. And...

Her belly tightening at the possibilities, she curled up in bed with the ebook she'd downloaded. She got through only a few pages before she dozed off.

* * *

The phone jerked her from sleep. She fumbled among the covers, finally found it and came more fully awake when she recognized Dev's number.

"Did you let them all out of the conference room?" she asked with a smile.

"I did. They're printing the modified contracts as we speak. They'll be ready to sign tomorrow morning."

"Congratulations!"

She was happy for him, she really was, even if it meant the termination of their arrangement.

"I'm on my way back to the hotel. Is it too late for a celebration?"

"I don't know. What time is it?"

"Almost one."

"No problem. Just give me a few minutes to get dressed. Do you have someplace special in mind? If not, I know several great cafés that stay open until 2:00 a.m."

"Actually, I was hoping for a private celebration. No dressing required."

She could hear the smile in his voice, and something more. Something that brought Gina forcefully to mind. Her sister always claimed she felt as though she was tumbling through time and space whenever she fell in love. Sarah hadn't scoffed but she *had* chalked the hyperbole up to another Gina-ism.

How wrong she was. And how right Gina was. That was exactly how Sarah felt now. As though Dev had kicked her feet out from under her and she was on some wild, uncontrollable slide.

"A private celebration sounds good to me," she got out breathlessly.

She didn't change out of the teddy and bikini briefs she'd worn to bed, but she did throw on the peony robe and make a dash to the bathroom before she answered Dev's knock.

As charged up as he'd sounded on the phone, she half expected him to kick the door shut and pin her against the wall again. Okay, she kind of hoped he would.

He didn't, but Sarah certainly couldn't complain about his altered approach. The energy was there, and the exultation from having closed his big deal. Yet the hands that cupped her face were incredibly gentle, and the kiss he brushed across her mouth was so tender she almost melted from the inside out.

"Jean-Jacques told me to thank you," he murmured against her lips.

"For what?"

"He thinks I finally agreed to his company's design for the pneumatic turbine assembly because I was so damned anxious to get back to you."

"Oh, no!"

She pulled back in dismay. She had no idea what a pneumatic turbine assembly was, but it sounded important.

"You didn't concede anything critical, did you?"

"Nah. I always intended to accept their design. I just used it as my ace in the hole to close the deal. *And* to get back to you."

He bent and brushed her mouth again. When he raised his head, the look in his eyes started Sarah on another wild spin through time and space.

"I don't want to risk any more mangled verbs," he said with a slow smile, "so I'll stick to English this time. I love you, Sarah St. Sebastian."

"Since...? Since when?"

He appeared to give the matter some consideration. "Hard to say. I have to admit it started with a severe case of lust."

She would have to admit the same thing. Later. Right now she could only try to keep breathing as he raised her hand and angled it so the emerald caught the light.

"By the time I put this on your finger, though, I was

already strategizing ways to keep it there. I know I black-mailed you into this fake engagement, Sarah, but if I ask very politely and promise to be nice to your ditz of a sister, would you consider making it real?"

Although it went against a lifetime of ingrained habit, she didn't fire up in Gina's defense. Instead she drew her brows together.

"I need a minute to think about it."

Surprise and amusement and just a touch of uncertainty colored Dev's reply. "Take all the time you need."

She pursed her lips and gave the matter three or four seconds of fierce concentration.

"Okay."

"Okay you'll consider it, or okay you'll make it real?"

Laughing, Sarah hooked her arms around his neck. "I'm going with option B."

Dev hadn't made a habit of going on the prowl like so many crew dogs he'd flown with, but he'd racked up more than a few quality hours with women in half a dozen coun-tries. Not until *this* woman, however, did he really appreci-ate the difference between having sex and making love. It wasn't her smooth, sleek curves or soft flesh or breathless little pants. It was the sum of all parts, the whole of her, the elegance that was Sarah.

And the fact that she was his.

He'd intended to make this loving slow and sweet, a sort of unspoken acknowledgment of the months and years of nights like this they had ahead. She blew those plans out of the water mere moments after Dev positioned her under him. Her body welcomed him, her heat fired his. The primi-tive need to possess her completely soon had him pinning her wrists to the sheets, his thrusts hard and deep. Her head went back. Her belly quivered. A moan rose from deep in her throat, and Dev took everything she had to give.

* * *

She was still half-asleep when he leaned over her early the next morning. "I've got to shower and change and get with Girault to sign the contracts. How about we meet for lunch at your grandmother's favorite café?"

"Mmm."

"Tell me the name of it again."

"Café Michaud," she muttered sleepily, "rue de Monttessuy."

"Got it. Café Michaud. Rue de Monttessuy. Twelve noon?"

"Mmm."

He took his time in the shower, answered several dozen emails, reviewed a bid solicitation on a new government contract and still made the ten o'clock signing session at Girault's office with time to spare.

The French industrialist was in a jovial mood, convinced he'd won a grudging, last-minute concession. Dev didn't disabuse him. After initialing sixteen pages and signing three, the two chief executives posed for pictures while their respective staffs breathed sighs of relief that the months of intense negotiations were finally done.

"How long do you remain in Paris?" Girault asked after pictures and another round of handshakes.

"I had planned to fly home as soon as we closed this deal, but I think now I'll take some downtime and stay over a few more days."

"A very wise decision," Girault said with a wink. "Paris is a different city entirely when explored with one you love. Especially when that one is as delightful as your Sarah."

"I won't argue with that. And speaking of my Sarah, we're meeting for lunch. I'll say goodbye now, Jean-Jacques."

"But no! Not goodbye. You must have dinner with Elise and me again before you leave. Now that we are partners, yes?"

"I'll see what Sarah has planned and get back to you."

* * *

The rue de Monttessuy was in the heart of Paris's 7th arrondissement. Tall, stately buildings topped with slate roofs crowded the sidewalks and offered a glimpse of the Eiffel Tower spearing into the sky at the far end of the street. Café Michaud sat midway down a long block, a beacon of color with its bright red awnings and window boxes filled with geraniums.

Since he was almost a half hour early, Dev had his driver drop him off at the intersection. He needed to stretch his legs, and he preferred to walk the half block rather than wait for Sarah at one of the café's outside tables. Maybe he could find something for her in one of the shops lining the narrow, cobbled street. Unlike the high-end boutiques and jeweler's showrooms on some of the more fashionable boulevards, these were smaller but no less intriguing.

He strolled past a tiny grocery with fresh produce displayed in wooden crates on either side of the front door, a chocolatier, a wine shop and several antique shops. One in particular caught his attention. Its display of military and aviation memorabilia drew him into the dim, musty interior.

His eyes went instantly to an original lithograph depicting Charles Lindbergh's 1927 landing at a Paris airfield after his historic solo transatlantic flight. The photographer had captured the shadowy images of the hundreds of Model As and Ts lined up at the airfield, their headlamps illuminating the grassy strip as the *Spirit of St. Louis* swooped out of the darkness.

"I'll take that," he told the shopkeeper.

The man's brows soared with surprise and just a touch of disdain for this naive American who made no attempt to bargain. Dev didn't care. He would have paid twice the price. He'd never thought of himself as particularly sentimental, but the key elements in the print—aviation and Paris—were what had brought him and Sarah together.

As if to compensate for his customer's foolishness, the shopkeeper threw in at no cost the thick cardboard tube the print had been rolled in when he himself had discovered it at a flea market.

Tube in hand, Dev exited the shop and started for the café. His pulse kicked when he spotted Sarah approaching from the opposite direction. She was on the other side of the street, some distance from the café, but he recognized her graceful walk and the silky brown hair topped by a jaunty red beret.

He picked up his pace, intending to cross at the next corner, when a figure half-hidden amid a grocer's produce display brought him to a dead stop. The man had stringy brown hair that straggled over the shoulders and a camera propped on the top crate. Its monster zoom lens was aimed directly at Sarah. While Dev stood there, his jaw torquing, the greaseball clicked off a half-dozen shots.

"What the hell are you doing?"

The photographer whipped around. He said something in French, but it was the careless shrug that fanned Dev's anger into fury.

"Bloodsucking parasites," he ground out.

The hand gripping the cardboard tube went white at the knuckles. His other hand bunched into a fist. Screw the lawsuits. He'd flatten the guy. The photographer read his intent and jumped back, knocking over several crates of produce in the process.

"Non, non!" He stumbled back, his face white with alarm under the greasy hair. "You don't…you don't understand, Monsieur Hunter. I am François. With *Beguile.* I shoot the photos for the story."

For the second time in as many moments, Dev froze. "The story?"

"Oui. We get the instructions from New York."

He thrust out the camera and angled the digital display.

His thumb beat a rapid tattoo as he clicked through picture after picture.

"But look! Here are you and Sarah having coffee. And here you walk along the Seine. And here she blows you a kiss from the balcony of her hotel room."

Pride overrode the photographer's alarm. A few clicks of the zoom button enlarged the shot on the screen.

"Do you see how perfectly she is framed? And the expression on her face after you drive away. Like one lost in a dream, yes? She stays like that long enough for me to shoot from three different angles."

The anger still hot in Dev's gut chilled. Ice formed in his veins.

"She posed for you?" he asked softly, dangerously.

The photographer glanced up, nervous again. He stuttered something about New York, but Dev wasn't listening. His gaze was locked on Sarah as she approached the café.

She'd posed for this guy. After making all those noises about allowing only that one photo shoot at Cartier, she'd caved to her boss's demands. He might have forgiven that. He had a harder time with the fact that she'd set this all up without telling him.

Dev left the photographer amid the produce. Jaw tight, he stalked toward the café. Sarah was still a block away on the other side of the street. He was about to cross when a white delivery van slowed to a rolling stop and blocked her from view. A few seconds later, Dev heard the thud of its rear doors slam. When the van cut a sharp left and turned down a narrow side street, the sidewalk Sarah had been walking along was empty.

Eleven

Dev broke into a run even before he fully processed what had just happened. All he knew for sure was that Sarah had been strolling toward him one moment and was gone the next. His brain scrambled for a rational explanation of her sudden disappearance. She could have ducked into a shop. Could have stopped to check something in a store window. His gut went with the delivery van.

Dev hit the corner in a full-out sprint and charged down the side street. He dodged a woman pushing a baby carriage, earned a curse from two men he almost bowled over. He could see the van up ahead, see its taillights flashing red as it braked for a stop sign.

He was within twenty yards when the red lights blinked off. Less than ten yards away when the van began another turn. The front window was halfway down. Through it Dev could see the driver, his gaze intent on the pedestrians streaming across the intersection and his thin black cigarillo sending spirals of smoke through the half-open window.

Dev calculated the odds on the fly. Go for the double rear doors or aim for the driver? He risked losing the van if the rear doors were locked and the vehicle picked up speed after completing the turn. He also risked causing an accident if he jumped into traffic in the middle of a busy intersection and planted himself in front of the van.

He couldn't take that chance on losing it. With a desperate burst of speed, he cut the corner and ran into the street right ahead of an oncoming taxi. Brakes squealing, horn blaring, the cab fishtailed. Dev slapped a hand on its hood, pushed off and landed in a few yards ahead of the now-rolling van. He put up both hands and shouted a fierce command.

"Stop!"

He got a glimpse, just a glimpse, of the driver's face through the windshield. Surprise, fear, desperation all flashed across it in the half second before he hit the gas.

Well, hell! The son of a bitch was gunning straight for him.

Dev jumped out of the way at the last second and leaped for the van's door as the vehicle tried to zoom past. The door was unlocked, thank God, although he'd been prepared to hook an arm inside the open window and pop the lock if necessary. Wrenching the panel open, he got a bulldog grip on the driver's leather jacket.

"Pull over, dammit."

The man jerked the wheel, cursing and shouting and trying frantically to dislodge him. The van swerved. More horns blasted.

"Dev!"

The shout came from the back of the van. From Sarah. He didn't wait to hear more. His fist locked on the driver's leather jacket, he put all his muscle into a swift yank. The bastard's face slammed into the steering wheel. Bone crunched. Blood fountained. The driver slumped.

Reaching past him, Dev tore the keys from the ignition. The engine died, but the van continued to roll toward a car that swerved wildly but couldn't avoid a collision. Metal crunched metal as both vehicles came to an abrupt stop, and Dev fumbled for the release for the driver's seat belt. He dragged the unconscious man out and let him drop to the pavement. Scrambling into the front seat, he had one leg over the console to climb into the rear compartment when the back doors flew open and someone jumped out.

It wasn't Sarah. She was on her knees in the back. A livid red welt marred one cheek. A roll of silver electrical tape dangled from a wide strip wrapped around one wrist. Climbing over the console, Dev stooped beside her.

"Are you okay?"

"Yes."

Her eyes were wide and frightened, but the distant wail of a siren eased some of their panic. Dev tore his glance from her to the open rear doors and the man running like hell back down the side street.

"Stay here and wait for the police. I'm going after that bastard."

"Wait!" She grabbed his arm. "You don't need to chase him! I know who he is."

He swung back. "You *know* him?"

When she nodded, suspicion knifed into him like a serrated blade. His fists bunched, and a distant corner of his mind registered the fact that he'd lost the lithograph sometime during the chase. The rest of him staggered under a sudden realization.

"This is part of it, isn't it? This big abduction scene?"

"Scene?"

She sounded so surprised he almost believed her. Worse, dammit, he wanted to believe her!

"It's okay," he ground out. "You can drop the act. I bumped into the photographer from *Beguile* back there on rue de Monttessuy. We had quite a conversation."

Her color drained, making the red welt across her cheek look almost obscene by contrast. "You...you talked to a photographer from my magazine?"

"Yeah, Lady Sarah, I did. François told me about the shoot. Showed me some of the pictures he's already taken. I'll have to ask him to send me the one of you on the balcony. You make a helluva Juliet."

The sirens were louder now. Their harsh, up-and-down bleat almost drowned out her whisper.

"And you think we…me, this photographer, my magazine…you think we staged an abduction?"

"I'm a little slow. It took me a while to understand the angle. I'm betting your barracuda of a boss dreamed it up. Big, brave Number Three rescues his beautiful fiancée from would-be kidnappers."

She looked away, and her silence cut even deeper than Dev's suspicion. He'd hoped she would go all huffy, deny at least some of her part in this farce. Apparently, she couldn't.

Well, Sarah and her magazine could damned well live with the consequences of their idiotic scheme. At the least, they were looking at thousands of dollars in vehicle damage. At the worst, reconstructive surgery for the driver whose face Dev had rearranged.

Thoroughly disgusted, he took Sarah's arm to help her out of the van. She shook off his hold without a word, climbed down and walked toward the squad car now screeching to a halt. Two officers exited. One went to kneel beside the moaning van driver. The other soon centered on Sarah as the other major participant in the incident. She communicated with him in swift, idiomatic French. He took notes the entire time, shooting the occasional glance at Dev that said his turn would come.

It did, but not until an ambulance had screamed up and two EMTs went to work on the driver. At the insistence of the officer who'd interviewed Sarah, a third medical tech examined her. The tech was shining a penlight into her pupils when the police officer turned his attention to Dev. Switching to English, he took down Dev's name, address while in Paris and cell-phone number before asking for his account of the incident.

He'd had time to think about it. Rather than lay out his suspicion that the whole thing was a publicity stunt, he stuck to the bare facts. He'd spotted Sarah walking toward him. Saw the van pull up. Saw she was gone. Gave chase.

The police officer made more notes, then flipped back a few pages. "So, Monsieur Hunter, are you also acquainted with Henri Lefèvre?"

"Who?"

"The man your fiancée says snatched her off the street and threw her into the back of this van."

"No, I'm not acquainted with him."

"But you know Monsieur Girault and his wife?"

Dev's eyes narrowed as he remembered Sarah telling him about the goons Girault had employed to do his dirty work. Was Lefèvre one of those goons? Was Jean-Jacques somehow mixed up in all this?

"Yes," he replied, frowning, "I know Monsieur Girault and his wife. How are they involved in this incident?"

"Mademoiselle St. Sebastian says Lefèvre is Madame Girault's former lover. He came to their table while they were at lunch yesterday. She claims Madame Girault identified him as a gigolo, one who tried to extort a large sum of money from her. We'll verify that with madame herself, of course."

Dev's stomach took a slow dive. Christ! Had he misread the situation? The kidnapping portion of it, anyway?

"Your fiancée also says that the manager of your hotel told her Lefèvre made inquiries as to her identity." The officer glanced up from his notes. "Are you aware of these inquiries, Monsieur Hunter?"

"No."

The police officer's expression remained carefully neutral, but he had to be thinking the same thing Dev was.

What kind of a man didn't know a second- or third-class gigolo was sniffing after his woman?

"Do you have any additional information you can provide at this time, Monsieur Hunter?"

"No."

"Very well. Mademoiselle St. Sebastian insists she sustained no serious injury. If the EMTs agree, I will release her to return to your hotel. I must ask you both not to leave Paris, however, until you have spoken with detectives from our *Brigade criminelle*. They will be in touch with you."

Dev and Sarah took a taxi back to the hotel. She stared out the window in stony silence while he searched for a way to reconcile his confrontation with the photographer and his apparently faulty assumption about the attempted kidnapping. He finally decided on a simple apology.

"I'm sorry, Sarah. I jumped too fast to the wrong conclusion."

She turned her head. Her distant expression matched her coolly polite tone. "No need to apologize. I can understand how you reached that conclusion."

Dev reached for her hand, trying to bridge the gap. She slid it away and continued in the same, distant tone.

"Just for the record, I didn't know the magazine had put a photographer on us."

"I believe you."

It was too little, too late. He realized that when she shrugged his comment aside.

"I am aware, however, that Alexis wanted to exploit the story, so I take full responsibility for this invasion of your privacy."

"*Our* privacy, Sarah."

"Your privacy," she countered quietly. "There is no us. It was all just a facade, wasn't it?"

"That's not what you said last night," Dev reminded her, starting to get a little pissed.

How the hell did he end up as the bad guy here? Okay, he'd blackmailed Sarah into posing as his fiancée. And, yes, he'd done his damnedest to finesse her into bed. Now that he had her there, though, he wanted more. Much more!

So did she. She'd admitted that last night. Dev wasn't about to let her just toss what they had together out the window.

"What happened to option B?" he pressed. "Making it real?"

She looked at him for a long moment before turning her face to the window again. "I have a headache starting. I'd rather not talk anymore, if you don't mind."

He minded. Big time. But the angry bruise rising on her cheek shut him up until they were back at the hotel.

"We didn't have lunch," he said in an effort to reestablish a common ground. "Do you want to try the restaurant here or order something from room service?"

"I'm not hungry." Still so cool, still so distant. "I'm going to lie down."

"You need ice to keep the swelling down on your cheek. I'll bring some to your room after I talk to Monsieur LeBon."

"There's ice in the minifridge in my room."

She left him standing in the lobby. Frustrated and angry and not sure precisely where he should target his ire, he stalked to the reception desk and asked to speak to the manager.

Sarah's first act when she reached her room was to call *Beguile*'s Paris offices. Although she didn't doubt Dev's account, she couldn't help hoping the photographer he'd spoken to was a freelancer or worked for some other publication. In her heart of hearts, she didn't want to believe *her* magazine had, in fact, assigned François to shoot pictures of her and Dev. Paul Vincent, the senior editor, provided the corroboration reluctantly.

"Alexis insisted, Sarah."

"I see."

She disconnected and stared blankly at the wall for several moments. How naive of her to trust Alexis to hold to her word. How stupid to feel so hurt that Dev would jump to the conclusion he had. Her throat tight, she tapped out a text message. It was brief and to the point.

I quit, effective immediately.

Then she filled the ice bucket, wrapped some cubes in a hand towel and shed her clothes. Crawling into bed, she put the ice on her aching cheek and pulled the covers over her head.

The jangle of the house phone dragged her from a stew of weariness and misery some hours later.

"I'm sorry to disturb you, Lady Sarah."

Grimacing, she edged away from the wet spot on the pillow left by the soggy hand towel. "What is it, Monsieur LeBon?"

"You have a call from *Brigade criminelle.* Shall we put it through?"

"Yes."

The caller identified herself as Marie-Renee Delacroix, an inspector in the division charged with investigating homicides, kidnappings, bomb attacks and incidents involving personalities. Sarah wanted to ask what category this investigation fell into but refrained. Instead she agreed to an appointment at police headquarters the next morning at nine.

"I've already spoken to Monsieur Hunter," the inspector said. "He'll accompany you."

"Fine."

"Just so you know, Mademoiselle St. Sebastian, this

meeting is a mere formality, simply to review and sign the official copy of your statement."

"That's all you need from me?"

"It is. We already had the van driver in custody, and we arrested Henri Lefèvre an hour ago. They've both confessed to attempting to kidnap you and hold you for ransom. Not that they could deny it," the inspector added drily. "Their fingerprints were all over the van, and no fewer than five witnesses saw Lefèvre jump out of it after the crash. We've also uncovered evidence that he's more than fifty thousand Euros in debt, much of which we believe he owes to a drug dealer not known for his patience."

A shudder rippled down Sarah's spine. She couldn't believe how close she'd come to being dragged into such a dark, ugly morass.

"Am I free to return to the United States after I sign my statement?"

"I'll have to check with the prosecutor's office, but I see no reason for them to impede your return given that Lefèvre and his accomplice have confessed. I'll confirm that when you come in tomorrow, yes?"

"Thank you."

She hung up and was contemplating going back to bed when there was a knock on her door.

"It's Dev, Sarah."

She wanted to take the coward's way out and tell him she didn't feel up to company, but she couldn't keep putting him off.

"Just a minute," she called through the door.

She detoured into the bedroom and threw on the clothes she'd dropped to the floor earlier. She couldn't do much about the bruise on her cheek, but she did rake a hand through her hair. Still, she felt messy and off center when she opened the door.

Dev had abandoned his suit coat but still wore the pleated pants and pale yellow dress shirt he'd had on earlier. The shirt was open at the neck, the cuffs rolled up. Sarah had to drag her reluctant gaze up to meet the deep blue of his eyes. They were locked on her cheek.

"Did you ice that?"

"Yes, I did. Come in."

He followed her into the sitting room. Neither of them sat. She gravitated to the window. He shoved his hands into his pants pockets and stood beside the sofa.

"Have you heard from Inspector Delacroix?"

"She just called. I understand we have an appointment with her at nine tomorrow morning."

"Did she tell you they've already obtained confessions?"

Sarah nodded and forced a small smile. "She also told me I could fly home after I signed the official statement. I was just about to call and make a reservation when you knocked."

"Without talking to me first?"

"I think we've said everything we needed to."

"I don't agree."

She scrubbed a hand down the side of her face. Her cheek ached. Her heart hurt worse. "Please, Dev. I don't want to beat this into the ground."

Poor verb choice, she realized when he ignored her and crossed the room to cup her chin. The ice hadn't helped much, Sarah knew. The bruise had progressed from red to a nasty purple and green.

"Did Lefèvre do this to you?"

The underlying savagery in the question had her pulling hastily away from his touch.

"No, he didn't. I hit something when he pushed me into the van."

The savagery didn't abate. If anything, it flared hotter and fiercer. "Good thing the bastard's in police custody."

Sarah struggled to get the discussion back on track. "Lefèvre doesn't matter, Dev."

"The hell he doesn't."

"Listen to me. What matters is that I didn't know Alexis had sicced a photographer on us. But even if she hadn't, some other magazine or tabloid would have picked up the story sooner or later. I'm afraid that kind of public scrutiny is something you and whoever you *do* finally get engaged to will have to live with."

"I'm engaged to you, Sarah."

"Not any longer."

Shoving her misery aside, she slid the emerald off her finger and held it out. He refused to take it.

"It's yours," he said curtly. "Part of your heritage. Whatever happens from here on out between us, you keep the Russian Rose."

The tight-jawed response only added to her aching unhappiness. "Our arrangement lasted only until you and Girault signed your precious contracts. That's done now. So are we."

She hadn't intended to sound so bitter. Dev had held to his end of their bargain. Every part of it. She was the one who'd almost defaulted. If not personally, then by proxy through Alexis.

But would Dev continue to hold to his end? The sudden worry that he might take his anger out on Gina pushed her into a rash demand for an assurance.

"I've fulfilled the conditions of our agreement, right? You won't go after my sister?"

She'd forgotten how daunting he could look when his eyes went hard and ice blue.

"No, Lady Sarah, I won't. And I think we'd better table this discussion until we've had more time to think things through."

"I've thought them through," she said desperately. "I'm going home tomorrow, Dev."

He leaned in, all the more intimidating because he didn't touch her, didn't raise his voice, didn't so much as blink.

"Think again, sweetheart."

Twelve

Left alone in her misery, Sarah opened her hand and stared at the emerald-and-gold ring. No matter what Dev said, she couldn't keep it.

Nor could she just leave it lying around. She toyed briefly with the thought of taking it downstairs and asking Monsieur LeBon to secure it in the hotel safe, but didn't feel up to explaining either her bruised cheek or the call from *Brigade criminelle*.

With an aching sense of regret for what might have been, she slipped the ring back on her finger. It would have to stay there until she returned it to Dev.

She was trying to make herself go into the bedroom and pack when a loud rumble from the vicinity of her middle reminded her she hadn't eaten since her breakfast croissant and coffee. She considered room service but decided she needed to get out of her room and clear her head. She also needed, as Dev had grimly instructed, to think more.

After a fierce internal debate, she picked up the house phone. A lifetime of etiquette hammered in by the duchess demanded she advise Dev of her intention to grab a bite at a local café. Fiancé or not, furious or not, he deserved the courtesy of a call.

Relief rolled through her in waves when he didn't answer. She left a quick message, then took the elevator to the lobby. Slipping out one of the hotel's side exits, she hiked up the collar of her sweater coat. It wasn't dusk yet, but the temperature was skidding rapidly from cool to cold.

As expected this time of day, the sidewalks and streets were crowded. Parisians returning from work made last-minute stops at grocers and patisseries. Taxis wove their erratic path through cars and bicycles. Sarah barely noticed the throng. Her last meeting with Dev still filled her mind. Their tense confrontation had shaken her almost as much as being snatched off the street and tossed into a delivery van like a sack of potatoes.

He had every right to be angry about the photographer, she conceded. She was furious, too. What had hurt most, though, was Dev's assumption that *Beguile* had staged the kidnapping. And that Sarah was part of the deception. How could he love her, yet believe she would participate in a scam like that?

The short answer? He couldn't.

As much as she wanted to, Sarah couldn't escape that brutal truth. She'd let Paris seduce her into thinking she and Dev shared something special. Come so close to believing that what they felt for each other would merit a padlock on the Archbishop's Bridge. Aching all over again for what might have been, she ducked into the first café she encountered.

A waiter with three rings piercing his left earlobe and a white napkin folded over his right forearm met her at the door. His gaze flickered to the ugly bruise on her cheek and away again.

"Good evening, madame."

"Good evening. A table for one, please."

Once settled at a table in a back corner, she ordered

without glancing at the menu. A glass of red table wine and a croque-monsieur—the classic French version of a grilled ham and cheese topped with béchamel sauce—was all she wanted. All she could handle right now. That became apparent after the first few sips of wine.

Her sandwich arrived in a remarkably short time given this was Paris, where even the humblest café aimed for gastronomic excellence. Accompanied by a small salad and thin, crisp fries, it should have satisfied her hunger. Unfortunately, she never got to enjoy it. She took a few forkfuls of salad and nibbled a fry, but just when she was about to bite into her sandwich she heard her name.

"Lady Sarah, granddaughter to Charlotte St. Sebastian, grand duchess of the tiny duchy once known as Karlenburgh."

Startled, she glanced up at the flat screen TV above the café's bar. While Sarah sat frozen with the sandwich halfway to her mouth, one of a team of two newscasters gestured to an image that came up on the display beside her. It was a photo of her and Gina and Grandmama, one of the rare publicity shots the duchess had allowed. It'd been taken at a charity event a number of years ago, before the duchess had sold her famous pearls. The perfectly matched strands circled her neck multiple times before draping almost to her waist.

"The victim of an apparent kidnapping attempt," the announcer intoned, "Lady Sarah escaped injury this afternoon during a dramatic rescue by her fiancé, American industrialist Devon Hunter."

Dread churned in the pit of Sarah's stomach as the still image gave way to what looked like an amateur video captured on someone's phone camera. It showed traffic swerving wildly as Dev charged across two lanes and planted himself in front of oncoming traffic.

Good God! The white van! It wasn't going to stop!

Her heart shot into her throat. Unable to breathe, she saw

Dev dodge aside at the last moment, then leap for the van door. When he smashed the driver's face into the wheel, Sarah gasped. Blobs of béchamel sauce oozed from the sandwich hanging from her fork and plopped unnoticed onto her plate. She'd been in the back of the van. She hadn't known how Dev had stopped it, only that he had.

Stunned by his reckless courage, she watched as the street scene gave way to another video. This one was shot on the steps of the Palais de Justice. Henri Lefèvre was being led down the steps to a waiting police transport. Uniformed officers gripped his arms. Steel cuffs shackled his wrists. A crowd of reporters waited at the bottom of the steps, shouting questions that Lefèvre refused to answer.

When the news shifted to another story, Sarah lowered her now-mangled sandwich. Her mind whirled as she tried to sort through her chaotic thoughts. One arrowed through all the others. She knew she had to call her grandmother. Now. Before the story got picked up by the news at home, if it hadn't already. Furious with herself for not thinking of that possibility sooner, she hit speed dial.

To her infinite relief, the duchess had heard nothing about the incident. Sarah tried to downplay it by making the kidnappers sound like bungling amateurs. Charlotte was neither amused nor fooled.

"Were you the target," she asked sharply, "or Devon?"

"Devon, of course. Or rather his billions."

"Are you sure? There may still be some fanatics left in the old country. Not many after all this time, I would guess. But your grandfather… Those murderous death squads…" Her voice fluttered. "They hated everything our family stood for."

"These men wanted money," Sarah said gently, "and Dev made them extremely sorry they went after it the way they did. One of them is going to need a whole new face."

"Good!"

The duchess had regained her bite, and her granddaughter breathed a sigh of relief. Too soon, it turned out.

"Bring Devon home with you, Sarah. I want to thank him personally. And tell him I see no need for a long engagement," Charlotte added briskly. "Too many brides today spend months, even years, planning their weddings. I thank God neither of my granddaughters are prone to such dithering."

"Grandmama…"

"Gina tends to leap before she looks. You, my darling, are more cautious. More deliberate. But when you choose, you choose wisely. In this instance, I believe you made an excellent choice."

Sarah couldn't confess that she hadn't precisely chosen Dev. Nor was she up to explaining that their relationship was based on a lie. All she could do was try to rein in the duchess.

"I'm not to the point of even thinking about wedding plans, Grandmama. I just got engaged."

And unengaged, although Dev appeared to have a different take on the matter.

"You don't have to concern yourself with the details, dearest. I'll call the Plaza and have Andrew take care of everything."

"Good grief!" Momentarily distracted, Sarah gasped. "Is Andrew still at the Plaza?"

Her exclamation earned an icy retort. "The younger generation may choose to consign seniors to the dustbin," the duchess returned frigidly. "Some of us are not quite ready to be swept out with the garbage."

Uh-oh. Before Sarah could apologize for the unintended slight, Charlotte abandoned her lofty perch and got down to business.

"How about the first weekend in May? That's such a lovely month for a wedding."

"Grandmama! It's mid-April now!"

"Didn't you hear me a moment ago? Long engagements are a bore."

"But…but…" Scrambling, Sarah grabbed at the most likely out. "I'm sure the Plaza is booked every weekend in May for the next three years."

Her grandmother heaved a long-suffering sigh. "Sarah, dearest, did I never tell you about the reception I hosted for the Sultan of Oman?"

"I don't think so."

"It was in July…no, August of 1962. Quite magnificent, if I do say so myself. President Kennedy and his wife attended, of course, as did the Rockefellers. Andrew was a very new, very junior waiter at the time. But the letter I sent to his supervisor commending his handling of an embarrassingly inebriated presidential aide helped catapult him to his present exalted position."

How could Sarah possibly respond to that? Swept along on a relentless tidal wave, she gripped the phone as the duchess issued final instructions. "Talk to Devon, dearest. Make sure the first weekend in May is satisfactory for him. And tell him I'll take care of everything."

Feeling almost as dazed as she had when Elise Girault's smarmy ex-lover manhandled her into that white van, Sarah said goodbye. Her meal forgotten, she sat with her phone in hand for long moments. The call to her grandmother had left her more confused, more torn.

Dev had risked his life for her. And that was after he'd confronted the photographer from *Beguile*. As angry as he'd been about her magazine stalking him, he'd still raced to her rescue. Then, of course, he'd accused her of being party to the ruse. As much as she wanted to, Sarah couldn't quite get past the disgust she'd seen in his face at that moment.

Yet he'd also shown her moments of incredible tenderness in their short time together. Moments of thoughtfulness and laughter and incredible passion. She couldn't get past those, either.

Or the fact that she'd responded to him so eagerly. So damned joyously. However they'd met, whatever odd circumstances had thrown them together, Dev Hunter stirred—and satisfied—a deep, almost primal feminine hunger she'd never experienced before.

The problem, Sarah mused as she paid her check and walked out into the deepening dusk, was that everything had happened so quickly. Dev's surprise appearance at her office. His bold-faced offer of a deal. Their fake engagement. This trip to Paris. She'd been caught up in the whirlwind since the day Dev had showed up at her office and tilted her world off its axis. The speed of it, the intensity of it, had magnified emotions and minimized any chance to catch her breath.

What they needed, she decided as she keyed the door to her room, was time and some distance from each other. A cooling-off period, after which they could start over. Assuming Dev wanted to start over, of course. Bracing herself for what she suspected would be an uncomfortable discussion, she picked up the house phone and called his room.

He answered on the second ring. "Hunter."

"It's Sarah."

"I got your message. Did you have a good dinner?"

She couldn't miss the steel under the too-polite query. He wasn't happy that she'd gone to eat without him.

"I did, thank you. Can you come down to my room? Or I'll come to yours, if that's more convenient."

"More convenient for what?"

All right. She understood he was still angry. As Grandmama would say, however, that was no excuse for boorishness.

"We need to finish the conversation we started earlier,' she said coolly.

He answered with a brief silence, followed by a terse agreement. "I'll come to your room."

Dev thought he'd done a damned good job of conquering his fury over that business with the photographer. Yes, he'd let it get the better of him when he'd accused Sarah's magazine of staging her own abduction. And yes, he'd come on a little strong earlier this evening when she'd questioned whether he'd hold to his end of their agreement.

He'd had plenty of time to regret both lapses. She'd seen to that by slipping out of the hotel without him. The brief message she'd left while he was in the shower had pissed him off all over again.

Now she'd issued a summons in that aristocratic lady-of-the-manor tone. She'd better not try to shove the emerald at him again. Or deliver any more crap about their "arrangement" being over. They were long past the arrangement stage, and she knew it. She was just too stubborn to admit it.

She'd just have to accept that he wasn't perfect. He'd screwed up this afternoon by throwing that accusation at her. He'd apologize again. Crawl if he had to. Whatever it took, he intended to make it clear she wasn't rid of him. Not by a long shot.

That was the plan, anyway, right up until she opened the door. The mottled purple on her cheek tore the heart and the heat right out of him. Curling a knuckle, he brushed it gently across the skin below the bruise.

"Does this hurt as bad as it looks?"

"Not even close."

She didn't shy away from his touch. Dev took that as a hopeful sign. That, and the fact that some of the stiffness went out of her spine as she led him into the sitting area.

Nor did it escape his attention that she'd cut off the view that had so enchanted her before. The heavy, room-darkening drapes were drawn tight, blocking anyone from seeing out…or in.

"Would you like a drink?" she asked politely, gesturing to the well-stocked minibar.

"No, thanks, I'm good."

As he spoke, an image on the TV snagged his glance. The sound was muted but he didn't need it to recognize the amateur video playing across the screen. He'd already seen it several times.

Sarah noticed what had caught his attention and picked up the remote. "Have you seen the news coverage?"

"Yeah."

Clicking off the TV, she sank into an easy chair and raised a stockinged foot. Her arms locked around her bent knee and her green eyes regarded him steadily.

"I took your advice and thought more about our…our situation."

"That's one way to describe it," he acknowledged. "You come to any different conclusions about how we should handle it?"

"As a matter of fact, I did."

Dev waited, wanting to hear her thoughts.

"I feel as though I jumped on a speeding train. Everything happened so fast. You, me, Paris. Now Grandmama is insisting on…" She broke off, a flush rising, and took a moment to recover. "I was afraid the news services might pick up the kidnapping story, so I called her and tried to shrug off the incident as the work of bumbling amateurs."

"Did she buy that?"

"No."

"Smart woman, your grandmother."

"You might not agree when I tell you she segued immediately from that to insisting on a May wedding."

Well, what do you know? Dev was pretty sure he'd passed inspection with the duchess. Good to have it confirmed, especially since he apparently had a number of hurdles to overcome before he regained her granddaughter's trust.

"I repeat, your grandmother's a smart woman."

"She is, but then she doesn't know the facts behind our manufactured engagement."

"Do you think she needs to?"

"What I think," Sarah said slowly, "is that we need to put the brakes on this runaway train."

Putting the brakes on was a long step from her earlier insistence they call things off. Maybe he didn't face as many hurdles as he'd thought.

His tension easing by imperceptible degrees, Dev cocked his head. "How do you propose we do that?"

"We step back. Take some time to assess this attraction we both seem to…"

"Attraction?" He shook his head. "Sorry, sweetheart, I can't let you get away with that one. You and I both know we've left attraction in the dust."

"You're right."

She rested her chin on her knee, obviously searching for the right word. Impatience bit at him, but he reined it in. If he hadn't learned anything else today, he'd discovered Sarah could only be pushed so far.

"I won't lie," she said slowly. "What I feel for you is so different from anything I've ever experienced before. I think it's love. No, I'm pretty sure it's love."

That was all he needed to hear. He started toward her, but she stopped him with a quick palms-up gesture.

"What I'm *not* sure of, Dev, is whether love's enough to overcome the fact that we barely know each other."

"I know all I need to know about you."

"Oh. Right." She made a wry face. "I forgot about the background investigation."

He wouldn't apologize. He'd been up front with her about that. But he did attempt to put it in perspective.

"The investigation provided the externals, Sarah. The

time we've spent together, as brief as it's been, provided the essentials."

"Really?" She lifted a brow. "What's my favorite color? Am I a dog or a cat person? What kind of music do I like?"

"You consider those essentials?" he asked, genuinely curious.

"They're some of the bits and pieces that constitute the whole. Don't you think we should see how those pieces fit together before getting in any deeper?"

"I don't, but you obviously do."

If this was a business decision, he would ruthlessly override what he privately considered trivial objections. He'd made up his mind. He knew what he wanted.

Sarah did, too, apparently. With a flash of extremely belated insight, Dev realized she wanted to be courted. More to the point, she *deserved* to be courted.

Lady Sarah St. Sebastian might work at a magazine that promoted flashy and modern and ultrachic, but she held to old-fashioned values that he'd come to appreciate as much as her innate elegance and surprising sensuality. Her fierce loyalty to her sister, for instance. Her bone-deep love for the duchess. Her refusal to accept anything from him except her grandmother's emerald ring, and then only on a temporary basis.

He could do old-fashioned. He could do slow and courtly. Maybe. Admittedly, he didn't have a whole lot of experience in either. Moving out and taking charge came as natural to him as breathing. But if throttling back on his more aggressive instincts was what she wanted, that was what she'd get.

"Okay, we'll do it your way."

He started toward her again. Surprised and more than a little wary of his relatively easy capitulation, Sarah let her raised foot slip to the floor and pushed out of her chair.

He stopped less than a yard away. Close enough to kiss,

which she had to admit she wouldn't have minded all that much at this point. He settled for a touch instead. He kept it light, just a brush of his fingertips along the underside of her chin.

"We'll kick off phase two," he promised in a tone that edged toward deep and husky. "No negotiated contracts this time, no self-imposed deadlines. Just you and me, learning each other's little idiosyncrasies. If that's what you really want…?"

She nodded, although the soft dance of his fingers under her chin and the proximity of his mouth made it tough to stay focused.

"It's what I really want."

"All right, I'll call Patrick."

"Who? Oh, right. Your executive assistant. Excuse me for asking, but what does he have to do with this?"

"He's going to clear my calendar. Indefinitely. He'll blow every one of his fuses, but he'll get it done."

His fingers made another pass. Sarah's thoughts zinged wildly between the little pinpricks of pleasure he was generating and that "indefinitely."

"What about your schedule?" he asked. "How much time can you devote to phase two?"

"My calendar's wide-open, too. I quit my job."

"You didn't have to do that. I'm already past the business with the photographer."

"You may be," she retorted. "I'm not."

He absorbed that for a moment. "All right. Here's what we'll do, then. We give our statements to the *Brigade criminelle* at nine tomorrow morning and initiate phase two immediately after. Agreed?"

"Agreed."

"Good. I'll have a car waiting at eight-thirty to take us downtown. See you down in the lobby then."

He leaned in and brushed his lips over hers.

"Good night, Sarah."

She'd never really understood that old saying about being hoisted with your own petard. It had something to do with getting caught up in a medieval catapult, she thought. Or maybe hanging by one foot in a tangle of ropes from the mast of a fourteenth-century frigate.

Either situation would pretty much describe her feelings when Dev crossed the room and let himself out.

Thirteen

Sarah spent hours tossing and turning and kicking herself for her self-imposed celibacy. As a result, she didn't fall asleep until almost one and woke late the next morning.

The first thing she did was roll over in bed and grab her cell phone from the nightstand to check for messages. Still nothing from Gina, dammit, but Alexis had left two voice mails apologizing for what she termed an unfortunate misunderstanding and emphatically refusing to accept her senior layout editor's resignation.

"Misunderstanding, my ass."

Her mouth set, Sarah deleted the voice mails and threw back the covers. She'd have to hustle to be ready for the car Dev had said would be waiting at eight-thirty. A quick shower eliminated most of the cobwebs from her restless night. An equally quick cup of strong brew from the little coffeemaker in her room helped with the remainder.

Before she dressed, she stuck her nose through the balcony doors to assess the weather. No fog or drizzle, but still chilly enough to make her opt for her gray wool slacks and cherry-red sweater coat. She topped them with a scarf doubled around her throat European-style and a black beret tilted to a decidedly French angle.

She rushed down to the lobby with two minutes to spare and saw Dev had also prepared for the chill. But in jeans, a black turtleneck and a tan cashmere coat this morning instead of his usual business suit. He greeted her with a smile and a quick kiss.

"*Bonjour, ma chérie.* Sleep well?"

She managed not to wince at his accent. "Fairly well."

"Did you have time for breakfast?"

"No."

"I was running a little late, too, so I had the driver pick up some chocolate croissants and coffees. Shall we go?"

He offered his arm in a gesture she was beginning to realize was as instinctive as it was courteous. When she tucked her hand in the crook of his elbow, she could feel his warmth through the soft wool. Feel, too, the ripple of hard muscle as he leaned past her to push open the hotel door.

Traffic was its usual snarling beast, but the coffee and chocolate croissants mitigated the frustration. They were right on time when they pulled up at the block-long building overlooking the Seine that housed the headquarters of the *Brigade criminelle.* A lengthy sequence of security checkpoints, body scans and ID verification made them late for their appointment, however.

Detective Inspector Marie-Renée Delacroix waved aside their apologies as unnecessary and signed them in. Short and barrel-shaped, she wore a white blouse, black slacks and rubber-soled granny shoes. The semiautomatic nested in her shoulder holster belied her otherwise unprepossessing exterior.

"Thank you for coming in," she said in fluent English. "I'll try to make this as swift and painless as possible. Please, come with me."

She led them up a flight of stairs and down a long corridor interspersed with heavy oak doors. When Delacroix pushed through the door to her bureau, Sarah looked about with interest. The inspector's habitat didn't resemble the bull pens depicted on American TV police dramas. American bull pens probably didn't, either, she acknowledged wryly.

There were no dented metal file cabinets or half-empty cartons of doughnuts. No foam cups littering back-to-back desks or squawking phones. The area was spacious and well lit and smoke free. Soundproofing dividers offered at least the illusion of privacy, while monitors mounted high on the front wall flashed what looked like real-time updates on hot spots around Paris.

"Would you like coffee?" Delacroix asked as she waved them to seats in front of her desk.

Sarah looked to Dev before answering for them both. "No, thank you."

The inspector dropped into the chair behind the desk. Shoulders hunched, brows straight-lined, she dragged a wireless keyboard into reach and attacked it with two stubby forefingers. The assault was merciless, but for reasons known only to French computer gods, the typed versions of the statements Sarah and Dev had given to the responding officers wouldn't spit out of the printer.

"Merde!"

Muttering under her breath, she jabbed at the keyboard yet again. She looked as though she'd like to whip out her weapon and deliver a lethal shot when she finally admitted defeat and slammed away from her desk.

"Please wait. I need to find someone who can kick a report out of this piece of sh— Er, crap."

She returned a few moments later with a colleague in a blue-striped shirt and red suspenders. Without a word, he pressed a single key. When the printer began coughing up papers, he rolled his eyes and departed.

"I hate these things," Delacroix muttered as she dropped into her chair again.

Sarah and Dev exchanged a quick look but refrained from comment. Just as well, since the inspector became all brisk efficiency once the printer had disgorged the documents she wanted. She pushed two ink pens and the printed statements in their direction.

"Review these, please, and make any changes you feel necessary."

The reports were lengthy and correct. Delacroix was relieved that neither Sarah nor Dev had any changes, but consciously did her duty.

"Are you sure, mademoiselle? With that nasty bruise, we could add assault to the kidnapping charge."

Sarah fingered her cheek. Much as she'd like to double the case against Lefèvre, he hadn't directly caused the injury.

"I'm sure."

"Very well. Sign here, please, and here."

She did as instructed and laid down her pen. "You said you were going to talk to the prosecuting attorney about whether we need to remain in Paris for the arraignment," she reminded Delacroix.

"Ah, yes. He feels your statements, the evidence we've collected and the confessions from Lefèvre and his associate are more than sufficient for the case against them. As long as we know how to contact you and Monsieur Hunter if necessary, you may depart Paris whenever you wish."

Oddly, the knowledge that she could fly home at any time produced a contradictory desire in Sarah to remain in Paris for the initiation of phase two. That, and the way Dev once again tucked her arm in his as they descended the broad staircase leading to the main exit. There was still so much of the city—*her* city—she wanted to share with him.

The moment they stepped out into the weak sunshine a blinding barrage of flashes sent Sarah stumbling back. Dismayed, she eyed the wolf pack crowding the front steps their news vans parked at the curb behind them. While sound handlers thrust their boom mikes over the reporters' heads, the questions flew at Sarah like bullets. She heard her name and Dev's and Lefèvre's and Elise Girault's all seemingly in the same sentences.

She ducked her chin into her scarf and started to scramble back into police headquarters to search out a side exit. Dev stood his ground, though, and with her arm tucked tight against his side, Sarah had no choice but to do the same.

"Might as well give them what they want now," he told her. "Maybe it'll satisfy their appetites and send them chasing after their next victim."

Since most of the questions zinged at them were in French, Sarah found herself doing the translating and leaving the responding to Dev. He'd obviously fielded these kinds of rapid-fire questions before. He deftly avoided any that might impact the case against the kidnappers and confirmed only that he and Sarah were satisfied with the way the police were handling the matter.

The questions soon veered from the official to the personal. To Sarah's surprise, Dev shelved his instinctive dislike of the media and didn't cut them off at the knees. His responses were concise and to the point.

Yes, he and Lady Sarah had only recently become engaged. Yes, they'd known each other only a short time. No, they hadn't yet set a date for the wedding.

"Although," he added with a sideways glance at Sarah, "her grandmother has voiced some thoughts in that regard."

"Speaking of the duchess," a sharp-featured reporter commented as she thrust her mike almost in Sarah's face, "Charlotte St. Sebastian was once the toast of Paris and New York. From all reports, she's now penniless. Have you insisted Monsieur Hunter include provisions for her maintenance in your prenup agreement?"

Distaste curled Sarah's lip but she refused to give the

vulture any flesh to feed on. "As my fiancé has just stated," she said with a dismissive smile, "we've only recently become engaged. And what better place to celebrate that engagement than Paris, the City of Lights and Love? So now you must excuse us, as that's what we intend to do."

She tugged on Dev's arm and he took the hint. When they cleared the mob and started for the limo waiting a half block away, he gave her a curious look.

"What was that all about?"

She hadn't translated the last question and would prefer not to now. Their engagement had been tumultuous enough. Despite her grandmother's insistence on booking the Plaza, Sarah hadn't really thought as far ahead as marriage. Certainly not as far as a prenup.

They stopped beside the limo. The driver had the door open and waiting but Dev waved him back inside the car.

"Give us a minute here, Andre."

"*Oui*, monsieur."

While the driver slid into the front seat, Dev angled Sarah to face him. Her shoulders rested against the rear door frame. Reluctantly, she tipped up her gaze to meet his.

"You might as well tell me," he said. "I'd rather not be blindsided by hearing whatever it was play on the five-o'clock news."

"The reporter wanted details on our prenup." She hunched her shoulders, feeling awkward and embarrassed. "I told her to get stuffed."

His grin broke out, quick and slashing. "In your usual elegant manner, of course."

"Of course."

Still grinning, he studied her face. It must have reflected her acute discomfort because he stooped to speak to the driver.

"We've decided to walk, Andre. We won't need you anymore today."

When the limo eased away from the curb, he hooked

Sarah's arm through his again and steered her into the stream of pedestrians.

"I know how prickly you are about the subject of finances, so we won't go there until we've settled more important matters, like whether you're a dog or cat person. Which are you, by the way?"

"Dog," she replied, relaxing for the first time that morning. "The bigger the better, although the only one we've ever owned was the Pomeranian that Gina brought home one day. She was eight or nine at the time and all indignant because someone had left it leashed outside a coffee shop in one-hundred-degree heat."

Too late she realized she might have opened the door for Dev to suggest Gina had developed kleptomaniac tendencies early. She glanced up, met his carefully neutral look and hurried on with her tale.

"We went back and tried to find the owner, but no one would claim it. We soon found out why. Talk about biting the hand that feeds you! The nasty little beast snapped and snarled and wouldn't let anyone pet him except Grandmama."

"No surprise there. The duchess has a way about her. She certainly cowed me."

"Right," Sarah scoffed. "I saw how you positively quaked in her presence."

"I'm still quaking. Finish the story. What happened to the beast?"

"Grandmama finally palmed him off on an acquaintance of hers. What about you?" she asked, glancing up at him again. "Do you prefer dogs or cats?"

"Bluetick coonhounds," he answered without hesitation. "Best hunters in the world. We had a slew of barn cats, though. My sisters were always trying to palm their litters off on friends, too."

Intrigued, Sarah pumped him for more details about

his family. "I know you grew up on a ranch. In Nebraska, wasn't it?"

"New Mexico, but it was more like a hardscrabble farm than a ranch."

"Do your parents still work the farm?"

"They do. They like the old place and have no desire to leave it, although they did let me make a few improvements."

More than a few, Sarah guessed.

"What about your sisters?"

He had four, she remembered, none of whom had agreed to be interviewed for the *Beguile* article. The feeling that their business was nobody else's ran deep in the Hunter clan.

"All married, all comfortable, all happy. You hungry?"

The abrupt change of subject threw Sarah off until she saw what had captured his attention. They'd reached the Pont de l'Alma, which gave a bird's-eye view of the glass-roofed barges docked on the north side of the Seine. One boat was obviously set for a lunch cruise. Its linen-draped tables were set with gleaming silver and crystal.

"Have you ever taken one of these Seine river cruises?" Dev asked.

"No."

"Why not?"

"They're, uh, a little touristy."

"This is Paris. Everyone's a tourist, even the Parisians."

"Good God, don't let a native hear you say that!"

"What do you say? Want to mingle with the masses for a few hours?"

She threw a glance at a tour bus disgorging its load of passengers and swallowed her doubts.

"I'm game if you are."

He steered her to the steps that led down to the quay. Sarah fully expected them to be turned away at the ticket office. While a good number of boats cruised the Seine, picking up or letting off passengers at various stops, tour agencies tended to book these lunch and dinner cruises for large groups months in advance.

Whatever Dev said—or paid—at the ticket booth not only got them on the boat, it garnered a prime table for two beside the window. Their server introduced herself and filled their aperitif glasses with kir. A smile in his eyes, Dev raised his glass.

"To us."

"To us," Sarah echoed softly.

The cocktail went down with velvet smoothness. She savored the intertwined flavors while Dev gave his glass a respectful glance.

"What's in this?"

"*Crème de cassis*—black-currant liqueur—topped with white wine. It's named for Félix Kir, the mayor of Dijon, who popularized the drink after World War II."

"Well, it doesn't have the same wallop as your grand-mother's *Žuta Osa* but it's good."

"'Scuse me."

The interruption came from the fortyish brunette at the next table. She beamed Sarah a friendly smile.

"Y'all are Americans, aren't you?"

"Yes, we are."

"So are we. We're the Parkers. Evelyn and Duane Parker, from Mobile."

Sarah hesitated. She hated to be rude, but Evelyn's leopard-print Versace jacket and jewel-toed boots indicated she kept up with the latest styles. If she read *Beguile,* she would probably recognize Number Three from the Sexiest Singles article. Or from the recent news coverage.

Dev solved her dilemma by gesturing to the cell phone Evelyn clutched in one hand. "I'm Dev and this is my fi-ancée, Sarah. Would you like me to take a picture of you and your husband?"

"Please. And I'll do one of y'all."

The accordion player began strolling the aisle while cell phones were still being exchanged and photos posed for. When he broke into a beautiful baritone, all conversation on the boat ceased and Sarah breathed easy again.

Moments later, they pulled away from the dock and glided under the first of a dozen or more bridges yet to come. Meal service began then. Sarah wasn't surprised at the quality of the food. This was Paris, after all. She and Dev sampled each of the starters: foie gras on a toasted baguette; Provençal smoked salmon and shallots; duck magret salad with cubes of crusty goat cheese; tiny vegetable egg rolls fried to a pale golden brown. Sarah chose honey-and-sesame-seed pork tenderloin for her main dish. Dev went with the veal blanquette. With each course, their server poured a different wine. Crisp, chilled whites. Medium reds. Brandy with the rum baba they each selected for dessert.

Meanwhile, Paris's most famous monuments were framed in the windows. The Louvre. La Conciergerie. Notre Dame. The Eiffel Tower.

The boat made a U-turn while Sarah and Dev lingered over coffee, sharing more of their pasts. She listened wide-eyed to the stories Dev told of his Air Force days. She suspected he edited them to minimize the danger and maximize the role played by others on his crew. Still, the war-torn countries he'd flown into and the horrific disasters he'd helped provide lifesaving relief for made her world seem frivolous by comparison.

"Grandmama took us abroad every year," she related when he insisted it was her turn. "She was determined to expose Gina and me to cultures other than our own."

"Did she ever take you to Karlenburgh?"

"No, never. That would have been too painful for her. I'd like to go someday, though. We still have cousins there, three or four times removed."

She traced a fingertip around the rim of her coffee cup.

Although it tore at her pride, she forced herself to admit the truth.

"Gina and I never knew what sacrifices Grandmama had to make to pay for those trips. Or for my year at the Sorbonne."

"I'm guessing your sister still doesn't know."

She jerked her head up, prepared to defend Gina yet again. But there was nothing judgmental in Dev's expression. Only quiet understanding.

"She has a vague idea," Sarah told him. "I never went into all the gory details, but she's not stupid."

Dev had to bite down on the inside of his lower lip. Eugenia Amalia Thérése St. Sebastian hadn't impressed him with either her intelligence or her common sense. Then again, he hadn't been particularly interested in her intellectual prowess the few times they'd connected.

In his defense, few horny, heterosexual males could see beyond Gina's stunning beauty. At least not until they'd spent more than an hour or two in the bubbleheaded blonde's company. Deciding discretion was the better part of valor, he chose not to share that particular observation.

He couldn't help comparing the sisters, though. No man in his right mind would deny that he'd come out the winner in the St. Sebastian lottery. Charm, elegance, smarts, sensuality and...

He'd better stop right there! When the hell had he reached the point where the mere thought of Sarah's smooth, sleek body stretched out under his got him rock hard? Where the memory of how she'd opened her legs for him damned near steamed up the windows beside their table?

Suddenly Dev couldn't wait for the boat to pass under the last bridge. By the time they'd docked and he'd hustled Sarah up the gangplank, his turtleneck was strangling him. The look of confused concern she flashed at him as they climbed the steps to street level didn't help matters.

"Are you all right?"

He debated for all of two seconds before deciding on the truth. "Not anywhere close to all right."

"Oh, no! Was it the foie gras?" Dismayed, she rushed to the curb to flag down a cab. "You have to be careful with goose liver."

"Sarah…"

"I should have asked if it had been wrapped in grape leaves and slow cooked. That's the safest method."

"Sarah…"

A cab screeched to the curb. Forehead creased with worry, she yanked on the door handle. Dev had to wait until they were in the taxi and heading for the hotel to explain his sudden incapacitation.

"It wasn't the foie gras."

Concern darkened her eyes to deep, verdant green. "The veal, then? Was it bad?"

"No, sweetheart. It's you."

"I beg your pardon?"

Startled, she lurched back against her seat. Dev cursed his clumsiness and hauled her into his arms.

"As delicious as lunch was, all I could think about was how you taste." His mouth roamed hers. His voice dropped to a rough whisper. "How you fit against me. How you arch your back and make that little noise in your throat when you're about to climax."

She leaned back in his arms. She wanted him as much as he wanted her. He could see it in the desire that shaded her eyes to deep, dark emerald. In the way her breath had picked up speed. Fierce satisfaction knifed into him. She was rethinking the cooling-off period, Dev thought exultantly. She had to recognize how unnecessary this phase two was.

His hopes took a nosedive—and his respect for Sarah's

willpower kicked up a grudging notch—when she drew in a shuddering breath and gave him a rueful smile.

"Well, I'm glad it wasn't the goose liver."

Fourteen

As the cab rattled along the quay, Sarah wondered how she could be such a blithering idiot. One word from her, just one little word, and she could spend the rest of the afternoon and evening curled up with Dev in bed. Or on the sofa. Or on cushions tossed onto the floor in front of the fire, or in the shower, soaping his back and belly, or…

She leaned forward, her gaze suddenly snagged by the green bookstalls lining the riverside of the boulevard. And just beyond the stalls, almost directly across from the renowned bookstore known as Shakespeare and Company, was a familiar bridge.

"Stop! We'll get out here!"

The command surprised both Dev and the cabdriver, but he obediently pulled over to the curb and Dev paid him off.

"Your favorite bookstore?" he asked with a glance at the rambling, green-fronted facade of the shop that specialized in English-language books. Opened in 1951, the present store had assumed the mantle of the original Shakespeare and Company, a combination bookshop, lending library and haven for writers established in 1917 by American expatriate Sylvia Beach and frequented by the likes of Ernest Hemingway, Ezra Pound and F. Scott Fitzgerald. During her year at the Sorbonne, Sarah had loved exploring the shelves crammed floor to ceiling in the shop's small, crowded rooms. She'd never slept in one of the thirteen beds available to indigent students or visitors who just wanted to sleep in the rarified literary atmosphere, but she'd hunched for hours at the tables provided for scholars, researchers and book lovers of all ages.

It wasn't Shakespeare and Company that had snagged her eye, though. It was the bridge just across the street from it.

"That's the Archbishop's Bridge," she told Dev with a smile that tinged close to embarrassment.

She'd always considered herself the practical sister, too levelheaded to indulge in the kind of extravagant flights of fancy that grabbed Gina. Yet she'd just spent several delightful hours on a touristy, hopelessly romantic river cruise. Why not cap that experience with an equally touristy romantic gesture?

"Do you see these locks?" she asked as she and Dev crossed the street and approached the iron bridge.

"Hard to miss 'em," he drawled, eyeing the almost solid wall of brass obscuring the bridge's waist-high grillwork. "What's the story here?"

"I'm told it's a recent fad that's popping up on all the bridges of Paris. People ascribe wishes or dreams to locks and fasten them to the bridge, then throw the key in the river."

Dev stooped to examine some of the colorful ribbons, charms and printed messages dangling from various locks. "Here's a good one. This couple from Dallas wish their kids great joy, but don't plan to produce any additional offspring. Evidently seven are enough."

"Good grief! Seven would be enough for me, too."

"Really?"

He straightened and leaned a hip against the rail. The breeze ruffled his black hair and tugged at the collar of his camel-hair sport coat.

"I guess that's one of those little idiosyncrasies we should find out about each other, almost as important as whether we prefer dogs or cats. How many kids *do* you want, Sarah?"

"I don't know." She trailed a finger over the oblong hasp of a bicycle lock. "Two, at least, although I wouldn't mind three or even four."

As impulsive and thoughtless as Gina could be at times, Sarah couldn't imagine growing up without the joy of her bubbly laugh and warm, generous personality.

"How about you?" she asked Dev. "How many offspring would you like to produce?"

"Well, my sisters contend that the number of kids their husbands want is inversely proportional to how many stinky diapers they had to change. I figure I can manage a couple of rounds of diapers. Three or maybe even four if I get the hang of it."

He nodded to the entrepreneur perched on his overturned crate at the far end of the bridge. The man's pegboard full of locks gleamed dully in the afternoon sun.

"What do you think? Should we add a wish that we survive stinky diapers to the rest of these hopes and dreams?"

Still a little embarrassed by her descent into sappy sentimentality, Sarah nodded. She waited on the bridge while Dev purchased a hefty lock. Together they scouted for an open spot. She found one two-thirds of the way across the bridge, but Dev hesitated before attaching his purchase.

"We need to make it more personal." Frowning, he eyed the bright ribbons and charms dangling from so many of the other locks. "We need a token or something to scribble on."

He patted the pockets of his sport coat and came up

with the ticket stubs from their lunch cruise. "How about one of these?"

"That works. The cruise gave me a view of Paris I'd never seen before. I'm glad I got to share it with you, Dev."

Busy scribbling on the back of a ticket, he merely nodded. Sarah was a little surprised by his offhanded acceptance of her tribute until she read what he'd written.

To our two or three or four or more kids,
we promise you one cruise each on the Seine.

"And I thought *I* was being mushy and sentimental," she said, laughing.

"Mushy and sentimental is what phase two is all about." Unperturbed, he punched the hasp through the ticket stub. "Here, you attach it."

When the lock clicked into place, Sarah knew she'd always remember this moment. Rising up on tiptoe, she slid her arms around Dev's neck.

She'd remember the kiss, too. Particularly when Dev valiantly stuck to their renegotiated agreement later that evening.

After their monster lunch, they opted for supper at a pizzeria close to the Hôtel Verneuil. One glass of red wine and two mushroom-and-garlic slices later, they walked back to the hotel through a gray, soupy fog. Monsieur LeBon had gone off duty, but the receptionist on the desk relayed his shock over the news of the attack on Lady Sarah and his profound regret that she had suffered such an indignity while in Paris.

Sarah smiled her thanks and made a mental note to speak to the manager personally tomorrow. Once on her floor, she slid the key card into her room lock and slanted Dev a questioning look.

"Do you want to come in for a drink?"

"A man can only endure so much torture." His expression rueful, he traced a knuckle lightly over the bruise she'd already forgotten. "Unless you're ready to initiate phase three, we'd better call it a night."

She was ready. More than ready. But the companionship she and Dev had shared after leaving Inspector Delacroix's office had delivered as much punch as the hours they'd spent tangled up in the sheets. A different kind of punch, admittedly. Emotional rather than physical, but every bit as potent.

Although she knew she'd regret it the moment she closed the door, Sarah nodded. "Let's give phase two a little more time."

She was right. She did regret it. But she decided the additional hours she spent curled up on the sofa watching very boring TV were appropriate punishment for being so stupid. She loved Dev. He obviously loved her. Why couldn't she just trust her instincts and…

The buzz of her cell phone cut into her disgusted thoughts. She reached for the instrument, half hoping it was Alexis trying to reach her again. Sarah was in the mood to really, really unload on her ex-boss. When her sister's picture flashed up on the screen, she almost dropped the phone in her excitement and relief.

"Gina! Where are you?"

"Lucerne. I…I waited until morning in New York to call you but…"

"I'm not in New York. I'm in Paris, as you would know if you'd bothered to answer any of my calls."

"Thank God!"

The moaned exclamation startled her, but not as much as the sobs her sister suddenly broke into. Sarah lurched upright on the sofa, the angry tirade she'd intended to deliver instantly forgotten.

"What's wrong? Gina! What's happened?"

A dozen different disasters flooded into her mind. Gina had taken a tumble on the ski slopes. Broken a leg or an arm. Or her neck. She could be paralyzed. Breathing by machine.

"Are you hurt?" she demanded, fear icing her heart. "Gina, are you in the hospital?"

"Nooo."

The low wail left her limp with relief. In almost the next heartbeat, panic once again fluttered like a trapped bird inside her chest. She could count on the fingers of one hand the times she'd heard her always-upbeat, always-sunny sister cry.

"Sweetie, talk to me. Tell me what's wrong."

"I can't. Not…not over the phone. Please come, Sarah. *Please!* I need you."

It didn't even occur to her to say no. "I'll catch the next flight to Lucerne. Tell me where you're staying."

"The Rebstock."

"The hotel Grandmama took us to the summer you turned fourteen?"

That set off another bout of noisy, hiccuping sobs. "Don't…don't tell Grandmama about this."

About *what?* Somehow, Sarah choked back the shout and offered a soothing promise.

"I won't. Just keep your phone on, Gina. I'll call you as soon as I know when I can get there."

She cut the connection, switched to the phone's internet browser and pulled up a schedule of flights from Paris to Lucerne. Her pulse jumped when she found a late-night shuttle to Zurich that departed Charles de Gaulle Airport at 11:50 p.m. From there she'd have to rent a car and drive the sixty-five kilometers to Lake Lucerne.

She could make the flight. She had to make it. Her heart racing, she reserved a seat and scrambled off the sofa. She started for the bedroom to throw some things together but made a quick detour to the sitting room desk and snatched up the house phone.

"Come on, Dev. Answer!"

Her quivering nerves stretched tighter as it rang six times, then cut to the hotel operator.

"May I help you, Lady Sarah?"

"I'm trying to reach Monsieur Hunter, but he doesn't answer."

"May I take a message for you?"

"Yes, please. Tell him to call me as soon as possible." Hell! Where was he?

Slamming the phone down, she dashed into the bedroom. She didn't have time to pack. Just shove her laptop in her shoulder tote, grab her sweater coat, make sure her purse held her passport and credit cards and run.

While the elevator made its descent, she tried to reach Dev by cell phone. She'd just burst into the lobby when he answered on a husky, teasing note.

"Please tell me you've decided to put me out of my misery."

"Where are you?" The phone jammed to her ear, she rushed through the lobby. "I called your room but there wasn't any answer.

"I couldn't sleep. I went out for a walk." He caught the tension in her voice. The teasing note dropped out of his. "Why? What's up?"

"Gina just called."

"It's about time."

She pushed through the front door. The fog had cleared, thank God, and several taxis still cruised the streets. She waved a frantic arm to flag one down, the phone clutched in her other fist.

"She's in some kind of trouble, Dev."

"So what else is new?"

If she hadn't been so worried, the sarcastic comment might not have fired her up as hot and fast as it did.

"Spare me the editorial," she snapped back angrily. "My sister needs me. I'm on my way to Switzerland."

"Whoa! Hold on a minute…"

The taxi rolled up to the curb. She jumped in and issued a terse order. "De Gaulle Airport. Hurry, please."

"Dammit, Sarah, I can't be more than ten or fifteen minutes from the hotel. Wait until I get back and we'll sort this out together."

"She's *my* sister. I'll sort it out." She was too rushed and too torqued by his sarcasm to measure her words. "I'll call you as soon as I know what's what."

"Yeah," he bit out, as pissed off now as she was. "You do that."

In no mood to soothe his ruffled feathers, she cut the connection and leaned into the Plexiglas divider.

"I need to catch an eleven-fifty flight," she told the cab-driver. "There's an extra hundred francs in it for you if I make it."

The Swiss Air flight was only half-full. Most of the passengers looked like businessmen who wanted to be on scene when Zurich's hundreds of banks opened for business in the morning. There were a few tourists scattered among them, and several students with crammed backpacks getting a jump start on spring break in the Alps.

Sarah stared out the window through most of the ninety-minute flight. The inky darkness beyond the strobe lights on the wing provided no answers to the worried questions tumbling through her mind.

Was it the ski instructor? Had he left Gina stranded in Lucerne? Or Dev's Byzantine medallion? Had she tried to sell it and smacked up against some law against peddling antiquities on the black market?

Her stomach was twisted into knots by the time they landed in Zurich, and she rushed to the airport's Europcar desk. Fifteen minutes later she was behind the wheel of a rented Peugeot and zipping out of the airport. Once she hit the main motorway, she fumbled her phone out of her purse and speed-dialed her sister.

"I just landed in Zurich," Sarah informed her. "I'm in a rental car and should be there within an hour."

"Okay. Thanks for coming, Sarah. I'll call down to reception and tell them to expect you."

To her profound relief, Gina sounded much calmer. Probably because she knew the cavalry was on the way.

"I'll see you shortly."

Once Sarah left the lights of Zurich behind, she zoomed south on the six-lane E41. Speed limits in Switzerland didn't approach the insanity of those in Germany, but the 120 kilometers per hour max got her to the shores of Lake Lucerne in a little over forty minutes.

The city of Lucerne sat on the western arm of the lake. A modern metropolis with an ancient center, its proximity to the Alps had made it a favorite destination for tourists from the earliest days of the Hapsburg Empire. The Duchy of Karlenburgh had once constituted a minuscule part of that vast Hapsburg empire. As the lights of the city glowed in the distance, Sarah remembered that Grandmama had shared some of the less painful stories from the St. Sebastians' past during their stay in Lucerne.

She wasn't thinking of the past as she wound through the narrow streets of the Old Town. Only of her sister and whether whatever trouble Gina was in might impact their grandmother's health. The old worries she'd carried for so long—the worries she'd let herself slough off when she'd gotten so tangled up with Dev—came crashing back.

It was almost 3:00 a.m. when she pulled up at the entrance to the Hotel zum Rebstock. Subdued lighting illuminated its half-timbered red-and-white exterior. Three stories tall, with a turreted tower anchoring one end of the building, the hotel had a history dating back to the 1300s.

Even this early in the season, geraniums filled its window boxes and ivy-covered trellises defined the tiny terrace that served as an outdoor restaurant and *biergarten.*

Weary beyond words, Sarah grabbed her tote and purse and left the car parked on the street. She'd have a valet move it to the public garage on the next block tomorrow. Right now all she cared about was getting to her sister.

As promised, Gina had notified reception of a late arrival. Good thing, since a sign on the entrance informed guests that for safety purposes a key card was required for entry after midnight. A sleepy attendant answered Sarah's knock and welcomed her to the Rebstock.

"Lady Eugenia asked that we give you a key. She is in room 212. The elevator is just down the hall. Or you may take the stairs."

"Thank you."

She decided the stairs would be quicker and would also work out the kinks in her back from the flight and the drive. The ancient wooden stairs creaked beneath their carpeted runner. So did the boards of the second-floor hallway as Sarah counted room numbers until she reached the one at the far end of the hall. A corner turret room, judging by the way its door was wedged between two others.

She slid the key card into the lock and let herself into a narrow, dimly lit entryway.

"Gina?"

The door whooshed shut behind her. Sarah rounded the corner of the entryway, found herself in a charming bedroom with a sitting area occupying the octagonal turret and came to a dead stop. Her sister was tucked under the double bed's downy duvet, sound asleep.

A rueful smile curved Sarah's lips. She'd raced halfway across Europe in response to a desperate plea. Yet whatever was troubling Gina didn't appear to be giving her nightmares. She lay on one side, curled in a tight ball with a hand under her cheek and her blond curls spilling across the pillow.

Shaking her head in amused affection, Sarah dropped her tote and purse on the sofa in the sitting area and plunked down on the side of the bed.

"Hey!" She poked her sister in the shoulder. "Wake up!"

"Huh?" Gina raised her head and blinked open blurry eyes. "Oh, good," she muttered, her voice thick with sleep. "You made it."

"Finally."

"You've got to be totally wiped," she mumbled. Scooting over a few inches, she dragged up a corner of the comforter. "Crawl in."

"Oh, for…!"

Sarah swallowed the rest of the exasperated exclamation. Gina's head had already plopped back to the pillow. Her lids fluttered shut and her raised arm sank like a stone.

The elder sister sat on the edge of the bed for a few moments longer, caught in a wash of relief and bone-deep love for the younger. Then she got up long enough to kick off her boots and unbelt the cherry-red sweater coat. Shrugging it off, she slid under the comforter.

As exhausted as she was from her frantic dash across Europe, it took Sarah longer than she would have believed possible to fall asleep. She lay in the half darkness, listening to her sister's steady breathing, trying yet again to guess what had sparked her panic. Gradually, her thoughts shifted to Dev and their last exchange.

She'd overreacted to his criticism of Gina. She knew that now. At the time, though, her one driving thought had been to get to the airport. She'd apologize tomorrow. He had sisters of his own. Surely he'd understand.

Fifteen

Sarah came awake to blinding sunshine and the fuzziness that results from too little sleep. She rolled over, grimacing at the scratchy pull of her slept-in slacks and turtleneck, and squinted at the empty spot beside her.

No Gina.

And no note, she discovered when she crawled out of bed and checked the sunny sitting room. More than a little annoyed, she padded into the bathroom. Face scrubbed, she appropriated her sister's hairbrush and found a complimentary toothbrush in the basket of amenities provided by the hotel.

Luckily, she and Gina wore the same size, if not the same style. While she was content to adapt her grandmother's vintage classics, her sister preferred a trendier, splashier look. Sarah raided Gina's underwear for a pair of silky black hipsters and matching demibra, then wiggled into a chartreuse leotard patterned in a wild Alice In Wonderland motif. She topped them with a long-sleeved, high-skimming wool jumper in electric blue and a three-inch-wide elaborately studded belt that rode low on her hips.

No way was she wearing her red sweater coat with these

eye-popping colors. She'd look like a clown-school dropout. She flicked a denim jacket off a hanger instead, hitched her purse over her shoulder and went in search of her sister.

She found Gina outside on the terrace, chatting with an elderly couple at the next table. She'd gathered her blond curls into a one-sided cascade and looked impossibly chic in pencil-legged jeans, a shimmering metallic tank and a fur-trimmed Michael Kors blazer. When she spotted Sarah, she jumped up and rushed over with her arms outstretched.

"You're finally up! You got in so late last night I… Omigod! What happened to your face?"

Sarah was more anxious to hear her sister's story than tell her own. "I got crosswise of a metal strut."

"I'm so sorry! Does it hurt?"

"Not anymore."

"Thank goodness. We'll have to cover it with foundation when we go back upstairs. Do you want some coffee?"

"God, yes!"

Sarah followed her back to the table and smiled politely when Gina introduced her to the elderly couple. They were from Düsseldorf, were both retired schoolteachers and had three children, all grown now.

"They've been coming to Lake Lucerne every spring for forty-seven years to celebrate their anniversary," Gina related as she filled a cup from the carafe on her table. "Isn't that sweet?"

"Very sweet."

Sarah splashed milk into the cup and took two quick, lifesaving gulps while Gina carried on a cheerful conversation with the teachers. As she listened to the chatter, Sarah began to feel much like the tumbling, upside-down Alices on the leotard. Had she fallen down some rabbit hole? Imagined the panic in her sister's voice last night? Dreamed the sobs?

The unreal feeling persisted until Gina saw that she'd downed most of her coffee. "I told the chambermaid to wa until you were up to do the room. She's probably in there now. Why don't we take a walk and…and talk?"

The small stutter and flicker of nervousness told Sarah she hadn't entered some alternate universe. With a smile for the older couple, Gina pushed her chair back. Sarah did the same.

"Let's go down to Chapel Bridge," she suggested. "We can talk there."

The Rebstock sat directly across the street from Lucerne's centuries-old Church of Leodegar, named for the city's patron saint. Just beyond the needle-spired church, the cobbled street angled downward, following the Reuss River as it flowed into the impossibly blue lake. Since the Reuss bisected the city, Lucerne could claim almost as many bridges as Venice. The most famous of them was the Chapel Bridge, or *Kapellbrücke*. Reputed to be the oldest covered wooden bridge in Europe, it was constructed in the early 1300s. Some sections had to be rebuilt after a 1993 fire supposedly sparked by a discarded cigarette. But the octagonal watchtower halfway across was original, and the window boxes filled with spring flowers made it a favorite meandering spot for locals and tourists alike.

Zigzagging for more than six hundred feet across the river, it was decorated with paintings inside that depicted Lucerne's history and offered wooden benches with stunning views of the town, the lake and the snowcapped Alps. Gina sank onto a bench some yards from the watchtower. Sarah settled beside her and waited while her sister gnawed on her lower lip and stared at the snowy peaks in uncharacteristic silence.

"You might as well tell me," she said gently after several moments. "Whatever's happened, we'll find a way to fix it."

Gina exhaled a long, shuddering breath. Twisting around on the bench, she reached for Sarah's hands.

"That's the problem. I came here to fix it. But at the last minute, I couldn't go through with it."

"Go through with what?"

"Terminating the pregnancy."

Sarah managed not to gasp or groan or mangle the fingers entwined with hers, but it took a fierce struggle.

"You're pregnant?"

"Barely. I peed on the stick even before I missed my period. I thought… I was sure we were safe. He wore a condom." She gave a short, dry laugh. "Actually, we went through a whole box of condoms that weekend."

"For God's sake, I don't need the details. Except maybe his name. I assume we're talking about your ski instructor."

"Who?"

"The cuddly ski instructor you texted me about."

"Oh. There isn't any ski instructor. I just needed an excuse for my sudden trip to Switzerland."

That arrowed straight to Sarah's heart. Never, *ever* would she have imagined that her sister would keep a secret like this from her.

"Oh, Gina, why did you need an excuse? Why didn't you just tell me about the baby?"

"I couldn't. You've been so worried about Grandmama and the doctor bills. I couldn't dump this problem on you, too."

She crunched Sarah's fingers, tears shimmering in her eyes.

"But last night… After I canceled my appointment at the clinic…it all sort of came down on me. I had to call you, had to talk to you. Then, when I heard your voice, I just lost it."

When she burst into wrenching sobs, Sarah wiggled a hand free of her bone-crushing grip and threw an arm around her.

"I'm *glad* you lost it," she said fiercely as Gina cried into her shoulder. "I'm *glad* I was close enough to come when you needed me."

They rocked together, letting the tears flow, until Gina finally raised a tear-streaked face.

"You okay?" Sarah asked, fishing a tissue out of her purse.

"No, but…but I will be."

Thank God. She heard the old Gina in that defiant sniff. She handed her the tissue and hid a grin when her sister honked like a Canadian goose.

"I meant to ask you about that, Sarah."

"About what?"

"How you could get here so fast. What were you doing in Paris?"

"I'll tell you later. Let's focus on you right now. And the baby. Who's the father, Gina, and does he know he is one?"

"Yes, to the second part. I was so wigged-out last night, I called him before I called you." She scrunched up her nose. "He didn't take it well."

"Bastard!"

"And then some." Her tears completely gone now, Gina gave an indignant sniff. "You wouldn't believe how obnoxious and overbearing he is. And I can't believe I fell for him, even for one weekend. Although in my defense, he gives new meaning to the phrase sex on the hoof."

"Who *is* this character?"

"No one you know. I met him in L.A. My company catered a party for him."

The bottom dropped out of Sarah's stomach. She could have sworn she heard it splat into the weathered boards. She stared at the snow-covered peaks in the distance, but all she could see was the surveillance video of Gina. At Dev's house in L.A. Catering a private party.

"What's…?" She dragged her tongue over suddenly dry lips. Her voice sounded hollow in her ears, as though it came from the bottom of a well. "What's his name?"

"Jack Mason." Gina's lip curled. "Excuse me, John Harris Mason, the third."

For a dizzying moment, Sarah couldn't catch her breath. She only half heard the diatribe her sister proceeded to pour out concerning the man. She caught that he was some kind of ambassador, however, and that he worked out of the State Department.

"How in the world did you hook up with someone from the State Department?"

"He was in L.A. for a benefit. A friend introduced us."

"Oh. Well…"

Since Gina seemed to have finally run out of steam, Sarah asked if she'd eaten breakfast.

"No, I was waiting for you to wake up."

"The baby…" She gestured at her sister's still-flat stomach. "You need to eat, and I'm starved. Why don't you go back to the hotel and order us a gargantuan breakfast? I'll join you after I make a few calls."

"You're not going to call Grandmama?" Alarm put a squeak in Gina's voice. "We can't drop this on her long-distance."

"Good Lord, no! I need to call Paris. I raced out so fast last night, I didn't pack my things or check out of the hotel."

Or wait for Dev to hotfoot it back to the Hôtel Verneuil. Sarah didn't regret that hasty decision. She wouldn't have made the Swiss Air flight if she'd waited. But she did regret the anger that had flared between them.

No need to tell Gina about Dev right now. Not when she and Sarah were both still dealing with the emotional whammy of her pregnancy. She'd tell her later, after things had calmed down a bit.

Which was why she waited until her sister was almost to the exit of the wooden tunnel to whip out her phone. And why frustration put a scowl on her face when Dev didn't answer his cell.

She left a brief message. Just a quick apology for her spurt of temper last night and a request for him to return her call as soon as possible. She started to slip the phone back into her purse, but decided to try his hotel room. The house phone rang six times before switching to the hotel operator, as it had last night.

"May I help you?"

"This is Sarah St. Sebastian. I'm trying to reach Monsieur Hunter."

"I'm sorry, Lady Sarah. Monsieur Hunter has checked out."

"What! When?"

"Early this morning. He told Monsieur LeBon an urgent business matter had come up at home that required his immediate attention. He also instructed us to hold your room for you until you return."

For the second time in less than ten minutes, Sarah's stomach took a dive.

"Did he…? Did he leave a message for me?"

"No, ma'am."

"Are you sure?"

"Quite sure, ma'am."

"I see. Thank you."

The hand holding the phone dropped to her lap. Once again she stared blindly at the dazzling white peak. Long moments later, she gave her head a little shake and pushed off the bench.

Gina needed her. They'd work on her problem first. Then, maybe, work on Sarah's. When she was calmer and could put this business with Dev in some kind of perspective.

The scene that greeted her when she walked into the Lebstock's lobby did nothing to promote a sense of calm. If anything, she was jolted into instant outrage by the sight of a tawny-haired stranger brutally gripping one of Gina's wrists. She was hammering at him with her free fist. The receptionist dithered ineffectually behind the counter.

"What are you doing?"

Sarah flew across the lobby, her hands curled into talons. She attacked from the side while Gina continued to assault the front. Between them, they forced the stranger to hunch his shoulders and shield his face from fifteen painted, raking fingernails.

"Hey! Back off, lady."

"Let her go!"

Sarah got in a vicious swipe that drew blood. The man, whom she now suspected was the overbearing, obnoxious ambassador, cursed.

"Jesus! Back off, I said!"

"Not until you let Gina go."

"The hell I will! She's got some explaining to do, and I'm not letting her out of my sight until…"

He broke off, as startled as Sarah when she was thrust aside by 180 pounds of savage male.

"What the…?"

That was all Mason got out before a fist slammed into his jaw. He stumbled back a few steps, dragging Gina with him, then took a vicious blow to the midsection that sent him to his knees.

Still, he wouldn't release Gina's wrist. But instead of fighting and twisting, she was now on her knees beside him and waving her free hand frantically.

"Dev! Stop!"

Sarah was terrified her sister might be hurt in the melee. Or the baby. Dear God, the baby. She leaped forward and hung like a monkey from Dev's arm.

"For God's sake, be careful! She's pregnant!"

The frantic shout backed Dev off but produced the opposite reaction in Mason. His brown eyes blazing, he wrenched Gina around to face him.

"Pregnant? What the hell is this? When you called me last night, all weepy and hysterical, you said you'd just come back from the clinic."

"I *had* just come back from the clinic!"

"Then what...?" His glance shot to her stomach, ripped back to her face. "You didn't do it?"

"I...I couldn't."

"But you couldn't be bothered to mention that little fact before I walked out on a critical floor vote, jumped a plane and flew all night to help you through a crisis you *also* didn't bother to tell me about until last night."

"So I didn't choose my words well," Gina threw back. "I was upset."

"Upset? You were damned near incoherent."

"And you were your usual arrogant self. Let me go, dammit."

She wrenched her wrist free and scrambled to her feet. Mason followed her up, his angry glance going from her to their small but intensely interested audience. His eyes narrowed on Sarah.

"You must be the sister."

"I... Yes."

His jaw working, he shifted to Dev. "Who the hell are you?"

"The sister's fiancé."

"What!" Gina's shriek ricocheted off the walls. "Since when?"

"It's a long story," Sarah said weakly. "Why don't we, uh, go someplace a little more private and I'll explain."

"Let's go." Gina hooked an arm through Sarah's, then whirled to glare at the two men. "Not you. Not either of you. This is between me and my sister."

It wasn't, but Dev yielded ground. Mason was forced to follow suit, although he had to vent his feelings first.

"You, Eugenia Amalia Therése St. Sebastian, are the most irresponsible, irritating, thickheaded female I've ever met."

Her nostrils flaring, Gina tilted her chin in a way that would have made the duchess proud. "Then aren't you fortunate, Ambassador, that I refused to marry you."

* * *

Her regal hauteur carried her as far as the stairwell. Abandoning it on the first step, she yanked on Sarah's arm to hurry her up to their room. Once inside, she let the door slam and thrust her sister toward the sofa wedged into the turret sitting room.

"Sit." She pointed a stern finger. "Talk. Now."

Sarah sat, but talking didn't come easy. "It's a little difficult to explain."

"No, it's not. Start at the beginning. When and where did you meet Dev?"

"In New York. At my office. When he came to show me the surveillance video of you lifting his Byzantine medallion."

Gina's jaw sagged. "What Byzantine…? Oh! Wait! Do you mean that little gold-and-blue thingy?"

"That little gold-and-blue thingy is worth more than a hundred thousand pounds."

"You're kidding!"

"I wish I was. What did you do with it, Gina?"

"I didn't do anything with it."

"Dev's surveillance video shows the medallion sitting on its stand when you sashay up to the display shelves. When you sashay away, the medallion's gone."

"Good grief, Sarah, you don't think I stole it, do you?"

"No, and that's what I told him from day one."

"*He* thinks I stole it?"

The fury that flashed in her eyes didn't bode well for Devon Hunter.

"It doesn't matter what he thinks," Sarah lied. "What matters is that the medallion's missing. Think, sweetie, think. Did you lift it off its stand? Or knock it off by accident, so it fell behind the shelves, maybe?"

"I did lift it, but I just wanted to feel the surface. You know, rub a thumb over that deep blue enamel." Her forehead creased in concentration. "Then I heard someone coming and... Oh, damn! I must have slipped it into my pocket. It's probably still there."

"Gina!" The two syllables came out on a screech. "How could you not remember slipping a twelfth-century Byzantine medallion in your pocket?"

"Hey, I didn't know it was a twelfth-century *anything*. And I'd just taken the pregnancy test that morning, okay? I was a little rattled. I'm surprised I made it to work that evening, much less managed to smile and orchestrate Hunter's damned dinner."

She whirled and headed for the door. Sarah jumped up to follow.

"I'm going to rip him a new one," Gina fumed. "How *dare* he accuse me of..." She yanked open the door and instantly switched pronouns. "How *dare* you accuse me of stealing?"

The two men in the hall returned distinctly different frowns. Jack Mason's was quick and confused. Dev's was slower and more puzzled.

"You didn't take it?"

"No, Mr. High-and-Mighty Hunter, I didn't."

"Take what?" Mason wanted to know.

"Then where is it?"

"I'm guessing it's in the pocket of the jacket I wore that evening."

"So you *did* take it?"

"Take what?"

Sarah cut in. "Gina was just running a hand over the surface when she heard footsteps. She didn't want to be caught fingering it, so she slipped it into her pocket."

"Dammit!" the ambassador exploded. "What the hell are you three talking about it?"

"Nothing that concerns you," Gina returned icily. "Why are you in my room, anyway? I have nothing more to say to you."

"Tough. I've still got plenty to say to you."

Sarah had had enough. A night of gut-wrenching worry, little sleep, no breakfast and now all this shouting was giving her a world-class headache. Before she could tell everyone to please shut up, Dev hooked her elbow and edged her out the door. With his other hand, he pushed Mason inside.

"You take care of your woman. I'll take care of mine."

"Wait a minute!" Thoroughly frustrated, Gina stamped a foot. "I still don't know how or when or why you two got engaged. You can't just…"

Dev closed the door in her face.

"Ooh," Sarah breathed. "She'll make you pay for that."

He braced both hands against the wall, caging her in. "Do I look worried?"

What he looked was unshaven, red-eyed and pissed.

"What are you doing here?" she asked a little breathlessly. "When I called the Hôtel Verneuil a while ago, they told me you had some kind of crisis in your business and had to fly home."

"I had a crisis, all right, but it was here. We need to get something straight, Lady Sarah. From now on, it's not *my* sister or *your* business. We're in this together. Forever. Or at least until we deliver on that promise to give kid number four a cruise on the Seine."

Sixteen

The prewedding dinner was held on the evening of May 3 at Avery's, where Dev had first "proposed" to Sarah. He reserved the entire restaurant for the event. The wedding ceremony and reception took place at the Plaza the following evening.

Gina, who'd emerged from a private session with the duchess white-faced and shaking, had regained both her composure and some of her effervescence. She then proceeded to astonish both her sister and her grandmother by taking charge of the dinner, the wedding ceremony and the reception.

To pull them off, she'd enlisted the assistance of Andrew at the Plaza, who'd aged with immense dignity since that long-ago day he'd discreetly taken care of an inebriated presidential aide during Grandmama's soirée for the Sultan of Oman. Gina also formed a close alliance with Patrick Donovan, Dev's incredibly capable and supremely confident executive assistant.

All Sarah had to do was draw up her guest list and select her dress. She kept the list small. She wanted to *enjoy* her wedding, not feel as though she was participating in a carefully scripted media event. Besides, she didn't have any family other than Grandmama, Gina and Maria.

She did invite a number of close friends and coworkers— including Alexis. *Beguile*'s executive editor had admitted the Paris thing was a mistake of epic proportions, but swore she'd never intended to publish a single photo without Sarah's permission. As a peace offering/wedding present, she'd had the photos printed and inserted into a beautifully inscribed, gilt-edged scrapbook. Just to be safe, Sarah had also had her hand over the disk with the complete set of JPEGs.

Dev's guest list was considerably longer than his bride's. His parents, sisters, their spouses and various offspring had flown to New York four days before the wedding. Dev had arranged a whirlwind trip to New Mexico so Sarah could meet most of them. She'd gotten to know them better while playing Big Apple tour guide. She'd also gained more insight into her complex, fascinating, handsome fiancé as more of his friends and associates arrived, some from his Air Force days, some from the years afterward.

Elise and Jean-Jacques Girault had flown in from Paris the afternoon before the wedding, just in time for dinner at the Avery. Sarah wasn't surprised that Elise and Alexis formed an instant bond, but the sight of Madame Girault snuggled against one of Dev's friends during predinner cocktails made her a tad nervous.

"Uh-oh," she murmured to Dev. "Do you think she's trying to seduce him?"

"Probably."

She searched the crowded restaurant, spotted Monsieur Girault happily chatting with Gina and relaxed.

Her wedding day dawned sunny and bright. Gina once again assumed charge. She'd accepted Dev's offer of payment without a qualm and arranged a full day at a spa for the women in the wedding party. She, Sarah, the duchess,

Maria, Dev's mother and sisters and the two little nieces who would serve as flower girls all got the works. The adults indulged in massages, facials, manicures, pedicures and hair treatments. The giggling little girls had their hair done and their fingernails and toenails painted pale lavender.

Sarah had enjoyed every moment of it, but especially treasured the half hour lying next to her sister on side-by-side massage tables while their facial masks cleaned and tightened their pores. According to the attendant, the masks were made of New Zealand Manuka honey, lavender oils and shea butter, with the additive of bee venom, which reputedly gave Kate Middleton her glowing complexion.

"At fifty-five thousand dollars per bottle, the venom better produce results," Gina muttered.

Only the fact that their masks contained a single drop of venom each, thus reducing the treatment price to just a little over a hundred dollars, kept Sarah from having a heart attack. Reaching across the space between the tables, she took Gina's hand.

"Thanks for doing all this."

"You're welcome." Her sister's mouth turned up in one of her irrepressible grins. "It's easy to throw great parties when you're spending someone else's money."

"You're good at it."

"Yes," she said smugly, "I am."

Her grin slowly faded and her fingers tightened around Sarah's.

"It's one of the few things I *am* good at. I'm going to get serious about it, Sarah. I intend to learn everything I can about the event-planning business before the baby's born. That way, I can support us both."

"What about Jack Mason? How does he figure in this plan?"

"He doesn't."

"It's his child, too, Gina."

"He'll have as much involvement in the baby's life as he wants," she said stubbornly, "but not mine. It's time—past time—I took responsibility for myself."

Sarah couldn't argue with that, but she had to suppress a few doubts as she squeezed Gina's hand. "You know I'll help you any way I can. Dev, too."

"I know, but I've got to do this on my own. And you're going to have your hands full figuring how to meld your life with his. Have you decided yet where you're going to live?"

"In L.A., if we can convince Grandmama to move out there with us. Maria, too."

"They'll hate leaving New York."

"I know."

Sarah's joy in her special day dimmed. She'd had several conversations with the duchess about a possible move. None of them had ended satisfactorily. As an alternative, Dev had offered to temporarily move his base of operations to New York and commute to L.A.

"I just can't bear to think of Grandmama alone in that huge apartment."

"Well..." Gina hesitated, indecision written all over her face. "I know I just made a big speech about standing on my own two feet, but I hate the thought of her being alone, too. I could...I could move in with her until I land a job. Or maybe until the baby's born. If she'll have me, that is, which isn't a sure thing after the scathing lecture she delivered when I got back from Switzerland."

"Oh, Gina, she'll have you! You know she will. She loves you." Sarah's eyes misted. "Almost as much as I do."

"Stop," Gina pleaded, her own tears spouting. "You can't walk down the aisle with your eyes all swollen and red. Dev'll strangle me."

As Dev took his place under the arch of gauzy netting lit by a thousand tiny, sparkling lights, strangling his soon-to-be sister-in-law was the furthest thing from his mind.

He was as surprised as Sarah and the duchess at the way
Gina had pulled everything together. So when the maid of
honor followed two giggling flower girls down the aisle,
he gave Gina a warm smile.

She returned it, but Dev could tell the sight of the unexpected, uninvited guest at the back of the room had shaken
her. Mason stood with his arms folded and an expression on
his face that suggested he didn't intend to return to Wash-
ington until he'd sorted some things out with the mother
of his child.

Then the music swelled and Dev's gaze locked on the
two women coming down the aisle arm in arm. Sarah
matched her step to that of the duchess, who'd stated bluntly
she did *not* require a cane to walk a few yards and give her
granddaughter away. Spine straight, chin high, eyes glowing with pride, she did just that.

"I hope you understand what a gift I'm giving you,
Devon."

"Yes, ma'am, I do."

With a small harrumph, the duchess kissed her granddaughter's cheek and took her seat. Then Sarah turned to
Dev, and he felt himself fall into her smile. She was so luminous, so elegant. So gut-wrenchingly beautiful.

He still couldn't claim to know anything about haute
couture, but she'd told him she would be wearing a Dior
gown her grandmother had bought in Paris in the '60s.
The body-clinging sheath of cream-colored satin gave Dev
a whole new appreciation of what Sarah termed vintage.
The neckline fell in a soft drape and was caught at each
shoulder by a clasp adorned with soft, floating feathers.
The same downy feathers circled her tiny pillbox cap with
its short veil.

Taking the hand she held out to him, he tucked it close
to his heart and grinned down at her.

"Are you ready for phase three, Lady Sarah?"

"I am," she laughed. "So very, very ready."

Epilogue

I must admit I approve of Sarah's choice of husband. I should, since I decided Devon Hunter was right for her even before he blackmailed her into posing as his fiancée. How absurd that they still think I don't know about the deception.

Almost as absurd as Eugenia's stubborn refusal to marry the father of her child. I would respect her decision except, to borrow the Bard's immortal words, the lady doth protest too much. I do so dislike the sordid, steaming cauldron of modern politics, but I shall have to learn more about this Jack Mason. In the meantime, I'll have the inestimable joy of watching Eugenia mature into motherhood—hopefully!

From the diary of Charlotte,
Grand Duchess of Karlenburgh

* * * * *

LET'S TALK
Romance

For exclusive extracts, competitions
and special offers, find us online:

- facebook.com/millsandboon
- @MillsandBoon
- @MillsandBoonUK

Get in touch on 01413 063232